A WHOLE NEW BALL GAME

A Whole New Ball Game

Gary Thacker

www.1889books.co.uk
ISBN: 978-1-915045-03-4

For Polly

Departures and Arrivals

As with most airports, the one at Alicante, serving the coastal towns of Costa Blanca, is a place of arrivals and departures, a place of greetings and goodbyes, a place of beginnings and endings. During the spring, summer and early autumn months, tourists throng its halls and corridors, anxious to cast aside the cares and concerns of their workaday world for a couple of weeks, intent on dipping toes into the Mediterranean and themselves into a better lifestyle. Then, all too quickly, they return, compelled to pick up their bundles of belongings and responsibilities once more, head home to pay bills and save for their next escape.

Almost 12 months earlier, Jon Moreton had arrived at the same airport, contemplating an equally brief stay in Spain, nervous and unconvinced about an uncertain stay in a foreign land. On that day, it had been a step into an unclear future; one that he had convinced himself would inevitably be short, before returning to the more comfortable and accustomed surroundings he was used to. Of course, that would mean returning home having failed, but at least he would have honoured his debt to a friend who had given him so many opportunities. The seductive prospect of wrapping the comfort blanket of familiar places and people around him would soothe any pangs of failure.

On this day though, as the airport buzzed with the activity of holiday makers, excited arrivals and downcast departures, Moreton could not contemplate the thought of leaving a country that had gifted him the treasured relationships of new friends and the love of a woman he had known nothing of those many months ago.

A half-consumed, now cold, cup of coffee was his only companion as he sat in the café, elbows on the table, fingers interlocked supporting his chin, watching the slowly rotating doors of the airport entrance. As it turned, the door had a melancholy converse nature, welcoming those who were leaving, and expelling those arriving. Moreton had little doubt which group he belonged to. What he had once considered to be the irresistible siren calls of a permanent return to England were now merely distant seductive whisperings that he had resolved to overcome.

Upon arriving at the airport, Moreton had glanced up at the large clock on the far wall of the large hall. As he watched, the digital display clicked over to read 10.58, precisely two hours before his planned flight back to England. That mattered little now though. The solitude of the taxi ride to the airport had been sufficient to clear his mind of doubts, and resolve on action.

Instead of joining the obligatory queue for the phalanx of automated check-in portals and baggage checks ranged in front of him, he searched for the airline desks selling tickets for internal fights. A brief arternet search on his phone had suggested that the *Escuela Naval Militar* based at the town Pontevedra in Galicia was the most likely place for Alvaro to be, and therefore where he would find Sophia.

Finding the ticket desk, he was greeted by a smiling and helpful young man, wearing a blue uniform jacket, with 'Ricardo' on the name badge.

'Do you speak English?' Moreton enquired hopefully. Although he had conquered a few words and phrases of Spanish, conducting his planned conversation with Ricardo in the language of his adopted country would have been considerably beyond his capabilities.

'Yes,' came the encouraging reply, accompanied by a smile.

In response to Moreton's enquiry about travel to Pontevedra, Ricardo suggested that the nearest available commercial airport was in the Galician city of Vigo. He was unsure as to how travel arrangements were from there but, as the airport was only around 28 kilometres or so from Pontevedra, a bus, train or even a taxi would be possible options to see him reach his destination. Sensing a potential sale, Ricardo enquired as to whether Moreton would like to purchase a ticket for the next flight there.

'Fortunately,' he added after a quick glance at the computer screen. 'A limited number of seats are still available for today's flight.' He was trying to close the deal.

'When is the flight scheduled to leave?' Moreton enquired.

A glance back to the computer screen revealed the required information '15.50' came the reply. 'The journey takes a little over 90 minutes, so you would be arriving in time to confirm your onward travel arrangements, and book into a hotel for dinner before setting off bright and early in the morning. We do have hotel partners in the city that we could recommend.'

Moreton nodded absently. In the taxi, as his plans had become fixed in his mind, he had even considered the possibility that, had a pre-lunch departure been available, Sophia may even have been booked on the same flight. Her text message, from the previous day, had said, *I've spoken to Alvaro, and am going to him in the morning.'*

'How many flights are there to Vigo, each day?' he asked.

'Only one. And there are only four flights per week,' came the reply.

Moreton mused for a moment. He had deduced that heading to the Ponteverda *Escuela Naval Militar* was the most likely way to find Alvaro and the place where Sophia was headed. The internet search had been efficient, but was only capable of responding to the queries posed. Moreton had tapped "Galicia naval academy" into the search engine.

"Ponteverda *Escuela Naval Militar*" was the first item on the results page, and fitted perfectly with all of the information he had – Galicia Naval training academy – but, what if it was wrong? What if Alvaro had been transferred somewhere else? Sophia had mentioned Galicia during one of their first, often awkward and clumsy fumbling, conversations almost a year ago. Anything could have happened since then.

If this was the only flight that day, how could Sophia be flying there "*in the morning*"? Perhaps she hadn't been planning to fly. Maybe she had decided to travel by train, or bus. Then the thought that perhaps he was heading in the wrong direction bubbled to the surface again. He had to start somewhere though.

The money Charlie Broome had paid him would be sufficient to fund Moreton's search for a while. When the deception had been revealed to him, he had considered the money paid to him as toxically tainted but, on reflection, accepted that as Broome's malign plans had torn them apart, using the money to find Sophia again carried a kind of justice. Additionally, the low cost of living in Spain had meant that he hadn't spent much of the money he had been earning as a coach back in England. Financial prudence was hardly a key concern at the moment anyway. He'd willingly spend it all to find Sophia again.

Ricardo waited patiently.

Any action was better than doing nothing, Moreton decided. 'Yeah, one ticket please.'

'Sure, no problem, sir. One-way or return?'

'One way, please. I'm not sure when I'll be back' The words "Or if" were only added in Moreton's mind.

The rapid clicking sound of keyboard operation was followed by the compliant hum of a printer, and Morton was handed a new ticket.

'Is there anything else that I can help you with?' The ticket was handed across with a further inquiry. 'Would you like some leaflets that cover places of interest in the area?'

Moreton shook his head slowly, looking at the ticket. 'No thanks.'

By this time though, the leaflets were already being handed to him. 'Vigo is a nice city if you have time to explore there. Also, it's very close to Cape Finisterre. It's beautiful there, if a little rugged.'

Moreton took the leaflets and nodded briefly, but without much interest.

By now though, Ricardo was in full travel agent flow. 'It's called Cape Finisterre because the Romans thought it was the end of the world. If you have time, it's worth going to.'

Moreton had already turned to walk away, but Ricardo's explanation about Cape Finisterre's name stuck him like a bolt. Perhaps his journey would take him to the end of his own personal world, if Sophia wasn't there.

Regardless of what else he had lost, the team, the players, the way of life that he had settled into so quickly, he was never more certain about one thing. He could not lose Sophia. He would not give up on her, even if she had given up on him.

He had walked back to the café, and ordered a cup of coffee, sitting down at a vacant table after dropping his ticket, with 'BHX' marked as the destination, into the café's recycling bin alongside discarded cardboard sandwich packaging and unwanted receipts.

The digital clock now told him it was 11.24. With check-in time for his flight to Vigo a little over four hours away, there seemed little else to do but sit and wait as his coffee slowly went cold.

Although there was lots of activity going on around him, little of it provided any distraction for Moreton. He sat in sullen solitude with a mind that refused to consider anything but the events of the previous 24 hours. A time that had seen his life turned upside down and so many things, so many people, that he had relied on, believed in, fade to dust before his eyes – and then there was Sophia.

Although the text message he had received from her the previous evening was merely words on a screen, each time he remembered it, his mind tormented him with thoughts of her saying the words to him, face to face, and a chill ran through his soul. *'Never try to contact me again.'* It felt like a door slamming in his face. How could someone he had shared so much with, so much joy, sorrow, elation and disappointment, so much passion and belief, so much love, now be so cold? He saw her face again. He heard the words again. *'Never try to contact me again.'* He bowed his head, looking down at the table, then closed his eyes, but there was no escape.

There was the voice again. 'Jon, Jon!' it said. The same voice, but the words were different. 'Jon' – again in a voice now louder and quivering with emotion. Moreton looked up from the table, towards the airport's rotating door, and saw Sophia running towards him.

He jumped to his feet sending the chair falling away to the floor behind him. Clipping the table as he rose, his cold coffee spilled across the laminated surface, running towards the edge before dripping slowly onto the floor. This was no time to cry over spilt milk – or coffee – though.

In the middle of the airport hall, Moreton and Sophia fell into each other's arms. For a few seconds they embraced, neither willing to let the other go, lest they might slip away again. A small crowd had gathered around them, some smiling, others applauding softly.

Airports are places of arrivals and departures, a place of greetings and goodbyes, a place of beginnings and endings. Sometimes though, they are also a place of staying, rather than arriving or departing, of renewing relationships rather than greetings or goodbyes, of renewals, rather than beginnings or endings.

As Moreton and Sophia held each other tightly, on this day, Alicante airport was one of those places.

Embraces

Two minutes later, after realising that their reunion had created a small stir, they kissed tenderly but briefly, before walking back, hand-in-hand, towards the upturned chair and coffee-stained table where Moreton had left his bag, as his surely forlornly resigned dream had become real.

They arrived as a waitress from the café was wiping down the table and picking up the chair. Moreton looked at her apologetically.

'*Lo siento,*' he said in abashed apology.

The waitress smiled at him, then at them both, and winked slightly at Sophia. '*De nada,*' she replied before turning away to leave them on their own.

Sitting down opposite each other, Moreton spoke first. 'I thought I'd lost you.'

'You could never do that.'

'What… ?'

'When Billy told everyone that you and he were involved in Broome's plan to destroy the club, no one believed it at first, but then a few wavered and when he said that you'd sent him on to score an own goal, more doubts followed.'

The pain of that memory was written on Moreton's face.

'I wouldn't believe it,' Sophia continued. 'But then Paco said that perhaps it was true. Why would Billy lie, he asked? We were all very emotional, then everyone was shouting. Only Kiko and Victor defended Billy. They refused to believe it, insisting there had to be some other explanation. I had to get out, so Paco took me away. I went to his house to stay with him and his wife. They looked after me, and Paco took my phone so that I could sleep in peace. He promised that he would tell me if you tried to call.'

'I did,' Moreton protested. 'I tried to call you so many times, but there was no answer.'

'I know, Jon.' She paused. 'Well, I know now. Yesterday Paco had my phone though and never told me. Well, not until today.'

'Paco! But why?'

'Jon, you have to understand, he was trying to protect me. You know that don't you.'

'But what about that text message you sent me, about going to Alvaro and saying that I should never try to contact you again?'

He looked at Sophia

'You didn't send it. Paco sent it.' Then again: 'Paco sent it, not you.'

'Yes, Jon. He did.' She paused for a moment. 'I would never do something like that. I wouldn't treat Alvaro like some fallback option, a second choice. It would not have been fair to him. My time with Alvaro was over when you and I met. It's only you, Jon.'

'So, Paco sent that message to put me off? To keep me away. To tell me that there was no hope for us.'

'Yes, a little, but also to test you, your sincerity.' Sophia pursed her lips, before continuing. 'Do you trust me, Jon?'

There was never any doubting Moreton's reply. It duly came. 'Of course.'

'And I trust you. Please wait here a moment for me.'

Sophia got up from the table and walked back towards the rotating doors, and out through them. Moreton's heart skipped a beat as the door swung around to reveal the empty compartment where Sophia had entered.

Four minutes passed, then five, then ten. Moreton felt lost again. Then he saw Sophia return through the door, now accompanied by a short, muscular, older man. It was Paco Jiménez. For a moment Moreton was unsure what to do. Here was the man who, he now knew, had seen his calls, probably listened to his messages intended for Sophia, but had done nothing. He was angry and he was hurt, but he also knew that he needed to suppress such emotions. He had told Sophia that he trusted her and wouldn't break that bond.

Sophia and Paco settled into chairs opposite Moreton. As she did so, Sophia reached out to Moreton's hand and squeezed it gently, before looking at Paco and giving a nod of encouragement.

'Mister...' he said to Moreton.

'Paco.'

'I was not sure of you,' he said. 'You know that don't you. I tried, but always were doubts. Do you remember when I told you never to...' he paused, a little embarrassed looking towards Sophia as if revealing some guilty secret. It was quite the opposite. 'That I told you', he continued. 'Never to hurt her?'

'And I told you that I never would. And I never have.'

'OK,' Paco said. 'But I swore my word to García that I would always protect her. I do not say sorry for that.'

Moreton remembered how Sophia had told him about the 'blood oath' that she said Paco had sworn to García to protect her, as if she was "a princess with a knight in armour to make sure I'm OK, and protected from anything – or anyone – bad." Despite feeling wronged, his anger towards the Spanish man was fading slightly as empathy rose in its place.

'You should not apologise for that, Paco,' Moreton admitted, drawing a smile from Sophia.

'Umph' Paco grunted in grudging response.

It was hardly sufficient for Sophia. 'Paco!' she insisted.

'Yes, sorry. Thank you, Mister. I'm pleased you understand.' It was sincere enough, but still carried an undeniable measure of doubt.

'I do,' Moreton jumped in quickly, sparing the older man any further embarrassment. 'But why did you keep my calls from Sophia?'

'I wanted to prove that you were not good for her.' Paco confessed 'Did I believe what Billy Swan had said about you? I was not sure. None of us were sure, but I thought it could be true. I never trusted Broome. Even from the premier day we met. I didn't like him and I think he knew that. He wasn't honest, too much there ...' he paused pointing to the ground, looking for the correct English word. 'My English is not perfect when I get angry.'

'Deep?' Sophia ventured.

'Yes, yes,' Paco replied. 'Yes, too much deep.' It wasn't perfect, but the message was effectively delivered. 'So, as you were his friend, you too may be the same. I decided not to tell Sophia until this morning, after 10am. Then we would know. Had you stayed in Retama to fight for Sophia because you were innocent and because you truly loved her, or had you fled back to England – run away with or without your friend and his money?'

'Paco!' Sophia scolded.

'OK,' the accused conceded. 'It was not an easy test. A tough test, but could you pass it? When I showed Sophia the missed calls, she listened to your messages, she tried to call you. It was just after 10am, but you had left. For me, you had failed the test. But she would not give up. She made me drive her here to see what you were doing. And here you are. I checked. The flight to England leaves just before 1pm. You should go and check-in now. Perhaps my test was hard, but you failed it.'

Sophia's head sank a little.

Moreton shook his head slowly as a smile began to play across his lips. 'No, I didn't,' he said reaching into his pocket for the airline ticket had purchased from Ricardo. He passed it to Paco.

'Not England, Paco. Not running away from anything or anyone. I was running after something, after someone.' His eyes quickly flicked towards Sophia.

In the next few minutes, Moreton explained how he had devised a plan to track down Alvaro and find Sophia. How he had reasoned that Ponteverda and the *Escuela Naval Militar* there was the best place to start. Paco looked at the ticket. The 'VGO' listed as the destination airport confirmed Moreton's account. Sophia looked across and saw the same letters, and then she looked to Moreton and their eyes met. For her, the three letters simply spelt out the justification that she had been right to trust Moreton, to trust love. Paco handed back the ticket.

'I was wrong,' Paco said, head bowed in remorse. 'I am sorry.' Sophia wrapped an arm around the Spaniard's shoulder and hugged him close to her.

'You were,' Moreton added, rising to his feet. It could have been an act of triumphalism, but instead it was one of compassion. He held out his hand. 'But, I'm often wrong as well. I was wrong about Charlie Broome, but you weren't. And I was wrong to trust Billy as well. My mistakes were because I too easily trusted people. Yours was because you found it difficult to trust me, and you wanted to protect Sophia.' He paused. 'We both failed each other. Shall we forgive each other?' Paco rose and took his hand, but instead of merely shaking it, he walked around the table and embraced Moreton.

As he did so, Moreton whispered in his ear. 'You are a fiercely loyal and honest man, Paco. I can only value such virtues in a friend.'

Paco smiled as they separated, patting Moreton on the shoulder, 'You passed,' he confirmed with a smile. *Mi amigo. Si?*'

'Si,' Moreton confirmed.

Across the table Sophia beamed at the reconciliation, before Paco returned to sit beside her.

'So,' he said. 'Shall I drive you both back to Retama? I do not think you will need that ticket to Vigo any more.'

It wasn't difficult to discern that Moreton was less than enthusiastic about Paco's invitation, and Sophia quickly spotted his discomfort.

'No, Paco,' she said. 'You go on. You need to get back for work. Jon and I will stay here for a while. Perhaps get something to eat and talk about things.'

Moreton smiled in affirmation, and nodded barely perceptively.

Understanding that three had become a crowd, Jiménez rose to his feet, shook hands with Moreton once more before kissing Sophia on her cheek and leaving.

'Thanks,' Moreton said after he had left. 'After what went on yesterday, I'm not sure that I'm ready to go back to Retama yet. My mind is still in a whirl and, to be honest, I just feel a bit lost.' He paused. 'Does that sound strange?' It felt like the wrong time for questions and explanations, but also that there would never be a better time.

'It wasn't true,' he began. 'You know that, don't you? What Billy told you. What he told you all about me. It wasn't true.'

Sophia nodded. 'I know.'

Moreton blew out his cheeks. His emotions were in turmoil. 'I was conned by Broome – and by Billy. I should have known better, but Charlie had been such a good friend in the past. At least I thought he had, and I was blinded by that. Perhaps he'd planned this all along. I don't know.' Moreton shook his head in sad recognition. 'I don't know what to believe any more. I'm so lost.' Then he looked up and smiled at Sophia. 'At least I was until a few minutes ago.' He raised her hand to his lips and kissed it, as she spoke.

'I know much of what happened, but not all of it. I know about Broome's plan to sell the business and land of Retama Azulejos, also the land of the club to Cerámica Internacional.'

'How do you know about that?'

'You forget that my father was an accountant in Retama for many years. Many of the most successful and wealthy people in the town were his clients. It's how he was able to develop a consortium to try and buy the club a while ago, before Broome beat him to it. This morning, he has spoken to a few people that he knows. Some are members of the local *ayuntamiento*. It quickly all became clear. The people at the *ayuntamiento* were persuaded to agree to the proposed land deal, and grant permission for the development. It was sold to them as bringing more employment to the town and helping to promote it as a growing and prosperous location.' She paused a moment. 'Now, they are having second thoughts, though. The sale of Retama Azulejos was apparently all signed and sealed weeks ago, but the issue of the club is being reviewed. Perhaps they will decide that a football club is more important to the town than a new factory and business.'

'Let's hope so,' Moreton said.

'Yes,' Sophia agreed. 'But what about Billy? Esteban said he found him crying in the dressing room afterwards with wounds on his head. Did you fight?'

Moreton related the exchanges with Billy Swan when he found him alone in the dressing room, and how he had hit his head against the wall several times in anger and self-disgust.

Sophia winced at the description. 'Why did he help Broome? After the game, in the dressing room, Billy said that you both had been bribed as part of the plan to destroy the club, but, in one of your messages, you said that he was being blackmailed.'

'He was,' and then Moreton paused correcting himself. 'Perhaps you could call it blackmail, or perhaps bribery. I'm not really sure what to call it.'

Moreton explained how Swan had been in debt to people who were unlikely to be patient about payment and feared for his safety. He explained about the nightclub incident and how it was so easy for people to believe that, given his history, the tabloid version of the events was true. He told her how, when he had suggested an approach to Swan to come out to Retama, that Broome had probably seen an opportunity for some kind of insurance policy, just in case the club was looking likely to get promotion. It was something he could throw in to make sure things went his way. Broome had offered Swan a way out, so that he could pay off his debts. He was literally in fear for his life, and that was the hold that Broome had over him.

'To be honest, given what I know about Charlie now, I wouldn't put it past him to have even threatened Billy with telling those psychos where they could find him.'

'So, Billy was a victim as well?'

Moreton shook his head. 'I'm not so sure of going that far. Billy was always looking out for number one. It was something he'd always say. He wasn't ashamed of it, and truthfully, I don't think he really cared about anyone or anything except himself. I guess I was a fool to trust him. It's not as if I shouldn't have known better.

Sophia was clearly less than convinced. 'No, Jon. It's been a traumatic time for us all. Now isn't the time to decide who was to blame, Sophia replied sympathetically. 'Apart from Charlie Broome!'

'Thanks, I just need a bit of time to clear my head, before going back to Retama. I want to go back, to go back with you, but I need some time to work out how to get back into some kind of control of things.'

Sophia smiled, trying to ease his confusion by placing her hand on his. 'I think I have the perfect solution.'

'What?'

'Well, my parents are in Retama for a few weeks. My father has some business there and they are staying for a while to look up some old friends.'

'OK,' Moreton conceded without appreciating the implication.

'It means Jon, that their house in Árboles Altos is empty. We could go there for a couple of weeks or so, spend some time on our own, away from everything, be together and find out where we're going. There's always plenty of food there and the shops in the village are only a couple of hundred metres away if we need anything. It's very beautiful, very tranquil and some time away from things will help us both.'

It sounded like a perfect solution to Moreton. 'That would great, Sophia,' he confirmed. 'Some quiet time, just the two of us, would be wonderful.'

'Let's do that then,' Sophia said, rising to her feet. 'You have your bag here and I have plenty of clothes at the house. We can get the shuttle bus into the city and then one from there out to the village. If we get going now, we can be there by dinner time, and in a few hours, we can be sitting on the balcony looking out over the countryside eating pasta with a nice bottle of wine from my father's cellar.'

'That sounds perfect,' Moreton agreed as he stood to join her, picking up his bag. 'One thing though.'

'What?'

'Wherever we decide to go, whatever we decide to do. We are together forever,' he said, smiling. *'Claro?'* he added.

'Claro!' Sophia confirmed.

As they left, Moreton dropped the airline ticket to Vigo into the café's recycling bin. Amongst all of the other discarded rubbish, it landed neatly on top of the earlier discarded ticket for Birmingham airport.

Families and Friends

The journey from Alicante bus station to Árboles Altos took around 90 minutes and, after eating lunch in the cafeteria above the area where buses leaving to travel across Spain awaited their passengers before dispersing in varied directions, Moreton and Sophia made their way to the allotted platform for their bus.

The electronic board above their heads told them that it would depart at 15:50. It was precisely the same time that Moreton's flight to Vigo would have been accelerating along the runway back at Alicante airport. When the bus arrived, Moreton threw his bag into the luggage area, climbed aboard and settled down next to Sophia, with an audible sigh. It didn't go unnoticed. Sophia patted him on the leg.

'OK?' she enquired.

'More than OK!' Moreton reached across and kissed her, then settled back into the comfort of the seat, his hand holding hers. Before the bus had left the environs of Alicante, he was asleep. The previous night had hardly been restful and he willingly fell into the comforting arms of Morpheus.

An hour or so later, he awoke as the bus began to climb into the mountains towards Árboles Altos. Stretching slowly, he turned to his left to find Sophia smiling at him indulgently. 'Did you have a nice sleep?'

Moreton yawned a little, smiled back and then leant across to kiss her. 'I did,' he admitted. 'After last night, I think I needed it.'

Sophia raised her index finger to his lips to stop him speaking. 'No more talk of yesterday for now. For a few days at least, let's forget about the past, about football and Retama. For now, all that matters is you and me. A few days' peace and quiet and then there'll be plenty of time for that sort of thing.'

'Vale.' Moreton agreed.

The next few days passed precisely as planned. They slept late into the mornings, and left their bed even later. Even in the mountains, the summer Spanish sun was still delivering on its contractual obligations, and the frequent mountain breezes delivered a pleasantly cooling zephyr allowing long lazy walks around the neighbouring countryside and opportunities to sample the bars and restaurants of the village. Breakfasts, plus any lunches or dinners spent at the house, were taken on the first-floor balcony that afforded panoramic views down into the valley below the forests adorning the mountains that gave the village its name. For one of the very seldom periods in his life, Jon Moreton's mind was lost to football.

Two telephone calls arriving on the same day though, halfway through their second week in Árboles Altos would change all that. The first was received by Sophia as they sat in quiet contemplation eating lunch on the balcony. After a glance to check the caller identification, Sophia opened her phone. Moreton could only hear one side of the conversation, but it quickly became clear that Sophia was speaking to her father.

Hola papá – Sí, los dos estamos bien, gracias – ¿Qué t'al? – Está bien – ¿Como le fue?

Sophia closed out the call, placed the phone back on the table and looked at Moreton. She clearly had something to say, but took a sip of wine before beginning. Curious, Moreton decided to open the conversation.

'Your father?'

Sophia nodded in reply as she swallowed the wine. 'Jon, there are some things that I need to tell you.'

'What?'

'Well, firstly, while we have been here, Retama have completed both legs of their first round play-off fixtures. They lost both games. The club will not be promoted this season. García took control for the games, but it was mostly Alejandro trying to organise things. The players even drove to the away leg near Valencia in their own cars as Broome had frozen the club's accounts at the bank, so there was little money to pay for anything.'

Moreton blew out his cheeks.

'I know,' Sophia continued. 'Do you remember that I told you Esteban had found Billy crying in the dressing room after you had left?'

'Sure.'

'Some of the players had told Esteban what had been said but, a little like Kiko and Victor, he found it difficult to believe.' She paused a moment. 'He always liked Billy, you know?'

'Yeah, I know.' The memory of the unlikely relationship between Billy Swan and the guardian of CD Retama's traditions and honour brought an unconscious smile to his face, as Sophia continued.

'He called Kiko, who then contacted Victor and they both rushed back to the club and took care of Billy. Kiko drove him back to the hotel where he was staying. Then they arranged with Sebastián to look after him, and arrange his flight back to England.'

'Wow,' Moreton replied. 'That was great of them, especially after what happened to the team.'

'It happened to Billy as well, Jon. Remember that. He was a victim of Broome's schemes as well.'

Moreton nodded, half-heartedly.

'Anyway,' Sophia continued. 'Afterwards, Esteban collected up all of the kits from the dressing room, took them away and washed them. Then, using some of the blue paint that was left over from when we painted the dressing room, he painted over the white patch that had read Broome Cerámica in green letters. Finally, he hand-painted "Retama" in white on there instead. The players wore that kit bin the play-offs. Some dirf the players on the other team laughed at the shirts, but Alejandro said it just made them stronger. My father wanted to make sure that I told you this.'

Moreton shook his head slowly, not in any negative way, but in undisguised admiration at the dedication of the people he had come to know and respect – but never more so than at that moment. 'That's amazing,' he said. 'The people at the club are so …' he searched for the right word, before finding it. 'So inspiring.' Then, looking at Sophia. 'We can't let the club die,' he declared with resolve. 'We can't. These people, Esteban, Alejandro, Kiko, Victor, all of them. Paco, as well. They've been dealt such a crap hand, but they don't give up. They never quit. This is our family. We can't quit either.'

Sophia's smile was washed with the hint of a tear at Moreton's reaction, but there was more to follow. 'I know Jon, and we are fighting back against Broome and his plans. He and Cerámica Internacional have lots of money, but Retama, our family, is strong.'

'Fighting? How?' He paused, before adding another question. 'Does your father know all about us. Does he know the truth about what Charlie did to Billy and me? All the lies and deceit?'

Sophia nodded. 'Of course. I called him from Paco's car on the way to the airport and told him that I knew you would never do any of those things. He believed me even then but, when I briefly left you at the airport to get Paco, I called him again to say that I was correct, everything was good, and we were together.'

'That's great,' Moreton said relieved.

'Then, he called me while you were sleeping on the bus. I knew he had plans when he went to Retama, but I wasn't sure what he was going to do. He's spoken with the people who were interested in buying the club with him last year, before they lost out to Broome. He is trying to put the consortium together again. Some of these people are very important in the town, and the region. They have a lot of influence. Now, they are trying to get the *ayuntamiento* to rescind the permission they had granted to CI for development on the club's grounds. The story of what Broome did, has caused a lot of resentment in the town. It is very difficult, very complicated. There are lots of talks going on. This will take some time but, as I said, we are fighting.'

Moreton was taken aback by the things that had been going on while he was away from Retama. 'I had no idea.'

'I know', Sophia confessed. 'I wanted to tell you, but my father said to wait until things were set up properly with the group of people he was contacting. He didn't want to build hopes up just to see them fall apart. But now… ' Sophia paused.

'Things are going our way?'

'Perhaps it's too early to say that, Jon. But, we are fighting.'

'Do you think he'll win. Your father, do you think he can make this work?'

Sophia smiled. 'I told you that I called him and told him that you were innocent and that we would be together again, yes?'

Moreton nodded.

'He trusted me to be correct. He believed in me. And I trust him and believe in him as well.'

Moreton picked up his glass of wine to offer a toast. Sophia responded in kind. 'To Joaquín, CD Retama and success,' he said.

'To family,' Sophia replied as they touched glasses.

The second call came later in the day. Sophia was preparing dinner in the kitchen as Moreton tidied up around the house. At first, the ring tone on his own phone, the one he had brought with him from England and had hardly used since Broome had given him the Spanish one that was still sitting on the table back in Retama, surprised him. He hadn't heard it for so long, and only then, when his parents had called him, if he had neglected to speak with them for a few days.

He walked across to the bedroom, and picked up the phone to check the caller's name, fully expecting it to be his parents. Instead, the name on the screen was "Bobby Broome." He hesitated. What had Charlie's father been told? Had he been painted a picture by his son that was as far from the truth as the one that Charlie had painted for him?

He opened the phone with a cautious 'Hello?'

Moreton's concerns were quickly dismissed though when Bobby Broome's first words revealed that he was at least partly aware of what had happened. 'I'm so sorry for what Charlie has done to you, you and those people over there, to the town,' the older man confessed sadly.

Bobby Broome went on to explain that his son had called an emergency board meeting of Broome Interiors, involving father and son, plus the accountant, where he revealed the approach from Cerámica Internacional to buy out the business. He told Moreton how he had dismissed the offer out of hand, but Charlie had insisted on a vote and, when the accountant sided with his son, voting to accept, the implications became clear. Not only was his business, the thing he had built up from nothing being taken away from him, but it was his son that had contrived to make it happen behind his back.

After the meeting, when the accountant left to arrange all of the required paperwork with the company solicitors and those in Spain, Charlie had regaled his father with the full extent of how he had put the plan together involving both Spain and Broome Interiors.

On the other end of the call, Moreton could easily detect the emotional pain that Bobby Broome was enduring at both the memory of his son's betrayal and the apparent delight he had taken in revealing it to his father. Trying to forestall any further discomfort for both parties, Moreton felt compelled to speak. 'I'm sorry.'

The voice of Bobby Broome still carried pain as he replied. 'Sorry? No, lad. You've got nothing to be sorry for. You were conned just like me and the people over there and Billy Swan. Charlie used us all to get away with what he wanted.'

There was little that Moreton could offer, except for a measure of empathy. 'I know, we've all been victims of his scheme. We've all suffered.'

'You and the people over there more than most,' came the reply. 'At least the deal has brought me loads of money in the bank, not that I'm going to live long enough to spend it all.' There was a pause before Broome continued. 'Look, Jon. I want to talk to you about something, not on the phone, it's the sort of thing that's best said face to face. Are you coming back to England any time soon?'

It was something that Moreton had been thinking about for some time, at least that is until the events after Retama's last game blotted out any other thoughts. After the season had finished, he had planned to take Sophia to England to meet his parents, but events had pushed such thoughts to the back of his mind. Bobby Broome's words reminded him that he hadn't seen his parents since Christmas, and that he should still go back to see them, and introduce Sophia at the same time.

'Nothing definite,' he replied. 'But perhaps in a few weeks. Things are still a bit up in the air at the moment.'

'Well, when you do, give me a call. I'd like to have that chat. OK, lad?'

'Sure, of course.'

Moreton closed the call and placed the phone down, walking back into the living room. Sophia was standing there, drying her hands on a towel. 'Who was that, Jon? Your parents?'

'No,' he replied. 'Just an old friend, checking in for a quick chat.' The words came tripping off his tongue without hesitation. He wasn't sure why he hadn't been more honest, but shielding her from the name 'Broome' felt like the right thing to do, and he took comfort in the fact that, he hadn't lied to Sophia. 'I want to talk to you about something,' he added.

'Can it wait until dinner? I'm in the middle of cooking at the moment and it will be easier then.'

'Sure, no problem.'

Sophia turned to walk back to the kitchen, but Moreton called after her. 'Hey.' Sophia stopped and turned to face him. 'I love you,' he said. She blew him a kiss and disappeared back into the kitchen.

Later that evening, after dinner as they sat on the sofa listening to music, Moreton told Sophia that he wanted to go back to England for a week or so to see his parents, and asked her to go with him. She was reluctant however.

'I'm not sure Jon. I think I need to be here. With all the work my father is doing for the club, I should be here in case he needs me.'

Moreton found it difficult to suppress his disappointment. 'It's only for a week, Sophia. I'm sure he'll be fine with that.'

She wasn't to be convinced. 'No, you go, Jon. It may be a good idea for us to spend some time alone with our own families, anyway. A week apart will give us both some time to clear our heads. When you get back, if all goes well, the club will need both of us at our best.'

He was unconvinced by the argument, and not a little disappointed, but reluctantly agreed. They finished dinner and Moreton used his iPad to book the flight.

Three days later, Moreton and Sophia sat, drinking coffee, in the same café in Alicante airport that had seen their reconciliation, what seemed like a lifetime ago. He had suggested making the bus journey alone, but Sophia had decided to return to Retama to be on hand should her father need her support or to liaise with the players. Going to the airport and then taking a bus to Retama from there, was hardly any diversion, so they had travelled together. Now, with Moreton's flight leaving in a couple of hours, it was time for him to go through check in and on to Departures.

They walked slowly across the 20 metres or so to the electronic gates where Moreton needed to scan his ticket to gain access, reluctant to reach the destination that would mean their separation. Arriving, Moreton drew Sophia close to him and they held each other for a few seconds before kissing and, simultaneously saying 'Call me' and then laughing. They hugged again before Moreton went through the gate, waving as he headed towards the security check. Sophia stood watching until he had disappeared, before turning away.

As she did so, a couple of tears traced down her cheeks. A week later she would know if there would be more to follow. Moreton had passed Paco's test. He didn't know it, but now he had to pass hers, too.

Following Bobby Broome's call, after dinner, Moreton had been washing the dishes when Sophia went into the bedroom to change. Seeing Moreton's phone on the bedside table, she couldn't resist the temptation of tapping the button to see the identity of his "old friend." She hated herself for doing it, but also knew that much of the blame for her curiosity could be levelled at the events of a few weeks ago. The name "Bobby Broome" chilled her. She knew that this was Charlie's father, and that he had employed Moreton as a coach at a club he owned. Was he asking Moreton to go back and work for him again? Was the call somehow linked to Charlie Broome? Why had he not been honest with her? Then, when Moreton suggested going back to England, her concerns were given renewed impetus.

She was sure that such thoughts were merely collateral emotional damage from the trauma at the club – at least that's what she told herself – but there remained the unstilled voice that worried her. She should let him go and, if he came back, all would be good, but the next seven days would be a trying time. In his attempt not to concern Sophia unnecessarily, Moreton had caused precisely the issues he had sought to avoid. Seven days felt like a long time to wait for reassurance. Fortunately, she wouldn't have to wait that long.

Confessions

Moreton knew nothing of the anguish his description of Bobby Broome's call had caused. In almost any other time during their relationship, each would have been more honest with the other. He would have told Sophia who the call was from, and she would have not been tempted to look at his phone. The recent events, however, had led to both of them deceiving the other, with the most benign of intents that had only led to potential anguish. The malign influences and implications of Charlie Broome's planning had inflicted wounds that only time and renewed trust would heal.

After spending so much of the previous twelve months in Spain, and becoming accustomed to the lifestyle there, the hectic environment of England jarred with Moreton. Everything seemed so urgent and frantic. Even after settling into the familiar surroundings of his parents' home, it was difficult for him to relax and his first night there brought little sleep. Many times, he had turned over in bed expecting to see the dark hair of Sophia, framing her face, and to breathe in the warm scent of her body, but there was only emptiness. The unpalatable prospect of losing her, a fear soothed away by the time they had spent together at Árboles Altos, forced its way back into his thoughts and dreams as he slept uneasily, wrestling with the spectres that dwell in the twilight hours.

When he awoke, it was with a resolution to never let Sophia slip away again. He had two items on his agenda for that day. He had already called Bobby Broome and agreed to meet him later that morning. As soon as he had done so, he would also call Sophia and tell her about the meeting, and explain why he had been reluctant to do so while in Spain.

A few hours later, Moreton was welcomed into Bobby Broome's house with a warm, affectionate embrace from the older man.

'Coffee?' Broome asked as he guided Moreton towards the elegantly, but far from ostentatiously, decorated sitting room.

'No thanks,' he replied. 'I've not long had breakfast.'

Dropping down uneasily in an armchair and inviting Moreton to sit opposite, Bobby Broome, moved an open newspaper to one side of the table and looked at his young visitor, offering up a sigh.

'I know I've said it before, Jon. But I'll say it again.' He paused a little. 'I'm so sorry about all of this mess.'

Moreton pursed his lips, and tried to offer an understanding response.

Bobby Broome shook his head slowly. 'I knew Charlie could be a bit wild sometimes, but I never… ' He paused again, shaking his head, before blowing out his cheeks. 'I never thought he could do something like this.'

'Charlie's mother died while he was very young,' he began. 'You know that, don't you, Jon?'

'Sure. Yes, of course.'

'Well, even that was probably my fault. I should have been there, at home, more. The business took up far too much of my time and, look where it's got me. In the end, it's cost me my family.'

Moreton bowed his head sadly. He had no words to offer that would provide any kind of comfort.

Broome continued. 'If I'd have been at home more, I'd have seen the signs, that she wasn't well. I could have done something, but I wasn't there. I was so wrapped up in the business that I never found out until it was too late. I had neglected her. It was my fault. It was all my fault.'

The older man rested back into his chair. The thing he had created, his business, had been the beast that consumed him. He had been devoured by the monster of his id.

'So,' Broome began again. 'What did I do with Charlie, eh? I messed that up as well. I gave him everything he wanted. As a kid, I'd had a pretty hard upbringing, and wanted him to have a better life. I wanted to show him that I loved him, so I tried to buy his love. The problem was that it wasn't for sale. He took all the things I gave, but he needed the one thing I didn't give. I made the same mistake. I never gave him my time. The way he's become, the things that have happened. They're all my fault, Jon. All my fault.'

He was clearly trying to hold back tears, but his watery eyes illustrated that it was a fight he was losing. Moreton felt compelled to say something, and he reached out.

'You can't say that,' he offered. 'People are who they are for lots of reasons. Charlie is who he is, looks at the world the way he does, has done the things he has, because that's who he is. It's his personality. It's his character. I can't believe that you ever did anything other than try and point him in the right direction, to be the sort of man you'd want him to be.' He paused, reflecting slightly. 'Look, for many years Charlie was my friend. He did lots of things for me. Getting me the job with your club, for example. That was nothing to do with how things turned out years later. He was a good guy then.' Another pause, and a way to open a fire door occurred to him, just as Bobby Broome's mind was burning in anguish. 'Perhaps he was just led astray by the money. When he first bought the business in Spain, he may have just wanted to prove himself to you, but when the potential of big money was flashed before him, it might have just led him astray. He was always ambitious, and there's nothing wrong with that. Suddenly, he was offered a chance of getting into the big time, and he took it.'

Bobby Broome offered an unconvinced smile. 'You're a good lad, Jon,' he said. 'Thanks for saying that. I'm not sure how true it is. I'm not sure how much you even believe it yourself, but thanks anyway.'

Moreton nodded. He hadn't been sure it was accurate either. In fact, he doubted it very much but, if it offered even a brief respite for Bobby Broome's troubled soul, he gave it willingly. Both men were trying to square the circle of a relationship with Charlie Broome that had been revealed as something far different than what they had perceived it to be. Bobby Broome looked to move things forwards.

'Jon, anyway. I didn't ask you to come over here just to listen to me make confessions. The way I see things is that what Charlie did hurt a lot of people, you among them and, at the same time, it meant me ending up with loads of money that I really don't need.' He paused briefly, sighing before continuing. 'To be honest Jon, I'm not well. It's nothing desperate, just a bit of old age catching up on me, but the doctors have told me to take things easy. When all this money landed, I thought about trying to buy the club here in the town back from those shysters but, the doctors told me that I'd be dead in six months and that wouldn't solve anything. So, I settled on doing something else, but before I tell you about that, and what followed, I wanted to make you a promise.' Bobby Broome leant forward, emphasising the sincerity of his words.

'So, here's the deal, Jon. If you want to buy a house for you and your Spanish girl, don't bother with banks, come to me. I don't mean as a loan or anything like that. It'll be a gift. It'll be my way of paying you back a bit for the crap that my son, the man that my lifestyle made, caused. The money caused the problem, so it's only fair that I use it to make things a little easier for people it hurt, if I can.'

Moreton was taken aback by what he heard. 'I couldn't possibly...' he began before Bobby Broome's insistent waving hand brought his protests to a halt.

'I don't want to hear any of that. No arguments, Jon. The simple fact is that I already had plenty of money before this CI deal was done, and now it's just sitting there in a bank. I want it to do some good. It's much more than I could ever spend and, if I don't use it for something useful, it'll just end up in Charlie's pocket when I'm gone and,' he paused as he leant forward, an earnest expression on his face. 'We don't want that to happen, do we?' The conspiratorial wink, sealed the deal. 'It's always here. OK, Jon?'

'OK,' Moreton conceded, still a little less than fully accepting that what he thought he had been told was real. His mind spinning.

'There's something else I want to show you,' Bobby Broome continued as he passed the open newspaper across to Moreton, drawing him back into the present. 'The back page,' the older man advised.

Moreton turned over the newspaper. The headline on the back page read: "Bad boy Billy comes good!" Beneath it was a picture of Billy Swan juggling a football with his feet, surrounded by a group of teenage boys in football kits. Moreton eagerly scanned the text for an explanation. The report revealed that "former footballing bad boy Billy Swan has formed a charity to set up a series of soccer schools around the East End of London targeting underprivileged children with the aim of keeping them off the streets, playing football, and back into schools." There was even a quote from Swan. "I've done some bad things in my life and let people, my friends, down. Now I've got the chance to help these kids out, give them something I never had, to play football, get proper coaching and get back into school." Moreton dropped the newspaper and looked up at the man smiling at him from across the table. Bobby Broome smiled warmly in acknowledgement.

For the next 30 minutes or so, he explained the events of a few weeks ago to Moreton. He had contacted Swan when he returned to England and asked to meet him. At first it had been difficult, his calls went unanswered, but he persisted and, eventually, Swan agreed to meet him. 'Even though,' Broome explained, with a smile. 'He probably thought it was the only way to get rid of me!'

When they met, Swan had looked completely different to what Broome had expected. Instead of the swaggering drunkard of tabloid infamy, he was quiet and subdued. He had told Broome that, what had happened to him in Spain, had changed his life. Not only how he had been forced to be part of Charlie Broome's scheme, and betrayed Moreton, the players and people who had welcomed him, but more importantly how he had been treated afterwards by Kiko, Victor, Esteban and Sebastián. Swan had also told Broome that he had given up alcohol, and was trying to get a job, hopefully working with local radio again. Bobby Broome, though, had suggested something different.

'I just want to do some good things with all this wealth,' he explained. Using some of the money received from CI, Broome had set up a foundation in his local town to give teenagers a chance to play football, tied to their attendance at school. This was what he had settled on after being advised not to get into football club ownership again. The scheme had worked well and Broome had offered to set up a similar project with Swan in London's East End, if the former professional was prepared to front it. Broome didn't want the publicity, but having someone like Billy Swan, a local lad who was looked up to by the kids of the area, fronting the foundation would give it great PR presence. The deal was, though, that, much like the teenagers that the scheme was set up to help, Swan would have to do the right things as well. Behave himself, work at the foundation and keep on the straight and narrow.

Swan had been unsure, but Broome had convinced him. 'If you're a changed man,' he had challenged. 'Prove it. Don't talk it. Walk it!' he had demanded. A week later, with Broome using the same management firm to run the charity that had set up the local foundation, the project was launched.

'Wow,' was all Moreton could offer in reply.

'So far, so good,' Broome concluded. 'Billy even rings me most days to say how much he's enjoying himself, how great it is to be working with kids from his own area and,' he chuckled softly, 'to keep thanking me.'

Moreton shook his head in surprise. 'Wow,' he repeated. 'And you funded this?'

A little nod confirmed the answer. 'Doing something positive with all that money, Jon. You should get in touch with him. I know he'd appreciate it. You won't believe the man he is now.'

Moreton pursed his lips. He wanted to be convinced, but even more he didn't want to be deceived again.

An hour later Moreton was sitting in his hired car outside his parents' home calling Sophia. After exchanging brief pleasantries, Sophia spoke first. 'I have something that I need to tell you, Jon.' She was going to confess about looking at his phone, but Moreton got his confession in first.

'OK, but can I say this first please?' He explained how the call that he described as being from an "old friend" was in fact from Charlie's father, but he hadn't known what the situation was and didn't want to worry her about it until he did. He then went on to detail the conversation with Bobby Broome, the way he felt about what his son had done, how he wanted to make up for it in some way, and how he had made Moreton promise to take him up on the offer about a house.

Sophia was as taken aback by what Moreton told her as he was when Bobby Broome had spoken to him. 'That's amazing,' she said.

'I know, I don't really want to take anything from him but, as he explained, it would be more like taking money from Charlie than him, so that felt so much better.'

'What are you going to do about it?' Sophia asked.

'Well, nothing for now, but it's nice to know that the offer is there, isn't it?' In reality, he had thought about little else. Living with Sophia in her parents' house at Árboles Altos had convinced him that this was what he wanted, and suddenly, the means to make it happen had been dropped into his lap, when the time was right.

'Yes, of course,' she replied.

Moreton then went on to explain what Bobby Broome had told him about the foundations he had set up, about his intentions to use the money for good, and about Swan. 'Well, that's my news. What did you want to tell me?'

After Moreton's confession about the true source of the call there was no real need for Sophia to tell him about her falling prey to temptation and checking his phone. He had passed her test, though, and she couldn't now fail her own. There was an easy way to delay that though for a moment.

'Have you called Billy?'

There was silence from the other end of the call.

'Jon, have you called Billy?'

'No, not yet,' came the hesitant reply. 'I'm just not sure...' His voice trailed off and Sophia decided it was now her turn to confess. She did and was instantly forgiven. They spoke each day for the remainder of the week, and Moreton found news of football's reformed "bad boy" Billy Swan difficult to ignore as more newspaper and even television coverage focused on the story of the ugly duckling who had turned into a laudable Swan.

Meetings

Walking out through passport control and into the main hall of Alicante airport, Moreton beamed as he saw Sophia waiting for him. They rushed towards each other and embraced tightly, each reluctant to release the other from their arms. Ten minutes later, they sat beside each other on the bus heading to Retama.

'Well,' Sophia suggested. 'You had an interesting time in England, didn't you?'

'Yeah, just a bit, I guess.'

'Did you speak to Billy?'

Moreton blew out his cheeks in reply. It wasn't the answer Sophia was hoping for.

'Jon, do you not see how wrong this is? You, me, the players, the club, everyone has forgiven each other, understood each other. There was only one bad person in this whole mess and that was Charlie Broome. Everyone else...' she paused before repeating the words, with added emphasis. '*Everyone else* was a victim!'

She reached into her bag and pulled out a newspaper, passing it to Moreton at an open page. It was one of the English-language publications popular among the British exiles living in the area that often carried both local news and items from England. Sophia pointed at a photograph and story.

Moreton sighed as he realised that it was another account of the reformed Billy Swan and his work at the soccer schools Broome had set up in his name.

'Even here in Spain,' Sophia said. 'We have news of what Billy is doing. Look,' she said, pointing to particular part of the article. 'See what he says about being sorry for all the bad things he's done and betraying people, letting down his friends.' She stopped and looked Moreton in the eye. 'He is not a bad person, he was paying the price for being weak, not for being bad. The players understand this, all of them, not just Kiko and Victor. Not just Esteban, all of them, all of us. Why can't you?'

Moreton knew that the argument was unanswerable, but the pain of being deceived, the fear of leaving himself open to it happening again, was difficult to overcome.

'Jon, he was your friend. He made a mistake and Charlie Broome put him in an impossible position. What else could he do? Would you rather have seen those people you spoke of injure him?'

Moreton sighed, and Sophia delivered the argument to which he had no answer other than resigned acquiescence. 'He is part of our family.'

'OK,' he conceded. 'You're right. Of course, you're right.'

Sophia took his hand, and smiled. 'That's good Jon, and... because you have agreed that I am right, I have some news for you.'

'About the club?'

A nod and smile suggested it was something positive. 'There have been many discussions with the *ayuntamiento*, representatives of CI and friends of my father. At first CI would not consider anything changing. They had signed contracts for the purchases and written agreement from the *ayuntamiento* for the development. They argued that the actions of the man selling the properties to CI was nothing to do with them, and that he hadn't broken any laws anyway, had he? It was a difficult time, but then my father took one of his friends with him to the next meeting. Rodrigo Hernández was a client of my father's many years ago when he owned two local newspapers. Then, however, his business grew and he left Retama to move to Valencia, but they remained very good friends, and he was part of the consortium that was interested in buying the club. He now owns many newspapers serving the area.' She pointed to the newspaper with the story about Billy Swan in it. 'Including that one,' she added.

'OK,' Moreton acknowledged, but Sophia could tell that he was unsure of where the story was leading.

'CI is a very big organisation. But their only clients are the public, the people. Of course, they are correct that they had broken no laws, but everyone in the room knew that they had been aware of what Charlie Broome was doing, and that's where Hernández comes in. He let it be known that he would consider it an important public service to use his newspapers to publicise the events that led up to their development taking place in Retama. He made it clear that he would not be saying that CI had been involved in anything underhand, but it would be up to his readers to decide who was profiting most from the situation.'

'Bad publicity for the business?' he said thinking aloud.

'That's right. For so many towns in Spain, their football club is an intrinsic part of their community, and that's even more the case with bigger clubs in the cities. CI could see how it could potentially damage sales and, their big fish, taking control of Broome Interiors, was already landed. Would they be prepared to risk the potential damage to their image that the much smaller development in Retama may cause?'

'So, they've backed out,' Moreton suggested, hopefully.

'No, but their people have gone back to discuss the issue. There's another meeting planned for tomorrow, and we should have a better idea of how things are looking by then.'

'Well, there's some hope then.'

'There's always hope, Jon. You have only failed when you stop trying to succeed.'

An hour later, they arrived back in Retama, and an uneasy concern wrapped its chilly arms around Moreton as they approached the gate at the complex where he had lived opposite Sophia for so many months. So many times, he had passed through the gate and turned left to climb the stairs to his old apartment, and he couldn't help but look up at the door and the shuttered windows. It was like an episode in his life had been locked down.

Sensing his troubled mind, Sophia took his hand and led him up to her apartment, opening the door and inviting him into a new chapter of his life. Walking in, Moreton dropped his bag on the floor as Sophia smiled at him.

'Welcome home,' she said, and Moreton subconsciously relaxed.

Sitting on the apartment balcony drinking a coffee cortado later, Moreton gazed around at the view it afforded. Unlike the one from his old apartment with panoramic views over the rooftops to the mountains in the distance, the scene from Sophia's balcony was merely of the row of apartments opposite, the external road to the right and across into the complex towards the swimming pool to the left.

'The view isn't as nice as from your old apartment,' Sophia suggested.

Moreton smiled in response, before taking a sip of his coffee. 'I don't know,' he said playfully, looking directly at her. 'It looks pretty good from here.'

Sophia stood from her chair and kissed him on the forehead as the took his empty cup away into the apartment. 'Jon,' she said, pausing at the doorway. 'Shall we have dinner at Bella Cucina afterwards?'

'After what?'

Sophia paused slightly. She'd been postponing raising a subject for most of the time since they met at the airport, but now she'd laid the trap for herself and was committed. 'After the meeting,' she said looking at Moreton as he turned to face her.

'Meeting?'

'I should have said this earlier, but I wanted to be sure you felt comfortable and relaxed first.'

Moreton fidgeted uncomfortably in his chair, concerned at what was about to be revealed to him.

'While you were away, I spoke with García about the club and what should happen if we can play next season. Tío said that he was too old to be involved full time again, but that if the negotiations to save the club were successful, it should be you taking over again as coach.' Sophia was acutely aware of Moreton's hesitancy, but she was also convinced that what she was doing was right.

'The meeting,' she continued, 'is at the club. All of the players will be there. I'll be there, so will García.' she paused. 'And, so will you.'

'I'm not sure that's a good idea. At least not at the moment.'

'Yes, it is. This is our family Jon. When we were at my parents' house, you said that we needed to help save the club. This is how we start. Other people, my father and his friends have other tasks to accomplish. This is what we can do. It's what we can do now to help save the club. Tío has spoken to the players. They will all be there. You, we can't let them down.'

Moreton exhaled heavily, reluctantly conceding the point. 'OK, he said.

The walk from the apartment to the home of CD Retama only took 15 minutes or so, but Moreton felt no urgent need to reach his destination. Sophia had assured him that the players now understood what had happened and that he hadn't been involved as part of Charlie Broome's plan but, even if that was the case, it was still his naïve trust of people that had led to the problem. People accepting that he had no malicious intent was one thing, but they must still have considered him to be the sort of gullible fool who led them astray. It was the real reason why he had hesitated about contacting Billy Swan, and was why, despite his conversation with Sophia on the bus to Retama, that he had still not done so.

Reaching the club and standing by the gates, Moreton looked up at the rusting sign declaring it to be the Estadio Antonio Núñez. A year or so earlier, he had walked through those same gates with trepidation of the unknown, now his concerns were different, but no less intense.

'Come on,' Sophia encouraged as she held his hand. They pushed the gates open, walked in, up the steps and across the pitch towards the open door of the dressing room from where a quiet hum of conversation drifted out. Sophia walked through the door ahead of him. The room fell quiet as he followed her into the dressing room. Moreton swallowed hard.

The benches around the walls of the dressing room were filled by the players, all of whom seemed to be there. With them, in the corner nearest the door, sat the large, portly figure of Vicente García. Climbing slowly to his feet, the old man kissed Sophia on the cheek then embraced Moreton. It was a gesture intended to portray solidarity, reassuring Moreton, and did so, spectacularly well.

As García sat back down again, Moreton felt more confident. He nodded to the group of players before offering a quiet 'Lo siento.'

Paco Jiménez was the first to respond. He stood up and, looking at Moreton spoke to the group in Spanish. The words were delivered far too quickly and beyond Moreton's limited vocabulary to understand, but Sophia whispered, what was being said, to him.

'He's telling them that he doubted you, and had done for a long time, and that he was one of the first to accept what Billy had told them after the game. It had confirmed his suspicions, and fitted with what he wanted to believe. He's saying that he felt betrayed and angry.'

To Moreton it hardly sounded like the ringing endorsement he was hoping for and the anger in Jiménez's husky tones only made the account sound worse but, as the veteran goalkeeper paused and looked down at the floor, and then up again and pointing at Moreton, his tone had clearly changed.

'Now he's saying that he was wrong,' Sophia translated. 'He, and all of them had been deceived, but not by the Mister, by Señor Broome. This man was also a victim. He was cheated by Broome, and to make matters worse, we all blamed him for what happened. He was down and, instead of helping him to his feet, as we would have done with any of our family, most of us kicked him and walked away.' The passion of the last few words caused Jiménez to pause and gather himself before speaking again. As he did so, Sophia took Moreton's hand in hers and squeezed it gently.

'Now he's saying that we, the team, all of us, should be ashamed.' Sophia failed to translate the part when he said about her never losing faith in Moreton, quickly passing over it to continue. 'When you're hurt, it is natural to lash out at someone, to blame someone, but that is wrong. I was wrong about the Mister. I was wrong about Billy. He was a victim too, but he's not here now. He's gone. The Mister has come back and the first thing he does is apologise. I have given him my apology, and it's right that I was the first to do so, because I was the first to condemn him.' Then the finger was pointed at Kiko and Victor, inevitably sitting together, before continuing. 'They stood by their friend. They stood by Billy. They believed in him. We did not.'

His speech finished, he walked the few steps towards Moreton and offered his hand, but Moreton pushed it aside, embracing Jiménez again, as he had at the airport weeks earlier. As he did so, the applause began, slowly at first but then swelling as everyone joined in as the goalkeeper sat down again.

At the far side of the room, Alejandro Sanz raised his hand to ask for quiet. The captain of CD Retama's leadership was undiminished and the gesture was sufficient to silence the room. Without rising, the gnarled defender spoke with quiet authority. The words were Spanish but spoken intentionally slow enough for Moreton to understand their meaning.

'*Soy Retama,*' he said, softly.

Then, pointing at Paco Jiménez, '*El es Retama.*'

Then, at Kiko and Victor, '*Ellos son Retama.*'

At Sophia, '*Ella es Retama.*'

Finally waving his hand all around the room. '*Todos somos Retama.*'

Sanz paused for a moment before pointing directly at Moreton. '*Todos creemos que eres Retama, también.*'

Then, he asked Moreton for confirmation. '*¿Eres tú?*'

Moreton nodded before offering it with firm conviction. '*Si, mi capitán. Soy Retama. Somos Retama para siempre.*'

The applause broke out again and trying to make himself heard over the noise and cheers, Moreton called out '*¡Mi familia!*' No one heard. No one needed to.

That night, their first spent together since Moreton's return from England, both slept soundly. The morning would bring news of hope, problems and a possible solution.

International Rescue?

Moreton and Sophia had slept late, the emotional dam breached at the players' meeting the previous evening had released a flood of relief and growing contentment that washed away immediate concerns. When Sophia's phone rang at 9.10 the following morning, it woke them both with the shock of a 5.00 alarm call.

Sophia flicked open the phone and spoke sleepily into it, her tones betraying her drowsy state. Moreton was still half-asleep and heard little of the conversation but, when Sophia closed out the call, placed the phone back on the bedside table and leant across to kiss him, he sighed contentedly. The relaxation would not last long.

'Jon,' Sophia said with a newly gathered sense of urgency. 'Come on, we need to get up and dressed. My parents are on their way round. They have news.'

Moreton was still trying to reconnect with the conscious world. 'News? Good or bad?'

'I'm not sure, but we'll find out soon. We've got ten minutes.'

Sophia jumped out of bed and headed into the bathroom clicking the shower on as she did so.

'Make coffee!' she called over her shoulder as her naked torso disappeared behind the closed bathroom door.

Moreton shook himself and climbed out of bed, throwing on a pair of jogging bottoms and a vest top. It wasn't until the bubbling sound and rising aroma from the coffee machine assailed his senses that he realised that he would soon be facing Sophia's parents for the first time since everything had fallen apart. Suddenly he felt anxious.

At that moment, Sophia appeared from the bathroom dressed in tracksuit trousers and his old training top that she would often wear without the accompanying trousers, but that was for his eyes only. He couldn't help but smile at the memory, and his concerns were abated for a while.

A few minutes later, Sophia was peering out of the window as a black Range Rover drew up outside. She opened the door and trotted down the steps towards the gate to let her parents into the complex, kissing each of them on the cheek as they passed her.

Joaquín Garrigues was the first to enter the apartment, beaming a smile towards Moreton as he did so. 'Jon,' he exclaimed offering his hand and then turning it into an embrace.

'*Hola Señor Garrigues,*' Moreton offered in reply, before the traditional '*¿Que t'al?*'

The older man stepped back for a moment, before offering a mock admonishment. 'Jon, you must always call me Joaquín,' he insisted. 'And we can speak in English.'

Moreton smiled in acknowledgment

'And you must call me Dolores,' Sophia's mother added as she followed her husband into the apartment, kissing Moreton on both cheeks, before sitting down on the sofa. Garrigues settled down next to her as Sophia brought the coffee flask in from the kitchen and Moreton drew the chair from in front of the table that served as Sophia's desk, to sit alongside the guests. Seconds later, as she was pouring the coffee into the waiting cups, Sophia enquired as to what the news was, and whether CI had backed down.

Garrigues, pursed his lips as if searching for an answer. 'Well, not really,' he began before hesitating. 'Well perhaps a little.' He raised his coffee cup and took a small sip before placing it down and leaning forwards, as Sophia moved to lean against the table by Moreton.

'So, this morning we heard that CI had made a decision. As you, know, there was a further meeting planned with them for later today, but they sent an email early this morning instead. They had an offer for us, but it was a strict take it or leave it situation and, if we chose to reject it, they would go ahead with their plans and,' he paused offering up the "air speech marks" gesture. 'And let the lawyers deal with the consequences.' He paused and waited for the inevitable question.

Sophia provided it. 'What was the offer?'

Her father took another sip of coffee before continuing. 'Well, it pretty much boils down to this. CI will offer a one-year moratorium on the agreement and allow the consortium I have built up to buy the club from Broome, under certain conditions. If the club can prove its worth to the town by winning promotion, they will continue with the development of the existing site they have already taken over, but look elsewhere for a location nearby to build their factory, and expect that the ayuntamiento will be amenable to help them find one. From their point of view, it solves the potential PR problem as they can project themselves as being benevolent and having supported the town's club, even if it still fails.

'So, we have a chance,' Sophia declared, but the assumption was abruptly deflected by her father's cautioning raised hand.

'That's not all though, and here's where the problem lies. CI say that, even assuming the club fails and they can go ahead with purchasing the ground where the stadium is and building the factory there, the year's delay will have cost them a substantial amount of money. If that happens, my consortium will then be contractually obliged to sell them the club and its location for €10. If, however, the club survives, and they have to look elsewhere for a new site, there will also be costs, even assuming that the ayuntamiento help them to find a new location.'

Moreton thought that he could see the looming problem that Garrigues had alluded to. 'How much are they looking for?' he asked.

The former accountant was well used to discussions concerning large amounts of money in business dealings, but there was an emotional stake in this situation, and his normal matter-of-fact demeanour was difficult to maintain.

'They require the club's prospective owners, the consortium I have built up or a different guarantor, to post a bond with them for the sum of €250,000. The money has to be there for the entire season. If, for any reason, the guarantor withdraws from the agreement, my group is then obliged go through with the sale of the club and its location for €10. If the money remains in place, and club fails to win promotion, they can go ahead with their plans, they will require the full payment of the money. If the club wins promotions, it will survive and they will only require €100,000 to fund the search for an alternative location. The remainder can be redeemed by the guarantor.'

Having delivered the information, Garrigues sighed and settled back in the sofa as his wife looked at him with concerned empathy. 'Of course, the problem is that neither I, nor all of my group combined, can afford to risk such an amount.' He paused. 'I have to say that, from CI's point of view, it gives them a win-win situation and, whichever way it plays out, they can paint a picture of themselves for public consumption as being very reasonable people. I'm afraid that us bringing the issue of public opinion into the discussion with Hernández's newspapers has been turned against us.'

Sophia blew out her cheeks in disappointment. 'So, we've lost', she conceded. Moreton reached out his hand to take hers, squeezing it gently. 'Have we?' he asked, looking at her father questioningly.

The answer offered a little hope. 'Well, I have to say that it looks that way at the moment, but perhaps there is a slight chance.'

Moreton and Sophia's attentions were focused as they leant forward in eager anticipation of further details to follow, but the retired accountant was keen to counsel caution.

'This is only a small window, but perhaps it may offer some light. Please, don't be too hopeful at this stage.' Garrigues was keen to dampen any overoptimistic expectations, but even the glimmer of a possible solution, had sparked hope, so he continued.

'You know of course of the Bella Cucina restaurant near here.' Both Moreton and Sophia nodded barely perceptively. 'Do you also know that this is just one restaurant in a chain that has similar locations across the Mediterranean coast and in most of the bigger cities in Italy, Greece, southern France and of course here in Spain?'

'I've seen many of them here, and also while I was in Madrid,' Sophia answered. 'But I didn't know they were that big.'

'Well, yes they are.' Her father continued. 'They are all part of the same organisation based in Italy and owned by the Barbieri family, and Gianni Barbieri in particular.'

The information was new to Moreton, and he was unsure as to how it affected the fortunes of CD Retama. It was not something Garrigues was unaware of. He continued.

'Gianni Barbieri is currently in Valencia. He is speaking with the regional Valenciana authorities about extending the chain of restaurants already open here, and looking for favourable financial considerations for bringing employment into the different areas of the region.' He paused, flicking up his eyebrows as he did so, before continuing. 'It's the way business is done these days, and Barbieri is apparently always keen to see his name linked with something positive across the media.'

Moreton was still less than clear how this situation could be to CD Retama's advantage, but that was about to become clear.

'It's also the way business is done these days that publicity, good publicity, is like an energy drink. It boosts business. In the past, Barbieri has looked to give the local media some 'good news' stories when announcing his expansion plans. It helps to put a positive spin on things, increases the profile of the business, and Barbieri can see his name in the press linked with something positive. Hernández has an appointment with him tomorrow. As the owner of a number of local newspapers, he was able to get access. He will try to sell the idea to Barbieri of him supporting CD Retama with the guarantee. In exchange, Hernández can offer him some very positive reports for both himself and his business in his newspapers and suggest to other people he knows in the media to do the same.'

With everything now dropped into place, Moreton could appreciate both the rationale behind the plan, and how fragile it sounded. He asked the inevitable question. 'Will it work?'

The sigh inadvertently released by Garrigues offered an impromptu answer, but he followed it up anyway. 'In all honesty, I cannot say, Jon. I have never met Barbieri. I've read a lot about him and his ways. He's certainly very successful and such men can often be swayed by a little flattery. They have more money than they need, but there's always that desire to feel that they are appreciated, and receive what they consider to be the correct amount of ...' he paused, searching for the correct English word. Moreton helped him out. 'Adulation?' Garrigues smiled. 'Yes, adulation. That's correct, Jon. Plus, you must understand that Hernandez is also a very good businessman. He was a journalist, and knows how to sell a story. So, let's see. As soon as the meeting ends tomorrow, he has promised to call me. When he does, I'll let you both know of course.' Then, turning to Sophia. 'It's probably best not to say too much to the players or others at the club at the moment. Just tell them that talks are continuing.' A brief pause and slight smile. 'After all, it's the truth.'

After Sophia's parents had left, she sat down of the sofa next to Moreton, placing a hand and then her head on his shoulder. 'What do you think, Jon?'

'I don't know. It all sounds very complicated to me, but if there's a chance to save the club, we have to hope for the best. Do you know Hernández? Is he as persuasive as your father thinks?'

'No, not really. He came to dinner a few times, but I was very young then. By the time I came back to Retama from Madrid, he had left and moved to Valencia, but if my father has faith in him, then I do too.'

'Me, too,' Moreton said.

The following day passed slowly as Moreton and Sophia waited for the call from Garrigues. The summer sun was bright and warming so they spent the morning swimming and then lazing by the side of the pool in the complex, only returning to the apartment for lunch. It was as they were drinking coffee after their meal that Sophia's phone rang. Within a couple of seconds, she had reached for it and flipped the call open.

'Your father?' mouthed Moreton silently to her as she spoke to the caller. A nod gave the answer in the affirmative. As Sophia spoke, Moreton tried to discern the flow of the conversation from her responses, and what it all meant.

Hola papá.

A pause.

Si. ¿Qué significa eso?

A pause

¿Quién es él?

A long pause

Vale, claro

A pause.

Necesitaré hablar con Jon. Debería decidir.

Por supuesto.

Te devolveré la llamada en breve.

A pause.

A luego.

Sophia closed out the call, placed the phone down on the table and looked across at Moreton.

'Well?' he asked, although the question was unnecessary.

Sophia paused briefly as if arranging her thoughts before delivering the answer.

'Is everything OK?' Moreton asked again. The answer was unexpected.

'Well, Jon. Apparently that depends on us.'

'On us?' A more detailed explanation was required and delivered

'So, Hernández pitched the idea to Barbieri and after some discussion, he seemed interested, but there's a catch.'

Moreton sighed.

'Well,' Sophia continued. 'I say a catch, it might actually be a bonus for us.'

Sophia explained that despite Hernández's persuasive ways, there may have been another reason for Barbieri showing interest. The billionaire has a son, from his first marriage, called Daniele. He was keen a footballer and had been a very promising prospect as a youngster. He had been inducted into the Milan academy at Milanello, staying there for a couple of years, but eventually he left after falling out with some of the coaches there, and thought he was being bullied by them. That had been around three years ago now though, and Daniele was keen to play football again and looking for a club where he could restart his career. Moreton thought he saw where the conversation was heading. He was partially right, but not completely.

'And he wants to have a trial with us, play for a season or so to get fit, and then try to get a break with a big club again?'

'Well, not quite,' came Sophia's guarded reply. 'Barbieri says that he will guarantee the bond to CI, apparently Hernández said that talking with Barbieri about €250,000 was like discussing how big a tip to leave the waiter after dinner, but his son does not want a trial with us.'

'He doesn't,' Moreton asked feeling he had lost the thread.

'No,' Sophia confirmed. 'He wants to play. That's the deal. He has to play in every game that he wants to.' Sophia shrugged her shoulders. 'So, that is why it is up to us, to you and me. Well, you really. If we agree to this, the club has a chance to survive. If we say no, then this last chance will be gone.' She paused. 'And the club will die.' Moreton realised the implication, but still struggled against what was now an obvious reality.

'OK,' he protested. 'But we can't just agree to that. What if he's not good enough? What if he's absolute crap? It'll be like killing the club anyway.'

Sophia, nodded in acceptance, but added that perhaps that wouldn't be the case.

'Remember Jon, that for two years he was with the Rossoneri at Milanello. He must have some talent to be accepted there.'

'I guess so.' It was grudging acceptance at best, but Moreton couldn't deny the validity of Sophia's point. 'OK,' he concluded. 'I guess we have to say yes, don't we?' It was hardly a question at all. 'If you agree, I think we should ask your father to tell Hernández that we agree. We can get …' he paused trying to recall the name of the player who had been thrust front and centre into Retama's coming season, the one that would be their last chance of survival.

'Daniele,' Sophia inserted.

'Yes, Daniele, into a few training sessions and see how it goes.' He flicked his eyebrows up optimistically. 'Perhaps he'll be a decent player. As you say, he could be a bonus.' The words had been positive, but a doubt remained, gnawing at Moreton's mind. He resented having someone imposed on him; someone who could demand inclusion in the team. If he really was such an accomplished player, why would he need such a commitment?

Sophia picked up the phone to call her father, but Moreton placed his hand on hers, pausing her for a moment.

'Look, I don't want to be less than honest with all of the guys, especially after what has already happened but, do you think it's a good idea not to tell the players about having to select Daniele? It may not go down well with them and, even if we do tell them, it may just cause resentment, and damage the team spirit.'

Sophia thought for a moment, then smiled. 'Yes, I think that's best. I'll tell my father too. He'll understand,' she said tapping out Garrigues' number on the phone. Her first words, confirmed that CD Retama would live to fight another day.

Hola papá.

Sí, estamos de acuerdo.

Sophia smiled at Moreton as she spoke to her father. Neither of them, however, were aware of what lay ahead. Four weeks later, at the first pre-season training session for CD Retama, there would be one exit and three arrivals, albeit one arriving later than the other two. The new season would be just as dramatic as the previous one – if not more so.

Late Arrivals and Early Starts

It was early August when Moreton and Sophia next walked through the gates of the Estadio Antonio Núñez. They climbed the steps that led up to the gap in the wall and then down the other side, slipped over the perimeter wall and walked onto the pitch. Instantly, now in his own environment, Moreton felt comforted.

Intentionally arriving earlier than the players, Moreton and Sophia wanted a few minutes of quiet contemplation of their own as they savoured the unexpected opportunity that had been granted to them of saving CD Retama. Strolling over to the coaches' bench, Moreton laid his bag down and sat looking across the pitch, as Sophia settled beside him.

As well as the established squad, three new recruits were expected to join the club's first training session ahead of the new season. Alongside the expected arrival of Daniele Barbieri, Nicolás, the partner of Sophia's friend Elena, had suggested that a couple of players from his youth squad were now ready for a higher level of football and suggested that he bring them along for Moreton and Sophia to assess. They had readily agreed and, as they sat silently together, a feeling of expectation washed over them.

'We have another chance,' she said.

Moreton smiled.

Just then, the shuffling steps of Esteban announced his arrival from the dressing room behind them. Sophia smiled and the old man responded in kind. She rose, and gently kissed the new arrival on both cheeks before stepping to one side as the old man moved to embrace Moreton. 'Mister,' he said in his inimitably croaky voice. *'¡Este año ganamos!'* he insisted. Esteban's husky voice, made the words barely discernable, and Moreton was unsure what the old man had said. Sophia stepped in. 'This year we win!' she translated. Moreton wanted to agree but a natural caution tempered the optimism. *'Yo espero,'* he offered nervously glancing at Sophia for confirmation that he said that that he hoped so. It arrived.

'No, esperanza no. Ganamos. Somos Retama. ¿Sí?' the old man insisted. It seemed that hope was not enough, but the final words gave Moreton a convenient way out.

'Si, amigo. Somos Retama.'

It was deemed sufficient by Esteban. He snorted approval and ambled away.

As Moreton and Sophia watched the man who carried the tradition of CD Retama in his soul shuffle back towards the dressing room, Sophia's phone rang. Clicking the call closed, briefly afterwards, she related to Moreton that the fixtures for the new season had been produced and her father had emailed the details across to the apartment.

'Perhaps after training and a shower, I can print out the information, we can go down to Carlito's and discuss things over a couple of glasses of wine. Yes?' Moreton's smile was sufficient as an answer. Although he had only been in Spain for just over a year, Moreton had quickly become accustomed to the local bar being a place to meet friends and relax over one or two drinks, usually wine. The English approach of spending all night in a bar, often drinking too much, felt like an alien concept from another time and place, a million years and a million miles away.

Sophia was placing her phone in her bag when the first few players began to arrive. They were greeted with an embrace from Sophia and Moreton as they passed towards the dressing room to prepare for the training session.

As more and more of the players arrived, Moreton spotted Nicolás amongst their number, accompanied by two teenagers wearing football kits. Both were tall and slim but their hairstyles were very different. One had short-cropped hair, the other a mass of curls that tumbled from his head like an irresistible flood of water hurtling with untrained vigour over a series of rapids. Moreton walked to meet the trio and Nicolás introduced him to Elías and Mateo. The former had the short hair and the latter the abundance of curls. Moreton called across to Santi who had just arrived with Guido and asked them to take the newcomers into the dressing room and introduce them to the other players. The four strolled away as Moreton turned to Nicolás. 'So, can you give me a bit of background?'

'Sure, Elías is very quiet. Not only for most of the time anyway, but also, he is the same during games. You won't notice him for a while, then a chance will fall to him and 'bang', he clapped his hands unexpectedly to illustrate the point. 'He'll score. Probably don't expect too much from him too quickly though, he's a little shy as well.'

Moreton nodded, mentally noting down the comments.

'Mateo usually plays as a centre-back for us. He's tall and athletic, perhaps a little lightweight, but also very determined. He rarely gets bullied from the ball, has a good turn of pace and is skilful on the ball. I'm sure he could also play in midfield, but he always prefers being at the back. Very calm, not as quiet as Elías, but not very vocal either. There may be a complication however for him. His parents are from Italy originally and he told me that they are looking to return there as the company where his father works is opening a new office in Turin. He's likely to be transferred there, and Mateo will obviously be going with his parents. I'm not sure how long he will be here for, so you'll just have to see how things go, I guess.

'OK,' Moreton agreed. 'That's fair enough.

Nicolas continued. 'They're good friends to be honest. So, it would be ideal if you took them both, rather than just one, as they would not feel alone in a strange group then.' He paused for a moment, realising how his last comment could have been misunderstood. 'Only if you think they are both good enough of course. Then, if Mateo does leave, at least Elías will settled into the group by then.'

Moreton appreciated Nicolás's concern, and addressed it quickly with a disarming smile. 'Of course, I understand.' Before leaving, Nicolás mentioned that both Elías and Mateo lived near to the ground so would be finding their way home themselves, but asked if either Moreton or Sophia would ring him later and let him know how his players had fared. 'Of course,' Sophia confirmed.

With two new arrivals safely ensconced in the dressing room, Moreton and Sophia waited for the arrival of Daniele Barbieri to complete the squad but, as time ticked on and the players began to spill out of the dressing room and warm up ahead of the training session, no one appeared. After waiting an additional five minutes beyond the scheduled starting time, Moreton's patience was exhausted. 'Right,' he said, turning to Sophia. 'Let's get going.'

The irritation was clear in his voice, and Sophia tried to ease the situation. 'Perhaps he's been delayed,' she offered, without much conviction. Adding, 'or had trouble finding us.'

'Yeah, that's probably it,' Moreton replied, even less convinced. It had hardly been an ideal start for CD Retama's new player, and the absence was noted by the players, as well as by both coaches.

Moreton had planned a few gentle sessions over the coming couple of weeks to ease the players back into football after the summer break – and the traumatic end of the last term. A couple of passing and shooting drills were followed by a short-sided game played at walking pace, and in silence, with the rationale that it required players with the ball to look for team-mates with heads up rather than concentrating on the ball at their feet. The eerie silence of this final phase of the session was interrupted by the throaty roar of a high-powered car drawing up outside of the ground.

The violent intrusion into the sedate environment of the game caused all to stop and look towards the end of the ground that led to the gate. Even Moreton and Sophia temporarily lost concentration, but the latter was about to signal the game to restart when a figure dressed in a red and black tracksuit appeared at the gap in the wall at the top of the steps. The restart was delayed with all attention focused on the figure who stood for a moment, apparently looking around at the surroundings that comprised the Estadio Antonio Núñez, before descending the steps and making his first entrance onto the home ground of CD Retama.

The game had been set up on the far side of the pitch, so the newcomer's journey to reach where Moreton, Sophia and the players stood was around 60 metres, but the leisurely stroll to cover it suggested no real urgency. When the gap had been reduced to a mere dozen metres or so, Moreton could discern that the arrival was young, in his early twenties, slim and tanned, with swept back dark hair and wearing mirrored sunglasses. He ventured a guess as to who it was. 'Daniele?'

A hand raised the sunglasses onto the top of his black hair and Daniele Barbieri announced his arrival with a nod and a further glance around that hardly seemed designed to impress. '*Si,*' came the answer.

Moreton held out his hand. 'Jon Moreton,' he announced.

'*Ciao*' came the relaxed and self-assured reply.

'And this,' Moreton continued, indicating to Sophia standing a few metres away, 'Is Sophia.'

This time the reply carried more interest. '*Ciao, Sophia. ¿Cómo estás en este día? Me llamo Dani, Dani Barbieri.*' The proficiency of the Dani's language skills was impressive, but hardly had that effect on Sophia. The difference in responses offered by the newcomer was hardly lost on Moreton either.

'¿*Habla inglés?*' He asked, Then in hesitant and unconvincing Italian. '*Lei parla inglese?*'

Dani Barbieri smiled, and laughed a little. 'Yes,' he replied. 'I speak English.' Then, turning to Sophia, he added in Spanish, '*Y hablo inglés mejor que él habla español o italiano,*' with a conspiratorial wink and confident smile.

Moreton was unsure of the translation, but Sophia's shrug and turn away to indicate the players to restart the game at least hinted at the remark. It gave him the opportunity to talk to Barbieri without the audience that the young Italian clearly seemed to enjoy performing for.

'I know that this is your first time here, but I require all players to attend training on time, and be ready to take a full part in the session.' If Barbieri's father had compelled Moreton's hand in including Dani in his team, he was going to do so on his terms.

'I am ready to play,' Dani confirmed, unzipping his tracksuit top to reveal an Azzurri shirt beneath it, and then slipping off his tracksuit trousers.

'Maybe,' Moreton replied. 'But you are late. You've missed most of the session.'

Dani offered a disarming smile. 'I apologise,' he said. 'But this is the first training of pre-season. Yes?'

Moreton was unable to argue.

'Then this is about fitness. Yes?' As he was talking, Dani looked over Moreton's shoulder and noticed that Sophia was watching the conversation. With the 'silent game' offering no distraction, she was drawn to the conversation. He pulled of his blue shirt and stood in white shorts, tensing the muscles of his tanned torso and arms. He flicked his eyebrows up in Sophia's direction, before turning back to Moreton. 'You see. I am fit. I am ready to play.' The true reason for Dani's display had not escaped Moreton and his resulting irritation was clear.

'Well, we'll see about that. Put your shirt back on and we'll get you involved in the game. Let's see how hard you try to impress me.' The last word was delivered with obvious emphasis. Dani pursed his lips and nodded. 'Sure, which team am I playing with?'

A few minutes later, after the teams had been adjusted to fit in the new member of the squad, and the 'silent' rule removed, Sophia and Moreton watched as Dani took his place in the game. There was no doubt that the young Italian had talent. He was confident in possession, happy to display a variety of tricks and flicks to beat opponents and delighted in doing so. The quiet Mateo particularly falling prey to his ability. After watching Dani also score a couple of solo goals Moreton could only admit that having an ability like that in his team would surely be of benefit, if it could be harnessed for the good of the team, rather than merely for the self-indulgence of Dani Barbieri.

Once too often though Dani overindulged when faced by Adrián. Little knowing of the teak tough defender's reputation, a casual saunter forward with the ball and a couple of elaborate stepovers induced the sort of robust challenge that the other Retama players were well aware of, and so careful to avoid. Dani screamed out as the burly full back's challenge hurled him to the floor. It was

Adrián's own form of welcome. *¡Bienvenidos a Retama!'*

Dani held his leg screaming out abuse. *'Cretino! Culo! Figlio un cane!'* It was as well that Adrián understood little Italian. He reached a conciliatory hand down to pull Dani to his feet, but the Italian brushed away the gesture. *'A fanabla!'* He rolled away from the figure who stood over him and struggled to his feet, limping away towards where Moreton was watching in undignified, if subdued, quiet satisfaction.

'Is he crazy?' he asked rhetorically as he reached the Englishman.

'No, he's not crazy. He's just showing you that he has skills as well.'

The young Italian was still muttering inaudibly to himself as he returned to the game, barely acknowledging the hand proffered by Adrián.

Ten minutes later, Moreton brought the session to a halt and the players disappeared towards the dressing room to shower and change – with one exception. Dani headed in the opposite direction, away from the dressing room and across the pitch back towards the concrete steps and gate that stood behind them. Sophia noticed and pointed it out to Moreton.

'Hey,' he shouted. 'Hey, Dani.'

The young Italian stopped, half-turned and waited as Moreton trotted to catch up with him. 'Are you not showering? He asked.

'Sure,' came the reply. 'But not here. Back at the hotel.'

Moreton nodded slowly. He had quickly established that there was precious little chance Dani would ever be a fully integrated member of the Retama family, but he clearly had talent and could still be valuable to the team.

'OK,' Moreton conceded. 'Look, you're a good player. We could definitely use you. Do you want to play for us?'

Dani looked up at the sky as if contemplating the offer. 'Perhaps. I will come to the next few training sessions and let's see.'

'OK, but you were late today. It doesn't look good.' He checked himself as he spoke. 'It isn't good. We are a team and we show disrespect to each other if we don't arrive on time. Yes?'

Dani Barbieri had clearly heard such talk before, and flicked his eyebrows up, slightly rolling his eyes in apparent disdain.'

'Sure,' he replied with a throwaway nonchalance. 'Sure.'

'Dani, this is important.'

'OK, I said sure. I understand. Your town is new to me, and I don't know the area well yet. It made me late. OK?'

Moreton almost felt he was conceding the point by agreeing, but did so anyway, albeit somewhat reluctantly. 'OK'

'But, you tell that mad man not to keep kicking me. He should save that for the guys on the other team. OK?'

Moreton nodded and smiled tolerantly, but inside he was thinking, 'Well don't act like a twat then.'

An hour later, Moreton and Sophia had returned to the apartment, showered and walked down to Carlito's bar. As they did so, Sophia called Nicolás and told him that Retama would like to have both Mateo and Elías in the squad for the new season. Arriving at the bar, they sat at a table near the big window and toasted each other with a glass of wine, served by Elena. *'Salut.'*

Sophia spoke first. 'So, what do you think of Dani, then?'

'Well, that all depends which Dani you're talking about.'

Sophia smiled, fully understanding Moreton's reply. 'What about Dani himself?'

Moreton didn't hold back. 'To be honest, I think he's a spoilt brat and used to having his own way. I'm not sure he's ever committed to anything other than having fun. Plus,' he hesitated while taking a sip of wine before continuing. 'I think he's coming on to you a bit.'

'Well,' Sophia teased gently. 'He is a good-looking boy. Are you jealous, Jon?'

'No,' came the far too rapid answer. 'Well, yes.' A smile broke out across his face. 'Of course, I am,' he conceded. 'Shall I take my shirt of for you now?' he added in a mock Italian accent and with a self-deprecating laugh.

'Don't worry, Jon. He really isn't my type. You are. Well, what about Dani as the footballer?'

'He's got talent. There's no doubt about that. I can see why people rated him as a good prospect. The trouble is that I can also see why he frustrated people.' He paused. 'Especially at somewhere like Milanello. Having ability is a prerequisite to being an outstanding footballer, but it won't carry you all the way. If you don't have the will to succeed as well, it won't happen. You have to drive yourself. I'm not sure Dani has that desire.'

Sophia smiled gently.

'What?' Moreton asked.

'Do you know who you were describing then?' she asked.

Moreton looked at her inquisitively before simultaneously they delivered the same answer. 'Billy'.

'I guess so,' Moreton readily conceded, but then corrected the error. 'Billy's motivation was not ideal, but it was certainly there.'

It handed Sophia a key. She unlocked and opened the door. 'Well, his motivation is much better now, isn't it?'

She reached across, and handed Moreton one of the English language newspapers lying on the next table. The front page carried a picture of a smiling Billy Swan standing in front of a sign declaring "Billy Swan Soccer School". The text beneath the picture revealed how successful the foundation had become in both encouraging young people from the area to keep out of trouble and attend school. Youth crime was down in the area, as was truancy. Billy Swan was hailed as a local hero, a force for good in the community.

Walking through the door, she delivered the message. 'You need to talk to him Jon.'

'I know, I know.' It was a difficult issue to dispute, but at least he could delay the matter with a little diversion. 'Have you got the fixture list that your father sent. We should talk about that. Perhaps Dani will get bored of Retama before the season starts and decide that he couldn't be bothered to play. He won't be an issue then, but we'll still need to know who we're up against in the new season.'

Sophia realised it was the wrong time to push the matter. She reached into her bag and pulled out the sheets of paper from the email her father had sent her.

'Well,' she began. 'You know most of the clubs from last season, but there are a few changes. Firstly, Parque del Rey and UD Aragaza were relegated, and Estrella Azul have been promoted through the play-offs.'

'What about Torreaño? Didn't they make it through the play-offs for promotion then?'

Sophia shook her head. 'No, they came close but, in the deciding game, Montero was sent off for retaliation. I understand that he had been head-butted off the ball and then punched the player who did it. Then there was a big fight and another Torreaño player was also dismissed. They had been three goals up from the first leg, but lost the return game 5-0 with nine men. They missed out.'

'Wow, they'll be really up for it in the new season then.'

'Yes, and guess who we have, away, on the last game of the season?'

'No, really?'

'Yes, Jon. Retama's last game of the season is Torreaño away.'

'OK, that's one game sorted. Who are the new clubs and who do we have in the first few games?'

Sophia explained that the club relegated and taking Estrella Azul's place in the league was called CD Bugroño. Last season, they had a poor defence and had conceded 101 goals in 34 games. They had changed coach twice in the season and sacked the last one at the end of the season. For the new season, they had employed an English coach. When asked, Sophia explained that she didn't know his name, but understood that he had been a lower league player in England before taking up coaching and apparently moving to live in Spain, where he owned a bar. He had also signed three English players for the club.

'That's interesting,' Moreton mused almost to himself.

'Perhaps, Jon. But I don't think they'll be near the top of the table. I'm not sure that bringing in three players and a new coach who know little of the Spanish game is going to solve the club's defensive problems and turn things around that quickly.'

'I guess not.' Moreton agreed, but without much conviction. 'What about the promoted clubs?'

'Well, this might be more interesting, especially with one of them. Córuel is a large town around 20 kilometres away. They have had a club there for quite a while, but it's never been very successful. A couple of years ago though, a large and very successful software organisation called El Celo, moved into the town. It's a university town and El Celo tapped into a lot of the graduate talent. They also started to sponsor the football club, FC Córuel. Last season they signed a lot of new players and won the league by 12 points. They have apparently infected the club with a serious dose of ambition.'

'Hmm, I guess it's a kind of computer virus, then,' Moreton suggested, chuckling to himself at the quip. Sophia didn't seem to appreciate the joke though, so he quickly stilled the self-congratulation and took a sip of wine to cover his embarrassment.

Sophia moved on quickly. 'And, we play them at home in the game before travelling to Torreaño. Our last two games are likely to be difficult.'

'And hopefully important,' Moreton added.

'The other club is Castillo Viejo. They finished as runners-up last season and progressed through the play-offs, defeating UD Aragaza on penalties in the final to take their place. They are only a small club, so may struggle to stay up.'

Sophia folded the paper and placed back in her bag. 'So, there you go, Jon. That's the size of our task for the new season.'

Moreton paused briefly, chewing over in his mind the consequences of what Sophia had told him.

'OK, this is how I see it,' he began. 'Torreaño will definitely be a big danger and the same will probably be true for Córuel. Politanio as well, perhaps, depending on the sort of players they put into their B team.'

Sophia nodded, agreeing with each point in turn.

'Then there's Bugroño,' he added scratching his chin contemplatively.

'Bugroño? Why?'

'Well, the club have employed this guy after what was a disastrous season and allowed him to bring in three players from England. Why have they done that? They must have some reason to believe that he knows what he's doing.'

Sophia remained unconvinced, but they agreed that the first few games would show who was right.

'On the subject of the first few games,' Sophia added. 'Our season starts at home to San Esteban. Then we travel to Desorio before playing Castillo Viejo at home and then we go up into the mountains to play Árboles Altos.'

'It sounds like a reasonable start,' Moreton said.

'Yes, hopefully after the first few games, we should have established some momentum with a settled team and get some early points on the table, Jon.'

Sometimes, however, things simply don't go to plan.

When Your Number's Up

Sophia's phone rang, just as she and Moreton were preparing to leave the apartment and head out to the Estadio Antonio Núñez on the Wednesday before Sunday's first game of the season. She took the call on the balcony, as Moreton collected the necessary equipment together in his bag.

For the last couple of weeks Moreton had experienced contrasting emotions about CD Retama's prospects for the coming season. There was a growing confidence as the team progressed, building on last season and the way that Elías and Mateo had fitted in. They were both young, but offered cover for a number of positions and would develop as the season went on.

The optimism, though, was tempered with concerns about the way in which Dani remained outside, and aloof, from the group. On occasions, during training, his contribution would be electric, especially when he had the ball at his feet. At others though, there was a clear disinterest about his attitude. It was something not lost on the other players, and Moreton feared that when he selected the team to play the first game, and included Dani as he was committed to do, there may well be some level of resentment.

Moreton had just zipped up his bag when a beaming Sophia joined him from the balcony.

'I have good news,' she declared.

'I can tell.'

'That was my father. He took a call from someone at Barbieri's organisation. When we get to the stadium there will be some new kits waiting for us, all courtesy of Señor Barbieri and the Bella Cucina group.'

'That's great,' Moreton said. 'It'll give the guys a terrific lift just ahead of the season.'

'That's what I was thinking,' Sophia agreed.

When they entered through the gates of the stadium, Esteban was waiting for them, and beckoned Sophia over to him. 'You go,' Moreton said. 'I'll carry on and get things set up.'

With that, he climbed the concrete steps, descended the other side, hopped over the wall and crossed the pitch to the coaches' bench. Dropping his bag and settling down on the bench, he began scribbling in his notebook as the players arrived. Sebastián was the last to do so, except for Dani who would trail in a couple of minutes later. Instead of walking towards the dressing room, Sebastián headed directly in the direction of Moreton. Seeing him approach, Moreton climbed to his feet. *'Hola, Seb,'* he said. *'Que t'al.'*

'Si, muy bien, gracias,' the younger man replied, before seamlessly dropping into English. 'I have a slight problem,' he related. 'My responsibilities at the hotel are increasing, and I've just begun a distance business studies course with the university in Córuel. It all takes up so much of my time now that I don't think I

can keep attending training and playing for the team.' He paused a little, looking down at the floor with apparent guilt. 'At least for a while anyway.'

'I understand,' Moreton said. 'That's no problem and I really appreciate you coming to speak to me about it.'

'Of course. I wouldn't simply stop turning up. That wouldn't be fair on everyone and, I'll still try to come to some training sessions and, if there's ever an emergency and you need me for the odd game, I'll always try and be there.'

'That's great,' Moreton said. 'I can ask no more than that, but you must always put your parents' business and your studies first. Yes?'

Sebastián nodded and Moreton patted him on the back as the younger man walked on towards the dressing room.

A few minutes later, Sophia arrived and told Moreton that Esteban had the box with the new kits and that she had told him to bring it into the dressing room after training, when everyone was showered. 'That's perfect,' said Moreton. 'We can hand the kits out then. I've roughed out some ideas as to who should have what. Here,' he said, passing Sophia the notebook with the scribbles he had made while she way away. She nodded as she read his suggestions. 'Yes, I think that all looks good.'

He then told her about Sebastián. She sighed in both disappointment and understanding. 'He's such a good kid.'

'I know,' Moreton agreed. 'But it can't be helped.'

With the opening game of the season only a few days away, Moreton was keen to ensure that both this training session and the one on Friday, when the team would be selected, was delivered at a gentle pace. Injuries were to be avoided and, with a few weeks training already completed, he was satisfied that the squad was in good physical shape to give the club a strong start to the new term.

When the session was completed, after the warm down, Moreton asked Sophia to tell the players to wait in the dressing room after they had showered and changed. Fifteen minutes later, with the dressing room door open to signify that the players were ready, Moreton and Esteban brought in the box with the new kits in.

Moreton opened the box and, on top, wrapped in cellophane was a bright green shirt with the number one. Moreton reached inside and passed it to Paco Jiménez, together with shorts and socks. Beneath it was number two, which went to Alejandro Sanz. The Retama captain removed the shirt from its bag and held it aloft for everyone to see, as a quiet murmur of approval and nods spread around the room at the dark blue shirt with the Bella Cucina logo as sponsor on the front.

Much of the shirt allocation was straightforward, simply repeating the numbers from the previous season, with the new players dropping into the gaps remaining. At least, that was Moreton's intention as he continued. Numbers three to seven went to Adrián, Samuel, Kiko, Victor and Antonio Vasquez. Each shirt was received by the player with a shake of the hand and a polite *'Gracias.'* That established practice would not last much longer. The number eight shirt was next, and Moreton passed it to Esteban, accompanied by an approving round of applause. The old man held it to his chest, and beamed tearfully.

In the previous season, the number nine shirt had initially been allocated to Tomás Bendonces, before being taken up by Guido after his number twelve shirt had been torn apart in the game against Desorio. This time, Moreton had decided to allocate it to Dani, but that was not what the young Italian had expected. Instead of taking the proffered shirt, Dani, crossed his hands in front of him in a cancelling gesture. *'No, no nueve. No!'*

Moreton was confused as to the problem, but all quickly became clear as Dani sprang to his feet and reached into the box for the next shirt. He lifted the cellophane wrapped item and held it up to Moreton. Above the white number ten, in the same colour, the name "Dani" identified its intended owner. Satisfied, Dani returned to his seat, but clearly had more to say.

'Diez. Ten. *Dieci,'* he declared in three different languages to ensure the message had been received. *'Baggio è il numero dieci. Del Piero è il numero dieci. Maradona è il numero dieci.'* He paused as if the conclusion was obvious for all to see, then delivered it anyway. This time he spoke in Spanish so that everyone would understand. *'Números decenas. Somos los Fantasistas,'* he explained. Then in English, directly to Moreton. *'*Number tens are the fantasy players. Dani is number ten. Always number ten!' It was a statement that invited no dissent and, now satisfied that any disrespect had been dispelled, he settled down and, with a wave of his hand, indicated for Moreton to continue his deliberations.

The tension was palpable and Moreton, feeling more than a little humiliated by the wanton challenge to his authority in front of the entire squad of CD Retama, plus Sophia and Esteban, collected his thoughts as he quickly flicked through the remaining shirts in the box. No others had names on them, as Dani clearly knew would be the case.

The young Italian clutched his shirt and offered an affected nonchalance at Moreton's discomfort. Sophia reached out a hand, placing it on his arm in a gesture both of support and restraint. Despite Dani's father holding the future of the club in his hands, Moreton was sorely tempted to kick Gianni Berbieri's son out of the squad, right there and then.

It was Revi who came to the rescue. Jumping to his feet, he claimed the number nine shirt still in Moreton's hands. *'Nueve es mi número favorito. Es mi numero de la suerte,'* he declared, regaining his seat with an overly obvious broad smile, at the same time winking towards Juan Palermo who was sitting opposite him. The muscular forward responded. *'¿Número once para mí? ¿Sí?'* He took the shirt, shorts and socks that Moreton unconsciously handed to him. Then in turn, Guido followed the established lead. *'¿Doce, Mister?'*

The moment had passed, as the Retama players' actions smoothed out the tension, but for all who were there, the memory of Dani's behaviour would remain. Mateo was given number 13, Sebastián 15, Elías 17, Matías 18, Santi 19 and José Palermo 21. The other goalkeeper kit, bearing number 22 was passed to Juan Torres. There had been one number missing in the sequence, but the problem of Dani was still at the forefront of Moreton's mind, and he hadn't noticed. Few others did either. Only Sophia did, and that was because she was the one who had already removed the shirt.

Twenty minutes later, Moreton and Sophia were walking back towards the apartment. The evening was quiet, and still, but not as quiet and still as the lack of conversation between them. 'Don't let it get to you, Jon.'

Moreton's reply was less than honest. 'I'm not,' he lied. 'It's fine.'

'Really, Jon?' It was hardly a question.

Moreton exhaled noisily, as if the action was to expel a malevolent demon from his consciousness, then laughed a little. 'No, not really. He's a little shit, isn't he?'

Sophia couldn't help but laugh. Moreton hardly ever used bad language, especially when speaking to her, but even that comment felt inadequate. 'No,' she replied. 'He's a big shit.' They both laughed. It was certainly big enough to have broken the ice.

'You know,' Moreton said. 'Over the years, I've had plenty of players give me a bit of lip during training or in a game. Most of the time, you let it go and it's forgotten in a few minutes. You shake hands, accept it was a heat of the moment thing, and move on. This was different though. He knew what he was doing. He has us over a barrel. Well,' Moreton corrected himself. 'His father does anyway.'

'I know, it's difficult, Jon'

'Don't worry about it. This isn't about me or Dani Barbieri. It's about keeping CD Retama alive for the town, for everyone and, if I have to cope with someone like Dani to make that happen, I can do that.'

Sophia reached up and kissed him on the cheek.

Much as with Wednesday evening, the training on Friday was low key and easy paced and, at the end of the session, before they disappeared to the dressing room to shower and change, Moreton gathered the players around him by the coaches' bench. With Sophia translating, he announced the team that would open the season in the home game against San Esteban two days later.

There was little surprise in the formation that Moreton wanted. The past couple of weeks had concentrated on working in a system with a 4-2-3-1 formation. The team would have Jiménez in goal with Sanz, Kiko, Víctor and Adrián as the back four. Samuel would start alongside Revi playing in a deeper role. In front of them Antonio Vasquez and Guido would have the flanks, with Dani playing behind Santi, filling the role that, last season, had been the preserve of Billy Swan. Only the members of the squad who spoke English, and Sophia, noticed the particular emphasis that Moreton used when describing the young Italian's role as being the Number Ten in the system, although the subject in question seemed totally oblivious.

As the players dispersed and headed towards the dressing room, Jiménez stood apart from the others, and then walked back to where Moreton and Sophia were standing. He spoke hesitantly at first.

'Mister', he said addressing Moreton. 'We are good to be honest with each other now, yes?'

'Sure, Paco.'

'I never question your team selections. You are the Mister. That is your job.'

Moreton nodded. He knew what was coming.

'But I have to ask. Why Dani? Revi can play there. Matías can play with Samuel. Dani is a ...' the veteran goalkeeper searched for the word he was looking for.

'Little shit? Big shit?' thought Moreton, but kept his musings to himself.

'I don't know the word, but he is difficult, not friendly, not part of the team, not part of the club, not part of the family.'

Although Jiménez's command of English was far from complete, he had captured the essence of Dani Barbieri's relationship to CD Retama with exquisite precision.

Moreton wanted to agree with the assessment. He did agree, but only internally. That reality wasn't for public consumption, if the scenario with Gianni Barbieri was to be preserved. 'I understand Paco,' he said with no little empathy. 'But there is something valuable about him for the team, for the club. I want him to play, to see how he behaves in a game. He has a lot of talent and could be very valuable for us.'

It was clear that Jiménez was far from convinced but, having asked the question, he deferred to the decision of the coach with a quiet, 'Vale,' turned and walked away.

Sophia watched the elder man disappear and then looked at Moreton. 'I know you wanted to tell him, Jon. But it could have been disastrous. If the players find out that we have to let Dani play, it will cause all kinds of trouble.' Moreton blew out his cheeks. 'I know, but I really hate not being totally honest, especially with Paco.' He flicked his eyebrows up. 'Let's just hope Dani decides to play well on Sunday. It'll make the whole thing a lot easier.'

Some you win...

Sunday morning was bright and sunny. Moreton flicked open his eyes as the morning light pushed its way through the narrow gaps in the blinds shielding Sophia's bedroom from the sun's insistent rays. Instinctively he turned over in the bed, expecting to see Sophia, but the space next to him was empty and the sound of spraying water from the bathroom informed that she was already up and showering.

He sat up, rubbed his eyes, stretched and yawned. Then he remembered. It was game day. Not any game, but the start of a new season. Suddenly he felt exhilarated and sprang out of bed, just as the sound of the shower stopped. Grinning to himself, he stood outside of the bathroom door, with his nose pressed against it, sniggering silently. Seconds later, Sophia opened the door, startled for a moment to see him there. 'Jon!' she exclaimed in mock fright. He reached his arms around her pulled her naked body towards him, laughing as he did so. The scent of the shower was still fresh on her hair as Sophia's head rested on his chest. *'Buenos dias señorita,'* he said in overly polite tones. *'Hola,'* she replied softly, easing her body against his. Laughter and a militaristic agenda were the last things she expected in reply.

Easing her away from him by the shoulders, he declared in brusque tones: 'No time for any of that sort of thing. Shower, dressed, coffee, swim, breakfast, plan for the game, lunch, game, win, celebrate, dinner… ' he paused, kissing her softly on the lips. 'And then, mi amor, bed.'

'Hmm,' Sophia replied. 'I think you've forgotten something before shower.' She took his hand led him back into the bedroom.

Five hours later, with Sophia's addition to the agenda – plus half-a-dozen other tasks – completed, Moreton and Sophia arrived at the Estadio Antonio Núñez. Esteban was waiting for them at the gate, wearing his new CD Retama shirt. He pulled open the gates for them, kissing Sophia on both cheeks as she entered. As Moreton followed, the old man shook hands with him, then reached up and punched the badge on the chest of his shirt. Moreton responded in kind with the badge on his tracksuit top.

'Do you remember our results against San Esteban last season?' Moreton asked as they sat down on the coaches' bench.

Sophia thought for a moment. '0-0 both games.'

'You're good. It was that away game where Santi got injured early on.'

'And Jose and Alejandro clashed heads and had to come off. We had a lot of bad luck in that game. But for Juan saving that late penalty it would have we would have lost.'

Moreton nodded. 'In a run of ten games, we won nine of them. San Esteban was the exception. Their coach will know that they stopped us scoring in both games and will be drilling it into his players to remind them of it, and convince them that they can do it again. A good start, and an early goal will be very important. If they keep us out until half time, they'll believe they can do it again. We need a good start.'

Ninety minutes later, with the players warmed up, the CD Retama team sat in the dressing room awaiting Moreton's final team talk. Locking into the theory that flattery would be the best tool to inspire Dani, Moreton told the young Italian how important he was to the team and that he was their 'magician', the one that could open defences and create chances. It felt a little hollow to Moreton as he spoke, but Dani seemed to be pleased with the compliment, and that was the important thing. The coach also emphasised how he wanted a strong start to the game and an early goal to get the season underway.

A dozen minutes into the game, Moreton nearly had that early strike. Dani received a pass from Revi inside the centre circle, a sharp turn took him away from his marker and galloping towards the visitors' back line. Closed down by a defender, he decided to shoot from 20 metres. Striking the ball with the outside of his right foot, the shot curled towards the top corner, but the San Esteban goalkeeper got enough contact on the ball to divert it onto the bar and away for a corner.

From the restart, Retama succeeded in doing something they had failed to do across two entire games during the previous season, as Santi scored with a header from Antonio Vasquez's corner. Moreton and Sophia jumped to their feet and celebrated with the substitutes as Santi high-fived the mop-haired Vasquez, receiving congratulations from his other team-mates.

The pattern of the game was set and, despite Dani hardly being the most communicative or popular player in the home team, his undoubted ability shone like a beacon as he dominated the game. Had he been more prepared to pass when it was the obvious option, rather than shoot from tight angles, more goals would have doubtlessly followed inside the first half-hour and, with the break approaching, the single goal was scant reward for Retama's domination.

On 39 minutes though, the scoreline took on a more realistic view. A cross from the left fell to Dani on the edge of the box and his crisp volley cast the San Esteban goalkeeper in the role of impotent observer as the ball whistled past him and thundered against the crossbar. Ever alert, it was Santi reacting the quickest to collect the rebound and fire it home to double Retama's lead. This time, the goal scorer rushed to Dani to applaud his skill and celebrate with him as the others joined in. On the sidelines, Moreton stood and clapped, as Sophia and the substitutes followed suit.

At the break, as the teams walked to the dressing rooms, it was Dani receiving the plaudits from the other Retama players, and clearly basking in the adulation. After allowing the players time to take a drink and calm down, Moreton made it clear how impressed he had been and that, on another day, they would be four or five goals clear. He particularly made a point of praising Dani, offering a single word, *Magnifico.*'

The second half followed a similar pattern to that before the break. Retama were clearly in control and with the home defence hardly troubled by barely sporadic attacks from the isolated San Esteban forwards, Moreton realised that the points from the opening game were fairly safe. With 20 minutes to play, he decided to make a few changes and offer some early season playing time to a few of the substitutes.

First, Matías was sent on to replace Samuel and then Felipe Blanco took over on the left flank of the Retama back line from Adrián. With the defence hardly involved in the game, it was a low-risk move, and Moreton could see good value in getting as many players as possible involved in what was, by now, a more than comfortable win. The final change however was less planned.

With two minutes to play and no further scoring, Dani powered forward with the ball after exchanging passes with Guido on the left side of the Retama attack. Cutting infield, he skipped between two defenders. A stepover confounded the third and put him into the area with just the goalkeeper to beat. A drop of the shoulder saw him play the ball around the diving goalkeeper, but the collision brought the Retama forward sprawling to the floor as the ball was cleared downfield. It was the most obvious of penalties and Dani jumped to his feet, calling for the ball and clearly intent on exacting his revenge.

Retama captain Sanz had collected the cleared ball as it drifted into the Retama half of the field and, instead of passing it to Dani as the Italian demanded, gave it to Santi instead. Clearly annoyed that he was being denied his goal, Dani shouted in frustration, but such protests would cut little ice with Alejandro Sanz. The captain wagged a critical finger to Dani who then turned towards Moreton, arms spread wide appealing for intervention. Moreton stood motionless though. Santi had taken over as the club's penalty taker since Swan had left the club, scoring twice from 12 yards in the play-off games that Retama had lost at the end of last season and, as far as Sanz was concerned, nothing had changed.

Seeing little reaction from Moreton, Dani then dropped to the floor, holding his ankle, then rotating fingers in the air to indicate a substitution. Moreton bowed his head slightly and puffed out his cheeks, before calling to José Palermo. Dani limped off the pitch, behind the goal and sat on the wall as the younger Palermo brother replaced him.

Santi converted the spot kick comfortably and, as he did so, Moreton noticed the figure of Dani vaulting up the concrete steps past a small gathering of Retama fans, and disappearing through the gap in the wall leading towards the stadium gates.

Before the referee ended the game, the unmistakable sound of Dani's sports car being gunned into life and driven away at speed filled the air. Moreton glanced to Sophia shook his head and sighed. The game ended in a 3-0 win for Retama. On the field, it was all Moreton could have asked for. Off it however, the issue of Dani Barbieri that, for so much of the game, had looked to have been heading towards a positive conclusion, was once more front and centre in the mind of Jon Moreton.

Despite the inappropriate disappearance of Dani at the end of the game, on the whole the opening encounter of the season had produced a hugely encouraging win for CD Retama and, as he sat on the balcony of Sophia's apartment a few hours later, sipping at a glass of wine, Moreton tried to comfort himself with that fact. Sophia had just joined him after a shower when her phone rang. She picked it up and, after checking the incoming caller's name, mouthed the word 'Seb' to Moreton as she answered the call.

'*¿Hola?*

'*Hola Seb? Que t'al?*'

'*Vale*'

There was a pause as Sophia listened to the information Sebastián was passing on, before she spoke again.

'*Si, entiendo.*'

'*Claro.*'

'*Gracias, Seb.*'

'*Hasta luego.*'

'What did Seb want?' Moreton enquired warily.

As Sophia puffed out her cheeks before answering, Moreton knew the information would not be positive. 'He said,' she began, 'that Dani had asked him to tell us that his injury would mean he would not be at training next week or be available for the game against Desorio.'

Moreton shook his head sadly, but there was more.

'He also said that Dani was certain that he would not be fit for training the following but would play in the next home game.'

Moreton sighed. 'Injury?' he offered scornfully. 'The only injury, he has, is to his pride and ego.' Although both knew that to be the case anyway, Moreton felt better for saying it and having Sophia agree.

The mood of the evening suddenly felt sombre.

'Let's go for a walk, Jon,' Sophia suggested.

'I'm not sure I'm in the mood,' he replied.

'Well, let's go for walk instead then,' she replied with an impish smile.

It raised Moreton from his solemn mood. "Yeah, OK then.'

As the training session began on Tuesday evening Dani's absence was hardly worthy of mention. His late arrival was now very much expected and, it was only around fifteen minutes later that some of the players realised that perhaps it wasn't due to a matter of serial tardiness. As Sophia brought the initial passing drill to a halt and the players took drinks Revi raised the inevitable question to Moreton. 'Dani is not coming?' he asked in perfect English.

Moreton shook his head. 'Injured.' He suggested without conviction before adding. 'His ankle.'

Revi flicked up his eyebrows in genuine surprise. 'Really?'

'That's what I was told.'

'Well, OK. I guess that's how it is then.'

Moreton only offered a wry smile in reply, but in his mind the phrase, "That's how it is then," summed up his feelings neatly.

Regardless of his opinions on Dani's absence, however, and how it was considered as Revi passed on the news to his team-mates, there was little

Moreton could do to change matters. He had to accept it and organise his team accordingly.

Moreton and Sophia had already discussed how to restructure the team to cover for Dani's absence in Sunday's game away to Desorio. As with their opening day opponents, CD Retama had drawn both games against the team from the town along the coast during the previous season. In the home game, a seemingly comfortable victory had been squandered when Swan had been sent off for an apparently Charlie Broome-inspired indiscretion. Then, in the return fixture, Kiko had suffered a similar fate. In his case however, there was clear injustice.

For all that, it was unlikely to be an easy game, and Sophia had suggested moving Revi forward to play behind Santi and then slotting Matías in alongside Samuel in midfield to strengthen the defence. It was an obvious solution, but Moreton was reluctant for two reasons. Firstly, it would mean changing Revi's role and potentially making him feel that he was simply second best to Dani, rather than first choice in his deeper position. Secondly, despite the always earnest endeavours of Samuel and Matías, neither had the creativity of Revi and, consequently, the team's ability to build from deep would be compromised. In the end though, he was persuaded to go with Sophia's suggestion as it would at least give the team a solid pairing in front of the defence and be able to compete in the more physical demands of the game.

After the opening drills in this training session, and the ones on the following evening and on Friday, the emphasis would be to work on Revi's amended role and the partnership of Matías and Samuel. When the team was announced, therefore, following Friday's training, there was little surprise in those changes being the only ones made from the team that had eased past San Esteban.

As the coach carrying the Retama party exited the coastal town of Desorio following the game on Sunday however, much of what Moreton feared may be the case, had come to pass. The game had been competitive, and Sophia's idea of pairing Samuel and Matías in front of the back line had worked well as the pair had been solid in the face of some aggressive play, whilst always maintaining a discipline that meant Retama only suffered a single yellow card in the game, and that was for Revi complaining to the referee after he had been pulled down for the third time in five minutes by the same home player, a defender with a misshapen nose.

The team's attack however had looked largely sterile and, even when Juan Palermo had been sent on with 20 minutes to play, replacing Samuel with Revi dropping back to his more usual role, the home defence remained solid. At full time, the goalless draw that had felt increasingly inevitable as the game wore on, was confirmed. Despite the team's defence holding firm and not conceding in the opening two games, the early momentum of that three-goal win over San Esteban had now stalled. Moreton and Sophia were compelled to face the unpalatable reality that, for all the problems he brought with him, Dani Barbieri was probably as important to the salvation of CD Retama as his father's money.

Rolling with the punches

The training sessions for the following weak presented Moreton with a dilemma. Dani had said he wouldn't be available for training that week, but would play on Sunday against Castillo Viejo. It meant that the team would need to work on a formation during in the week without a key element of it being present. In the back of Moreton's mind was the nagging thought that a late call from Dani claiming he wasn't fit to play would cause even more disruption. It was, therefore, a surprise when on Friday morning another phone call to Sophia from Sebastián suggested that the errant Italian would attend Friday training, but only be able to participate in some of the session.

Sure enough, as the players completed their warm up ahead of training that evening, the roar of Dani's sports car drawing up outside the stadium announced his arrival. There was a hush of quiet expectation as the players waited, both for the start of their next drill, and to see Dani Barbieri joining them.

A few seconds, later with an apparently less than comfortable stroll the young Italian walked down the concrete steps, over the wall and across the pitch he had left with a similar gait almost two weeks earlier. Moreton turned to Sophia. 'Ask him if you can check his ankle and see if you can help,' he suggested. Sophia nodded and, walking towards Dani, guided him to the bench as Moreton set the players into their next task. With one eye focused on the players' movement in the rondo he had set up, Moreton had the other firmly fixed on Sophia as she examined Dani's ankle, noticing her attention was focused on his left leg.

A few minutes later, she returned to Moreton's side, leaving Dani sitting on the bench. 'Well?' he enquired.

'There's certainly some swelling there,'

'Really?' There was clear surprise in Moreton's voice. 'Am I wrong? I thought it was his right ankle that had the problem.

'I'm not sure.' Sophia paused for a moment, trying to recollect the events of the game against San Esteban. 'He told me that it is a problem that first started when he was at Milanello. He had suffered a couple of challenges on the joint and was sent to the medical team, but they brushed it off saying it was nothing, and he has suffered with it ever since.'

Moreton's frown was sufficient to suggest that he had been less than convinced by Dani's explanation.

'I know,' Sophia agreed. 'The facilities and expertise at somewhere like Milanello are first class. It seems difficult to accept that they would react to an injury in that way.' She glanced back towards where Dani remained sitting on the bench, and received a wink in reply. 'Anyway, I've told him to sit this out and give the ankle more time to heal. He said that he'll be fine for Sunday and is keen to play again.'

Moreton had been drawn to look at Dani at the same time, and felt the wink given to Sophia was as much for his attention as it was for hers. It did little to cement the relationship between coach and player, but Moreton felt that, with Sophia's confirmation of the damage to the ankle, he at least had a cloak of justification for the player's absence, and return, despite his misgivings.

At the end of the session, Dani rose from the bench and walked haltingly with the other players towards the dressing room and, from the conversation, Sophia told Moreton that he had been repeating the Milanello story, and receiving sympathy in exchange. Twenty minutes later, Moreton had announced the team for the home game against Castillo Viejo, resorting to the line-up that played the opening game. Dani was back in the starting eleven.

The year was now moving into Autumn, and the heat of the Spanish sun was easing, although temperatures were still in the high thirties. In order to get some time away from football, Sophia suggested to Moreton that they visit the beach at Torre del Mar. It was where, the previous year, she had introduced Moreton to the simple delights of grilled sardines and cold beer while watching the waves gently rolling onto the golden sands of the beach. The following day, they took the short bus ride to the small resort town and then the hundred metres or so walk onto the sands where they set up their beach umbrellas, before running off into the waves.

An hour later, they were settled into the beachside restaurant hungrily devouring a plate of sardines, accompanied by a glass of cold beer. Together, they provided the perfect culinary symbiotic relationship. Moreton eased back into his chair as all that remained of the fish was a pile of heads, tails and bones. 'Do you think, that Dani flirts with you just to annoy me?'

'Maybe. But I am also very attractive.' She paused, adding,' Aren't I?' with a smile.

'Well, that's true,' Moreton laughed.

'Of course, he flirts, Jon. It's all just a game for him. He knows that his father's money has put us both in a difficult situation, and he uses that to try and play games with you. He does not want to be liked. He wants people to accept that his money gives him power over them, and then he can play silly games and be safe.'

'I guess so. What about you, though?'

Sophia was unsure as to the implication in the question.

'Does he play games with you? What I mean is, has he ever tried to push things with you?'

'No.' The answer was clear.

'I'm sorry,' Moreton conceded. 'I shouldn't have said that. It's just that his stupid little games are beginning to get under my skin a little.'

'Then you let him win, Jon.'

'I know. Of course, you're right.' He smiled at her.

'Anyway, how can he when you are there and, even when you're not, there's always Paco. And you know that Paco does not like him.'

Moreton laughed and nodded as he raised the glass to drain it of the last of the beer. 'I've always liked Paco.'

Following the goalless draw against Desorio, Sunday's visit of newly promoted Castillo Vieja to the Estadio Antonio Núñez offered Retama a chance to get things moving in the right direction again. Despite Moreton's continuing reservations about Dani, many of the players seemed content with the Italian's explanation for his absence from the previous game and training during the week. Fuelled by the boost that the player's presence gave to the team, it was easy to forgive and forget.

That tolerance was rewarded just six minutes into the game when Dani put the home team ahead. A cross from the right by Antonio Vasquez looked to have been drawn too far away from the goal and drifted behind where Santi had made his run towards the near post. The striker's threat though had grabbed the attention of the visitor's defenders and two of them trailed Santi, leaving space behind them. Vasquez had seen the decoy run and Dani advancing into the space created. His cross was perfectly timed to meet up with Dani's run and an adept chest control and searing volley into the roof of the net completed the move. As the ball ripped into the net, Dani simply stood on the edge of the penalty area, motionless from the point his foot had detonated on the ball, before shrugging his shoulders as if to dismiss such extravagant skill as the merely run-of-the-mill fare. The exuberant celebrations of his team mates quickly engulfing him however dismissed such stances. It was a goal of rare quality and, of the players wearing Retama blue, few others had the ability to deliver it with the skill exhibited by Dani Barbieri. Standing on the sidelines applauding, it was something that Moreton was compelled to accept as unarguable.

Despite his apparent nonchalance at the goal, it clearly inspired Dani. For the next half hour or so, he dominated the game, demanding the ball that was inevitably arrowed towards him by Revi, prompting the Retama attacks. Dani sprayed passes left and right bringing Retama's flank players into the game and repeatedly threatening to open up the visitors' overworked defence.

Twice, he threaded intricate passes through to Santi, only to see the forward's efforts thwarted, first by the post and then by the goalkeeper's legs as the striker's attempted flick past the last man in the visitors' defence was deflected wide. There was even a chance for Revi, as he charged forward following another pass to Retama's number ten. Dani was strolling around the field like a king surveying his underlings and it was only the frustrated over-physical challenges of a defence and midfield, run ragged, that halted his progress. A turn from Dani saw a shot struck from 25 metres that flew narrowly wide. Another goal was surely on the cards and, when it came, there was little surprise in who it was that found the back of the net.

With half-time just half-a-dozen minutes away, Moreton was becoming concerned that, for all their domination, and Dani's expansive play, Retama's lead remained slender. Those six minutes however would be highly significant. First, a long pass forward by Revi deceived the visitors' back line and with Santi in an offside position and unable to contribute, Dani chased after the ball. The advancing goalkeeper, Dani and the ball all arrived at the same time around the penalty spot. The goalkeeper threw up his arms to try and block the seemingly inevitable clip over his head from the Retama player, as Dani looked to loft the ball. Instead, he merely feigned contact with the ball, allowing it and him to move past the stranded goalkeeper. With no defender in sight, there was enough pace on the ball for it to roll unhindered into the net, but Dani chased after it, sliding into a touch just before it crossed the line, he confirmed the goal. Jumping to his feet afterwards, he folded his arms standing with a self-satisfied grin on his face. The skill inherent in the goal impressed Moreton, but the attendant need for self-aggrandisement irritated him in equal measure. Two minutes later, that irritation had evolved into anger.

From the restart, it was clear that Dani was intent on notching a hat-trick before the break. Retama quickly gained possession and a ball from Revi sent Guido scampering down the left flank. His cross was headed on by Santi, with Dani's run taking him past his marker and looking to be clear on goal. A desperate pull at his shirt however halted his progress and he fell to the floor. Irate at the cynical denial of his third goal, Dani quickly jumped to his feet, remonstrating with the referee, demanding a red card as sanction for the offence. When the official chose instead to deliver a yellow card and a caution instead, the already boiling temper of Dani exploded. Standing just a foot in front of the referee he decried the perceived injustice, waving his arms in the air in frustration. The anger was understandable, but inevitably brought a sanction of its own. A yellow card was insufficient to cool Dani's ardour and was quickly followed by a red one. Seconds earlier, Retama looked to be heading into a comfortable three-goal lead. That had now evolved into playing out the second-half without their best player. Wisely, Alejandro Sanz ran up field and, wrapping his muscular arms around Dani, guided him from the field to prevent any further punishment from the referee.

Two minutes later as the referee ended the first half, the Retama coaches and players returned to the dressing room to find a still fuming Dani awaiting them. As they entered the room, Dani sprang to his feet and headed straight for Moreton. 'Have you all walked off the field in protest at that idiot?' he demanded in English.

Moreton sought to maintain a level of calm. He shook his head. 'It was a poor decision, but that happens in football, Dani. You know that.'

It was an attempt to cool Dani's fury, but it fell on deaf ears as the young Italian reverted to his native tongue to vent his anger. *Lui è un stronzo! Pezzo di merda! Stupido!'* He waved his arms in the air, before collapsing back down onto his seat, ire temporarily spent. Moreton decided it was best to let the storm blow itself out and, for the next few minutes, he concentrated his attention on drilling into his team the importance of being solid for the first 15 minutes of the second period. If they conceded an early goal, they could be in danger of seeing the points slip away. With a ringing shout of *'Somos Retama!'* the players left the dressing room for the second half. Moreton nodded to Sophia to go with them as he sat down next to Dani, the younger man still muttering profanities to himself, anger simmering. The young coach saw a chance to build a relationship with his frustrating but hugely talented forward.

'Dani,' he began softly. 'I understand your anger but, if you lose your composure and get yourself sent off, it means that these players, who can only stop you by kicking, you or pulling you back, win. They are not fit to lace your boots, but when you lose control, they win. They are all out there for the second half, and you're …' He draped his arm around Dani's shoulders, 'stuck in here with me. Angry and pissed off at the injustice.' There was little response from the player, but even the silence was a measure of progress for Moreton. He pressed on.

'You remember when you claimed the number ten shirt?'

There was barely perceptible nod.

'Well, those players you mentioned. Baggio, Del Piero, Maradona. They were all kicked, pulled, tripped, or hacked down when their abilities humiliated opponents. Yes?'

This time the silent acknowledgement of the nod was clearer.

'And, sometimes, when they were younger, they also lost their temper,' Moreton continued. 'And paid the price for it, but they learnt from those experiences. They understood that each kick, each pull, every time they were fouled, it was a compliment. It was like someone saying "You are too good for me. This is all I have." They took the compliment, got up and carried on. They won games for their teams, and made sure those cheats suffered. It was the best lesson they could deliver. It was the best revenge. They won and the cheats lost.'

For the first time, Dani looked up and, into Moreton's eyes as if seeking some confirmation. It came with a smile and calm assurance. 'It's true, Dani.'

The second half of the game was almost 20 minutes old when Moreton returned to his seat alongside Sophia on the coaches' bench. 'How's it going?'

'Not bad,' she replied. 'There was a lot of pressure early, but the defence was solid. Kiko is a real giant in games like this. He and Victor are almost the finished article now. So sure, so composed, and Paco is experienced in these things.'

Moreton nodded contentedly, listening as he watched the game. A long hopeful cross into the Retama box was comfortably collected by Paco Jiménez. It signalled an increasing frustration in the visitors' play as their attacks against a diminished Retama team came to nought.

'How did it go with Dani?' Sophia asked.

'I'm not sure, to be honest. Not too bad, I think. At least I hope so.'

The conversation paused as a strong tackle from Adrián broke up another attack, and Moreton and Sophia loudly applauded, shouting encouragement.

'Go on,' Sophia asked, seeking more information as they settled down again.

'Well, we had a bit of a chat, and I tried to make him feel better and understand that sometimes things aren't fair, but you just have to roll with the punches.'

Despite Sophia's comprehensive command of the English language, the boxing metaphor passed her by. 'What punches?' she asked. 'Did you hit him?'

Moreton suppressed a laugh and explained, before continuing. 'I told him he would be suspended for two games, and he said he wanted to go back to Italy for a couple of weeks to visit his mother, as he hadn't seen her for a few months.

Apparently, he is quite close to Daniela Barbieri, and is named after her. It would mean him missing training, but perhaps the break would do him good, and he said he would be back for training on the Friday before the game against Sobrolepeña, so I agreed.'

'It's a good idea Jon. Perhaps your chat will help things.'

On the pitch, Retama continued to deny the attacks of the Castilla Vieja forwards and, with the game heading into the last quarter of an hour, Moreton opted to send some fresh legs on to see out the game. He called the curly-haired Mateo to warm up and a few minutes later Retama's new defender made his debut replacing a tiring Samuel. Felipe Blanco took over from Guido and Juan Palermo replaced Santi, with Moreton instructing the rugged forward to try and offer a long ball option for the defence and keep the ball up field as long as he could.

Finally, with the game entering the final couple of minutes, the other newcomer to the squad, Elías replaced Antonio Vasquez. The changes meant that, aside from the absent Sebastián, every member of the Retama squad had enjoyed some game time inside the club's first three fixtures and, when the final whistle went with the two-goal lead still intact, and considering the sending-off, Moreton had good reason to feel satisfied with the day's endeavours.

That evening they had arranged to have dinner with García, Sophia's great uncle. The man who had temporarily returned to take charge of the club for the play-off games at the end of the previous season had been in hospital for a minor operation on an old ankle injury from his playing days. Moreton and Sophia sat at their table in the Bella Cucina restaurant, they chatted about the game as they awaited Garcia's arrival. A few minutes later, the shuffling figure of Vicente García, apparently still struggling from the after effects of his operation arrived and made his way over to the table. After exchanging greetings, Moreton enquired about the older man's ankle.

'Ah, it's just the price old footballers pay for having the joy of playing the game,' García said stoically. 'But,' he continued. 'You know all about that, don't you, Jon?'

Moreton nodded, unconsciously reaching down to rub his injured right knee as he asked how García's injury had occurred.

'Well,' the old man related. 'Back in my playing days sports medicine was very basic. If you had an injury there was a sponge and some cold water.' He chuckled to himself at the cliché, before continuing. 'But this was something a bit worse. A tackle caused me to turn the ankle. It was painful, but I just got the medic to strap it up so I could continue. After the game though it went 'poof''. The old man expanded the gap between his hands rapidly to illustrate the swelling. I go to the doctor, but they say it is OK and, in a couple of days, the swelling goes down. But then it comes back when I play. Play, swell, rest. Play, swell, rest. It slowly becomes worse each time. For the rest of my career that is what I did. In the end, I stop playing as it becomes too painful. Later they found ligament damage, but it had been missed for many years. The scar tissue had caused further damage and it became difficult to walk, but hopefully now, I will be better.'

'That's good,' Moreton replied.

'Perhaps, Jon,' García added. 'In a few weeks you will give me a game with your team, yes?' He beamed a smile and laughed.

'Sure,' Moreton said, joining the laughter. 'Why not.'

The conversation continued as they ate, moving through the fortunes of CD Retama, family and future plans, but there was something at the back of Moreton's mind. Over coffee, he returned to the subject of poorly diagnosed football injuries, relating Dani's account of his injury and the problem at Milanello to García. The old man was clearly surprised by the story.

'Is that so?' he asked. 'That seems strange for an organisation with such an advanced medical facility and the care and investment that the club pour into player welfare.'

Moreton nodded in agreement.

'Very strange,' repeated García contemplatively. 'But these things can happen in the very best of places. Let's just hope that young Dani's injury isn't as bad as mine was, eh?'

Retama's next fixture would send them into the mountains to visit Árboles Altos. Sophia had told Morton that it would not be possible to meet up with her parents whilst in their village, as her father was in Milan, visiting the Bella Cucina headquarters, to sign some documents. It meant, Sophia added, that their house there was empty so, after the game they could stay there in the mountains for a few days and enjoy some peace together. Moreton had been tempted by the prospect, but thought it would seem like they were abandoning the team by sending them back to Retama on their own. Sophia was disappointed, but also understood the validity of Moreton's point.

Dani's absence from the Retama team for the next two weeks inevitably meant another reshuffle of the club's resources ahead of the game against Árboles Altos on the following Sunday. It meant that much of Moreton's time with Sophia on Monday was spent discussing what team should be selected for the game and how the formation should be laid out. The game against Desorio, with Revi further forward and Matías partnering Samuel in front of the defence had brought a draw. With a full team however, Moreton was convinced that they could have won the game. Despite the extra solidity in defence, there was a price to pay in not having Revi to instigate attacks from his deeper position, and the Retama threat was diminished. He was keen to avoid a similar situation. Options were discussed involving one or both of the Palermo brothers, or even bringing Elías in to play as the striker and dropping Santi back into the number ten role. In the end, they decided on something different.

Antonio Vasquez would be moved centrally from his wide position and played as the number ten and José Palermo would be drafted in on the right flank. There was little doubt that the tricky winger had the skill to play in the role behind the striker, but his natural aversion to the more physical rough and tumble of the middle of the field might compromise his desire to display his full repertoire of skills. It was decided, however, that it was a gamble worth taking, with the option of changes from the bench if things went awry.

The three training sessions of the week were focused on using Vasquez in this role, and encouraging him to look for opportunities to take on a defender and open up spaces for Santi ahead of him. When the team was announced on Friday, therefore, there was very little surprise among the players about selection and formation. The previous season, had seen Retama return from their trip to the mountains with a goalless draw. This time, they would fare less well.

The early period of the game was encouraging for Moreton and Sophia as they watched their team dominate possession. Revi repeatedly fed the ball into Antonio Vasquez, but the little winger seemed to struggle at first under the sharp pressure of the opposition midfield players seeking to deny him space but, as he eased into the game, his natural ability began to open a few doors. One pass inside of the full back saw the younger Palermo brother galloping into the area, but his cross flew narrowly wide of the far post. It was even more frustrating for Moreton when, with just a dozen minutes played, a sharp turn by Vasquez was brought to a sudden halt as he hobbled, before falling to the floor, holding his right calf. Sophia grabbed her medical bag and ran on to the field, but her twirling fingers signal to Moreton, indicating that a substitution was required, only confirmed what he had already feared.

It would have been harsh to call the decision to move the winger into the centre of the game a failure. Injuries can happen on any part of the field, but it still felt that way to Moreton. With the injury occurring so early in the game, he decided to take the safe option. Matías was sent on to partner Samuel and Revi was slid forward into the role behind Santi. At worst, it was a holding situation until Moreton could rethink his options at the break.

As Antonio Vasquez hobbled towards the sidelines, supported by Sophia, Moreton stood up and patted the little winger on the back as he passed on the way to a seat with the remaining substitutes.

'How bad?' He asked as Sophia sat down beside him after taping an ice back to Antonio Vasquez's calf.

'I don't think it's too bad, but he'll be out for a couple of weeks or so.'

It was what Moreton had expected to hear. Already denied the services of Dani, the injury to Retama's winger meant the truly creative options in the team were becoming increasingly limited.

As Moreton had feared would be the case, Matías and Samuel in partnership added a welcome solidity to the Retama defence but, the absence of a more creative mind to move the ball forwards stunted his team's attacking threat. Revi and Santi became isolated. At the break, the game remained goalless, and looked likely to stay that way unless anything changed. Moreton wasn't content with that prospect.

For the fourth game in succession, Samuel was removed from the action, but his natural gentle disposition produced nothing but a gentle nod of acceptance at the coach's decision. Revi was moved back to play alongside Matías, and Juan Palermo was sent on to play as the main striker with Santi dropping into the number ten role. The Retama defence had delivered successive clean sheets in the club's opening three games and, against a team that had failed to score against them in either of their games last season, Moreton felt confident that they could do the same again, whilst hoping the changes offered an increased chance of a goal at the other end.

The beginning period of the second half seemed to justify the decision, as Retama's attacks became more frequent and threatening. Over the previous season, Santi had matured into an outstanding forward, and was well capable of linking Revi's clever play with the pace of Guido on the left and the youthful exuberance of the younger Palermo sibling on the other flank, while the older brother caused problems for the home defence with his muscular play. Inside two minutes, a header from José Palermo, advancing in from the right to meet a cross from Guido, looked likely to bring tangible reward, but an acrobatic save by the goalkeeper tipped the ball over the bar.

The next chance came after a clever return pass from the same player set Santi running free, but he was foiled as the goalkeeper plunged at his feet and smothered the ball before he could get a shot off. The game was developing into a battle between the eager Retama forwards and the overworked home goalkeeper. Another chance fell to the younger Palermo brother inside the area, but he snatched at the ball and, from twelve yards out, his shot flew high over the bar. Fifteen minutes passed, and then 20, without a goal and, as more chances came and went, Moreton became increasingly frustrated that his team's pressure had failed to deliver any tangible reward. Were further changes the answer?

With 15 minutes to play, the momentum of the game had, if anything, swung even further in Retama's way. The home team had made changes too, but theirs had been to remove forward players for defenders to bolster the back line. Moreton decided it was time to act. Removing Adrián, he sent on the young Elías with instructions to join José Palermo in the striker role. It left the Retama defence a man short but, by this stage, there seemed little threat from the Árboles Altos forwards. Sometimes, however, that is when the danger is at its greatest.

Another save from the home goalkeeper, this time denying Guido, produced a corner on the Retama right. With both the Palermo brothers, Santi and Elías in the front line, the visitors carried plenty of aerial threat, but Moreton ushered Kiko forward as well to supplement the forwards. As Revi floated the ball into the area three minutes of the 90 remained on the clock.

The ball dropped towards the danger area, but a gloved fist from the goalkeeper cleared the immediate danger. Characteristically, Victor was the lone Retama sentinel hanging back around the halfway line as the ball bounced towards him and a lone home forward advanced in an apparently token effort to close him down.

For once however, the usually immaculately assured Victor misjudged the bounce. The ball passed under his foot and on into the Retama half. Seeing an unexpected opportunity drop into his lap, the home forward raced after the ball as Victor turned to chase. To all intents and purposes now, it was a contest between the forward and Jiménez. The Árboles Altos forward headed the ball on as it bounced up and continued the chase. Had he pushed it too far though? The veteran goalkeeper advanced towards the edge of his area, and threw up his arms as the Árboles Altos player caught up with the ball and tried to lift it over him. Jiménez had judged the situation well though and got enough contact on the ball to send it wide of the goal. The danger seemed to have passed.

Victor ran back towards Jiménez patting him on the back in thanks for baling out his slip, as both Moreton and Sophia shouted out in acclaim to their goalkeeper. They were instantly quietened however by the red card that the referee flourished in the face of Jiménez as soon as he had caught up on the play. Out on the left flank of the Retama defence, the linesman stood level with the edge of the Retama penalty area, with his flag raised, alleging that the goalkeeper had been outside of his area when the save was made.

For a moment all was quiet as the implications of the decision sank in. Moreton looked to Sophia. 'Was he?' he asked. A shrug was the only reply. It had been a hairline decision but, right or wrong, there was no changing it and Juan Torres quickly prepared to replace the expelled Jiménez.

Moreton decided to remove Guido so that Torres could take over in goal. At least Retama had a more than decent goalkeeper to deploy as cover, but that wouldn't save them from defeat. The resulting free-kick just outside of the area was fired in powerfully. It took a deflection from Santi in the wall, eluded Torres, and struck the post before nestling in the Retama net.

Moreton screamed out in anger and frustration as the home players celebrated what was surely now the most unexpected of victories. He picked up his water bottle and then hurled it to the floor again. Minutes later the referee blew for full-time and Retama had lost a game that they should have won.

The beaming Árboles Altos coaches walked across to shake Moreton and Sophia's hand, but Moreton's response was curt at best as he stood, hands on hips waiting for the referee as his players trooped slowly past him towards the dressing room. As he waited, Sophia took his arm and whispered into his ear. Moreton pursed his lips and nodded slowly in acceptance, bowing his head.

The referee and linesmen had seen the Retama coach waiting for them by the side of the pitch and their stone-faced demeanour suggested they were expecting a torrent of complaints. When they reached Moreton, however, he merely offered his hand to shake with each in turn and smiled. He then turned and jogged after the group of home coaches to apologise for his truculence and congratulate them, with Sophia's words in his mind. 'Roll with the punches.'

It's in our heads. It's in our hearts

The atmosphere on the coach journey back to Retama had been subdued and quiet. After the game Moreton had tried to emphasise to his team that the defeat had been massively undeserved, but that's just the way football goes sometimes and how important it was to not let the result distort the quality of the performance. 'Keep that level of play up, and we'll win far more games than we lose,' he had insisted. They were the correct words but, just as the coach had felt frustrated, that same emotion inevitably permeated through the squad, especially with Jiménez, who apologised to the players and coaches for his apparent misdemeanour. The *mea culpa* was quickly dismissed by Moreton who told the veteran that he didn't believe the goalkeeper had been at fault, but that was just the way things went sometimes. It was an assessment echoed among the players

For all the sincerity of Moreton's words about the defeat being unwarranted, the cost of Dani's red card was now making itself known. Each time, for various reasons, when he had been unavailable, the consequence had been an unsatisfactory make-do-and-mend approach that had compromised Retama's ability to win games. Given the volatility of the young Italian, and the likely prospect that other absences would be likely as the season progressed. It was a problem that occupied much of Moreton's time on the coach journey back to the coast, as Sophia dozed sleepily, resting her head on his shoulder.

Various options had gone through his mind, some echoed the thoughts of the previous season when, on occasions, the team had needed to cope without the talents of Billy Swan. A real solution had largely evaded him then, and still felt out of reach now, but would, at least temporarily, present itself in training on the following Tuesday evening.

Moreton and Sophia had promised themselves a free day on Monday to relax and agreed to meet Elena and Nicolás for lunch as it was fiesta day in the town. They rose late and decided to go for a swim before breakfast. The main holiday season had now passed and many of the apartments on the complex, owned by people who lived in Valencia or Madrid were empty, and they had the pool to themselves. The water was wonderfully relaxing and washed away the residues of disappointment caused by losing the game. An hour later, they sat on the balcony eating a light breakfast of fruit and yoghurt as Moreton distractedly prodded a piece of melon around his plate.

'Where are you, Jon?' Sophia asked softly.

'Sorry, what?'

'I asked you where you were, in your mind. That piece of melon will end up bruised if you move it around any more.'

Moreton smiled at her. 'Sorry.'

'Don't be sorry. Just invite me to the place you went to. I want to be there with you.'

Moreton beamed as he shook his head, searching for the correct words. 'I love you,' he declared locating them. 'You're so amazing. I don't deserve you.'

'Well, that's probably true, but we can talk about that later.' She laughed and reached across the table to take his hand. 'So, where were you?'

'Well, I guess I'm stuck in trying to work out how we replace Dani when we need to.' He paused. 'Because it's going to happen again this season, I'm sure of it and, if we don't solve the problem, it could cost us promotion in the end.'

Sophia nodded. 'I know, but the answer is there somewhere. It will come to us.'

'Replacing him with Revi looks the perfect solution. Revi is talented and can play the role, but we need to look for someone else instead because when we lose Revi from his deeper role it cuts off our supply line to the forward players. Samuel and Matías are both terrific but, as a pair, there isn't enough creativity there.'

'Yeah,' Sophia agreed. 'I know, but we'll work it out. Look, you're not going to find the answer hiding under a piece of melon. Let's go and get showered and we can head into town. A walk along the beach will help to clear our heads before we meet up with Elena and Nicolás at the restaurant.

Three hours later, they were sitting at a restaurant table, beneath a canopy offering shelter from the sun on Retama's Paseo Marítimo with the sea gently lapping onto the beach nearby, enjoying a paella. At the insistence of both Sophia and Elena, the conversation covered everything but football. Over coffee however, Nicolás enquired as to how Mateo and Elías were doing at the club.

'Great,' Moreton reported. 'They both seem like good lads and have fitted in with the rest of the squad really well.'

It was what Nicolás had expected to hear. He smiled in approval. 'That's good. I had a call from Mateo. He said that the two guys you have at centre-back, Kiko and Victor, are really good and he may struggle to get into the team for a while. I told him that it was a good challenge and he should work hard and earn his chance.'

'That's the perfect answer,' Moreton said, raising his glass of wine to Nicolás.

'Cheers', Nicolás said, accompanying the response with a smile. 'I also told him that defence wasn't the only place in the team. He has skill and pace, he can see a pass and carries the ball well, so there could be other options as well.'

Moreton agreed, and the conversation moved on to other subjects. The following evening at training however, Nicolás's words would flood back into Moreton's mind.

The issue of how to cope without Dani had troubled Moreton across the remaining hours of Monday and into Tuesday ahead of training that evening. As it was the first session after the defeat to Árboles Altos, Moreton had decided that a light-hearted session with plenty of fun and banter would help to dismiss the bad memory and focus attention on things moving forwards. The idea appeared to have been successful with plenty of laughs and chatter as the players went into short-sided game for the final 20 minutes of the session. It was then, watching the players, that the conversation over coffee with Nicolás came back into Moreton's mind.

Sophia had gone to find Esteban to tell him they would be leaving soon. When she returned, Moreton seemed transfixed by the game in front of him, so much so that he hardly heard when she spoke to him.

'Jon, Esteban will be here in about 30 minutes to lock up. I told him we'll be gone by then.' There was barely a response. 'Jon, did you hear me?'

'What, sorry. Yes, that's fine,' he said before turning towards her with broad smile.

'What?' She asked.

'Look,' he said, pointing at the game going on in front of him.

She did as Moreton suggested but the reason for his fascination as still lost to her. 'What, Jon?'

'Mateo. Watch him.'

The tall teenager with the mop of curly hair was playing just in front of Victor and Kiko for one of the teams, receiving the ball before running forward in possession or spraying off passes forwards or to the flanks.

'OK,' Sophia conceded. 'He looks good, but how does that help us. You don't expect him to play the number ten role, do you?'

Moreton shook his head and smiled at her. 'No, of course not. But I've realised that we've been looking at this problem the wrong way round. We shouldn't be looking for someone to replace Dani, that's not the problem. Revi does that job really well. The solution is to find someone who can play in Revi's place, and perform that role.'

'Mateo?'

'Yes, Mateo. Look at him. He's got all the assets. Reads the game well, he's quick, good on the ball and can pick a pass. Plus, he's got a defender's instincts as well. He could be perfect. Also, remember when he came on for Samuel in the game against Castillo Vieja. He was calm and cool under pressure.'

'He's very young though, Jon. Are we asking too much of him, too soon?'

Moreton thought for a second, reigning in his own enthusiasm. 'Perhaps, but it's worth a try, isn't it?'

Across the two following training sessions Moreton and Sophia paid particular attention to the form of Mateo, often using the drills deployed to test him out, offering different challenges to see how he fared. By the end of Friday's session, they had decided to start with Revi further forward and Mateo filling in ahead of the defence. When the team was announced, Elías reached an arm around his friend and hugged him as others patted him on the head in congratulation. He would play alongside Matias in front of the usual defence, albeit this time with Juan Torres in goal. Revi would play behind Santi with Guido on one flank and Juan Palermo on the other.

Sunday's fixture was against Costa Locos. Last year, they were the newly promoted team that started the term well, but fell away badly as the season progressed. The final table had seen them drop down to fourteenth position, only four points clear of the relegation play-offs. Without that bright start, their stay in the division would surely have been limited to a single season. It seemed therefore an ideal opportunity to test out Mateo in his new role.

Ahead of the game, Sophia had checked the league table and found that, in sharp contrast to the start of the previous season, their opponents had been struggling this term, with three defeats and a draw from their opening four games.

That form was reflected in the opening phase of the game as Retama pressed forward and the visitors were pushed onto the defensive. It soon became clear that, in this sort of game at least, playing Mateo in the deeper role usually occupied by Revi, was hardly a gamble. With little attacking coming from the Costa Locos forwards, he had plenty of time to settle on the ball and prompt play from deep.

In the same fixture last season, Retama had rattled in four goals when Costa Locos visited them in the second half of the season. The opening to this game suggested that something similar was highly likely. Inside the first 25 minutes, Santi had been denied three times by the visiting goalkeeper and, with Juan Palermo's height and power causing problems as he took up positions on the far post to meet up with Guido's crosses from the other flank, a goal seemed imminent. At half time however, despite overwhelming possession, and half-a-dozen other chances coming, and going, the score line remained blank.

Walking back to the dressing rooms, Moreton mulled over his options. Taking off a defender posed little risk when his team was so dominant but, against that, it was difficult to envisage how his team could play much better. 'What do you think?' he asked Sophia.

'I'm not really sure we need a back four and Matías, plus Mateo, to keep these out,' she answered candidly.

'Yeah, I know, but we're playing really well and, sometimes when you make changes, it disrupts the balance of the team. I'm not sure.'

'Give it 15 minutes and see how it goes?' Sophia suggested.

Moreton agreed. It was the sort of conclusion he had come to himself.

The start of the second period suggested that it had been a wise decision. The Retama attacks continued unabated but, by now, the visitors had virtually abandoned all thoughts of attack and, for the most part, had all eleven players back in defence. It meant there was precious little room for the Retama forwards, and Moreton surmised that adding further forward players to his team would merely compress the space even more. Time ticked on towards, and then past, the 15 minutes mark that Moreton and Sophia had earmarked as the time to consider changes. Play was still concentrated in the visitors' end of the pitch, but the Retama players were clearly becoming frustrated at their lack of success, resorting to long-range shots, as space further forwards to pick any kind of incisive pass was limited. It hardly helped, as most flew high and wide. In the Costa Locos ranks, the lessening threat only bred increasing confidence and resolution. Moreton needed to act.

Looking across to the options among his substitutes, the obvious attacking change would be to send on the younger Palermo brother, but would that merely be throwing another player into the game without changing anything. He needed to add something different. Instead, he called across Felipe Blanco.

At the next break in play, he made his change. Kiko was removed and Retama changed to a back three with Matías deployed in front of them and the incoming substitute told to push forward with Mateo and play alongside Revi, looking to create an opening. As he had feared, at first the change disrupted the flow of Retama's game, but, as Mateo and Felipe Blanco pressed forward, it allowed Revi to drift between the lines of the visitors' defence, disrupting their organisation. Heading towards the final 15 minutes, there was a new threat from the blue-shirted players as they began to infiltrate the opposition back line. Guido played a neat one-two with Mateo before driving into the box. He was felled by a crude tackle, but the referee waved away appeals for a penalty, pointing towards the corner flag, indicating the defender had played the ball. The crowd howled in dismay, but the decision was correct.

Revi was the fulcrum of the home attacks, receiving and giving off one-touch passes that denied the defenders time to restrict his space. One reverse pass put Juan Palermo into the area, but his shot deflected off the goalkeeper's shoulder, struck the bar and bounced clear. Two minutes later, it was Revi himself, feigning a pass, only to turn himself and clip a shot that flew narrowly wide. Inside the final two minutes, another effort from Santi was turned behind for a corner. Retama were entering the Last Chance Saloon, with the supporters in the ground sharing the frustration and roaring encouragement.

Revi floated the corner into the box. Santi leapt to challenge the goalkeeper, and the ball dropped towards Felipe Blanco on the edge of the area. His first time shot struck two defenders before falling to Guido five metres from goal. As he tried to control the ball a challenge forced it away from him, and the ball ran towards Juan Palermo standing on the penalty spot. His first shot was blocked back towards him. His second was deflected onto the post but, as he ran towards the rebound, a defender's boot sought to hack the ball clear. Instead, the attempted clearance struck the rugged Retama forward in the face and the ball spiralled into the air. Unperturbed, Juan Palermo threw himself at the ball as it dropped, heading it into the net from two metres as he collected both goalkeeper's fist and defender's boot to his head. Before the ball had crossed the line Juan Palermo's world had turned black.

After first celebrating the goal following the scramble in the box, it quickly became clear that all was not well, as players from both teams gathered around the stricken figure of Juan Palermo. Sophia grabbed her bag and ran onto the pitch, closely followed by the two ever-present *Protección Civil* volunteers. As Moreton watched from the sidelines, the medics got to work and, within a few minutes, he could see Juan Palermo sit up and talk to his younger brother. The two medics trotted back to the sidelines and collected the stretcher, taking it back onto the field as Sophia walked back towards Moreton. 'They think he's fine, but will take him to hospital anyway to check for concussion,' she explained as the older Palermo transferred himself onto the stretcher and was carried from the field, accompanied by his brother.

'I should go with them,' she added.

'Of course,' Moreton replied as she threw the apartment keys to him turning and heading towards the ambulance. 'I'll call you,' she shouted over her shoulder.

At that moment, the last thing on Moreton's mind was how to replace the stricken Juan Palermo for the last few minutes of the game, but that was brought back into focus by the figure of José jogging back towards him. At first Moreton was concerned, but as the younger Palermo brother spoke to Jiménez in Spanish, the smile on the suspended veteran goalkeeper, who had come to watch, put his mind at ease. Shaking his head softly, he explained to Moreton. 'José wanted to go with his brother,' he related. 'But Juan told him no. He was fine. He did not need him, but the team did. So, he sends him back to us.' Moreton couldn't help but smile as well.

José already had his shirt on and was ready to replace his brother, telling all the players that Juan was OK as he entered the field. A few minutes later, without the game really recovering into anything like a contest, the referee blew for full-time.

Standing in the dressing room with his players afterwards, Moreton felt humble amongst the group of men who had already shown such dedication to the cause of CD Retama. It was something brought home to him in sharp focus by the heroics of Juan Palermo. Sophia wasn't there to translate for him, so he asked Jiménez to help.

'Juan,' he began before emotionally pausing and taking a deep breath. 'Juan. He is Retama. It's in his head. It's in his heart.' Jiménez translated to a gathering chorus of nods. *'El es Retama. Está en su cabeza. Esta en su corazon.'*

José Palermo stood up and, quivering with emotion, delivered a phrase that would serve as CD Retama's motto for the remainder of the season. *'Retama. Está en nuestras cabezas. Está en nuestros corazones,'* he shouted.

Dutifully, Jiménez whispered across to Moreton. 'Retama. It is in our heads. It is in our hearts,' he translated.

Moreton placed an arm around the older Spaniard's shoulders. 'Yeah, I got that, Paco,' he said. *'Somos Retama!'* he shouted, receiving echoing calls in reply.

Four hours later, Moreton was sitting in the apartment sipping a glass of wine when his phone rang. Seeing 'Sophia' on the display he opened the call. Sophia told him that the hospital had completed a number of checks, diagnosed a very mild concussion, and sent Juan home. He was being collected by his girlfriend who had also offered to drop Sophia back at the apartment. The doctor had advised taking a couple of weeks' break from football, but it was hardly necessary. Moreton had come to appreciate the value of the older Palermo brother, not just today, but also recalling the incident in the play-off game against Atlético Santa Kristina when he'd collided with a post, saving a certain goal. 'Let's give him a three-game rest,' he suggested. Sophia agreed before hanging up. Two hours later, they were lying next to each other sleeping contentedly. Retama was in their heads and in their hearts.

Points proven as points lost

At training on the following Tuesday, whilst Sophia took the players through a warm up drill, Moreton reflected on how the team had coped without Dani Barbieri. He was pondering how Mateo had given him another option, freeing up Revi to play further forwards, when he saw Nicolás walking across the pitch towards him. As he did so, Mateo broke out of Sophia's group and jogged across to join the new arrival. The serious look on Nicolás's face suggested to Moreton that he wasn't about to deliver good news. After exchanging greetings, those suspicions were realised.

Mateo's father's transfer back to Italy had been confirmed and the family were moving at the weekend. The young footballer looked down at the floor as Nicolás explained that Mateo had played his last game for Retama, but had been too embarrassed to tell Moreton as he felt he was letting everyone down, especially after the game against Costa Locos where Moreton had given him his first chance in the starting eleven. It was a disappointment for the Retama coach, but there was very little he could do about the situation and appreciated Mateo's loyalty.

By this time, Sophia had joined them. As Nicolás repeated the news to her, Sophia reached out and placed her hand on Mateo's shoulder, patting it gently and explaining in Spanish that there was nothing to be sorry for and that the club were grateful for all his efforts while he was with them. Then, turning to Moreton, she explained what she had said. Moreton nodded in agreement. *'Gracias Mateo,'* he added.

'He really should go,' Nicolás added. 'His parents need him to be home and help with packing, but he wanted to come and say goodbye.'

Moreton smiled and thanked Mateo again, before the youngster jogged away to get his bag and returned holding his Retama shirt, shorts and socks, washed and neatly folded. He handed them to Moreton, but the coach shook his head. Turning to Sophia, he asked her to tell Mateo that he should keep the kit, because he'd earned it and, that whenever he wore it, he should remember the CD Retama family that he will always have here in Spain. Hearing the words, Mateo held the blue shirt close to him and shook hands with Moreton.

'Gracias, Mister. Retama. Está en nuestras cabezas. Está en nuestros corazones,' he said, before turning away with Nicolás, walking across the pitch, up the steps, through the gap in the wall and out of the CD Retama squad, offering a final wave to the other players.

'You should probably explain what has happened to the other guys,' Moreton suggested to Sophia.

'They already know,' she replied with a smile.

Ten minutes later, as Sophia set the players to work on their first drill of the training session, Moreton contemplated how his solution to the problem of

Dani's unavailability for the team had proven to be very short-lived. He decided to check on whether Dani would be back as promised for the weekend's game. Picking up his phone, he rang the hotel where Dani was staying. The ring tone was swiftly halted by the voice of Sebastián.

'Hello Seb. It's Jon Moreton.

'Oh, hi Mister.'

'I just wondered if it was possible to speak to Dani. Is he back yet?'

'No, not yet. He's still in town.'

'OK, can you ask him to call me please?'

'Of course, no problem, Mister.'

Moreton closed the call, dropped the phone back into his bag, and turned his attention to the two-touch passing and possession retention drill Sophia had set up.

'I've just tried to call Dani,' he explained to her. 'I wanted to be sure that he'll be here tomorrow and Friday so that he can play on Sunday. Seb is going to get him to call me back.'

Walking towards the stadium almost 24 hours later, Sophia asked Moreton whether Dani would be at training. 'I don't know,' he conceded guiltily. 'He never called. To be honest, I forgot all about it.'

'Perhaps he didn't call back as he was going to be here anyway,' Sophia suggested.

'Yeah, perhaps,' Moreton said, but without much conviction.

Arriving at the gates, it was no surprise that Dani's car was not outside. It was hardly significant. He was always one of the last to arrive. Moreton and Sophia entered and, 15 minutes later, had begun the warm up exercises for the session. There was still no sign of Dani. Moreton reached into his bag to retrieve the phone.

'You carry on,' he said to Sophia, walking a little distance away from the group, whilst tapping Sebastian's parents' hotel number into his phone. The voice on the other end was clearly not Sebastián.

'Hola, Hotel El Barco. ¿Puedo ayudarte por favor?' the female voice enquired.

'¿Habla inglés, por favor? Moreton asked.

'Yes, of course,' came the reply. 'Can I help you?'

Moreton explained who he was and asked if it was possible to speak to Dani Barbieiri. The enquiry was met with an enthusiastic response.

'Ah, Señor Moreton. I am Sebastián's mother. How are you?'

'I'm fine thank you. Is Dani there?'

'I think he is in the bar. One moment, please?'

The phone went quiet for a couple of minutes, and the next voice Moreton heard was that of Dani Barbieri.

'Hello, Mister?'

'Hi Dani. How are you? I was hoping to see you at training this evening.'

'I'm sorry, but I've only just got back and really tired. I will be there on Friday though and ready to play on Sunday.'

The reassurance was all that Moreton required. 'OK,' he said. 'See you then.' Before closing out the call though, he had one more question. 'Dani, did Seb pass on my message to you?'

'No, what message?'

'Don't worry, Dani. It doesn't matter. See you on Friday.'

'OK, Ciao.'

Moreton closed the call and dropped the phone in his bag on the way back to Sophia. 'All OK,' she asked.

'Yeah,' Moreton replied. 'He'll be here on Friday and ready to play on Sunday.'

'That's good. Why didn't he call you?'

'Seb forgot to give him my message,' Moreton said. As he did so though, there was something in his mind that didn't feel quite right. A couple of months later, all would become clear.

As he had promised, Dani turned up for training on Friday evening. It was just as well. With the departure of Mateo, plus the injuries to Antonio Vasquez and Juan Palermo, Moreton only had 13 outfield players available for Sunday's game against Sobrolepeña Industrial. Selecting the team would hardly be a complex matter.

With Jiménez sitting out the second game of his suspension, Torres was the only goalkeeper available, behind the regular back four. Revi was deployed alongside Matías and Felipe Blanco replaced the injured Juan Palermo on the right flank, with Guido on the left and Dani positioned behind Santi. In the previous season's encounters, Retama had comfortably won both games against the club owned by the large industrial organisation based in Sobrolepeña and, despite his depleted forces, Moreton felt confident that another victory was well within reach.

Last season, Guido had scored a hat-trick in the away fixture against the team in green and yellow-hooped shirts and started this game in similar vein, opening the scoring after just four minutes. It set the pattern for the game and further goals from Dani, and Santi before the break had settled the issue, well before Kiko headed home the fourth from a corner with five minutes to play. Moreton even had the luxury of resting a couple of players for the last 20 minutes, giving both Elías and Samuel the chance to play.

As the players left the field, Moreton made a point of congratulating each of them in turn on a job well done. When Dani reached him however, the young Italian's response tarnished the gloss on the coach's day.

'See, with me playing everything is fine. Dani scores goals. Dani makes goals,' he boasted.

Annoyed at the attitude, Moreton took hold of Dani's arm, stopping him in his tracks. 'You're one of a team, Dani. The team won, not you.'

There was a complacent arrogance about the reply. 'Sure, but when I'm not here, what happens, eh? You lose one game and then win one with a last-minute goal when someone nearly kills themselves scoring, yes? With me though, we win easily. The first game we win 3-0. Then I only play a half and we still win

2-0. Now we score four.'

With anger welling up inside him, Moreton felt compelled to react. 'We win games without you as well. How do you think we coped before you turned up?'

Dani pulled his arm free of Moreton's grasp. 'You win games without me?' It was hardly a question. 'Shall we see, yes?' Moreton was left standing there as Dani returned to the dressing room, but reappeared second later, still in his kit, with his bag slung over his shoulder. He headed across the pitch, towards the concrete steps and the gap in the wall. 'We shall see,' he called over his shoulder.

Moreton had decided not to say anything to Sophia about Dani's outburst, hoping it was just a heat of the moment comment that would quickly be forgotten. On Monday afternoon however, those hopes were dashed when he took a phone call from Sebastián. Dani had asked him to ring and say that he was ill, would not be at training that week and would not be able to play on Sunday. At the time, Sophia had gone to the local supermarket to buy food for dinner that evening.

On her return, Moreton told her of the conversation with Dani after the previous day's game, how he was sure that there was no illness, and how important it was for Retama to win next Sunday's game when the students of Universidad San Juan visited the Estadio Antonio Núñez. The complication was of course that, even though the university team were not one of the stronger clubs in the league, Retama's squad was increasingly threadbare It was decided that the training sessions the following week would necessarily be low key, to minimise any potential for injuries occurring.

Monday's session passed quietly, but on Tuesday, as Moreton and Sophia prepared to start training, they were greeted by the sight of Juan Palermo stripped into his kit and apparently ready to play. Moreton shook his head, held up his hand and called the forward to him and Sophia.

'¿Qué tal, Juan?' Moreton asked.

'Bien, muy bien. Mister,' he replied 'Y yo quiero jugar.'

'He wants to play,' Sophia explained, but Moreton had understood.

He shook his head again. 'No, Juan. Tres semanas. Tres semanas, sin entrenamiento, sin fútbol.' He would not let Palermo train or play for three weeks.

'*Pero te faltan jugadores. Puedo ser suplente en caso de lesiones,*' Palermo persisted, offering himself as a substitute, just to be used in emergencies to cover for injuries.

It was a tempting offer, given the straightened circumstance of the squad, but Moreton knew it would be wrong. 'Go home, Juan. Rest. Come back fit in a couple of weeks.' Sophia translated.

Juan Palermo blew out his cheeks in resignation. 'Vale, Mister,' he conceded. He turned and trudged back to the dressing room, appearing again ten minutes later and walking across the pitch to leave. '*Vete a casa.*' '*Descansar*' came the shouts of his team-mates as he trudged away.

'*Hasta luego,*' he shouted back.

Moreton watched the lonely figure stroll away, vault over the wall. Climb the steps and disappear through the gap in the wall. He turned to Sophia. 'If we could inject a little of Juan's passion and dedication into Dani, we'd have some player, you know.'

'Sure,' she replied, before smiling. 'But Juan is some player already, isn't he?'

'He is, and some man too.'

Now half-a-dozen games into the season, Moreton would have liked to rest a few of the players who had been on the pitch for every minute of every game so far but, with only a dozen outfield players to select from, his options were severely limited. Jiménez's suspension had been served, and he was available to be on the bench, but Moreton opted to retain Juan Torres in goal.

He decided to rest Sanz, with Felipe Blanco filling in, and the captain's armband passing to Adrián. Matias and Samuel played in front of the defence with José Palermo starting in place of his brother on the right, Guido on the left and Revi behind Santi.

On the way to the stadium, Moreton confessed to Sophia that he had hardly ever wished to win a game more than this one. In a tepid, frustrating encounter, however, he would be disappointed as the game ended in a goalless draw.

The subdued atmosphere as Moreton and Sophia walked back to the apartment after the game was driven by Moreton's frustration. Having such a depleted squad and playing out a goalless draw was, in subjective terms, not a bad result. Moreton's mind, however was not being ruled by subjective thoughts. He had little doubt that Dani Barbieri would not only bask in the schadenfreude generated by the result, but also take it as proof of his assertion that Retama were unable to win without him. Sophia knew Moreton's mind was churning with frustration.

'It was not a bad result, Jon,' she counselled. 'Another clean sheet for the defence and you managed to rest Alejandro for a game.

'Yeah, I know, but …'

'But what, Jon?'

Moreton pursed his lips, and shook his head. It was sufficient provocation for Sophia.

'You mean, Dani. Don't you?'

Moreton's guilt was complicit in his silence.

'This is crazy, Jon. This season cannot be about Dani Barbieri. It is about Retama, about the team, the club, all of us.' She rolled her eyes at him in frustration. 'Dani is one player and is someone we have to deal with, but winning games, losing them or drawing is not about him. It's about the team. Are his silly little games that important? You are letting him play you, Jon.'

Moreton knew that everything Sophia said was true. He had let Dani get under his skin. The game against the students was just one more fixture, no more important than any other in the league programme, but he had lost sight of that in his desire not to allow Dani the satisfaction of thinking he had been proved correct.

Accepting that he was in the wrong and actually admitting it to himself, and then Sophia, was much more difficult though. His sullen mood persisted and the uneasy tension between them carried on through dinner and afterwards. Around 11pm Moreton decided it was time for bed, hoping for a better day in the morning. He heard Sophia in the bathroom and waited for her to join him. Instead, the sound of the door of the spare bedroom closing told him that the night would be cold and lonely. For the first time since they had become committed to each other, they spent a night in the same house, but in different beds.

Last Dances

The rays of the early morning sun roused Moreton from his slumber the following morning. Sleepily, he turned over to move closer to Sophia, feel the warmth of her body and inhale her intoxicating fragrance. As he turned though, there was only empty space next to him. The events of the previous evening came flooding back. He looked up at the ceiling castigating himself for his pride and folly. 'You idiot!' He jumped out of bed, pulling on shorts and a vest top, and headed into the kitchen.

The door to the spare bedroom opened quietly and he looked inside to see Sophia still sleeping. This bedroom was on the opposite side of the apartment to the one he had slept in, was still in shadow, and only had a single bed in it. Moreton padded quietly inside, placed the cup of cortado coffee on the bedside table and sat softly on the bed, looking at Sophia's face with her dark hair falling across it. Not reaching out to touch her was more than he could bear. Leaning forward, he gently lifted the hair from across her face, causing her to murmur softly as he did so, and Morpheus freed her from his embrace. Her dark eyes blinked open and, seeing Moreton, she smiled.

'I made you coffee,' he said, nodding towards the steaming cup on the bedside table.

Sophia reached out a hand and softly stroked his arm. 'Thank you,' she said, still sleepily.

Moreton kissed her softly on the forehead and rose. 'I'll take a shower and then make breakfast,' he said. 'You stay here and drink your coffee.'

Sophia had other ideas though. She held his hand and threw back the covers on the side of the bed where he stood. The movement revealed a side of her naked body to him and, as she reached across with her free hand to pat the space in the bed invitingly, the covers fell back further.

'Come here,' she said. He slipped off the vest and shorts and got into the bed beside her, the narrowness of the bed compelling their bodies to be together. Moreton wrapped his arms around her and held her tightly.

'I'm sorry,' he said. 'I was total prat.'

Sophia reached her finger to his lips quietening him, but he still felt remorse.

'I was stupid, like some overgrown kid.'

'Shh', she whispered softly into his ear.

'I'm sorry.'

'I don't want to hear you say it,' she purred seductively. 'I want to feel you prove it,' and she rolled over on top of him.

At training on Tuesday, the players were delighted to be able to welcome Antonio Vasquez back into the group. The winger had been given leave to miss training in order to allow time for his calf strain to heal, but was now back, and in contention for selection for next Sunday's game. It felt like a positive step forward for Moreton, who had also resolved to brush off any barbed remarks that Dani Barbieri may have thrown at him. It proved unnecessary, however, as the Italian was absent, not even arriving late. As the evening progressed and ended with a short-sided game, Moreton asked Sophia to call Sebastián to check if Dani was there. She agreed and, while Moreton watched the game, conditioning the play to two-touches, she called the Hotel El Barco.

Five minutes later with the players indulging in banter as Revi forlornly tried to convince Moreton that it should only count as a single touch if he caught the ball between his knees, Sophia returned. Moreton looked at her questioningly, but she was caught up in the moment, as the other players teased Revi's confident assertions. Each one was pointing to one knee, and then the other. 'Uno, dos,' they shouted in unison, as Revi laughed at his own impudence. Sophia called out. '¡La cuenta es uno, Revi, dos, tres, cuatro!' Adrián wrapped a muscular arm around Revi's head, displacing the ever-present headband, holding him in a headlock and patting him on the head, repeating Sophia's count with each pat, before releasing him and slapping him on the back, as they both laughed.

'This is great,' Moreton said to Sophia temporarily forgetting about her errand. 'To see the guys happy and bonded with each other.'

Sophia smiled, but uncomfortably. The information she was about to relate would cast a shadow on Moreton's happiness and appreciation of his players' *esprit de corps*. 'He's not well,' she began, before correcting herself. 'I mean, he says that he's still not well.'

'What?'

'Seb says that Dani has told him that he is not well.'

Moreton snorted in irritation. 'Well, he could have let us know.'

'Apparently, Dani told Seb that if we enquired about him, he was to tell us that Dani was still unwell, but not to call us first.'

She paused, as the laughter from the pitch entered into Moreton and Sophia's consciousness again. She turned and clapped her hands in applause at the banter, before returning her attention to Moreton.

'I really think all of this is putting Seb into an awkward situation. Dani is a guest at his parent's hotel and he feels obliged to follow the requests given, but …' she paused again.

Moreton finished the sentence for her. 'But he knows that Dani is stringing us a line?'

'I'm sure he does, but when a guest asks him to pass a message on, what else can he do?'

'I know. Seb's a good kid, but he's got to do his job.'

Sophia squeezed Moreton's arm. 'Also,' she added. 'Dani told Seb that, if we asked, he was to tell us that he would not attend training this week until Friday when he would be feeling better.'

Moreton rolled his eyes, shaking his head. 'OK,' he conceded, having little other option. 'I'm not going to let him get to me,' he said, smiling. 'Is it OK though, if I still think he's a little shit?'

Sophia tried to suppress a laugh. 'No Jon,' she said. 'It's not OK. It's obligatory.' She reached up and kissed him on the cheek.

The Friday training session was 15 minutes old when the figure of Dani Barbieri wearing his red and black tracksuit, began a gentle stroll across the pitch to where the rest of the players were about to begin a pass and move drill, rotating around cones placed randomly within a ten metres square. The late arrival may well have been expecting more of a subdued greeting from the coach, and Moreton's cheery "Hi, Dani. Are you feeling better, mate?" took him a little by surprise.

Throughout the remainder of the session, Dani hardly over extended himself. Despite the urgings of Moreton and Sophia, and the players in the different groups with him, it was clear that there would be nothing beyond merely going through the motions. Moreton felt frustrated, but also committed not to let it show, and at the end of the evening, Dani's name was called out for the team to visit Torre del Olmos. Alejandro Sanz returned to his normal position on the right flank of an otherwise unchanged back four, with Matías and Revi ahead of them. The recovered Antonio Vasquez reclaimed his position on the right flank with Guido on the left and Dani behind Santi. If Moreton and Sophia had hoped that perhaps the lethargy displayed by Dani in training would be exchanged for a more enthusiastic outlook in the game however, they were to be disappointed.

It was as well for Retama that they weren't playing a team more accomplished than Torre del Olmos. Last season, the small club had finished near the bottom of the table, albeit comfortably clear of relegation worries, and this term looked to hold similar prospects. Despite a lethargic display by Dani, an early goal from Santi and a second by José Palermo after he had been sent on as a substitute replacing Guido, wrapped up the points. An injury time goal for the home team was significant only for statistical reasons.

On the face of it, the win should have been satisfactory for Moreton, and broadly it was, but the form and, more pertinently, the attitude of Dani was a growing concern. After the game, Moreton spoke with him and enquired whether he was still feeling weak after his supposed illness. The young Italian had another explanation though.

'My ankle is still not good. When I train, and then play, it causes me problems. I should have missed Friday. Perhaps I should not train, and then just play, yes?'

Moreton was hardly enthusiastic. 'I'm not sure, Dani,' he replied. 'If you miss training, it's not only the fitness issue, but you won't know what tactics we are looking at for the next game.' He not only felt that he was being played, but also that the footballer in front of him had written all of the rules of the game.

'Tactics?' Dani question dismissively. 'I play. I score. The team wins. You can have your tactics with the others. I just play. I do not need tactics. They do. You tell them. Give the ball to Dani and then everything will be good.'

Moreton was far from convinced.

'Look,' Dani insisted. 'I am fit, but my ankle makes me play like this if you make me train. The best Dani wins games. You want the best Dani, yes? From now, I play, I do not train.'

There was little that Moreton could do, and both men knew it.

The next game, at home to San Vicente seemed to justify Dani's stance. After missing all three training sessions across the week he opened the scoring after a dozen minutes, connecting with an astute through ball from Revi, before shimmying past the goalkeeper and rolling the ball into the empty net. Ten minutes after the restart he added his second, curling in a shot from outside of the area. Moreton had selected an unchanged team for the game, and was particularly delighted when Antonio Vasquez confirmed his return to fitness by adding the third goal, tapping in from the goalkeeper parrying Santi's shot with three minutes to play.

Given the quality of his performance in the game, Moreton had little justification for questioning Dani's non-training regime. It was a point not lost on the Italian as he walked from the field, arms outstretched, shrugging his shoulders, as if the game had confirmed all that he had said was the case. That would hardly be the case at the end of the next game though, when Retama visited UD Callosa.

Moreton made a couple of changes for the away fixture, with Samuel coming in for Matías and Juan Palermo offered a chance to rejoin the team, replacing Guido on the left flank of the attack. Even on the coach journey towards the well-equipped complex that housed the multi-faceted sporting club of Callosa, Moreton thought something was awry with Dani. Although he always sat on his own, with his bag next to him to dissuade anyone from joining him, he would usually spend the journeys to away games either tapping away on his phone, or playing video games. On this journey though, he merely slept and, when the squad arrived, Sophia had difficulty rousing him. It was a state that he carried onto the pitch with him. As the team toiled for a goal, without success, Dani was largely peripheral to all going on around him. At the break, Moreton asked him if he was OK to continue, but Dani insisted that he had just not slept very well and everything would be all right.

The reality on the pitch proved such claims to be fanciful. Moreton made changes as his team continued to labour without success. The understandably tiring Juan Palermo, returning after missing four matches was replaced by Elías, and José Palermo did the same for Vasquez. On two occasions, Moreton signalled to Dani to see if he wanted to come off, but was rebuffed. With ten minutes left to play however, he was about to take the issue out of his player's hands when Retama scored, with Dani as the architect.

A corner on the right was crossed in by Revi, but the home goalkeeper punched clear as Kiko challenged him in the air. Standing just outside of the Callosa penalty arc, Dani controlled the ball and eluded the first challenge switching the ball from left foot to right and then back again, before accelerating past the off-balance Callosa player. With Retama defenders up to support the attack on the corner, and the home team drawing all of their players back to defend, the penalty area was crowded. To open up a chance would take ebullient ability and outrageous confidence. Dani Barbieri had both. Flicking the ball up with his left foot, he fired in a volley with his right, almost in the same graceful movement. The home goalkeeper threw out a gloved hand to deflect the ball onto the crossbar and Kiko was there to head home from a couple of metres.

Retama had won the game and who could dispute that they may not have done so without Dani's impudence.

Later in the dressing room, with the players all congratulating Dani and the Italian wallowing in the adulation, Moreton felt ill at ease. Dani had won the game for the team at the last, but his lack of application, be it through tiredness, lack of fitness or some other reason had meant that 99% of his time on the pitch had been unproductive. And yet … And yet …, he counselled to himself, Dani had still won the game for Retama. To Moreton though it had felt like a last throw of the dice, something dredged up from the last puddles at the bottom of the well. It was a feeling he couldn't shake.

That evening, after dinner, Sophia flipped open her laptop to look at the other results and the league table. 'Jon,' she called excitedly as Moreton entered living area from the bathroom after a shower. 'Look at this.' Moreton dropped down next to Sophia on the sofa and peered at the laptop screen. The reason for Sophia's excitement was clear. At the top of the league with ten games played, sat Retama. Seven wins, two draws and a single defeat had put them on 23 points. Torreaño were second, on 20, with both FC Córuel and CD Bugroño a further point back. Given the struggling start that the club had endured last season, seeing Retama top of the table with almost a third of the season completed was a fillip to both of them, but Moreton still harboured concerns.

'It's good, Jon. Isn't it?' Sophia insisted.

'Yeah, of course it is. But there's a long way to go yet, and …' he hesitated. 'I can't help feeling that we're a bit fragile.'

Sophia was genuinely mystified. 'Fragile? We've lost once. We've scored 16 goals and only conceded three. That doesn't sound very fragile.'

It was difficult to dispute the logic of Sophia's assessment, but Moreton's concerns were more focused on the future than the past. 'Did you see how impotent we were today? Dani created that goal out of nothing at the end, but if he hadn't it would have looked like a terrible performance. Flat, uninspiring, unthreatening. It just gave me a glimpse of something I didn't like.'

Retama's next three games only served to confirm Moreton's foreboding. Retama had garnered 23 points from their first ten games. The remaining seven, running up to the mid-season break, would only add a further four.

Old friends and new ideas

With the club at the top of the table after ten games played, there should have been an established momentum driving the team on. Instead, there was almost apathy as Dani's performances continued to deteriorate. Very much as Moreton had feared, that late goal against UD Callosa had proven to be an isolated oasis in a desert of apparent lethargy.

A goalless home draw against Independiente Lacitana who were, at best, a mid-table team was hardly the form expected of league leaders and, in this game, there was no moment of inspiration from Dani to camouflage an insipid and thoroughly disinterested display from the Italian.

Dani's absence from training, explained by the player himself, as necessary to maintain his ability to play with the damaged ankle, had previously been justified to the other players by his performances in games. Although hardly welcomed by the remainder of the squad, the situation had been justified by outstanding displays. With his level of performance now dipping significantly, that reasoning was losing validity, beginning to cause tension within the group and damaging morale. It was a deteriorating situation hardly helped by the downturn in performances and results.

Moreton needed to change something to give the team a lift before the next game, a visit to CD Bugroño. Briefly, he contemplated explaining the true situation with regards to Dani to the other players, but it felt like the sort of nuclear option that would surely blow the club apart. Any developing antagonism that the players felt towards the Italian would only be intensified by the revelation. There may be a time for that in the future, but this wasn't it. Now faced by the club that he had forecast to Sophia would be significant challengers to Retama, he needed a decent result to get things back on track. With a number of players looking jaded and perhaps feeling that way too, he decided to make changes to the starting eleven. It was a gamble, but one he thought well worth taking and, after discussing the matter with Sophia, he made the announcement on Friday evening.

The Retama defence had only conceded three goals in eleven games. It would be dangerous to change too much in the back line but, with Adrián playing almost every minute of every game so far, in his typically fully committed way, giving the defender a break was probably less of a gamble than not doing so. Felipe Blanco replaced him on the left flank of the defence, with Matías and Revi in front of them. On the flanks though, Moreton selected the fiery passion of Juan Palermo and the potential talent of younger sibling José. Dani retained his place behind Santi. Moreton had contemplated giving the striker a rest, much as for the same reason as Adrián had been left on the bench, with Elías as a starting option, but Sophia persuaded him that doing the opposite might be the better move.

The stadium in the town of Bugroño had clearly seen better days. Playing at a higher level in the league pyramid had brought sizeable crowds to watch games but the spiralling fall into relegation and the rapid changing of coaches had clearly eaten away at the spirit of the fans. On the day of the game, the stadium that could comfortably hold 15,000 was populated by a tenth of that figure.

Moreton had sought to inspire his team to a positive performance, repeatedly invoking the *"Somos Retama. Está en nuestras cabezas. Está en nuestros corazones,"* mantras. They were met with mixed responses. Whilst some, like the Palermo brothers shouted their support, Dani sat quietly, looking at his feet. Fifteen minutes later, as the players were warming up, Moreton sat on the bench, doing very much the same as Dani had been doing. He was lost in contemplation, when a chirpy English voice roused him. 'All right, Jon?' enquired the Estuary accent. Moreton looked up at the figure in front of him, with a hand held out. He jumped to his feet and could now see the newcomer fully. He was around 60 years old stocky with a full moustache and, despite the warm weather, wore a zipped-up jacket over tracksuit trousers. A flat cap completing the ensemble.

'Derek Hart,' announced the newcomer, introducing himself. 'But call me Del, everybody does.'

'Jon Moreton.'

'Yeah, I know, mate,' said Hart, his Cockney accent now in full flow. 'I heard all about you back in England and how well you were doing as a young coach until that lot bought your club and shoved you out. I've been watching your team last year, and how well you did.' He put his hand to the side of his mouth, as if shielding his words from anyone else. 'In fact, it's because of you, that I got this job.'

Moreton was bemused by the revelation, and it showed.

'Yeah,' drawled Hart. 'I used to come up here and watch this lot regular like. Been a bit rough the past couple of years, had a right couple of clowns running the team. They were absolutely clueless, no organisation or nothing. A few of the top blokes here apparently heard about me. They're partners in a big regional estate agency around these parts. They saw what you did with me old mate Billy Swan and, next thing you know, they're banging on the door of my boozer offering me a job.'

'Really?' Moreton asked, as Sophia joined the two men.

'All right, darlin'?' Hart said, tipping his cap to Sophia. 'I mean *hola, que t'al?*'

Sophia smiled. '*Si bien gracias,*' she replied. '*¿Y tú? ¿Todo está bien?*'

'*Si muy bien, muchas gracias,*' Hart replied hanging onto the final syllable for too long. 'Sorry, I still struggle with the lingo a bit. Can't believe it after more than five years out here, can you? Maria, that's the missus, she's Spanish, keeps trying to teach me, but I'm a bit long in the tooth for all that grammar malarkey. We met in London when I was coaching there, been together for a while now. Can't understand why she puts up with me. She's far too good for me. So, I married her quick before she realised, and we came out here. She does all the organising and just tells me what to do in the bar.'

The information had come in waves, accelerated by Hart's rapid-fire conversation style, and much of it had washed over Moreton. One thing grabbed his attention though, and required clarification. 'You know Billy?'

'Billy Swan? Course I do, mate. What a player. I was coaching at my old club when he arrived. I'd packed up playing years before, problems with the old ankle. Got kicked on it too many times. Never quick enough to get away. Still gives me jip sometimes, especially in the damp. Not that we get much of that out here, eh?' Hart laughed gruffly. 'Anyway, they signed this scrawny looking kid, picked him up for a song from a local amateur side. They'd just bumped me up to work with the first team and me and Billy hit it off from the start. He was a top kid. A bit rough around the edges, you know, just like me, so me and him hit off from the start. Two peas in a pod, like. Some of the other blokes there didn't rate him, idle, selfish, too much of a showman, they'd say. Cobblers, I'd say to that. Even a blind man could see the talent he'd got. I kinda took him under my wing. "Just play your game, son," I'd tell him again and again. "These other clowns trying to coach you, they ain't got a bloody clue. Don't let them ruin you." Course, by the time he gets established in the team and then sold on for big brass, those plonkers were claiming the glory for making him the player he was. Jeez, what a con. To be honest, that's what finished me there. I'd had a couple of offers from down the leagues to go and be a manager myself, so I took one of them. Couldn't stand the crap any more. Travelled around a bit after that managing and coaching, before I met Maria and, as they say mate, the rest is history, ain't it?'

Sophia had taken an instant liking to the affable Del Hart. His warm and friendly chatterbox style made it difficult not to. She held out her hand to him. 'Sophia Garrigues,' she said with a smile. He returned the gesture. 'Yeah, I've heard of you too, Sophia,' he confirmed beaming. 'You don't get many women involved in football at this level. So, more power to you, girl. To you both,' he added. Hart chuckled to himself. 'Well, after today, of course.'

'Have you spoken to Billy recently?' Sophia asked.

Hart seemed surprised by the question. 'Of course. Part of the idea of getting me here was so that I could persuade young Billy to join and do for us what he so nearly did for you last season.' The expressions on Moreton and Sophia's faces quickly confirmed to Del Hart that his revelation had come as a surprise. He continued. 'Didn't you know? I gave him a bell and rolled the idea to him. He was just starting that charity thing with the football schools back on his old manor at the time.'

'So, he was too busy?' Sophia suggested.

'Well, a bit I suppose, but he told me that he was probably finished playing anyway, and only one club could ever make him change his mind. So, I moved on and got these three guys instead,' he said, waving his arm towards the team wearing yellow shirts and red shorts. 'There's George Clift. He used to play for me at a couple of clubs. Took him with me when I moved. He says he's 38 now, but I think he's 41. Legs have gone, lost his two front teeth years ago and he's as blind as a bat without his glasses, but he can't half read a game well. I just stick him at the back to organise things. Karl Bryant is the lad with the long hair. Plays in midfield. Should have done so much better. Could have played in the top league but loses his rag too easily. I told him when he came out here that he needed to cool it and, to be fair, he's been as good as gold. Proper hard, though. Don't half love a tackle. The best signing though was Alfie.' Hart pointed out the black player with the short-cropped hair wearing the number 13 shirt. 'His proper name is Alfonso Esteves Feliciano, from Angola originally, but moved to Portugal as a kid with his parents. He's a terrific bloke. I think he's 40 now, but he'd score goals in his fifties. He was recommended to me by a mate years ago when he was playing in minor league stuff up in Scotland and I was managing in England. I took a risk on him, but he's paid that back – and then some. When I asked him to think about moving over here, he told me it was nearer home, that's Lisbon, than back in the Smoke, so he signed. Notched eight goals already this season. Some of the kids who watch him here, love him. You'll hear 'em giving it the old "Alf-eee, Alf-eee, Alf-eee" chant if he scores.'

A call from the other bench drew Hart's attention to the fact that the referee was about to start the game. He turned to walk away, throwing a last remark over his shoulder. 'Catch you after the game, kids.' Moreton raised his thumb in confirmation, just as Sophia tugged at his arm.

'Only one club could ever make him change his mind,' she said, repeating Hart's words.

'I know,' Moreton replied with a smile.

Del Hart's knowledge of lower league English football had paid dividends for CD Bugroño. His three veteran players had clearly been influential in delivering an organised pattern of play and injecting determination into the squad. The results illustrated the success and, in the first half of the game, the home team dominated. Santi had been largely shackled by the home defence, calmly marshalled by George Clift and, further forward, with Dani largely irrelevant, Karl Bryant muscularly dominated the midfield, subduing any forward momentum coming from Revi.

The Palermo brothers were both forced deep to help the defence and, with Dani hardly involved, or seeking to be so, any link Retama had with possession of the ball was brief and tenuous at best. Only the solid defending and vigilance of Kiko and Victor prevented Feliciano from opening the scoring as he busied himself darting into spaces and astutely moving the pair around the pitch to create openings. The one time he managed to wriggle free from their attentions, it took a plunging dive from Juan Torres at the forward's feet to prevent a goal. The save hardly dampened the passion of the 40 or so children behind the goal, though, chanting his name incessantly, much as Hart had predicted.

At the break, with the game scoreless, Moreton decided that he needed to change things. He thought about removing Dani, pushing Revi further forward and putting Adrián into midfield to battle it out with Bryant. 'You need a break?' he asked Dani hopefully, but the shake of the Italian's head, and the potential after-effects of any accruing argument had he pushed the point, removed the possibility. Instead, he replaced the hard-working Felipe Blanco, restoring Adrián to his normal position and sent on Guido for José Palermo.

If Moreton hoped that adding steel and speed would bring his team more into the game, his hopes were shown to be fanciful and, with the pattern of the game still very much in favour of the home team, Alfie soon sent his small band of young fans into raptures. Turning past Victor, and evading the attentions of Kiko's sliding challenge, he coolly slipped the ball under the advancing Torres to put Bugroño ahead. 'Alf-eee. Alf-eee. Alf-eee' his starstruck band of young fans serenaded, as the goalscorer took his bow in front of them.

Moreton's head sank. For much of the game, his team had been very much second best and any chance of redemption looked slim. With Dani playing, his team were virtually down to ten men anyway, but Moreton felt hamstrung to do anything about it, without risking the club's existence. Yet, at the same time, leaving him on the field only increased the other players' dissatisfaction, and concerns about the coach's failure to make the obvious change, which may well have led to the same outcome anyway.

'We need to do something,' Sophia said softly.

'I know, but should I take Dani off? What happens then?'

Sophia sighed accepting the inevitable logic of Moreton's question.

'Give Elías a shout,' he said. 'Let's give the kid a chance for the last half hour and see what he can do.'

'Are you sure, Jon? It's a been difficult enough task for a player like Santi.'

'I know, but what have we got to lose?'

With 25 minutes to play, the young forward was sent on. At first all of the Retama players, except the Italian, were expecting Dani to be removed. Instead, it was Santi called over, and the exasperation and disapproval of those wearing the blue kit of Retama was clear.

The style of Retama's new front man was different to that of Santi. Whereas the club's regular striker was always busy looking for angles to create passing opportunities or making runs, Elías was more subdued. His moves were easily snubbed by Clift's disciplined defence, and he seemed to drift out of the game. Time moved on, with it looking increasingly likely that the home team wouldn't need another goal as Retama struggled to pose any threat. When the equaliser came, it was totally unexpected – as was its source.

Another home attack was broken down, and Sanz launched a long clearance up field. The ball drifted out wide and Juan Palermo headed it on. Guido had read the brawny forward's intention and raced into the middle of the field to collect the ball as he was closed down by one of the Bugroño centre backs. The Retama speedster got there first and flicked it past the defender towards a waiting Elías, now only opposed by George Clift. The veteran defender had faced many similar situations throughout his career and jockeying the younger man, he was clearly intent on avoiding being lured into a rash tackle. It was a cat and mouse situation encapsulated into a few brief seconds. Clift was poised ready to pounce, while Elías sought a route past him, with the ball still at his feet. With defenders recovering to support Clift, the time allowed to Elías was brief.

Opening his body, he shaped to play the ball wide, with Clift half turning to block the move. It was the gap that the young forward required. Playing the ball past Clift, he leapt over a clumsily lunging tackle as the widely-experienced defender fell to the ground. A clip over the advancing goalkeeper completed the move, and Retama had the most unlikely of equalisers. George Clift punched the ground in frustration. There had been no supporting Retama player when Elías had shaped to play the ball wide, but he had fell for the elaborate ruse. Elías ran towards the celebrating Retama bench and Sophia passed him a large towel with writing on it.

The young forward headed towards Adrián before holding out the towel so that the message was clear to read. *"¡Feliz cumpleaños Javi! ¡Te amamos!"* All the Retama players then made the baby-cradling motion, as Retama's teak-tough defender looked every inch the doting father he was. After that display of affection for his son's first birthday, there was no way that Adrián would allow Bugroño to score again.

A dozen minutes later, the referee ended the game and Retama had escaped with an unlikely draw. They would play much better in other games and lose, but Elías's trick had got them out of jail. Del Hart walked across to Moreton and Sophia shaking his head, and Moreton felt obliged to comment.

'Sorry, Del,' he commiserated. 'We didn't deserve that.'

'Ah, don't worry, Jon. That's football.' Hart paused, then sniggered to himself. 'To be honest, I'm thinking about staying out here for a while. Clifty is going to be hurling tea cups around in there after your kid did him up like a kipper for that goal. He'll be furious, and you can bet Karl will be reminding him of it for weeks. Still as the great man once said "Football eh, bloody hell!" I'd better go in and smooth out a few ruffled feathers I suppose. Catch you for the next game Jon, Sophia.'

He tipped his cap and returned to the home dressing room. Once he'd left, Moreton turned to Sophia. 'This can't go on,' he said with a sigh. 'If we don't sort the situation out with Dani one way or another, the other guys are going to get so hacked off about it, they'll end up throwing the towel in. Something has to change.'

He is not Retama. We are Retama!

After training on Tuesday evening, Jiménez and Sanz were the last of the players to leave the dressing room as Moreton and Sophia collected up the cones and balls from the session. When everyone else had left, Retama's captain and veteran goalkeeper walked slowly across to where Moreton and Sophia were packing the last items into their bags. There was clearly something on their minds and, looking up to see them approach, Moreton was convinced that it wasn't to offer an analysis of the training session. Jiménez spoke first.

'Mister, can we talk a little minute please?'

'Sure Paco, Alejandro. What can I do for you?'

'Do you remember when we spoke about being honest with each other?' The question immediately thrust pangs of guilt into both Moreton and Sophia, and their concerned expressions as they glanced at each other, seemed to confirm the suspicions of Jiménez and Sanz. 'We are thinking,' he continued, glancing across at the Retama captain, 'that you are carrying a heavy weight for the times, and you should not carry lonely.' He paused, looking at Moreton and Sophia. 'Dani.' He added conclusively.

Moreton bowed his head slightly and sighed.

'Alejo's nephew Cacho is working at a nightclub in the town. Every night, Dani is there until two or three in the night. He is dancing all the time. He is with girls. He is drinking very much. He is so much trouble there that the Cacho and the people there know him badly. Alejo's brother delivers Cacho to work, but was ill last night. Alejo took him instead. When they arrive, Dani was exiting out of a taxi and going in as well. Alejo said to Cacho if he knew who he was. Cacho laughed. He said to Alejo about the trouble Dani was there. He did not know it was the same person who his uncle had been talking about playing with for so many weeks. Cacho asked how someone could behave like Dani, and still train and play football. Alejo was most angry and came to see me. Today, I speak with García and asked him what to do. He said we must talk to you.'

Moreton knew that the two senior Retama players already knew too much of the truth for any kind of effective cover story, and he recognised that it was also an opportunity for the facts to come out anyway. 'I'm sorry,' he said slowly. 'Paco, Alejandro. I'm sorry. I've let you down.'

'No,' Sophia followed quickly, turning to Moreton and then Jiménez and Sanz. 'Not you, we.'

Jiménez held up his hand to quieten them. 'There is no reason for sorry, if what we think is true. We asked some questions. We think we know why you are carrying this weight.' He exchanged a few words in Spanish with Sanz before continuing. Moreton didn't understand, but the context quickly became clear. 'The club needed money to survive for this season. Bella Cucina is now sponsoring the club. Bella Cucina is owned by the Barbieri family. Dani Barbieri is playing for the club and, he plays bad, but is always select, yes?'

Sanz commented in Spanish '*¡Juega, pero no entrena!*'

Jiménez nodded to his team-mate. '*Si*' he said softly. 'Yes, he still plays, but does not train.'

Moreton was feeling just as guilty for doubting the players' ability to piece together the jigsaw as he did for deceiving them.

'So,' Jiménez continued. 'We think that you are forced to let his son play or Gianni Barbieri,' he paused. 'I think he is the father, yes? He is taking away the money and the club will be finished. Is that the weight you have been carrying, Mister?'

Moreton nodded his head, as Sophia wrapped her arm around his waist. 'Yes,' he admitted. Then to Sanz, '*Si, capitan.*'

'We did not want to say anything because we thought it would just cause problems,'

Sophia added quickly. 'And when Dani started playing so well, everything looked OK. Then when his ankle injury started to trouble him, and he stopped playing well, and couldn't train, it was all too late.'

Jiménez turned to Sanz. '*¡La lesión de tobillo de Dani, Alejo!*' It was said with a dismissive laugh. Sanz's reply was merely a snort of derision.

Moreton and Sophia were clearly confused, so Jiménez explained. 'The ankle injury is not from Milan,' he explained. 'Cacho told Alejo that one of the first times Dani was in the nightclub, he was very drunk. He was talking to lots of girls and being loud and bad to dance with him. Cacho and his friends wanted him out, but he was spending lots of money there and the owner said no. Then Dani chose the wrong girl. Her boyfriend was angry and chased Dani out of the nightclub. He tried to jump over a wall to escape, but was too drunk and fell instead. That was how his ankle became hurt, but it was a small thing, not big, and would have been good in a few days. He was not honest for it all.'

Moreton felt relieved of the burden of deception. Despite Jiménez's less than perfect English, he had summed up the situation perfectly. It was the weight that had been bearing down on him and Sophia since they had conceded to Gianni Barbieri's demands. The problem was, having it in the open didn't solve the original problem. Despite the burden now being shared, it hadn't gone away.

'So, now you know everything,' he said. 'In fact, you know more than we did. But where do we go from here? If Dani doesn't play, his father takes away the money and the club is probably finished.'

Throughout the conversation, Sanz's contribution had been typically short and unquestioned. Now he would take the lead and point the way forward.

'*Retama, el pueblo, el club, es del pueblo. No es de Gianni Barbieri ni de nadie como él. No es suyo para jugar como un juguete para su hijo. Si el club muere, morimos de pie, no de rodillas. ¡No es Retama! Somos Retama. ¡Nadie nos quitará eso!*'

Clearly moved by his sentiment, Sophia walked forward and kissed the CD Retama captain on the cheek. She beamed at Moreton who had failed to understand much of what had been said. 'He said that the club belongs to the people of the town, not Gianni Barbieri. It is not his plaything and, if it dies, it dies on its feet, not on its knees. I think we know what we need to do now.'

Moreton nodded with a smile and embraced Sanz and then Jiménez. 'Somos

'Retama,' he confirmed.

As had become the normal state of affairs over the recent weeks, Dani turned up at the end of the Friday training session, to hear the team selection for the next game. It would be the local derby game at home against Villanuevo. Wearing his red and black Milan tracksuit he sat in the dressing room as Moreton read out the names, unaware that every person in the room now knew what he still believed to be a secret.

The first change was a return to the starting team for Jiménez, and a rest for Juan Torres. The usual back four was in place with Samuel partnering Revi in front of them. Guido and Antonio Vasquez had the flanks with Dani in his usual position. After his goal against Bugroño, Moreton considered that Elías had earned a starting place in the team and with Santi rested, the young forward would lead the line. As the players drifted out of the dressing room, Moreton caught the arm of Dani Barbieri. 'No more free rides,' he said with cold determination.

Local rivalries are often the most fiercely contested, and games between Retama and Villanuevo were no different. Although the physicality didn't reach the extremes of Moreton's first experience of games between the two clubs, there was still plenty of robust challenges flying in from both teams, with precious little thoughtful play in between. The attitude of the rival supporters did little to quell the fires raging.

It quickly became clear that Elías was hardly suited to the physical demands of leading the line in such an encounter. Two ferocious tackles, the second of which could easily have been sanctioned by a red card, saw him limping after 30 minutes. Moreton withdrew the youngster and sent on the much more appropriate qualities of Juan Palermo.

Whilst the visiting defenders found the substitute much less easy to dominate, the change did little to influence the stop-go pattern of the game and, at the break, there had hardly been any meaningful chances, let alone goals. As Moreton watched his players walk back to the dressing room, he noticed Dani limping and then stopping to rub his ankle just in front of where Moreton and Sophia were standing. It was clearly a gesture intended for their consumption.

'Not his sort of game,' Moreton whispered to Sophia, trying hard to suppress a malicious pleasure at the turn of events. 'Struggling, mate?' He said to Dani as he drew level with them.

'My ankle' Dani replied. 'I should come off.'

'Yes, you should,' Moreton agreed.

As Dani sloped off to his car, together with Sophia, Moreton headed towards the dressing room to shuffle his team. For the second period, Matías joined Samuel in a more combative pairing in front of the defence with Revi moving into the position behind the elder Palermo brother. Whilst offering Retama a more resilient look, the move did little to increase their chances of a goal though as any brief attempts at constructive play were compromised by free-kicks and temporary halts to treat injured players. At the end of the game. Moreton was happy to take a point and come out of the game with no serious injuries, barring a few bumps and bruises.

A couple of hours later, the doorbell at Sophia's apartment rang. Looking through the window, she could see García standing by the gate. 'It's Tío,' she informed Moreton who was sitting on the sofa. She opened the door and descended the steps to open the gate, returning with her great uncle behind her. Moreton was already on his feet when the old man entered the room. *'Hola, Señor García,'* he said. *'¿Que t'al?'*

'I am well,' García replied. 'But, please Jon, call me Vicente, or perhaps Tío, as Sophia does. And,' he added.' Let's speak in English. It is good practice for an old man.'

Moreton smiled. 'Of course, Vicente.'

Sophia made coffee and returned to find the two men inevitably discussing football. 'It's good to see you, Tío,' she said passing him a cup.

'Ah,' he replied. 'I do not get out so much these days. I sometimes go and watch your team play when the weather is kind.' Then, adding with a wink. 'I sit at the back so no one sees me.' He took a sip of his coffee. 'Things have been a little difficult for you after a good start to the season,' he said, placing the cup down.

'Yeah,' Moreton agreed. 'This whole Dani thing has been like a cloud hanging over us.'

'Claro,' García acknowledged, nodding and dropping back into his native tongue.

'Paco and Alejandro tell me that they spoke to you when they worked out what the issue was, and you told them to speak to me. Thank you for that.'

García nodded. 'It was the correct thing to do.' He raised his cup and took another sip of coffee. 'I've always found that, if ever you do not know what to do, always do the right thing.' He laughed softly. 'And,' he continued. 'On that subject, I have something to tell you about young Dani Barbieri. After Paco and Alejo spoke with me, I contacted a few old friends to see what I could find out. It seems that the story about him being bullied at Milanello was totally false. In reality, he was ejected from the academy because of ill-discipline and missing training. He was a good prospect, but lacked application. It seems that he has a very fertile imagination, that boy.'

'I suppose that we shouldn't be surprised,' Moreton replied, glancing towards a nodding Sophia.

'No, indeed. But I thought you might want to know, anyway.'

'Of course, Yes, thank you Vicente. We really appreciate it.'

'Not a problem,' García confirmed. 'I was at the game against Villanuevo on Sunday,' he continued. 'Always a difficult game when we play them. They are …' he paused searching for the correct word. He found it. 'Scoundrels?'

Moreton chuckled at the choice, but agreed. 'Yes, they are.'

'At least,' García continued. 'They removed Diego. He was a not a good man, and a very bad coach. I think,' he added, pointing a finger playfully at Moreton, 'that you had something to do with that, didn't you?'

Moreton raised both his arms, palms forward, pleading mock innocence. 'No idea what you mean,' he said with a wink, and they both laughed as Sophia kissed the top of Moreton's head.

'Against the 'scoundrels' you substituted Dani,' García continued. 'That was good. It needed to be done. Whatever happens from there, it's better to die on your feet than to live on your knees,' he added.

'Well, I didn't really,' Moreton confessed uneasily, but wanting to "do the right thing" and be honest. 'He pretty much substituted himself. I think the game was a bit too rough and tumble for him. But, I would have no hesitation to do so now. He is nothing special to me. If it's best for the team that he comes off, then he will, and we'll deal with whatever follows.'

'That's good,' García said nodding. 'If you do not know what to do, always do the right thing,' he said, recalling his earlier advice.

'We will.'

'Anyway, I must be going. It is well past my bedtime.' García rose awkwardly, easing himself into an upright position. 'As you get older, you know, chairs always seem to be much lower down and harder to get up from.' He laughed as he embraced Moreton, and kissed Sophia on both cheeks before leaving.

The atmosphere at the following week's training was much more buoyant than had been the case recently. No one mentioned Dani or the reason he had always been selected to play, but Moreton was relieved that Jiménez and Sanz had clearly informed the other players in the squad with the same level of empathy for the difficulty both he and Sophia had been in. To many, if not all of them, Moreton and Sophia included, it felt like the conclusion of that particular issue, regardless of the consequences, was about to be played out.

With that in mind, and the prospect of Retama being without Dani any time soon, the old problem of how to configure the team to get the best from his resources occupied much of Moreton's thoughts and the way he structured the sessions. Before his injury had brought the experiment to an abrupt halt, the ploy of moving Antonio Vasquez into the middle to play just behind Santi had begun to look promising. With the distinct possibility that Dani may not be part of the squad for much longer, Moreton and Sophia used the training on Tuesday and Wednesday evenings to develop Vasquez's understanding of the role. They had decided to select Dani for the weekend's game against Politanio's B team, always assuming he showed up after training on Friday. If not, they had a solution primed and ready.

As Sophia was completing the warm down at the end of Friday's training session, the sound of Dani's sports car roaring onto the car park outside the Estadio Antonio Núñez announced the arrival of CD Retama's least loved squad member. Despite the understandable emotions of the other players, as directed by Jiménez and Sanz, there were no visible signs of animosity towards the young Italian as his name was read out in the starting eleven. Even his announcement that he would be driving to the game in his own car, rather than on the coach with the Retama party, brought little response.

Moreton's decision to use the experience and calming assurance of Jiménez for what was always going to be a bruising encounter against Villanuevo had proven to be sound and, having kept a clean sheet, it would have been harsh to then drop the veteran. Rare, compared to the other selection conundrums he would face, Moreton was privileged to consistently have two good options to choose from as goalkeeper. Before the mid-season break, in a few games' time, that luxury would be denied him, with severe consequences.

As Sophia had related to Moreton the previous evening, after consulting the league table, Politanio had experienced a mixed bag of results in the 13 games they had played so far. Six home wins, balanced out by the same number of away defeats, and a single draw, had left the club in a fairly undistinguished mid-table position. At the time, to both Moreton and Sophia, the obvious conclusion was an inconsistency of form. When they arrived at the training ground where the B team played their fixtures, in the shadow of the club's main stadium, the real reason became clear. It also quickly became clear why Dani had decided to drive to Politanio.

As the Retama coach pulled onto the car-park at the compact stadium, Moreton, Sophia and the players were greeted by the sight of Dani, in his tracksuit juggling a ball between feet, knees, head and shoulders to the apparent delight of two girls sitting on the side of his car, who offered whoops of joy and applause each time he paused and caught the ball on his foot. 'He's brought his own supporters' club,' Moreton said to Sophia as the climbed down from the coach.

'Dani,' Moreton shouted with undisguised irritation, as he and the remainder of the party headed towards the dressing room, beckoning the performance artiste to follow him. Blowing kisses to the two girls, Dani strolled nonchalantly to join the group.

'Who are they?' Moreton asked as Dani caught up with him.

'Just friends,' Dani replied with a self-satisfied smile. Looking back, to the two girls who were now realising that short skirts and high heels were hardly the best wear for playing football. Moreton shook his head, before closing the dressing room door behind him.

Thirty minutes later, as Moreton and his players left the dressing room to begin their warm-up, he was surprised to see the number of Politanio track-suited players already on the pitch. Pointing Sophia's attention to the large group, they walked towards the home bench to shake hands with the coaches there. While Moreton exchanged the customary pleasantries, Sophia took the opportunity to engage one of the coaches in conversation before returning to Moreton. 'They have two teams,' she revealed.

'What? Two teams?'

'Yes,' she confirmed. 'Apparently the club decided that, as they have a large group of young players, they have basically split their season in half with two teams, each playing 17 games. The better players play in the home fixtures and the others in the away games. That way, it makes it easier for the coaches from the first team to come across and watch and evaluate the best prospects, while the other players gain experience in the away games. Their coach also told me that it stops the young players having to play too many games as well. Apparently, it was all Francisco's idea. You remember him from last season. He is doing very well with the first team and will be here shortly to watch his players.'

Moreton raised his eyebrows at the news. 'It makes sense, I guess.'

'Yes, Jon. But it also means that we will, be playing their best team today. They have won all six of their games so far, scoring 18 goals and only conceding four. It's going to be a difficult game.'

Before kick-off, as the starting eleven home players peeled-off their tracksuits to reveal the red shirts and white shorts of their club colours, the others from the group took seats in the small stand behind the home coaches' bench. As they did so, Moreton felt a tap on his shoulder. Startled from his concentration on the pitch, he looked up to see the grey hair and smiling face of Francisco, now established as the first team coach of Politanio. He shook hands with Moreton then did the same with Sophia, each time offering a pleasant '*Hola,*' before retiring to sit beside his team of coaches for the game.

It very quickly became clear that the eleven players starting the game for Politanio were indeed their first choices. Much as had been the case in the first game Retama had played under Moreton last season, the blue shirted players were pulled around, impotently chasing the controlled and confident passing of the home team. Even Dani seemed to be working hard.

Possession was a rare luxury for Retama but when the ball was channelled forward to Dani, it was quickly lost as he set off on an impossible dribble trying to beat player after player. The brief, but quickly aborted dribbles, brought screams of delight from the two girls who had now positioned themselves in the stand opposite the Retama bench, but only frustration at the wanton squandering of preciously rare possession from Moreton, Sophia and the other Retama players.

With the pressure growing on the Retama defence, and no sustained respite available, a Politanio goal felt inevitable. It came after 15 minutes. A neat triangle of passes opened up the left flank of Retama's defence and a low cross was hammered home at the near post. 'Well, that was coming,' Moreton conceded, much as his team had done. Ten minutes later, they did so again. This time it was an attack from the other flank. A neat one-two opened up a gap between Sanz and Victor, with a final stepover defeating Kiko and allowing a free run into the area for the Politanio striker who slid the ball confidently wide of Jiménez.

With just 25 minutes played, the game was surely already lost, but the Retama players still pressed enthusiastically, and defended with dogged determination. Their tenacity and application only intensified the frustration as Dani insisted on lone runs with the ball that inevitably resulted in lost possession. 'Pass the ball, Dani!' Moreton yelled angrily, but the young Italian feigned not to hear. The people he was trying to impress were not in Retama blue, but sat in the stands on the opposite side of the pitch from where Moreton and Sophia were positioned, their frustration growing with each passing minute.

With the game in the bag, the Politanio players seemed satisfied with their two-goal lead and, while they still controlled the game, a slight let up in their attacking intensity allowed Retama to get to the half-time break without conceding again. In the dressing room, first Moreton praised the dedication and tenacity of almost all of his players. Then, turning to Dani, his expression changed.

'Here's how it is Dani,' he said with cold determination. 'Continue playing like a twat and you're off. Got it!'

Dani Barbieri pursed his lips and nodded slowly, but without the slightest hint of contrition. 'Sure,' he said, without conviction. 'Whatever you say.'

As the players emerged for the second period, Dani trotted across the pitch to where the two girls were seated. Standing on the touchline, he blew kisses to them, as they responded in kind. Watching, Moreton frowned and, turning to Sophia, declared. 'He's got five minutes to prove me wrong.' Moreton never expected it to happen – and it didn't.

At the referee's whistle, the game quickly assumed the pattern of the first half. Politanio garnered and cherished possession with the selfish greed of a spoilt child jealously refusing to share the only bar of chocolate in the shop.

More than ten minutes had passed before a Retama foot even touched the ball, as Samuel plunged into a tackle, driving the ball free and forward. It fell to Dani, who controlled and turned to run up field. Dropping a shoulder, he glided past his first opponent before trying to nutmeg the second and losing possession. 'That's it. Get Juan ready,' Moreton said to Sophia.

At the next break in play, he called the substitution. 'Ten' he shouted, calling Dani towards the touchline, receiving a shake of the head in reply. 'Ten,' Moreton repeated. 'Ten!' Dani Barbieri stood his ground, incredulous at the decision. It took the gentle persuasive tones of Alejandro Sanz, accompanied by a strong push in the back to convince him that his time in the game was over.

As Dani walked reluctantly towards the touchline, Moreton and Sophia were intent on passing instructions to Juan Palermo. He was to play on the right flank, with Antonio Vasquez replacing Dani in the middle. They paid scant attention to the furious Dani as he walked straight past them and into the dressing room, emerging ten minutes later in his tracksuit. Walking towards the bench where Moreton and Sophia's attention was fixed on the game, he halted ten metres or so away. 'Hey,' he shouted. Again, louder. 'Hey. Hey!'

Moreton stood and looked towards where the voice was coming from.

As he did so, Dani threw the blue Retama shirt onto the ground and stamped on it, throwing the shorts and socks on top of it. He raised the middle finger of his right hand and thrust it up at Moreton. From among the substitutes, José Palermo jumped to his feet, angered at the insult to his club, but Moreton restrained him.

'*Vaffanculo!*' Dani shouted from a safe distance. 'You're finished. You, your club, all of you.' He turned and walked away towards his car, beckoning at the girls opposite to follow him. Perhaps concerned that he may have provoked some reaction, he cast a look back over his shoulder, before delivering the final insult. '*Pezzo di merda.*' And, with that, Dani Barbieri walked out of the Retama squad, and would soon be on his way back to Italy.

Moreton walked to retrieve the kit that Dani had thrown on the ground, shaking it free of the dust and dirt. He folded it carefully and placed it in his bag, before turning his attention back to the game, whispering to Sophia.

'If I ever see that little shit again …' he paused as she placed her finger to his lips.

'He's gone, Jon,' she said softly.

'Yeah, I know. But what happens now.'

Sophia shook her head slowly. 'I don't know, but all we can do is concentrate on the football, yes?

'*Si, mi amor.*'

As they spoke, a whistle from the Politanio bench grabbed their attention and they turned to see Francisco nodding and clapping towards them. '*Muy bien,*' he said. '*Muy bien.*'

It may have been the exhilaration of watching Dani Barbieri leaving their club, the change on the pitch with Vasquez now in the number ten role, or the fact that the Politanio players had eased up but, in the remaining minutes of the game, Retama established something approaching equality in the game and, with five minutes to play, Juan Palermo headed a consolation goal from a Revi corner.

Despite losing, the mood in the Retama dressing room after the game was decidedly upbeat. Moreton related how proud he was of the team's spirit, and praised the players' commitment to the club and each other. After he had finished, Sanz spoke in his quiet but authoritative tone as Sophia translated for Moreton.

'You all know that the club may well be in a lot of trouble financially now,' she whispered as Sanz spoke. 'It may mean the end of the club, but we will not lie down and die. These people think they can buy us, buy the club.' He shook his head. 'They cannot. The club belongs to the town, to the people. We will fight.' He grabbed the badge on his chest and as Sophia translated, Moreton knew what was coming. '*Somos Retama!*'

As the darkness falls

For all the inspirational defiance of Sanz's oratory after the game, the consequences of Dani Barbieri leaving the club remained like the Sword of Damocles hovering menacingly over CD Retama. The following morning, Sophia called her father to explain what had happened with Dani, and ask how he saw things as a consequence. He told her that he would need to check the fine print of the contract with Cerámica Internacional and would call her back. Sophia closed out the call and told Moreton what her father had said. 'I guess all we can do now is wait,' he replied

It was lunchtime when the ringtone on Sophia's phone suggested that the wait may be over. The name on the screen merely confirmed it. Moreton watched as she spoke, forlornly trying to discern the contents of the call by Sophia's replies and her expression. As she ended the conversation with a *Hasta luego papá,*' and placed the phone down on the table, it was clear to Moreton that the news wasn't encouraging.

'OK, Jon,' she began. 'My father has checked with his friend, the solicitor who is looking after the club's legal situation as part of the consortium. At the moment, it seems that Gianni Barbieri has not formally declared his intention to withdraw his guarantee of funds but, given the situation with Dani, he thinks that's only a matter of time.'

I'm sure that's right,' Moreton agreed.

'The terms of the agreement then give the club 30 days to have that guarantee reinstated either by Barbieri, or someone else. After that period, the clause requiring the club to be sold to Cerámica Internacional for the fee of €10 becomes obligatory and, once active, it cannot be rescinded.' Moreton's suspicions were confirmed. It certainly hadn't been encouraging news.

'Did Joaquín give any indication whether he thinks there's a chance of raising the money from somewhere else?' he asked hopefully.

'He is going to try, but he told me not to be very hopeful. He and his friends are all successful businessmen, but the amount of money required is very large, especially with the possibility that it will all be lost and the club sold anyway. They really cannot afford to gamble such an amount. You have to understand that, Jon.'

'Of course,' Moreton agreed. 'Joaquín and his friends have done so much to give the club a second chance. We can't expect them to risk their livelihoods as well.'

Sophia continued. 'My father thinks our best hope is to try and persuade Barbieri to change his mind. He's going to speak with Hernández, you remember, his friend the newspaper owner, and see if he will talk to Barbieri, and try to persuade him that a decision to kill the club will only hurt his business interests. He's not convinced that it will be effective though. All the contracts with the local administration are now signed and completed, so the only weapon that Hernández could have would be the threat of bad publicity. We must remember of course, that Dani is unlikely to tell the truth about him leaving the club and will probably paint a picture for his father of being victimised or something like that and, Barbieri may well tell Hernández that he too can deliver bad publicity.'

'Well, I guess we at least have a little time until Barbieri gets his lawyers moving?'

At that moment, Sophia's phone interrupted the conversation. She picked it up and spoke to her father.

'Sí, papá.

Entiendo.

¿A partir de hoy?

Claro.

Claro.

Gracias, papá.

A luego.'

Sophia closed the call and looked sadly at Moreton. 'Barbieri has done it. The 30 days start today.'

Moreton and Sophia quickly agreed that hiding the reality from the players would be both wrong and pointless and, before training on the following evening they called the squad and Esteban, together in the dressing room. There was a silence in the room, save for the voice of Sophia explaining the situation in Spanish. Moreton understood most of what she was saying, and filled in the gaps with the knowledge gained from their conversations earlier in the day. When she had finished, there was a pause as the news was slowly digested.

Moreton felt compelled to speak. 'I'm sorry,' he said, as Sophia translated. 'If I hadn't taken Dani off, this wouldn't have happened …'

He was cut short by Alejandro Sanz. 'No, Mister. Hiciste lo correcto para CD Retama.' Sophia whispered to Moreton that the Retama captain was saying that he had done the right thing for the club. '*No vivimos de rodillas*,' Sanz continued. 'We do not live on our knees,' Sophia translated a little louder to Moreton, as the room burst into applause and cheers. There would be no lack of application in training that week. In the following Sunday's game though, the enflamed passion of the Retama players would have a cost.

Last season, UD Palancio had endured a difficult time in the league. The exit of Francisco back to Politanio and the subsequent exodus of players to Estrella Azul and their 2-2 draw with Retama towards the end of the season had contributed to them staying above the relegation zone, thanks to a superior head-to-head record against UD Aragaza who were relegated. As such, for a team in need of any kind of morale-boosting victory, they looked to be the ideal opponents.

Recognising the importance of a victory, Moreton took few chances when he announced the team after training of Friday. Jiménez was retained in goal behind the regular back four of Sanz, Kiko, Victor and Adrián. Ahead of them Samuel partnered Revi. Juan Palermo had the right flank, Guido the left, with Antonio Vasquez retained in the number ten role and Santi leading the line. No one knew it at the time, but this would be the last game for some while when Moreton was able to select his first-choice defence. The problems that lay ahead for the CD Retama would be more than merely financial.

When the game got underway, it was clear that there was a fiery determination in the Retama players and they hurled themselves forward against a team once more battling at the wrong end of the table. Chances quickly followed. Santi had two shots saved by the visiting goalkeeper, the second of which he fumbled out, but a charging Juan Palermo was just beaten to the rebound by a defender. Minutes later it was Palermo again causing problems. This time a header from a Guido cross just missed the far post. A mere 15 minutes had been played and Retama could have been two or three goals clear.

'This is good,' Sophia enthused to Moreton.

'Yeah, but we must not lose control and get carried away.'

It was a timely caution. Five minutes later, a slip by Kiko, as he received a pass from Victor, led to a breakaway by a Palancio forward. Kiko chased back to recover his error as the forward reached the edge of the box and was about to shoot, with just Jiménez to beat. Timing the challenge to perfection Kiko had made up the gap and plunged in to slide the ball clear as the forward fell to the ground over his outstretched leg. Moreton jumped to his feet, applauding the skill and pace of the athletic Kiko, but the referee's whistle halted his acclaim. Caught up field by the speed of the break, the official was still some 30 metres behind the play as Kiko made his challenge but, ignoring the lack of any confirming signal from his linesman his assessment was both harsh and uncompromising.

First, he stood waiting as Kiko climbed to his feet before brandishing a red card at the bewildered Retama defender, then walked purposefully into the Retama area and stood ramrod straight, pointing to the penalty spot. Moreton and Sophia both yelled from the touchline in protest. It was a call taken up by the players on the pitch, especially Adrián who became embroiled in a feverish argument with one of the Palancio players who took the easy option of falling to the floor holding his face, without any contact from the Retama defender. With a crowd of Palancio players crowding around their apparently stricken team-mate and calling for retribution, another red card was flourished and, in a few seconds, Retama had unjustly conceded a penalty and were down to nine men.

The official had clearly lost control of the situation and it took the authoritative figure of Sanz to calm the Retama players before any further sanctions were delivered by the flustered official. Eventually, after minutes of protests, claims and counterclaims, Kiko and Adrián were ushered from the field to be greeted by a seething but understanding Moreton, who embraced each player in turn as they passed him on the way to the dressing room.

While the penalty was driven low to Jiménez's left as the goalkeeper gambled right, Moreton and Sophia discussed how to reshape their depleted team with just 20 minutes played. Guido was quickly sent back to replace Adrián and Juan Palermo slotted in alongside Victor to give the coaches some thinking time. The moves diminished the attacking potential of Retama but, for now, that was of minor significance. Against a more accomplished team, Retama's patchwork defence might have struggled, but Palancio were unused to being in the lead, especially in away fixtures and instinctively dropped back to defend their ill-gotten gains.

As the game settled down, with neither team inclined to press forward, it gave Moreton and Sophia time to think. Ten minutes later, they made their changes. Given the game was now going to be largely one of attrition for the home team, the creative qualities of Revi and Vasquez were sacrificed, and Felipe Blanco and Matías sent on in their places. Leaving Juan Palermo as the replacement for Kiko meant that little was lost in terms of physicality at the heart of the Retama defence, although defensive nous was very much reduced. Felipe Blanco took over the left flank of the defence with Samuel and Matías providing a shield in front of them. The emphasis of the Retama attack would be provided by the speed of Guido and the goal scoring ability of Santi. If the defence could hold firm, Moreton was gambling on the new front pairing to find a goal from somewhere. Where the passionate opening of the game had led to Retama falling behind, Moreton was now betting on his players' obduracy in the face of injustice to find a way back into the game.

At the break, there had been no further goals and little threat of one. Palancio seemed content to play deep with their defenders heavily outnumbering the pair of Retama forwards, and choking off any hint of danger. At the other end, the elder Palermo brother had won his headers as required, with Victor tidying up around him, whilst Sanz and Felipe Blanco were calmly efficient on the flanks. In the Retama dressing room, Moreton emphasised the need not to concede again. Go two goals down and it would probably be all up for Retama. If they could remain solid at the back as the game wore on, there would be a chance for an equaliser if they could take it. 'Get a draw from this game and it will feel like a 5-0 win in other games,' he said as he sent the players out for the second period.

Sitting back down on the bench as the teams reappeared, Sophia placed her hand on his and squeezed it gently. 'Do you really believe we can get anything from here?'

'Maybe, but it doesn't really matter what I believe. It's what they believe that counts,' he replied, nodding towards the players. 'The problem isn't really about today, it's about the next few games. There's always been a danger about the centre of defence. What would happen if we lost Kiko or Victor? When Mateo came along, I thought we had an answer, someone who could slot in where needed, and could even give one of the guys a rest every now and then, but he's gone now. Juan will give everything he's got for us, but he's no Kiko. How could he be? And, without Kiko alongside him, Victor has so much more to do. Juan might be OK against a side like Palancio, but our next game is away to Córuel. That would be a tough game with our best team and, whatever happens between now and then, we're not going to have our best central defence available. With Felipe, we have cover for Alejandro and Adrián, but in the middle, we've always been one injury, one suspension, away from a crisis.' He paused as the referee restarted the game. 'And now we have one.'

Very much as Moreton had suggested, even without two of their regular players, the Retama defence coped with the occasional Palancio attacks without too many problems and, as time ticked on, with the prospect of an unlikely away victory for the visitors honing into view, they sank further and further back.

With 15 minutes to play, Moreton decided to gamble. Removing Samuel, he sent on the Elías to play up front with Santi, and moved Felipe Blanco forward to play next to Matías, leaving Retama with just three at the back. It meant an increased risk of conceding a second goal should Palancio push for it but, with the visitors' threat largely subdued by their own caution, that was unlikely.

Felipe Blanco advanced with the ball, as the Palancio players funnelled back to defend. On he went, across the hallway line and into the visitors' half of the field before he was challenged. Slipping the ball wide to Guido, he then raced forward to support Santi and Elías as the Retama wide man accelerated down the left flank before swinging in a cross. Arriving at speed the young substitute, leapt to meet the ball, crashing his header against the bar. The ball ricocheted out and struck the diving Palancio goalkeeper on the back and bounced on the goal line. A striker's instincts blaring in his mind, Santi had followed the header in and had the simple task of prodding the ball into the net to equalise.

The fragile confidence of the visitors quickly melted away and, in the final minute there was even a chance for Retama to snatch an unlikely winner, but Guido's shot from distance whistled past the post with the Palancio goalkeeper beaten.

At the end of the game, Moreton was delighted with the way his team had refused to bend the knee against what had seemed overwhelming odds. If only Joaquín Garrigues could conjure up a similarly unlikely outcome, perhaps the club could still be saved. At this stage though, there was very little that Moreton felt he could do to help achieve that end. His attention was concentrated on winning football matches and hoping that a white knight would gallop to the rescue. In a week's time, without two of his regular back line players, Retama would visit the highflying promoted club, FC Córuel, and that would demand all of his concentration.

A quick look at the league table on Monday had not only revealed to Moreton and Sophia how Retama's recent results had seen them tumble from the top of the table to seventh place. It also highlighted that their next opponents were very much on the rise, having scored 37 goals in their first 15 games, compared to Retama's relatively lowly 20. Their attack was clearly their strong point and, for the Retama team selected to face them, inevitably defence would be their weakness. It was hardly the ideal match up for Moreton and Sophia.

With both Kiko and Adrián suspended for the upcoming match, and the latter also missing the next two as well, the training sessions for the following week were concentrated on finding the most efficient solution. The easy part of the problem was playing Felipe Blanco instead on the left flank of the defence. The more taxing issue was to find the best replacement for Kiko. When he had been unavailable during the previous season, Moreton had tried a number of alternative options to cover the loss of the commanding centre back, at times deploying Samuel and Juan Palermo, at others coping by playing a five-man back line. None had been overly successful. There wasn't a perfect solution so, after discussing with Sophia over dinner on Monday evening, Moreton settled on what they considered would be the least imperfect option, and designed the training sessions for that week to repeatedly practise the formation.

Jiménez would have a five-man defence in front of him. Felipe Blanco would be on the right flank, with Guido dropping deeper to cover the left back role. Juan Palermo would play as the stand-in centre back alongside Victor, with Sanz deployed behind them as the last man and providing cover. Matías and Samuel would play in front of that line with Antonio Vasquez, Santi and José Palermo forming the attack. It was system designed to frustrate, protect and look to hit on the counterattack and, for much of the game that's how it would play out. But before he could bring that plan into being, Moreton would be compelled to make changes.

He was sitting on the balcony with Sophia enjoying breakfast when the doorbell rang. She jumped up and walked into the living area to look down towards the gate. 'It's Paco,' she shouted to Moreton, before opening the door and descending the steps to invite Retama's veteran goalkeeper in. By the time she returned with Jiménez, Moreton was waiting at the doorway and greeted the visitor with a cheery, *'Hola, Paco. Que t'al?'* The concerned look on Sophia's face, as she entered the apartment behind Jiménez, suggested problems.

'Paco has a problem,' she told Moreton as she closed the door.

'*Si*, Sorry, I mean yes, Mister,' Jiménez confirmed. 'Today, I have to travel to Valencia. My company completed some work at a business there a few weeks ago, but something is gone wrong. The owners are biggest of my clients, and they have insisted that I go to watch the work as everything must be completed correct so that the business can continue as is normal there on Monday morning. I do not know the full details yet, but it is very likely I will be there overnight and then for most of Sunday too.' He paused a moment, but the inevitable consequence was already clear to Moreton. 'I cannot play on Sunday,' Jiménez concluded unnecessarily. 'But Juan can play, of course,' he added.

'Of course, amigo,' Moreton replied. 'It cannot be helped and, as you say, we have Juan.'

'I want to say you myself as persons, not telephone you.'

'You're a good guy, Paco,' Moreton replied, patting the elder man on the shoulder. *'Muchas gracias, amigo.'*

'*Gracias, Mister*,' Jiménez said as he opened the door to leave.

'*De nada*,' Moreton replied. '*¡Suerte en Valencia!*'

Jiménez waved in acknowledgement as he opened the gate to leave the complex. Closing the door, Moreton turned to Sophia. 'We have Juan, so it shouldn't be much of a problem,' he said confidently. Six days later, that confidence would have evaporated.

For all the diligent work of coaches and players across the training sessions of the previous week, Moreton still felt strong pangs of apprehension as the Retama coach drew into the car park at the home of FC Córuel. The stadium was small but well maintained, and there were clear signs of renovation work beginning there, with a large sign welcoming any visitors as they passed through the gate. On a white background in bold read letters, it read *'El Celo. ¡Siempre aquí!'* Moreton asked Sophia what the name of the company sponsoring the club meant.

'It means "The Energy" …' She paused. 'No, that's not right. Perhaps, "The Enthusiasm"? No, that's not quite it. Ah, "The Zeal" is better. And then it says "Always here!" It's their slogan.' Moreton had understood the slogan but, as Sophia translated, the phrase struck a chord in his mind, but he couldn't think why - not at the time, anyway.

The sponsorship provided to the club by El Celo extended to the colours of FC Córuel. The white shirts of their players carried a broad red diagonal sash broken at the chest by a white patch and the name "El Celo" in red. Red shorts and socks completed the homage to the club's financial backers.

Appreciation of El Celo's largesse was certainly in order. Their support had allowed a team who had been champions of their league by a clear dozen points the previous season to add to their squad, and were now challenging at the top of the table. The opening phases of the game illustrated the success of that policy.

Adding an extra player to the back line inevitably had left Retama short in another department and, as Santi laboured to maintain at least a token presence for his team in attack, the Retama midfield quickly became outnumbered and overrun, with José Palermo and Antonio Vasquez forced to defend deeply. The confident Córuel attack were used to scoring goals and, as their team dominated possession and position, plenty of opportunities to do so followed.

Whilst Juan Palermo was well equipped to deal with crosses into the box, and more than held his own in the physical battles, when isolated in one-v-one situations, his lack of defensive experience was quickly exposed. It was something that the Córuel forwards quickly identified and targeted. In the first 15 minutes of the game, Sanz was repeatedly forced to advance and cover for the stand-in centre back as the home forwards drew him out of position. Inevitably, it led to openings and Juan Torres was called on to deal with a number of shots, but did so with a reassuring competence. It was clearly going to be a long 90 minutes for the Retama defence and their concerned coaches watching from the sidelines.

As the game progressed, Palermo became more accustomed to his adopted role. The home forwards found it less easy to create openings around him, but their play was still causing consistent problems for the Retama defence, with Torres's goal bombarded with attempts both from distance and when the Córuel forwards' neat interplay tore holes in the visitors' defence. Reaching the half hour mark and with his team barely able to break out of their own half, Moreton was fearing the worst. 'I'm not sure we can hold out,' he said to Sophia with concern etched on his face.

'I know,' she replied. 'But what can we change?'

Moreton shook his head slowly. He hadn't got an answer. A few minutes later though, a change would be required.

Once again, the home forwards forced a way through the Retama defence, and as Sanz was drawn forward to cover, a neat pass put a Córuel player clean through with just Torres to beat. The Retama goalkeeper stood up for as long as possible, denying his opponent the easy option of clipping the ball over him if he committed himself too early. It compelled the forward to try and dribble round the goalkeeper and, as he dragged the ball wide to Torres's left, the goalkeeper made his dive, pushing the ball behind for a corner, just as the forward was committed to the shot.

With the ball disappearing behind the goal line for a corner, the forward's boot contacted the goalkeeper's wrist. The discomforting crack and ensuing pain immediately told Torres that he had problems. Slowly climbing to his feet and cupping his left wrist in his right hand he signalled to the Retama bench. Grabbing her bag, Sophia dashed onto the pitch but could do little and, within seconds, was signalling to Moreton that Retama's only on duty goalkeeper couldn't continue.

Moreton's mind raced for the best solution. With Sebastián absent and Dani Barbieri merely a bad memory, the substitute options were limited. Santi was the emergency goalkeeper and Sophia called him across as Moreton decided who to send on to replace Torres. The obvious answer looked to be Elías. It would then be a forward coming on to take over the role that Santi's new assignment in goal had created. Instead, Moreton opted for Revi, shuffling his players accordingly. The newcomer would partner Matías. Samuel was switched to left back and Guido moved into attack, with the hope that his pace may create a chance for an unlikely goal.

With the instructions delivered, Moreton watched as Torres slowly walked from the pitch with Sophia. As they reached the bench one of the Córuel coaching staff came across and spoke to Sophia briefly.

She smiled and thanked him. 'He's asked me to take Juan to their dressing room to see what they can do to help him. They have some basic First Aid equipment there.'

'*Muchas gracias,*' Moreton said to the coach, adding his thanks to that already offered by Sophia.

A wave of the hand by the red and white track-suited coach and brief 'De nada,' dismissed the need for thanks, and he led Sophia and Torres away. Moreton turned towards the Córuel bench and, raising his arms in front of his face, offered his applause to the coaches remaining there. A wave served as their reply. As he settled back down on the bench again, his confident words to Sophia after Jiménez had told them about being unavailable for the game, came back to him. "It shouldn't be much of a problem." He chastised himself. A week later, that problem would be seen in even sharper focus. For now, the problem of helping his team to keep the eager Córuel forwards at bay was front and centre of his concentration.

In typical style, Sanz passionately rallied his team against the adversity they faced and with renewed resilience the defence tackled, harried and blocked to limit the opportunities for the Córuel forwards to pressurise their emergency goalkeeper. The introduction of Revi also offered a bonus as the gifted playmaker utilised the rare moments of possession to supply long passes forwards, feeding the pace of Guido. Inevitably the forays came to nought as the Retama speedster was swamped by defenders and subdued. His threat, however, at least meant the home defence were required to maintain sufficient numbers to deal with the threat, and gave a break to the overworked Retama defence. At the break, the make-do-and-mend Retama set-up had managed to defy the best that Córuel could throw at them. The scoreline remained goalless. As they arrived back in the dressing room, Moreton and the weary Retama players found Sophia and Juan Torres waiting there.

'What do you think?' Moreton asked Sophia as the players alternated between speaking with their injured goalkeeper, taking on liquid, or merely collapsing onto the red benches that fitted around the white walls of the dressing room.

'I'm not sure, to be honest. Their guy thinks it may only be badly bruised, but I'm not sure. He's strapped it for now to limit the swelling and the ice should help. If there's still pain in the morning though, I've told Juan that he should get an X-ray to check for any breaks.'

Moreton nodded slowly, taking in both the news and the consequences. Bruising might only mean one or two weeks out, even if it was a deep bruise. A break, though, could be anything up to six or eight weeks. The injury was a complete accident, just one of those things that happens in a sport where physical contact is all part of the game. To Moreton though, it felt like another blow to CD Retama when things were already at a low ebb, and defeat felt inevitable.

Other than praising the heroics performed so far against a team in rampant form, encouraging and cajoling even greater efforts in the second half, there was little help Moreton could offer his team tactically, so he opted for an emotional approach. He told the players that, even with injury time, the second half would last no longer than 50 minutes but, if they broke that down into five segments of ten minutes, it would feel much more manageable.

'So,' he said, as Sophia translated. 'Let's be solid for the first ten minutes to make sure there's no breakthrough, and I'll call out when we hit the end of that segment. After that, if we can repeat the success, we'll be almost halfway to the final whistle, and I'll call out the ten minutes mark again. Just concentrate on keeping them out for ten minutes each time, yes?'

A muffled grunt was all Moreton could reasonably have expected, but his words drew more than that. That there were shouts cheers and applause. Amongst it all, José Palermo stood up as the noise quietened. '¡Somos Retama!' he bellowed at the top of his voice. '¡Está en nuestras cabezas. Está en nuestros corazones!' The shout was echoed to the rafters and, as the players filed past Moreton back to the pitch, he high-fived each in turn, reserving a long embrace instead for the younger Palermo sibling. Turning to Sophia as they followed the players, he whispered, 'The first ten minutes is in the bag already!'

Accessing reserves of energy from new untapped reservoirs of passion, the Retama players revealed his comment to be a substantial understatement. After ten minutes, as promised, he climbed to his feet and holding both hands in the air, fingers and thumbs spread wide, he yelled 'Ten!' to his players. His defence had been solid and Santi had been required to do little other than catch crosses and field back passes. The next yell followed ten minutes later and very little had changed in the pattern of the game. Moreton knew, however, that the adrenalin rush fuelled by José Palermo's rallying call would run dry soon, and the last part of the game would surely be the most testing.

Sure enough, by the time that the coach signalled 30 minutes had been passed without a goal being conceded, signs of growing fatigue and falling levels of concentration were becoming increasingly evident. The Córuel forwards began to find openings again, as tired limbs agonisingly railed against the instructions passed down from equally weary minds. His team were in urgent need of fresh legs, but the only card Moreton had left in his hand was the young striker Elías.

Five more minutes passed and now the Retama formation had all but disintegrated with all ten outfield players back as defenders. Santi was coming under increased pressure as his defence creaked and groaned in front of him. Two smart saves, and then a block with his foot diverted another shot wide. From the resulting corner, a header struck the Retama bar before Victor could hack the ball clear. There would be little respite however as, with no one up field, the ball was immediately recycled by Córuel and another attack launched. Sanz organised as best he could and cajoled his team-mates to greater efforts, but a goal was surely on the way. With eight minutes to play it looked to have arrived.

Out on the Retama left, a Córuel forward skipped past a tired challenge by Guido, who was now serving as an extra full back, and then cut inside Felipe Blanco into the penalty area. The weary defender jabbed out a foot to try and intercept, but merely brought his opponent to the ground. It was a clear penalty and the referee confirmed the inevitable pointing to the spot. Moreton threw back his head and puffed out his cheeks in disappointment, as Felipe Blanco's head sunk to his chest, only to have the strong hands and persuasive tones of Sanz raise it up again.

With the ball placed on the spot, Santi looked every inch the outfield player dropped into an unfamiliar environment as he faced the penalty. Unlike Jiménez and Torres, he had never had to face the twelve-yard contest before in a game and hadn't contemplated what to do in such a scenario. He decided to put himself in the penalty taker's position. If he was taking a spot kick himself, where would he place the ball? From the shape of the Córuel player's run up, he could tell he was right-footed, as he was, and decided that he would have hit the ball hard to the goalkeeper's right-hand corner.

As the penalty was about to be struck, he hurled himself in that direction, a gloved hand reaching out towards the bottom corner. The sound and sensation of the ball hitting his gloved hand and bouncing clear brought waves of elation as he jumped to his feet, punching the air to be mobbed by his team-mates. The joy only lasted a couple of seconds though, before the urgent whistles of the referee halted things. The official had decided that Santi's dive had moved him off his line before the ball was struck, and ordered a retake. The descent from delight to disappointment drilled into the Retama players, but their protests were always doomed to failure.

What to do for the retake was now Santi's problem. He decided to go the same way again, but determined to wait that fraction of a second longer. The Córuel player ran up and hit the ball centrally as Santi dived to his right. This time there was no satisfying sound of ball on glove. In fact, there was no sound at all. Disturbed by the first miss, and striking the ball firmly, the Córuel player had lifted his penalty over the bar. Retama had escaped – at least for now.

Before the goal kick could be taken Moreton decided to send on Elías. There was now a chance that this could turn out to be the sort of game that is burnt into the memory of all who took part in it, and would serve as an inspiration for the future. He wanted all of his squad to feel a part of it. Calling the young forward across he said to Sophia. 'Tell him there are heroes out there, and he belongs among them.' The goal kick was hit long and headed out of play as a Córuel defender tried to send it back up field. Morton called off Antonio Vasquez and an enthused Elías raced on to the pitch.

There was now only five minutes to play and Córuel's studied play had been replaced by a desperate and constantly frustrated attempt to hit in shots from any distance as the sight of the finishing line, and Moreton's shout that another ten minutes had passed, fed new reserves of energy. The time dragged for those in blue, but they held out as the final minute approached. A final desperate cross into a crowded Retama penalty area was headed down by a Córuel forward, and pinged around as players sought to shoot or clear in turn. Finally, the ball dropped to Juan Palermo a couple of metres from goal and he tapped it into the arms of Santi. Córuel arms went up to appeal and were answered by the referee awarding an indirect free-kick for the goalkeeper picking up a back pass. If it had been possible, Moreton would have pleaded mitigation on the grounds that both players involved were playing out of position, and were less in tune with the laws of the game at that end of the field. Such details mattered little though.

With the entire Retama team stationed on the goal line, and the ball no more than a couple of metres from them, a Córuel player prepared to tap the ball to a team-mate to shoot. A couple of feints first drew a rush of blue charging from the line, before the referee sent them back. Finally, the ball was tapped back and the shot hit in. Although haphazardly formed, the sheer number of bricks in the blue wall made it unlikely that the ball would find an unhindered path into the net. It struck the knee of Sanz, and then the shoulder of Juan Palermo before hitting the bar and then the back of same player, seemingly bound for the back of the net. At the very last second though, Retama's late substitute threw himself into an acrobatic bicycle kick and hooked the ball clear. The final whistle sounded and Elías had fulfilled his coach's remit.

Sportingly, the Córuel coaches accepted the unjust result with good grace, shaking hands with Moreton and Sophia, and offering best wishes for Juan Torres's injury. An hour later, the Retama bus, full of physically and mentally spent players, pulled out of the car park, under the sign and began its journey back to Retama. Looking back over his shoulder, Moreton again saw the sign, and silently mouthed the words that Sophia had unnecessarily translated for him. *"¡Siempre aquí!"* Always here. It meant something to him, but he wasn't sure what.

Five minutes later, along with most of the other passengers on the coach heading back to Retama, Moreton drifted off to sleep.

On Monday morning, two pieces of news arrived with Moreton and Sophia, and any lingering elation from the draw hewed out of the visit to Córuel, were quickly banished. After the stresses of the previous day, time lazing in, and at the side of, the large swimming pool at the complex seemed the ideal way to recuperate following lunch. Moreton had just climbed out of the pool and settled down beside Sophia when her phone rang. She picked it up and walked away from the activity of the swimming pool to better hear the other person. A couple of minutes later she returned. The look on her face suggested the call had not been to deliver good news.

'Juan,' she said. 'He was still in pain this morning, although the swelling had gone down a little so he went to the hospital. They gave him an X-ray and it revealed a fracture in one of the bones in his wrist. It's not a major thing, but he'll be in a cast for a few weeks, and probably won't be able to play again for at least six.'

'Wow,' Moreton said slowly. 'Poor Juan. He's such a good kid as well. I always think that you have to be a bit crazy to be a goalkeeper. How they don't get hurt more often baffles me. How is he?'

Sophia smiled at Moreton's goalkeeper analysis. 'He's feeling a bit down, but he'll be OK. I've told him just to concentrate on resting up and not worrying about the team. We have Paco anyway.'

'Yeah,' Moreton agreed, lowering his head onto the sunbed.

A couple of hours later, as the sun began to dip behind the apartments surrounding the swimming pool and casting long, cool shadows across it, Moreton and Sophia collected their towels and headed back along the walkway towards the apartment. Moreton went in the shower first as Sophia hung out the towels to dry and then took her turn in the bathroom. By the time she re-emerged, with one towel covering her torso, and another wrapped around her head, Moreton was dressed in shorts and a vest top standing in the living area. He walked to her and drew her close to him, as the towel around her head fell to the floor.

'Your hair is wet,' he whispered softly into her ear. 'Are you wet everywhere?'

Sophia smiled seductively. 'Let's see,' she said, opening the towel that had been wrapped around her, allowing it to fall to the floor. 'Hmm,' she said, running a hand down her thigh. 'It looks like I am.' She reached up and kissed him on the lips, 'But you can help to dry me if you like.'

'I wouldn't dream of it,' Moreton lied, holding her tight against him, as the doorbell rang. 'What?' he said in disbelief at the timing. 'Whoever you are, go away. Are you having a laugh!'

Sophia picked the towel, and held it against her as she peered through the window to see who was at the gate. 'Paco.' she revealed. She turned away and hurried past Moreton into the bedroom, calling over her shoulder. 'I'll get dressed. You go and let him in.'

Moreton sighed in reluctant acceptance. 'Paco, you owe me big time, mate.' He mouthed to himself as he left the apartment to welcome the unwelcome visitor.

By the time the two men entered the apartment, Sophia was demurely dressed, dragging Moreton's consciousness back to the more mundane matters of things other than his lover's body.

'*Hola, Paco.*' she said with a broad smile. The visitor's expression was anything but reciprocal. '*Todo, bien?*' she asked.

'No,' Jiménez said shaking his head ruefully. 'The weekend was disaster. Everything is a big problem.' He reached up and rubbed his head.

'Sit down, Paco,' Moreton said sympathetically. 'Coffee?' A nod of the head sent Moreton into the kitchen as Jiménez explained to Sophia in Spanish.

Returning a couple of minutes later, Moreton placed three coffee cups on the table, before sitting down. Clearly worried, Jiménez looked at the floor as Sophia repeated to Moreton what she had been told.

'The business where Paco's company was working has lots of problems. It is old, and much of the electrical system that the machinery uses is outdated. They need Paco to install a new system but he can only do that when the machinery is not working, at the weekend. It is a lot of work and will probably take three weekends to complete. With the mid-season break nearly here, that will help and he will be finished before the season starts up again.'

'OK.'

'The problem is Jon, he has to start work on it this weekend, so will miss the Torreaño game.'

Jiménez looked up and nodded slowly. 'I am sorry, Mister.'

Sophia glanced at Moreton, and shook her head barely perceptively. He nodded in response.

'*Claro, amigo,*' Moreton said as cheerily as he could. 'You have to do this, Paco. You have no choice. Get everything completed and then be ready for the second half of the season.'

'But,' Jiménez countered. 'Without me and without Juan. What will you do? You have no goalkeeper.'

'We'll find a way to cope. Santi went in goal yesterday and the boys kept a clean sheet – even without Kiko and Adrián playing.'

'I could try again to delay the work perhaps,' Jiménez offered, but Moreton shook his head.

'That wouldn't really help, Paco. Juan is out for a couple of months maybe. Even if your clients agreed to delay the work so that you could play on Sunday, it would mean that you would miss at least one game when the season starts up again. No, you need to look after your business first.'

Even as he spoke the words, Moreton knew that without Joaquín Garrigues and his friends performing some kind of financial miracle, it was highly unlikely that the club would still exist after the mid-season break, but that was hardly Paco Jiménez's fault, and he already had enough worries to deal with.

After drinking his coffee and apologising a couple more times, Jiménez left.

As Moreton watched him go through the gate, he turned to Sophia.

'I didn't want to remind him, but the club may not exist after the mid-season break, you know. And the Torreaño game is probably going to be the most difficult home match of the season.'

'I know, but it was good that you did not remind him of that. He's a good man and has many problems already.'

'Yeah,' Moreton said with a smile. 'He is, but his timing's a bit crap.'

Sophia laughed and took him by the hand. 'Come with me,' she said.

Without either of his goalkeepers being available, Moreton had little choice other than to use Santi as the emergency cover. For the training sessions that week, the man normally relied on to score the goals for Retama was wearing the yellow goalkeeper's kit normally used by Juan Torres. Although it created a passable visual impression of a regular custodian, and his application to the task was laudable, there was little chance of converting the striker into a fully competent goalkeeper in three training sessions. Twenty of the allocated 30 days' leeway granted by the agreement with Cerámica Internacional to the owners of the cub would be spent by the time the CD Retama took the field for what was likely to be their last ever game. They would do so with their top goalscorer, playing in goal. Things were turned upside down. It felt somehow symbolic.

On the day of the game, Moreton had selected the players to start, but had also decided that, regardless of how the game was going, everyone would take some part in the game. He had also asked Sebastián if he could be available to play. If this was to be the club's final game, he wanted to ensure that all of the people who deserved to be honoured by playing on such an occasion had the opportunity to do so.

With Santi as the stand-in goalkeeper, the back line was Sanz, Victor and Kiko, with Sebastián returning to the team covering for Adrián. Samuel and Matías started in front of the defence with Antonio Vasquez and Guido on the flanks and Revi playing behind José Palermo.

As the players sat in the dressing room before the game, it was difficult for each not to feel a sense of loss. Moreton sought to instil some drive into them, but he too felt flat and his words lacked passion and belief. If it wasn't quite a funeral for CD Retama yet, there was a feeling that it soon would be, and the result of 90 minutes' football would hardly change that.

Three hours later, Moreton sat on the bench lost in his thoughts. Sophia had gone to find Esteban to ask him to lock up after she and Moreton had left. A five-goal defeat could have been so much worse but for the cussed determination of the Retama players who retained pride throughout the game, despite being pitted against overwhelming odds, much as the club itself was. Now it felt like a funeral. Each time Sophia had spoken with her father for an update on any kind of financial solution, the news had been disappointing. There were just ten days left in the life of CD Retama, and Moreton was unsure what would happen next for him, for Sophia, for them both.

He stood up and looked around, fully convinced that this would the last few minutes he would spend in a place that had become so special to him. As he did, so he saw Sophia walking towards him from the dressing room where she had left Esteban. He held out his arms as his lover approached and she readily fell into them.

'I still can't really believe it,' he said sadly. 'I always thought at the back of my mind, that something would happen, someone would think of something to save the day, but it's not going to happen, is it?'

Sophia shook her head slowly. 'I don't think so, Jon. We, you, me, the players, my father and his friends, we all fought as hard as we could but sometimes that isn't enough.'

He held her closer to him, looking for something solid and strong in a world where everything was falling apart. 'We still have each other and our love,' he said. 'I still have you and your love.'

'Yes, Jon. Whatever happens, you'll always have my love. Even on the darkest of days, it's always here.'

Moreton suddenly stepped away, startling Sophia. 'What did you say?' he asked with sudden urgency.

Sophia was taken aback, and not a little concerned by the sudden swing of mood. 'What do you mean?'

'What did you say then, Sophia? What did you say? Say it again.'

'I said I would always love you, Jon.'

Moreton shook his head. 'No, those weren't the words. What words did you say?'

Sophia's mind was racing. Why was this suddenly so important? She hesitated. 'I think I said you'll always have my love.'

'Yes, and then …,' Moreton pleaded.

'I think I said, "it's always here."'

'That's it!' Moreton exclaimed. 'I've got it now.' He punched the air. 'Do you think it's too late to get me on a flight to England tomorrow?' he asked.

'What?'

'Do you think it's too late to get me on a flight to England tomorrow?' he repeated, but more urgently.

'I don't know, but we can try when we get back to the apartment.'

'Come on, then,' he said, taking her hand and almost pulling across the pitch towards the gates.

'Jon, what's going on? Tell me!'

'Well, I can't promise anything,' he said excitedly. 'But I think I know how we might be able to save the club.'

'Really?' Sophia replied, now wrapped up in his excitement. 'Then what are you standing around here for?'

Holding hands, they ran across the pitch towards the gate laughing giddily.

A little over 24 hours later, Moreton knocked on the door of a large house in the West Midlands of England. It was opened by a grey-haired man with a warm smile. 'Hello, Jon,' said Bobby Broome.

The Returns

Even though it had only been the six months since Moreton had last sat in Bobby Broome's house, the elder man looked to have aged five years. Thin and drawn, and with cloudy eyes that had always sparkled with vitality. It was as if the very life force was slowly draining from him.

'How have you been, Jon?' Broome asked as he guided Moreton towards his sitting room.

'Not bad, thanks. In fact, pretty good to be fair. The lifestyle in Spain is healthy and I keep active.'

'Have you seen how well Billy is doing? His schools are becoming quite the thing. Apparently there a few other ex-pros helping him out there as well now. Not sure how much coaching he's actually doing, with so much glad-handing of celebrities and local dignitaries.'

'Yeah, so, I gather. Anyway, how are you?' Immediately the words fell from his lips, Moreton regretted making the enquiry.

'Well, there's a question,' Broome replied with a sigh. 'According to the doctors, the old ticker is playing up a bit. They've put me on this diet to try and lose a bit of weight as that will help ease things – apparently.' The last word conveyed all the scepticism that Broome felt. 'Look at me,' he said, patting his midriff. 'I'm wasting away, and buying new clothes all the time. It's costing me a perishing fortune.' His laugh turned into a spluttering cough. 'Still' he continued after a brief pause. 'Money isn't a factor, now is it, and if it gives me a few extra years, I shouldn't moan, should I.' Broome leaned forward and cupped his hand to his mouth as if about to whisper a deeply held secret. 'Tell you what though, Jon. I could murder a bacon sandwich right now.' They both laughed. 'A bacon sandwich in exchange for a couple of extra weeks. I think it would be worth it, don't you?' They laughed again. 'Between me and you, Jon,' Broome continued, looking left and right over his shoulder for anyone who may be eavesdropping, despite them being alone in the house. 'I do sneak an occasional one at the weekend.' He winked. 'It's my little treat and what the quacks don't know, won't hurt them.'

'Anyway, thanks for agreeing to see me,' Moreton said as he eased back into his chair.

'Ah,' replied Broome with a slight chuckle. 'That's no problem, Jon. I don't often get calls from the airport with someone asking if I would be available for a chat 30 minutes later. All very cloak and dagger. Have you come straight here?'

'Yeah,' Moreton conceded. 'I've phoned my parents though and I'm going to stay with them for a few days, but I needed to speak with you first.'

'Sounds pretty urgent, Jon. What can I do for you?'

Moreton had rehearsed this moment over and over again as the flight from Alicante traversed the length of the Iberian Peninsula, then flew over France and the English Channel, before landing at Birmingham. 'Well,' Moreton began. 'You remember that offer you made me in the summer ...'

Thirty minutes later, Bobby Broome closed out the phone call to his solicitors. 'It's done, Jon,' he confirmed. 'My guys already have established relationships with the Spanish legal eagles over at CI from when they bought out Broome Interiors. They assure me that all the paperwork will be completed in a couple of days, so your guarantee to CI will be all signed and sealed well ahead of your deadline.

'I really can't thank you enough,' Moreton replied. 'I've come here and asked you to put a quarter of a million quid on the line, that you may never see again, to help me save a club over in Spain that you know little about.'

Bobby Broome, shook his head. 'No thanks required, Jon.' He paused and then chuckled to himself. 'If you think about it, it's all a bit neat and tidy really, isn't it?'

Moreton was unsure.

'Well, it was CI's money-grabbing that put the club into peril in the first place, thanks to Charlie conniving with them. Then, they throw all this money at me to buy my business. And now …' he paused, and raised his right index finger in the air, indicating the key point was about to be delivered. 'And now, a little bit of that same money is returning to them to block their plans.' He laughed throatily. 'There's more than a bit of poetic justice in there, Jon.'

Moreton couldn't help but smile. He'd never seen someone sign off so much money and then take so much pleasure delighting in irony.

'When are you going back, Jon?'

'A few days. I'm spending Christmas with my parents, got a couple of things to do, and then I'm flying back.'

'Well, that's good, Jon. Anyway, you get off now, your parents will be waiting for you.'

'Yes, I should,' Moreton said getting up. 'Before I go though, there's one more thing I need to ask you.'

Ten minutes later, Bobby Broome followed Moreton to the door. As Moreton opened it, he turned to face the man who had thrown CD Retama a very expensive lifeline. 'Look,' he said. 'There are so many people in Retama who would want to thank you themselves, and explain why, what you have done, means so much. So, I'll try and do it for them.' He paused for a moment, searching for the best way to describe his feelings, and those of the people connected with CD Retama. 'Their football club is so important to them. It's part of who they are, and they've worked so hard to try and save it against crushing odds. It's such a great little club and the people there are some of the best that I've ever met. They were on the edge of a cliff, hanging on by their fingertips, without hope, but you've thrown them a lifeline. When the season gets underway again, they'll fight to make your gesture count. You can't imagine how many people in Retama you have made so happy.'

Bobby Broome's eyes were teary as he spoke. 'And you've made an old man here in England very happy, Jon. Being able to use that money to do some good is the best thing I can think of.' He hugged Moreton, and patted him on the back as they broke apart.

'Don't forget Jon,' he said. 'That offer of money for a house in Spain for you and your girl is still there. This little business deal changes nothing, OK? It's always here.' Moreton shook his head in disbelief at Broome's generosity. 'Anyway, clear off now,' he said, regaining his composure. 'Enjoy Christmas with your parents. Get done what you have to get done here and then get back to Spain and win promotion.'

Moreton hugged Broome once more. 'Don't worry,' he called over his shoulder as he headed for his hire car. 'As you, know, I've got a plan.'

Four days later on Saturday morning, Sophia and her father were standing at the Arrivals gate in Alicante airport. Unable to keep the exciting news under wraps for more than 30 seconds, Moreton had called her as soon as he closed the car door after leaving Bobby Broome's house. Two days later, Joaquín Garrigues had received official confirmation from Cerámica Internacional's solicitors that the new guarantee was confirmed in place. CD Retama were now able to complete the season, and news quickly spread around the club and, indeed, the town in general. They were the welcoming committee for the returning hero, but there was one additional item of news, and one item of luggage, that Moreton had yet to reveal.

The doors of the gate swung open and the passengers on the flight from Birmingham began to spill through. Many were greeted with hugs and kisses by awaiting family and friends, but none received the whoops of delight reserved for Moreton's appearance as he walked through the doors. Reaching the barrier, he was engulfed by Sophia's arms, as Joaquín Garrigues patted him on the back and then took his turn for a somewhat less passionate embrace. Whilst Sophia delivered her welcome in kisses, her father sought a more verbal approach.

'Welcome home, Jon,' he said, with a beaming smile. 'You are an amazing young man.'

Reluctant to release Sophia from their lingering hug, Moreton spoke over her shoulder. 'Not really, Joaquín. I just know some people who are.'

'Well, that'll do then. Come on, let's go,' Garrigues continued. 'Dolores is waiting in the car outside.'

Moreton eased himself away from Sophia, planting one final kiss on her lips, and looked over his shoulder back through the doors of the Arrivals gate. 'Just a minute,' he advised. 'I'm waiting …'

His words trailed away as the need for them became redundant. 'Wotcha, Sophie,' came the Cockney tones of the shuffling figure now approaching them.

'Oh, yeah,' Moreton said with affected forgetfulness. 'I've brought you a late Christmas present.'

'Billy!' Sophia shouted as she rushed to embrace him, then kissed him on the cheek.

'Steady on, gel,' Swan said, 'Your fella's over there. Don't want him getting any ideas, first day back do we.' Then whispering very loudly. 'Give it a day or two, then give me a shout, eh?'

Sophia slapped him on the arm in mock anger. 'It's so good to see you, Billy. Are you staying for long?'

'Well, that depends on the geezer over there, dunnit?' Swan replied nodding towards a smiling Moreton. 'As I understand things, there's a certain little football club around these parts who might need a bit of the old Billy Swan magic.'

'You're coming back to play for us again, Billy?' Sophia's excitement caused her voice to rise.

'Could be. All depends if I'm wanted.' The chirpiness of Swan's banter fell away. 'If the boys want me to come back. I'd understand if they don't. Jon says there's no problem, but I want to see for myself. I dropped them in some right shit last time.'

'Oh, Billy,' Sophia said wrapping her arm around his shoulder and guiding him towards to where Moreton and her father were standing. 'It wasn't your fault. We were all victims of Charlie Broome. You, me, Jon, everyone. No one blames you. We, everyone, understands what happened. Come on, let's head for Retama. Where are you staying?'

'Jeez, Jon!' Swan exclaimed to Moreton. 'Haven't you told her?'

'Think about it Billy, how could I, without ruining the surprise,' Moreton replied. He turned to Sophia. 'I said Billy could stay with us for a while until we get something sorted.'

'That's great,' Sophia agreed. Then to Swan. 'Isn't it "roomie"'?

On the way back to Retama Swan told the story of how Bobby Broome had contacted him and offered to set up the soccer school foundation in London. Initially, he had ignored the approaches but, in the end, had agreed to meet him just to stop the insistent calls. The meeting had changed his life. After returning from Spain, he had felt broken and unsure about everything. The way that Sebastián, Kiko, Victor and Esteban had helped him when they should have had nothing but contempt for the way he had betrayed them and the club had made him see things differently. He knew that he needed to change his life, but felt helpless to do anything about it. Then came the offer of the soccer schools and it opened a door for him.

'That man saved my life – it's that simple. Honest,' Swan insisted. 'My old man buggered off when I was four, leaving me mam to bring me up on her own. It was probably for the best. He was a right nob, so I never missed him. But, Bobby's been like a real dad to me. Picked me up and pointed me in the right direction. I owe him everything.' Swan's emotional attachment to Bobby Broome was clear. 'Course,' he explained, continuing after regaining his composure, 'then I'm sitting at home and Bobby rings me and says he's with this geezer who wants me to go back to Spain with him, I'm all: "Nah, thanks. Plenty to do here." I'd already turned down another chance from to go back there from an old mate.'

'Del Hart?' Moreton asked.

'Yeah, how did you know about that?'

'I'll explain later.'

'Anyway, then Bobby tells me it's Jon and there's a chance to go back to Retama. A chance to put things right and repair all the crap I caused. So, I say what about the schools, and he says it's no sweat 'cos the guys I've brought in, old local mates from my pro days, are coping fine. Then he says to me that if I don't go back, I'd regret it for the rest of my life. Course, he's right so, here I am.' He held his arms out wide. 'The prodigy's son returns, as they say.'

As the car drew up outside of the complex, Swan peered out of the window, looking at the walls and gate that marked its boundaries. 'Wow, I've never seen your gaff before Jon. Look at the size of the place. This is a bit of all right, init? Is it all yours, mate?' Everyone else in car laughed, but Swan was unsure why. 'Not quite, Billy,' Moreton said. 'Come on, and I'll show you.'

They exchanged farewells with Joaquín and Dolores Garrigues, and headed through the gate. Moreton explained that the complex housed a number of apartments and pointed out the one he shared with Sophia. With Sophia catching them up as she waved a last farewell to her parents, they climbed the steps and entered the apartment.

Diplomacy had never been one of Swan's strong suits, but he tried hard to cover up that inadequacy. 'It's very nice,' he said. 'It's what I hear they call bee's juice. All very up with the fashions and modern trendies.'

Moreton and Sophia both smiled at his effort. 'It's small Billy, but we like it,' Moreton explained, freeing Swan from feeling obliged to try harder, and showed him into the spare bedroom, as Sophia went to make coffee.

'Look, Jon,' Swan confided when they were alone. 'This is all good, but what about when you two want some, you know … private time?' Swan involuntarily flicked his eyebrows up as he said the final two words.

Moreton laughed softly.

'Tell you what?' Swan said. 'Point me in the direction of that pool you were telling me about, with a chair and I'll be fine.' He reached into his bag and pulled out three books. 'I'm proper into reading now you know? Ever since I gave up the booze, it gives me something to do. I've got these three to keep me going. One's called "Where the Cool Kids Hung Out." I thought it must have been about me with a title like that but it's about the UEFA Cup. There's this one called "Brazil 82". Again, I've got a bit of Brazilian magic in my feet so that's perfect for me, and this is "The Nearly Men" about the teams that should have won the World Cup.' He laughed, and nudged Moreton, 'Apparently all they were missing was someone like me to make the difference.'

'There are a few local bars as well, Billy, if you fancy that.'

Swan shook his head. 'Haven't been in a bar since I left here. No, don't you worry Jon. When you and Sophia want me to make myself scarce, just tip me the wink and I'll disappear for an hour for a bit of reading. All right?'

'Sure Billy,' Moreton said with a smile.

'Anyway, I'm not going to be here long to cramp your style Jon. I spoke with Seb. His parents are going to fix me up with a room at their hotel.'

'Can you afford that, Billy. It's a bit pricey there?'

'Yeah, no sweat, Jon. Seb's parents are giving me a decent discount. Bobby isn't skinny with wages and not going out on the razzle any more means I don't spend much. I've got enough to keep me going.'

'And you'll get expenses covered from the club, of course,' Moreton added.

'Yeah, if you guys can afford it, that'll be me sorted.' Swan's next words were something Moreton had never expected to hear him say. 'Anyway Jon, when's training start, I'm ready to rock and roll.'

Singing the Blues

Swan wouldn't have long to wait. After a couple of days spent with Moreton and Sophia, he moved out to take up the offer of a room at the Hotel El Barco. That same Tuesday evening, with the season about to restart the following weekend, Sebastián, who had been sworn to secrecy about Swan's return to Spain, dropped him off at the Estadio Antonio Núñez for training.

The remainder of the squad were already assembled there, as Moreton wanted everyone together when he revealed Swan's return. As Sophia was going through the regular warm up session, the shuffling figure of Billy Swan descended the concrete steps, hopped over the perimeter wall and walked towards the group of players and coaches. Sophia couldn't help a smile breaking over her face as she saw him approach, kitted up, with boots on and ready to play. Her focus on something behind them caught the attention of a number of the players, and they turned to see the cause of her distraction. With the setting sun behind him, at first it was difficult to discern who the approaching figure was. Then, as more players shaded their eyes from the glare, Swan's identity became clearer. 'Billy?' came the first whisper. Then another. Then louder, 'Billy!'

First two then three, then all of the group ran towards the approaching figure. At the front, Kiko and Victor drew their imaginary rapiers and waved then in the air as they ran, jumping on Swan and dragging him to the floor as the others piled in behind them, cheering and shouting. 'I hope they don't crush him,' Moreton quipped to Sophia, with a smile. 'We're going to need a fit Billy Swan for the opening game.'

Eventually, the crowd of players climbed to their feet, lifting Swan up from his position at the bottom of the pile, and walking back to where Moreton and Sophia stood beaming with pleasure at the welcome offered to Swan. Only Kiko and Victor remained, standing by Swan with their rapiers raised in the air. Swan dusted himself down, shaking his head at the pose struck by the Musketeers of Retama, but they would not be denied. Laughing, Swan finally accepted the inevitable and joined them, drawing his rapier too, as the waved them in the air in unison. All the other players cheered, as Moreton and Sophia applauded wildly. Kiko and Victor wrapped their arms around Swan's shoulders, guiding him back into the midst of the squad. The Musketeers were reunited and Billy Swan was back as a CD Retama player.

The week's training was full of enthusiasm and a renewed commitment. On Friday evening, Moreton announced the team that would open the second half of Retama's season with the visit to San Esteban. Although Swan had assured Moreton of his fitness after spending days and evenings at the soccer school back in London, Moreton was cautious, remembering the first game of the previous season when, playing a less than fully prepared Swan had led to an early injury, and an absence from the next few games. He didn't want to risk the same thing happening again. Already past the halfway mark of the season, it was no time to have Swan injured by gambling on his fitness.

With Jiménez now available after completing his contractual obligations in Valencia, Moreton was able to select a regular goalkeeper to wear the gloves for the opening game of second half of the season. Adrián was serving the final game of his suspension, so Felipe Blanco deputised in what was, otherwise, the regular back four. Cautious to ensure a solid start to the season, Moreton placed the solid pairing of Samuel and Matías in front of the defence with Guido and Antonio Vasquez on the flanks and Revi behind Santi. Billy Swan's second coming as a CD Retama player would begin with a spot on the bench. After the team had been announced, Moreton passed the number 20 shirt to Swan.

'Sorry, Billy,' he said. 'I don't know where the 14 shirt is.'

Sophia reached into her bag, pulling out a blue shirt with a flourish. 'I do,' she revealed. 'I kept it to one side when the kits were handed out before the season.'

Moreton was confused. 'Really?'

'Yes, number 14 is Billy Swan and no one else should wear that shirt if others are available.' She paused, before adding, 'And, I thought that if Billy came back, his number should be waiting for him.' Then in Spanish. '*El número catorce es* Billy Swan.'

Swan stood up and took the shirt as the other players applauded. 'Cheers darlin,' Swan chirped, kissing her on the cheek, before holding the shirt up and taking exaggerated bows with a dramatic sweep of his arm.

On the journey to the small village of San Esteban, the Retama coaches and players were in a subdued mood, despite the return of Swan. Even a few choruses of 'I've got the music in me,' struggled to rouse the contemplative mood of the group. After seven games without a victory, a run that had seen the club tumble from their position at the top of the table, the importance of the upcoming game wasn't lost on anyone. If there was to be anything like a realistic push for promotion, every point from here to the end of the season was vital.

It was a message that Moreton drilled into his players ahead of the game. The previous season had seen two goalless draws against the village team, and a 3-0 win on the opening day of this term meant that across three games, today's opponents had yet to score against Retama. It either meant that Moreton's defence had the comforting ability and confidence to shut out the home attack, or that San Esteban were due a goal. Less than 30 minutes into the game, it was clear that the latter had very much been the case.

With San Esteban equally keen on ensuring a good restart to the season, Retama had been under pressure from the start of the game as the home forwards eagerly pressed for an early goal. It came in fortunate circumstances after four minutes when a long-range shot, seemingly destined for the waiting gloves of Jiménez was diverted by Sanz's outstretched foot, leaving the goalkeeper stranded. Just two minutes later, a header from a corner had the home side two goals ahead, and Retama in serious trouble.

Whether the San Esteban players settled back to protect their lead, or

Retama came more into the game wasn't clear, but the outcome was the same, as the visitors got a foothold in the match and, for the remaining period of the first half, enjoyed a measure of equality. Despite that, at the break, the home team's lead remained intact. Moreton had decisions to make.

As the first half had ebbed away, it became clear that unless there was a change in personnel, tactics – or both – Retama's chances of taking anything positive from the game were limited. As the break had approached, Moreton and Sophia had considered their options and decided on what to do.

There was still a reluctance to throw Swan into the action after just a few days' training, and he was left on the bench, with the option of perhaps ten minutes or so late in the game if required. With the home team now settled deep into defence there was little space for Guido to exploit his speed and he was replaced by the younger Palermo brother. Samuel was taken off and Revi dropped back to play alongside Matías. Juan Palermo was sent on to play alongside Santi in what was now a 4-2-4 formation, with plenty of emphasis on attack. Less than two minutes into the game, Moreton's plans were in tatters. An attack from the San Esteban left flank looked to have been halted by Sanz as the Retama captain half-blocked an attempted cross. The ball ballooned into the area but with Jiménez and Victor both hesitating, a home forward stole in between them to gather the ball as it drifted to the left side of the Retama box. Desperate to retrieve the situation, Felipe Blanco reached out an arm to try and block the forward's run. The fall was theatrical, but achieved its aim as the referee pointed to the spot and flourished a red card at Felipe Blanco. Jiménez dived left as the ball flew into the opposite corner and Retama's plight now looked beyond redemption.

Another reshuffle was required, and Moreton moved Matías back to the left flank of Retama's defence, and pulled Juan Palermo back to play alongside Revi, hoping the elder sibling's commitment and determination would compensate for his lack of experience of playing a defensive role. In typical fashion, it did so, as Retama's adjusted line up held firm. The problem was, of course, that preventing any further damage was fine, but Moreton's team was still three goals down.

With a dozen minutes to play, Moreton decided to play his last card, and told Swan to get ready to go on. Sophia was unsure of the wisdom in the move. 'Is it worth risking a muscle injury in a game that's already lost?' She questioned.

Moreton had considered that possibility, but was keenly aware that his team's ambition had been severely deflated and seeing Swan back on the pitch again, may at least lift the mood of the team and offer confidence that better times were ahead. He explained his logic to Sophia, but she was less than convinced.

As the ball ran out of play behind Retama's goal, Moreton made his move. Antonio Vasquez was taken off, and Swan sent on with instructions to play in the middle and try and set opportunities up for either Santi or José Palermo as Retama abandoned the flanks in attack. Despite a spirited welcome from the other Retama players as Swan trotted onto the pitch, at first the change seemed to make little difference to the flow of the game. The action buzzed around Swan as he tried to pick up the pace of the play, but without much success. Then Juan Palermo muscled a San Esteban player out of possession and steered the ball forward to Retama's returning veteran player standing in the centre circle.

Collecting and controlling in an instant, Swan looked forward to see Santi making a run towards the San Esteban penalty area, and flighted the ball into the space ahead of the Retama forward. Reaching the pass ahead of the goalkeeper, Santi neatly lifted the ball over him and into the net. He punched the air in delight, running towards the corner flag, and was joined by the younger Palermo brother. In the centre of the field however, Swan stood alone, arms raised as Moreton applauded the dexterity of the pass.

There was now only five minutes to play, and Retama were still trailing by two goals. In half that time however, that deficit would be further reduced. From the kick-off, the ball was played forward into the Retama half and collected by Kiko, who then moved it on to Victor, and from him to Revi. Aware of the space on the flanks, as the San Esteban defenders had narrowed their back line having no Retama wide players to face, Swan drifted out to the left and Revi's precise pass found the veteran's feet.

Swan shuffled forwards, evading two inelegant challenges and drawing a third defender towards him. This time an uncompromising challenge brought Swan to the floor. Quickly collecting the ball as the referee confirmed the free-kick, Swan saw José Palermo make a run and slid a pass through to him. With the home defence unable to recover position, the younger Palermo brother raced into the area, and slipped the ball past the San Esteban goalkeeper. Swan's quick thinking had surely brought a second goal, but the ball struck the post and bounced back towards the penalty spot, running conveniently towards Santi, who had raced up in support. The Retama forward calmly passed the ball into the net and Retama were on the edge of the most unexpected of comebacks. Santi collected the ball and raced back towards the centre spot, placing it down ready for the restart. The ten men of Retama were suddenly playing like it was them holding the numerical advantage, rather than the now troubled home side.

Moreton glanced at his watch as the referee blew for the game to restart. It told him that there were just two minutes to play, plus any injury time. Anxious to preserve their dwindling advantage, the San Esteban players looked to keep possession of the ball from the restart, eating into the meagre amount of time remaining. The ball was played, back, sidewards and back again as Santi and José Palermo tried to press and force an error. Moreton waved the older Palermo brother forward as well to reinforce the outnumbered Retama forwards, and he galloped forwards in eager compliance.

Time ticked away, as the home players jealously hoarded possession of the ball. Eventually it went back to the goalkeeper who cleared long up field catching a home forward offside just inside the Retama half of the field. Jiménez gathered the ball and raced forward to restart the game, waving all of his team-mates forward as he did so. Another glance at Moreton's watch told him they were already three minutes past the scheduled 90, as the goalkeeper hit the ball long towards a crowded San Esteban penalty area.

Kiko rose to challenge for the ball, but the defender's efforts denied him a clean contact and the ball ran on towards the goalkeeper. Santi had anticipated the possibility, though, and, as the goalkeeper dived towards the ball, his contact with it was just ahead. The ball bobbled on towards the empty net, and gently nestled into the corner. The Retama players and coaches celebrated wildly as Santi ran around the pitch, hotly pursued by his team-mates, all considerations of fatigue now irrelevant, at least temporarily. Moreton embraced Sophia on the sidelines. 'You're a genius!' she yelled into his ear, but her words were lost in the cheering and shouts of the substitutes and substituted players celebrating with them. For a full minute, pandemonium reigned in all blue, with only the repeated, insistent whistles of the referee trying to rain on Retama's parade. As the elation calmed though, that whistle took centre stage.

Moreton looked across to where the referee stood in the San Esteban penalty area, with his arm in the air, next to the home goalkeeper who was now surrounded by his team-mates and apparently receiving treatment from the trainers. Moreton was confused, and held arms out, palms forward, in a gesture of enquiry. Shortly, that confusion would turn to furious anger.

The goalkeeper was helped to his feet, gingerly rubbing the side of his head. As the Retama players looked on in disbelief, the referee called for the ball and placed it down in front of the goalkeeper signalling for a free-kick, indicating that Santi's knee had struck the goalkeeper before diverting the ball into the net. He then called the Retama forward to him whose elation at scoring a hat-trick was replaced by the frustration of being shown a red card, as punishment for the perceived infringement. The goal had been ruled out, and Retama were now down to nine men for the remaining seconds of the game. As Moreton watched on in disbelief at the turn of events, the Retama players surrounded the referee in indignant rage at the injustice. Fuelled by righteous indignation, composure was lost and Moreton became concerned that the official could take further action.

Suddenly, there was a blue shirt placed between the referee and the other Retama players, easing his team-mates away and, at the same time, nodding reassuringly at the besieged official. Billy Swan, the unlikely voice of reason, slowly defused the situation and encouraged his team-mates back into their positions so that the game could restart. As he did so, a distraught Santi reached Moreton and Sophia. Wiping tears away with the sleeve of his shirt, he protested his innocence. 'No foul,' he insisted in English. 'No foul' He hit me!' Moreton placed his arm around Santi's shoulder as the other Retama players on the sidelines commiserated with their wronged team-mate in unison. '*Sabemos,*' Sophia said softly. '*No es tu culpa.*' Moreton nodded in agreement. Santi had done nothing wrong. The forward trudged back to the dressing room to join Felipe Blanco, and Moreton turned his attention back to the game as the referee blew for full-time.

Inevitably, a number of Retama players were still insistent on disputing the referee's crucial decision and marched stridently towards him. 'Go and shake the referee's hand,' Sophia whispered to Moreton.

'What? Why?'

'Look,' she said, pointing towards the gathering storm of blue-shirted players homing in on the referee. 'Do it, Jon,' she insisted urgently. 'Quickly!'

The message sank in, and Moreton raced onto the field, heading off the group of Retama players before they could reach where the official stood, in the centre circle with his linesmen. Moreton courteously shook hands with all three officials, before turning and ushering his players back to the dressing room, where their anger could be vented without sanction – and they did so.

Understanding the pent-up frustrations of his players, Moreton allowed them a couple of minutes to rage against the injustice, before calling for calm. He spoke slowly and with as much cool detachment as he could muster, as Sophia translated.

'That was unjust. We deserved more but, I have never been prouder of a group of players than I was out there today. Every one of you. Retama. Está en nuestras cabezas. Está en nuestros corazones.'

A chorus of applause broke out as he pointed to every player in the dressing room, his arm sweeping in a curve that wrapped each of them up in its sentiments, intentionally pausing longer when aligning with Felipa Blanco and Santi.

'Hey, Billy?' The voice of Sanz called out, recalling the incident when the Englishman had ushered his team-mates away from a confrontation with the official that could only have had bad consequences. Swan looked cross at Retama's captain in reply.

'*Gracias, amigo,*' Sanz added.

'Yeah, thanks, Billy,' Moreton agreed. 'You prevented a bad situation getting much worse, mate.'

Swan shook his head. 'Don't know what you're on about, Jon,' he said. 'I just wanted to deck the geezer and thought these blokes might beat me to it,' he said with a wink. The room erupted in laughter as Sophia translated, and the anger slowly evaporated.

Paybacks and paying your dues

For all the heroism and injustice in the game against San Esteban, Retama had failed to take a single point from the game. There were now just 16 games left in the season and the club were looking anything but promotion material. To justify the efforts of Joaquín Garrigues and his partners, plus the generosity of Bobby Broome, results needed to take an upswing before it was too late. One thing Moreton had been able to take from the 3-2 away defeat though was that Swan could well be the key to igniting the remainder of Retama's season. Those last ten minutes of the game had convinced him that Swan simply had to play.

With that harsh red card meaning Santi was suspended for the next two games, Moreton had the options of playing one of the Palermo brothers in the striking role, or opting for the untapped potential of Elías. Whilst the remainder of the team was fixed in his head for most of the training sessions across the following week, he delayed a decision as to who would replace Santi until just before the team was announced. As Sophia concluded the warm down on Friday, he shared his thoughts with her.

'I think we should go with Juan.' Sophia's expression suggested that she had other thoughts, and Moreton wanted to hear them. 'What do you think?'

'Juan will not let anyone down, he never does,' she replied. 'Sometimes though, as a striker he is best from the bench. When there is fatigue in the opposition, his strength, his power, is even more effective. Plus, Juan has played a part in almost every game. Giving him a break isn't a bad idea.'

Moreton nodded at the logic, as she continued.

'Elías is young and untested, but we have only given him substitute appearances, and one start, when we took him off. Desorio may be the ideal game for him. And with both José and Juan on the bench, we can change things if we need to.'

'OK,' Moreton conceded. 'But I think it would be good to give José a game anyway and give Guido a break. Yes?'

'Yes, that's a good idea.'

And, with that, the selection was decided. With Adrián's suspension now spent, he was free to return to the regular back four, in front of Jiménez. Revi was back in his deeper role alongside Mathias, Antonio Vasquez was on the right flank, with José Palermo on the left, and Swan playing behind Elías.

In the second game of the season, Retama had played out a goalless draw at Desorio, when Dani Barbieri had declared himself unavailable. This time, with Swan's return, they would have a creative talent to produce the opportunities. Ahead of the game, however, Moreton was concerned to remind the veteran of what happened in the game at the coastal town in the previous season, when Swan had been sent off for elbowing an opponent in the face. It was more than likely that Swan would be greeted with some rough treatment by the Desorio players when they recognised him. It may well have been easier to leave Swan out of the game to deflect any animosity, but results were now of paramount importance. Diluting the team's chances of victory simply wasn't an option. Moreton had to trust that the maturity Swan had shown in the game against San Esteban would be replicated.

Towards the end of last season, with Retama fighting for promotion, attendances at the Estadio Antonio Núñez had grown, but once the anticipation of success had disappeared, many of the fans had done so too, and as the team struggled again in the games ahead of the mid-season break, any hopes of them returning had proved to be fanciful at best, but the return of Swan had at least piqued interest and, for the first home game of the renewed season, Moreton was taken by the size of the crowd as he walked with Sophia from the dressing room ahead of his players.

'Wow,' he whispered to her. 'There's a few fans here today.'

Sophia nodded, looking around her. 'We need to give them a good reason to keep coming.'

'Start winning a few games, and that will take care of itself.'

'Let's start today then,' she said, squeezing Moreton's hand.

When the game got underway, Moreton's concerns about the Desorio players seeking revenge on Swan were quickly borne out. Whenever the ball reached the veteran, the tackles were swift and ferocious, usually just on the right side of the laws of the game, but often straying over the line, with the perpetrators willingly accepting cautioning words from the referee as the price for delivering what they considered to be payback for events in the game the previous season.

Throughout his career, Swan had become accustomed to such roughhouse tactics, often considering it as a compliment to his ability, and using his exquisite balance and sharpness of action to avoid the calamitous challenges. Inevitably, however, age had taken the edge from those previously razor-sharp reflexes and, whereas in the past he would have been able to evade such excesses now he was, more often than not, a victim of them.

Whether it was part of the design of the Desorio tactics, or merely the consequence of the vengeful attention to Swan, denying him any measure of time on the ball unbalanced the Retama attack, meaning that Elías was often isolated with Swan unable to link up the play with challenges rattling around his ankles.

As the break approached, with the game scoreless, Moreton mused about changes. Perhaps it would be wise to take Swan off. Much more of this sort of attention and he could get seriously injured. Plus, with the rhythm of the game dictated by the staccato stop-start of repeated free-kicks, there was precious little chance of Swan creating anything. As the referee ended the first-half and the players trooped towards the dressing room, Moreton waited for Swan, and walked back with him.

'You OK, Billy? Want to take a break for the second-half?'

Swan seemed genuinely insulted by the suggestion. 'No way, Jon!' he said firmly. 'These clowns think kicking me up hill and down dale is going to stop me. They can sod off. I've been kicked by proper tough guys. Blokes who could batter you all game and never get dinged by the ref. These lot are just fat sods with no brain and no stamina. Ten minutes into the second-half, they'll be knackered, and I'll run them a right dance then.'

'You sure, Billy? I don't want you getting hurt.'

Swan caught hold of Moreton's arm and stopped him, allowing the other players to pass them by. When they were on their own, he bent down and rolled the sock on his right leg down to the ankle. Already the marks of attention were clear on his calf and the areas around his shin pads. Bruises of violet and blue were forming.

'See these, Jon?' Swan indicated, pointing at his medals of battle. 'These are there to remind me how much I owe these yobs. Don't take me off, Jon. I need to deliver for the boys. Payback's gonna hurt these goons more than bruises hurt me. Right?'

It was an attitude Moreton had never seen before in Billy Swan. So often, in the past, he'd have been happy to be substituted so long as he didn't lose any money. But this was the new Swan. It wasn't about money. Moreton sensed it wasn't really about teaching the Desorio players a lesson either. It was about not letting his team-mates, his friends, down. Swan thought he owed them a debt and wanted to pay it in full.

Moreton nodded. 'OK, Billy.' At that moment, he knew that Retama would win the game.

As they reached the dressing room, Swan had one more thing to add. 'And don't take that Ellis off either, mate. I ain't give the kid a decent pass all half. He's worked his socks off making decent runs, and I owe him a goal.'

'Sure, Billy,' Moreton said as they entered the dressing room to join the other players and Sophia. 'No changes,' he whispered softly to her. 'Billy has it all sorted.'

A dozen minutes or so after the restart, Swan began to illustrate his point. Revi played the ball into the veteran's feet by the centre spot. Sensing the incoming challenge from behind, Swan flicked the ball a foot or so into the air and hopped over the lunging tackle, only pausing briefly to smile at his opponent before turning towards goal. A stepover beat the next over-exuberant challenge and Swan was bearing down on the edge of the area. He could have fired off a shot. Instead, he allowed the final defender to close on him before slipping the ball to his left and the waiting Elías, who curled a looping shot around the Desorio goalkeeper to give Retama the lead.

Walking back to the halfway line with the celebrating players, Swan was keen to give a wink and smile to the two Desorio players he had beaten on the way to setting up the goal. On the sidelines, after the applause for the goal had died down, Moreton turned to Sophia. 'It's show time,' he said.

For the next ten minutes, Swan ran the game, with fatigue now delaying any challenges from the weary Desorio players, he had earned the time to ease past tackles and even the occasional wildly swinging boot struck only thin air as Swan skipped aside. Whilst the Retama defence looked secure, offering little opportunity for the visitors to get back into the game, there was every prospect of more goals at the other end of the field.

The second goal came with 20 minutes to play. A corner from the right, was swung in by Antonio Vasquez, but the Desorio goalkeeper rose above Kiko to punch clear. The ball dropped to Swan standing on the edge of the penalty arc. Controlling the ball from his chest to his feet, he shaped to shoot, compelling two defenders to throw themselves to the floor in an attempt to block a shot that never came. Swan switched the ball to his right, skipped past the fallen defenders, nutmegged a third and then slipped the ball under the goalkeeper's forlorn dive. Shrugging his shoulders as if he had done nothing more taxing than taking the bins out, he strolled back to the middle of the field, offering a tip of an imaginary hat to the Desorio team as he did so, before accepting the congratulations of the Retama players.

The result was now beyond debate, but Swan had more payback to deliver. A Cruyff turn just inside the Desorio half, as he received a pass from Adrián, opened up the visitors' defence again. An astute through ball put Elías in the clear and the young forward finished with aplomb. There was one more goal to come. Before that, having seen Elías net his brace, Moreton withdrew the young forward with a couple of minutes to go, sending on Juan Palermo instead, as Retama won a corner. From Revi's cross, Kiko's header was blocked on the line, but the newly arrived substitute was on hand to prod the ball home.

At full-time, as Swan left the field, inevitably accompanied by the other Musketeers, Moreton wrapped his arm around the game's star performer. 'Brilliant, Billy,' he said. 'Bloody brilliant, mate. Look at the fans. They loved it, and we'll have more here for the next game as well.'

'Yeah,' Swan replied with a satisfied smile. 'But, my sodding legs are killing me now, though, Jon. Can I go and sit down for a bit?'

The full consequences of the physical battering that Swan had endured in the game against Desorio became evident at training on Tuesday evening. Kiko had now taken over the duties of collecting Swan from the hotel, and bringing him to training along with Victor, and the pair of centre-backs were clearly concerned about the health of their fellow Musketeer as they arrived, waving across to Sophia as they climbed over the wall and onto the pitch. Swan was walking with a pronounced limp, and a quick check by Sophia suggested that it would be wise for him to rest up for this session and allow some recovery time. As Sophia organised the session, it gave Moreton and Swan some time to reflect and look forward as they sat on the coaches' bench and watched.

'So,' Swan began. 'You gonna stay out here, Jon? I mean when this is all over.'

Moreton raised his eyebrows, surprised at the intimacy of the question. 'I want to, but it'll all depend on where we are at the end of the season, and what happens next.'

'You and Sophie, though. That's a full-time thing now, yeah?' Moreton sighed at his friend's repeated inability to remember her name, as Swan quickly recognised. 'Sorry, mate. Sophia,' he said, hanging onto the final letter for longer than required. 'But you're sorted now ain't you?'

'I can't imagine life without her, if that's what you mean.'

'Yeah, that's what I mean.'

Moreton thought for a while. 'You know, Billy. I've spent most of my life planning things in advance, mapping out the future, anticipating problems and how to deal with them.' He paused looking around, and then at Sophia. 'Since I've been here though, all that's changed. I've become someone different. This place, meeting Sophia, the people, it's all changed me. I've got my parents, other family and a few friends back home, but my life is here now. I really can't imagine leaving.

'Swan nodded absently. 'Yeah, me too, Jon.'

'Really?'

'Really, what?'

'You can't imagine leaving?' Moreton asked.

'No, I meant this place has changed me as well. All that shit last year. The way the guys looked after me afterwards. It changed me. It was what they call an "effipany," or something like that.' It was the sort of introspection Billy Swan had never really allowed himself previously, although the consequences of it were clear enough to him. 'Look at me now. Off the booze. Got a proper job, and bloody loving it by the way. I'm turning into a proper decent bloke. That dodgy geezer from the past is well gone now.'

Moreton put his arm around his friend's shoulder. 'That geezer wasn't all bad, Billy. Don't lose all of him, eh? Keep the good bits.'

'Cheers, Jon. But I'm not sure there were that many of them.'

They both laughed and the conversation fell silent for a while as they watched the players training, before Moreton spoke again.

'Oh, by the way, Billy,' he said. 'Sophia's been nagging me about getting in touch and seeing more of you. Going out for the day now and then, lunch, dinner or whatever. You must be bored in the hotel with nothing to do.'

Swan shook his head, looking down, and laughed. 'Bored? You've gotta be kidding, mate.'

Moreton looked at him questioningly.

'To be honest, Jon' he continued. 'I'm not in the hotel very often. Meldrew works up the road from the hotel at this computer shop. He sells all this Why-Fly interweb malarkey, computers and mobile phones. All sorts of jazzy gadgets, you know. So, most days, he'll either come round to the hotel for lunch, or we meet up somewhere else for a sandwich and glass of coke. Sometimes Kiki Dee hops round to join us as well, but he's training to be salesman at that big, posh car place, so most of the time he has his lunch on the fly. He's really ambitious and a busy kid. You know how it is.'

Moreton was impressed how Swan had settled into life in Retama, but there was more to come.

'Don't tell any of the boys,' Swan confided. 'But I've also been spending a bit of time here with old Esteban.

'What?'

'Yep,' Swan nodded. 'I got Seb to tell me how the buses work, so I caught one that drops you right outside here, just for a look around. I get on the bus, drop the driver a quick *"Hola"* and €1.50, and we're away. Anyway, last week, I got off the bus, and there was Esteban, painting one of the gates. So, we got to talking.

'Talking?' Moreton questioned. 'But Esteban doesn't speak English and you don't speak Spanish.' He paused. 'Don't tell me you've been having lessons on the quiet!'

'Nah, have a word with yourself, Jon,' Swan said with a self-deprecating laugh. 'I have enough trouble with English mate.' He chuckled to himself. 'No, we use the international language of football,' he said with overemphasised grandeur. 'He took me to this little shed he has behind the dressing room, where he keeps all his stuff. He's got some really old photos on the wall of when he was a player. Tell you what, looking at him now, you wouldn't recognise the skinny little kid he used to be.' Swan nodded slowly to himself. 'This must have been a decent club way back when. Some of the pictures he showed me had massive crowds in here. I mean, it's probably 50 years ago, but the old ground...' he paused as he looked around at the decaying state of the Estadio Antonio Núñez. 'It must have been buzzing in those days.' He paused again, adding with a sigh. 'It must have been great.'

'I'm sure it was, Billy,' Moreton agreed. 'At least we're trying get it back on the right direction again now, mate. Get the club and the ground back to its former glories.'

Swan sniggered to himself as Moreton finished.

'What's funny?'

'Jeez, Jon,' Swan answered. 'I can't believe I'm telling you about this, let alone doing it,' he replied. 'And don't ever tell the boys, or Sophia.'

Moreton was intrigued.

'Look,' Swan revealed, 'me and Esteban have a plan to spruce up the old place a bit. You know, a bit like when you and Sophia did with the dressing room. He's getting some paint organised and me and him are going to paint the wall, there,' he said, pointing to the boundary wall surrounding the pitch. 'He's spoken with one of the blokes from Sophia's old man's group who runs a decorating business and he's agreed to organise the paint, if we do the work. So, from next week, me and me old mucker Esteban will be up here on Saturdays painting that wall in proper Retama blue. He reckons that the whole wall, all the way round the pitch, is about 400 metres so, if we each paint a length 20 metres long each Saturday, we'll be finished before the end of the season. Don't mention it to the boys though, yeah? Let them think it's all Esteban's work. I told him that after we've finished people will be calling him Leonardo va Dinci, 'cos the painting will be as good as that Moaning Lisa thing that everybody bangs on about. Tell you what, Jon? He laughed at that and started calling me Raphael. I told him, we were mates, but we ain't reforming them Turtles off the telly!'

Moreton shook his head in delighted disbelief. 'Wow, Billy,' he said. 'I'm staggered. Honestly. But bloody delighted too.' Then, quietly to himself. *Retama. Está en nuestras cabezas. Está en nuestros corazones.*'

'Ah, stop being an old tart,' Swan said, seeking escape from his embarrassment in the chirpy demeanour of his previous personality. 'I can't let you and Sophia have all the painting glory, can I? You were just a clogging midfielder, Jon Moreton. Whereas I, Mr William Swan, was a true artiste of the game, a painter of beautiful pictures on that green canvas out there.'

'Yeah, whatever, Billy,' Moreton said, clipping his friend softly around the ear and laughing.

'I owe these guys,' Swan said with determined sincerity. 'These boys, this club. I owe them bad, Jon. You too, and Sophia, all of you.'

Moreton hastened to change the subject. 'Well, I guess that's your days sorted, but perhaps you fancy meeting Sophia and me for dinner on some evenings.'

'Hmm,' Swan mused. 'Can do, but I'll have to consult my social diary first,' Swan replied with mocked haughtiness.

'Oh yeah?'

'Well,' Swan continued. 'No kidding, I go around to Kiki Dee's mom and dad's for dinner on Tuesdays and Wednesdays after training. We have some dinner with his family there and then he drops me back to the hotel. And on Mondays, I go round to Meldrew's place to eat. Him and his girlfriend have a flat not far away from the hotel. His girl's a teacher, and bloody gorgeous by the way. He usually cooks. He ain't bad either, Jon. After training, on Friday nights, me and Meldrew go and watch Kiki Dee and his mates in his band at a bar in town for a few hours. I can't say it's my kind of music, but we're there to support him and his mates, so that's all right. I keep asking Kiki Dee to try some proper stuff. You know, Michael Jackson, George Michael, Boy George, but he says they've never heard of them. Cheeky sodding kids!'

'So, you're a busy boy then?'

'Yeah, and even on the odd nights when I'm not doing anything, Seb often comes and sits with me on his break, or I'll have my nose in a book.'

'Just a thought, Billy,' Moreton said with a note of caution. 'Probably best to call Victor and Kiko by their real names, eh?'

'You know what, Jon?' Swan replied. 'I did, but they told me not to. Seriously. You know even some of Kiko's mates in the band call him Kiki Dee now, and Victor's girlfriend has got into the habit of saying "I don't believe it!" when anyone tells her anything. Victor says it makes him laugh all the time.'

The two friends sat contemplating for a moment, before the conversation inevitably returned to football.

'So, how are the soccer schools going then? Bobby said they had been really successful in London. I don't know if you were aware, but it even made the local newspapers over here.'

'Yeah, they're all good. Bobby's guys who do the management stuff, so they pretty well run them now. I've got a few old mates in from a couple of clubs I used to play for and they've helped me to grow it. To be honest, I'm pretty much just the bloke with his name on the door now. I pop in and take a few coaching sessions with some of the kids every couple of days or so. It's good fun to be honest, and all the running around keeps me a bit fit as well. I meet a few celebs and donors who put some dosh in, just to have a few photos with me and the boys. I used to think gallivanting around with them sort of people was what I enjoyed, but it's all just cobblers really. Setting the whole thing up, getting kids involved, playing football with them, helping to improve their game, and do their education stuff as well. That's the best part.'

Moreton chuckled to himself. 'Billy, you've definitely have changed, mate.'

'Told ya, didn't I?'

'So, is that what you're going back to?'

Swan rubbed his hand over his forehead. 'I guess so, mate.' He paused. 'You know what I'd really like to do, though, don't you? Set up something like that attached to a club, see the boys develop and grow, girls too. The soccer schools are great but when the kids leave school, they leave the soccer schools as well. It's the only way we can keep enough places for younger kids coming in, but you just miss out on where they go afterwards. You want to think you've changed their lives for good but ...' His words trailed off.

'But once they've left you don't really know?'

'Yeah,' Swan agreed. 'Look, don't get me wrong, what Bobby has done for those kids is brilliant. His brass has given them something they never had before. It shows that someone cares about them and, I'll tell you what, Jon, some of those kids have changed from being the shitty little troublemaker that I was, and are now passing exams and talking about college and all that stuff. It's been unbelievable to watch.'

'It's not just Bobby,' Moreton said. 'It wouldn't have happened without you.'

Swan's face broke into a smile. 'Cheers, Jon. You know, I think it's probably the only worthwhile thing I've ever done in my life, and to see how those kids look at me, like some kind of bloody hero.' He shook his head, still unable to comprehend how he was perceived. 'It's a great feeling, Jon.'

Moreton wrapped his arm around his friend's shoulder, drawing Swan towards him, before pointing out across the pitch to where Sophia now had the players working on a passing and shooting drill. 'It's not the only worthwhile thing you've done, Billy.' He suggested. 'Look at what you've done for these guys here, for Retama, for Sophia and me. You're our hero too.'

'Cheers, mate. But I'm just paying my dues from last year. I owe these guys, the club, Sophia, and you most of all, Jon.'

'Get us promoted and we'll call it quits, yeah?'

'Sure, Jon. Sorted.'

Decisions, decisions

On the face of it, the defeat to San Esteban, with two players being dismissed should have been a blow to Retama, but for the club's coaches and players, it felt almost like a victory, and the crushing win over Desorio, with Swan delivering a virtuoso performance, only added to the growing confidence. There seemed little reason for Moreton to change a winning team.

After promotion, Castillo Viejo had found their enhanced status a mixed blessing. Advancing to this level, for the first time in their history, had come as a surprise. Mid-table for much of the season, only a late run of victories had allowed them to edge into third place, before victory in a couple of two-legged play-offs, both on penalties, confirmed their unexpected promotion.

The new season, had been a trial, however, and the first seven fixtures had passed without them recording a win. The 2-0 defeat to Retama in the third week of the season, being representative of the way things were shaping up for them. From then though, they had found a measure of resilience, becoming more accustomed to the higher level required and, although hardly climbing far from the foot of the table, had at least suggested that survival was a possibility.

A win and three draws in their last four games, the latter two against the strong clubs of Torreaño and FC Córuel had instilled a measure of hope into their players. It suggested that the game would be anything but an easy away victory for Retama, and that was very much how things panned out.

Following a tight, but goalless first-half, Revi put the visitors ahead with a free-kick ten minutes after the restart, curling the ball past a befuddled goalkeeper from 20 metres out. With Adrián now back to add his steel to the regular back line, and Samuel prowling in front of the defence, offering added security, Jiménez had enjoyed a fairly comfortable time in the win over Desorio and, despite a single goal lead only ever offering the most vulnerable of advantages, Moreton felt confident that a team struggling near the foot of the table was unlikely to breach his defence.

Entering the final five minutes, his confidence was being borne out. Retama continued to probe but, with Swan clearly still troubled by the physical treatment dished out to him by the over excessive challenges of the Desorio players, and consequently Elías having a quiet game. At the other end of the pitch, Castillo Viejo had only offered sporadic threats to endanger the victory Moreton felt increasingly confident about securing, with the likelihood of a 0-1 victory for Retama seemingly inevitable. At such times though fate can take a malicious turn.

Sanz was under no pressure as Jiménez played the ball out to him, but the Retama captain wasn't expecting the ball, with his attention drawn up field as he trotted forwards. An alarmed shout from the goalkeeper came too late. Sensing a gift in the making, a home forward, ran to intercept the pass and hit a low cross into the box. Victor sought to hook the ball clear, but it struck Kiko on the back and rebounded past a startled Jiménez, and into the net. After hardly being in the game offering any kind of threat, Castillo Viejo suddenly had the chance to steal a point, and keep their nascent undefeated run intact in the most unlikely of circumstances.

On the sidelines, Moreton threw up his arms in frustration. Was it too late to make any changes? Glancing at his watch with now just three minutes to play, it seemed that way. As he was contemplating, Revi received the ball from Samuel and looked to play forward to Swan but, now keen to hang onto their point, the home team was all back in defence and the Retama playmaker had little room to deploy his skills. Revi advanced with the ball, before deciding to swing it to the left and José Palermo.

The pass was over-hit, with the ball running towards the home defence. A last chance had surely gone. Reading the flight of the pass, Elías had gambled on the defence allowing the mishit pass to run through to the goalkeeper. Racing after the ball, with defenders suddenly realising the danger and chasing in his wake, the Retama forward reached the ball ahead of the goalkeeper and, falling away to his left, lifted it into the air and towards the gaping net. The goalkeeper was stranded, and helpless to intervene, but one of the recovering defenders was heading towards the goal line. He slid after the bouncing ball attempting to hook it clear, but his effort hit the bar and fell into the net anyway.

Much as Nicolás had suggested to Moreton before the start of the season, in a game where he had been anonymous for much of the time, Elías had turned up with a vital goal. Retama had their second successive win. The only problem to perplex Moreton now was whether to restore top scorer Santi for the following game with his suspension completed, or to retain Elías, who had now scored three goals in the two games he had started. It was a nice problem to have; at least it felt that way at the time.

After the demolition of Desorio, Moreton had suggested that the crowd for Retama's next home game would grow. He was right, and two people in particular helped to swell the numbers watching. The next visitors to the Estadio Antonio Núñez would be Árboles Altos, the team from the village where Sophia's parents had made their home after leaving Retama. Joaquín and Dolores Garrigues would travel to Retama to watch the game, and then stay overnight at the Hotel de Barco to give Joaquín the opportunity to meet up with other members of his group now in charge of CD Retama, before returning to their village in the mountains.

They had also insisted that Moreton, Sophia and Swan join them for dinner after the game. A similar plan for the previous season had led to disastrous consequences but, now safe from the malign influences of Charlie Broome, this year's event promised to be much less dramatic.

For much of the previous week's training sessions, and the time in between them as well, Moreton pondered on the selection issue as to who should be the team's front man in the upcoming game. The old maxim of "never change a winning team" kept pushing itself to the front of his mind but, once he had decided to bring a rested Guido back into the starting eleven in place of José

Palermo, such considerations were irrelevant anyway.

On the Friday afternoon, ahead of training, Moreton and Sophia had decided to go into town, for a walk along the beachfront, with the Retama coach hoping that the fresh sea air might uncloud his mind. Sitting at a bar with a glass of wine before heading home to prepare for training, however, the cooling sea zephyrs had failed to produce the solution.

Sophia was aware of the thoughts whirling around Moreton's mind.

'We could bring Santi back into the team and put him in goal again,' she said with an impish smile. It was enough to break the ice.

Moreton smiled at the quip. 'You know,' he said, 'if Santi's red card had been justified, it would be much easier to tell him he'd have to wait for his chance, if Elías keeps scoring, but he was sent off for doing nothing wrong. In fact, he was sent off for scoring a goal, his hat-trick goal. If we don't bring him back into the team, it'll mean he's lost his place for scoring three goals. That's hardly fair, is it?'

'I think,' Sophia offered. 'That what's fair, is less important than what's the best thing for the team. How many games are left now, a dozen or so? We don't really have the luxury of being nice. We need results. It's a simple question of who is the right choice to help us win the game.'

Moreton smiled at her. 'I love you. You know.'

'Of course, you do,' she beamed back at him. 'Who wouldn't?'

They both laughed. 'You're right of course. So, here's what I'm thinking. Elías is the man in possession. He's scored his goals, and won us the game against Castillo Viejo, he should play. Yes?'

Sophia put her index finger to her lip as in deep thought. 'Hmm, I'm not sure.'

'Really? Why?' He was both confused and perplexed.

She then burst into a giggle. 'I'm just kidding, Jon. Really. I think it's the right decision.'

Moreton shook his head in exaggerated condemnation. 'You know when I said I loved you, I'm not so sure now.'

Sophia smiled at him and winked as she rubbed her foot against the inside of his calf. 'Really? Are you sure?'

'Well, all right,' he said, reaching for her hand. 'You make a good point there, Well argued. Yes, I do love you.'

A few hours later, with training completed Moreton announced the team to face Árboles Altos on Sunday. With the goalkeeper and defence virtually selecting itself, Moreton announced that Matías would come in for Samuel as he rotated the defensive midfield position alongside Revi. Antonio Vasquez would be in position on the right with the returning Guido on the left. Swan would play behind the striker who was – Elías. Moreton couldn't help but glance at Santi when that last name was announced. He was hoping for a nod of understanding or something similar. Instead, Santi merely bowed his head and looked at the floor. For Moreton, although disappointing, the young forwards' reaction was also understandable.

An hour later, after Sophia had spoken with Esteban, she and Moreton walked out of the gate of the Estadio Antonio Núñez, to find Santi waiting outside. *'Hola, Santi,'* Moreton said. *'Todo bien?'*

The young Retama forward who had developed so much since being compelled to take over the main striker role for Retama after Tomás Bendonces had walked out of the club last season, looked nervous, and clearly everything wasn't good.

'Can I talk with you please?' he asked in perfect English

'Of course.'

'I have a problem. Well, an opportunity really.' He paused wobbling his head from side to side as if unable to decide. 'I don't know. A problem. An opportunity. Perhaps both, I'm not sure.'

Sophia sympathetically placed her hand on the Retama player's arm. *'¿De qué te preocupas?'*

Santi began to explain. 'You understand that here, I work for my father's transport company, in the office? It's fine there, but when I started it was only to be for a short while, until I secured a job doing what I want.' He paused a little, as if he knew the next part of the story would be difficult to tell. 'I studied at school and then college to be a *químico industrial,* a chemist, an industrial chemist. But, once I started working with my father, that dream sort of went away.'

Moreton was unsure where Santi's story was leading, but was increasingly concerned that he wouldn't like the destination. It was to prove a valid concern.

'Now,' Santi continued. 'I have this approach for a job as a *químico industrial* to learn all about the work with a big company.'

'That's great,' Moreton said. 'Congratulations, amigo.'

Santi shook his head. 'No, you don't understand. I'm not even sure it's a real job. It may be that it's just a temporary thing, not real.'

'I don't understand.'

Santi blew out his cheeks, the important part of the story couldn't be delayed any longer. 'I have been contacted by agents for Sobrolepeña Industrial. The job is with them, but they also want me to agree to play for their team as part of the arrangement.' Santi looked down at the floor. 'I'm not sure that it's a real job. Is it just to get me to play for them? It has to be, doesn't it? They know nothing about me, my qualifications, abilities, nothing. How can it be a real job?'

'I don't know Santi. Perhaps they plan to train you up anyway, teach you all the things you need to know.' Then he asked a question of his own. 'Do you want to go?'

'No sé, I don't know. I spoke with my father about it. He said he would support me whatever decision I make.' Santi looked down again. 'I told him that the team here needs me, but with Elías playing and scoring, I'm not sure that's true any more.'

It would have been easy for Moreton to say the words that Santi clearly wanted to hear, to say he would put him back in the team, to say he would always be selected, but he knew that would be wrong. He couldn't do it. He wouldn't do it. 'This can't be only about the team Santi. That can't be the thing that makes you decide. This could be a chance for you to achieve your dream and do the job you've always wanted to do. You have to make the best decision for Santi, not for Club Deportivo Retama.'

Santi nodded slowly.

'When do you have to tell them by?' Moreton asked.

'On Monday.'

'OK. Look, give it lot of thought. Forget Sunday's game. Take a break and give yourself some thinking time. Talk to your father. Talk to your friends. Listen to what they say. Remember though, that you must decide yourself. It's your life.'

Santi nodded again. 'I haven't told anyone in the team yet. I didn't know how to…'

His words drifted away as Moreton intervened. 'Don't worry about that now. Until you make a decision, there's nothing to tell anyway. I'll just tell the guys that I told you take a week off. That way, nobody's lying and when you decide what you're doing, we'll sort it out then. And, whether you go or stay, we will all still love you here. You will always be a part of the Retama family, of our family. OK?'

'*Gracias,*' Santi said, with a smile fighting its way onto his concerned young features. Moreton shook hands with him and Sophia planted a kiss on his cheek. Santi turned, and walked away in the opposite direction to Moreton and Sophia.

'Wow,' Moreton confided. 'That wasn't easy.'

'You did well,' Sophia said. 'You said all of the right things. I'm so proud of you.' She pressed her head into his chest. 'Fancy a glass of wine on the way home?'

'Yeah, I think I need one.'

Moreton and Sophia explained away Santi's absence on Sunday as the players gathered for the game saying that he looked tired and needed a weekend off. It wasn't the complete truth, but neither was it totally dishonest. As such the remainder of the squad accepted it without query. Moreton felt a little uncomfortable about it but was keen not to break Santi's confidence, and he quickly moved on to impress on his team the importance of a good start against a club they had beaten comfortably during in the previous season: a game that led to Charlie Broome organising Swan's fake injury after falling down the stairs at the hotel.

All of that was forgotten now, though, as Moreton merely concentrated on the events of the game when Swan's hat-trick was probably his best performance of the season. The team left the dressing room in confident and determined fashion and was greeted by a crowd much increased from the one that saw them score four times against Desorio. Two more were added to the growing number as well. Sophia's parents waved to her and Moreton as they headed towards the coaches' bench at the side of the pitch.

'Who do you think they're here to support?' Moreton asked playfully. 'Us or Árboles Altos?'

'I think you know the answer to that one,' Sophia replied with a smile.

If her answer meant that her parents were supporting Retama, they would be celebrating a goal inside the first 90 seconds as a neat first-time pass from Swan opened up a gap in the visitors' defence allowing Guido to scamper clear and drill the ball low past the goalkeeper as he came out to narrow the angle. It was only the Retama speedster's second goal of the season, but his third followed in quick succession. This time Revi was the provider.

Still inside the first ten minutes, he collected the ball from Matías and ran forward towards the halfway line as the opposition defence retreated. Again, Swan was the pivot as Revi fed the ball to him, before running on to collect a delicate one-two and driving into the penalty area. A simple cut back and side-foot finish by Guido doubled the home team's lead and, as a competition, the game was virtually over before it had even begun. For the remainder of the first period, Retama controlled the game, comfortably kept the rare Árboles Altos attacks at bay and walked back to the dressing room at the break in a satisfied mood, their early confidence having been fully justified.

Moreton, however, was concerned. He'd seen games like this before. One team goes ahead, looks totally in control of the game, and then concedes a sloppy goal. All of a sudden, they're in trouble and can't pick up the pace of the game again. Inevitably they concede and points are squandered, but what should he do? He confided his concerns to Sophia as they followed the players into the dressing room.

'Do I shout and bawl at them?'

She wasn't sure. 'We're winning and playing well. If you do that it may just damage the confidence, and perhaps cause problems.'

Opening the door, he still wasn't sure how to play things, but there was a quiet hum around the room, and he decided to play it cool. 'Great work, guys,' he said clapping his hands. 'Next goal is big though. Let's make sure we get it!'

The message seemed to have been successfully delivered. Retama restarted the game in determined fashion and scored the third goal ten minutes into the second-half as a series of corners finally saw Kiko heading home. The visitors did eventually score, but with only seconds to play as a long range shot deceived Jiménez, it hardly mattered. It looked like he had made the right decision at the break. Adopting a similar approach in the next game would have different consequences though.

Food for thought

Later that evening, Moreton was showered, changed and waiting for the taxi to take them to the hotel for the dinner appointment with Sophia's parents and Swan. Wearing a pristine new white shirt and blue tie, with his jacket thrown over the chair next to him, he gazed out of the apartment window, checking the road for the taxi. He glanced at his watch. It was nearly 7.30.

'Are you ready?' he asked towards the closed bedroom door where Sophia was changing. He looked, and felt, ill at ease. He sighed as he glanced both ways up and down the road.

'What's troubling you, Jon?' Sophia shouted from the bedroom.

'Ah, nothing really. You know me and these sorts of things though, don't you?' he called back. 'I'm always afraid that I'll use the dessert spoon for the soup or something like that.'

Sophia laughed. 'Well, don't have the soup then.'

'Yeah, all right then. I'm sorry. I just feel a bit weird dressed up in a shirt and tie, like a fish out of water.'

'Well, I'm dressed up too,' Sophia said, emerging from the bedroom wearing a full-length two-toned blue silk dress cut across one shoulder. 'Do I look weird?'

Moreton drew a sharp intake of breath. 'Wow,' he gasped, shaking his head slowly. 'No, you look amazing.'

She walked over to the window and kissed him tenderly. Her scent and the touch of her lips intoxicated his senses, while his mind was still reeling from the vision. 'We've got to go,' she said.

'What?' Moreton replied as his mind scrambled to remember where he was, temporarily lost in raptures.

'The taxi, Jon. It's here.'

'Oh, right yeah. OK.'

He picked up his jacket and slipped it on as Sophia walked out of the apartment. Following her, he closed the door and watched as she walked down the steps in front of him to the complex's gate, transfixed by the liquid movements of her body contained within the blue silk. 'Wow,' he whispered to himself.

Fifteen minutes later, Moreton and Sophia walked into Reception at the Hotel El Barco to be met by Sebastián. They hadn't seen him since the game against Torreaño, before the mid-season break when everyone had accepted that the club was doomed.

'I wanted to catch you before you went in,' the hotel owners' son revealed. 'We're now past the winter holiday season, and I've finished my exams for this year, so I can come to training most evenings now, if that's OK.'

'Of course, it is,' beamed Moreton. 'We've missed you, Seb?'

'That's great. I'll see you on Tuesday, then.'

'Sure, amigo. Are Joaquín, Dolores and Billy already in there?' Moreton asked, nodding towards the hotel restaurant

'Señor and Señora Garrigues haven't come down yet, but the other two are in there waiting.'

Moreton did a double-take. 'Other two?'

Sebastián nodded and smiled. Cocking his head to one side to encourage Moreton and Sophia to go into the restaurant. They followed his lead. The restaurant was sparsely populated. It was still early for dinner and, with only three tables occupied, it was easy to spot where Swan was sitting, and he wasn't alone. 'Hello,' Moreton said quietly to Sophia. 'What's going on here?'

Swan's companion had their back to Moreton and Sophia as they approached, but the jet-black hair set on the top of the head, and the slender black neck and shoulders beneath it, revealed that it was certainly a woman. Moreton spoke as they approached. 'Hi, Billy. You OK?'

Swan stood up, shook hands with Swan and kissed Sophia on both cheeks as his companion rose from her chair. Tall and elegant she smiled broadly at the newcomers, reaching out her hand in greeting.

'Hello' she said in a strong Spanish accent. 'I'm Isabella.'

Moreton and Sophia exchanged greetings with Isabella before sitting down at the table and ordering glasses of mineral water as they waited for Joaquín and Dolores Garrigues to arrive. After a few minutes, Isabella asked Sophia if she could direct to the ladies' room. 'Sure,' she said. 'Come on. I'll show you.' The two women were hardly out of earshot when Moreton's curiosity struggled free of its social constraints.

'Well?' he asked.

'Well, wot?'

'Billy!' Moreton insisted. 'Who's Isabella, then?'

'Oh, Izzy,' Swan replied in mock surprise. 'Didn't I mention to you about her?'

'No!'

'Well, I suppose that's fair enough. You never told me about Sophia, did you now?' The mischievous grin on Swan's face betrayed that he was enjoying the intrigue and Moreton was hooked.

'Billy!'

'OK, OK.' Swan signed with delicious enjoyment, waving his palms downwards encouraging Moreton to calm down. 'She's Kiko's aunt. His Mom's younger sister. I met her when I was round his parents for dinner, the first time I went there.'

'And?' Moreton was clearly anxious for more information before the two women returned and his window of opportunity for interrogation closed.

'And, we chatted a bit. Her English is great, but she's trying to teach me a bit of Spanish as well. Blimey, that ain't easy, Jon, I can tell you.'

'Forget the Spanish for a minute, Billy.' Moreton insisted. 'So, what are you two? An item? Friends or what?'

'Dunno really, mate. I always see her round Kiko's parents and she's gone with me to see his band a couple of times. Hmm, we've had lunch a few times and been on a few walks, erm…'

'Billy, you're a couple!' Moreton exclaimed triumphantly.

'Calm down, will yer!' Swan insisted. 'Look, I don't really know what the scheme is to be honest. I really like her, and for some stupid reason, I think she likes me too. When I told her about tonight, she asked if she could come along to meet you guys.' He paused. Before leaning in towards Moreton emphasising the confidentiality required in where the conversation was going. 'Look, Jon. Can you do this for me? Can you like her? It's really important to me. She's not just a bit of skirt like in the old days. She's nice.'

Moreton's face could hardly contain his pleasure. 'No worries, Billy,' he said. 'She seems great. And this is why you've been so busy I suppose.'

'Well, you know …'

At that moment Sophia and Isabella walked back into the restaurant laughing, just as Joaquín and Dolores Garrigues came down the stairs at the same time. They introduced each other on the way to the table and all four arrived together. There was no time for any more questions from Moreton.

The three couples settled into a pleasant evening, with Isabella quickly accepted as part of the group. The conversation covered food and football, work – Isabella explained that she had her own small business, an agency in the town that located exclusive properties for people – and football, the weather and football and, just occasionally, football. By the time they were drinking coffee, the subject had inevitably returned to football and, in particular the future of CD Retama. Garrigues explained that Cerámica Internacional had already deployed a company of surveyors to locate alternative potential sites for development in the town, should they have to honour their part of the agreement if the club win promotion.

Moreton was surprised. 'Wow,' he exclaimed. 'They have a lot of confidence in us, haven't they?'

'I'm sure they should, Jon,' Garrigues replied. 'But this is just how things work. Whichever way things turn out, they won't want to delay things, having postponed the development by twelve months already.'

'I guess so,' Moreton agreed.

'Can I ask,' Isabella said, 'have they identified any sites? It's just that, in my line of business, these things are important.'

'Of course,' Garrigues replied. 'There are a couple of places where preliminary discussions have taken place, but nothing definite. There's one site that I understand CI would be particularly interested in, on the edge of the town by the access to the *Autopista*, the toll motorway that runs up to Valencia. The location gives it good access routes of course, but the *ayuntamiento* had provisionally marked it up for housing development. Talks are very preliminary and conditional of course, but they may strike a deal if things fall that way.' He paused and turned to Moreton, Sophia and Swan. 'Which these three people will surely make happen. At the end of the day, of course, the *ayuntamiento* want the business for the benefit of the local economy and jobs for Retama inhabitants and CI want the development.'

An hour later, the party broke up. Garrigues didn't want to be up late as he had a meeting scheduled for early in the morning with members of his group. He and Dolores left for their room as the others headed into Reception so that Moreton and Sophia could organise their journey home. They offered to share their taxi with Isabella, but Swan told them that Kiko was coming to collect her later.

'Kiki Dee is a very good boy,' Isabella confirmed as Moreton and Sophia stifled their laughter at how Swan's nickname for Kiko had rapidly caught on with his family.

'See,' Swan said. 'I told you, didn't I?' Isabella clearly understood the comment and joined in the laughter.

'Oh dear,' she said. 'That's nothing. Thanks to Billy, I'm now Tía Izzy. Nobody in the family calls me Isabella any more. *Mi madre* would not have been happy with you, Billy,' she added, slapping him playfully on the arm.

'Then, is it OK if we call you Izzy as well?' Sophia asked.

'Of course, Sophia,' she replied.

Closing the door of the apartment behind them after leaving the taxi, Moreton took off his jacket and loosened his tie as Sophia went to the bathroom. 'Coffee?' he asked.

'Not for me, thanks,' came the reply.

'No, not me either, really,' he said to himself and slumped down on the sofa, finally ridding himself completely of the tie and undoing the top couple of buttons of his shirt, as Sophia re-entered the room. Moreton jumped to his feet.

'Can I hold you?' he asked politely. Sophia smiled and fell into his arms as Moreton sighed contentedly. 'I've wanted to do that all night, *mi amor*,' he confessed.

'Well, you should have said earlier, shouldn't you,' Sophia teased. 'It's a hotel, they have rooms, you know.'

'Yeah, right. I can just imagine me saying "Sorry Joaquín and Dolores, but while you have dessert, me and your daughter are off upstairs for a bit of roly-poly of our own. We'll be back in time for coffee!"' They both laughed and, after kissing, sat down next to each other on the sofa with Sophia lying against Moreton's arm.

'So,' he asked. 'What about Izzy, then?'

'She's nice.'

'Yeah,' mused Moreton. 'She is, isn't she.' He decided it was time to share their information and related what Swan had told him about how they met, the time they'd spent together and how he had asked Moreton to like her. 'Your turn,' he said afterwards. 'What did you talk about.'

'Well, not much really,' she said. 'Billy had told her about me, and us, so there wasn't much to tell from my side.' She wrapped Moreton's arm over her shoulder, resting her head on his chest. 'She likes Billy, I know that.'

'Really?' Moreton replied. 'Sorry, that sounded weird. It's just that the idea of Billy Swan being in any kind of a serious relationship with someone, anyone, is just … I don't know … weird, I guess.' He paused briefly, as a thought entered his mind. 'Does she know much about him?' he asked. 'Does she know about his past? About last year?' he added hesitantly.

'I think so. We didn't speak for very long of course, but she said that he had told her everything about him and what happened last season, about Charlie Broome and the blackmail.'

'That's amazing. He's really opened up to her, then?'

'Apparently, they went for a walk and ended up at a quiet park and he confessed everything to her, everything.'

'That must have taken some doing,' Moreton reflected, unconsciously holding Sophia closer to him. 'You, know, I don't think I know this new Billy Swan at all. I like him. I like him a lot, but I'm not sure I know him at all.'

'Well, Izzy does now. There's one thing though.'

'What's that?'

'She said that she doesn't want to get too involved, because he'll be going back to England in a few months and it'll be over.'

'Yeah, I guess so,' Moreton said with a resigned sigh. 'Anyway, I'm ready for bed now. You coming?'

'Of course. It's time for that dessert course.'

Losses and Gains

The following morning, Moreton and Sophia slept late before going into town for lunch, a stroll along the beach and then stopping at the local supermarket for some food shopping. By five o'clock, they had dropped off the shopping at the apartment and were sitting in the spring sunshine outside Carlito's bar. Moreton asked for a *caña*, and Sophia a glass of white wine. Elena brought them the drinks and Moreton raised his glass of beer with Sophia's wine to toast '*Salut*' to each other. As Moreton eased back into his chair, enjoying the sensation of the pleasantly cooling liquid swilling around his mouth, Sophia's phone rang. Picking it out of her bag, she looked at the caller's name. 'Santi,' she said.

Five minutes later, she closed out the call, and placed the phone down on the table in front of her. There was little need for confirmation of Santi's decision, Sophia's expression during the phone conversion told Moreton all he needed to know. Retama's leading striker and top scorer was leaving.

'He's going' Sophia confirmed unnecessarily.

Moreton looked up to the skies and blew out his cheeks. 'Yeah, OK,' he said resignedly.

'Santi said that it was a really difficult situation, but the conversation he had with us was important, and we had made it easier for him to make the decision that he really knew was right for him. He said to thank you for all you have done for him. I asked him if he wanted to speak with you, but I think he was too embarrassed.'

'Well done us, eh?' Moreton said with the merest hint of sarcasm, before correcting himself. 'No, that's not being fair. I understand. It's his chance for something he's wanted to do since he was at school. He's done the right thing and, if we made achieving his dream easier, then that's fine.'

Sophia smiled and raised her glass. 'To Santi and his dream, yes?'

'Yes, to Santi and his dream.' Moreton took a long draught of his beer before placing it down on the table. 'I guess we should tell the other guys.'

'No need,' Sophia replied. 'Santi's done it. He's spoken to everyone already. We were the last ones. Everyone was pleased for him and wished him well.'

'That's good. I'd have expected nothing less from the boys. Anyway, that doesn't make our situation any better. We've got three training sessions this week to work out how we cope without Santi for the visit to Costa Locos on Sunday.'

Sophia nodded. 'And you know what's after that Jon, don't you? We're at home to Sobrolepeña Industrial.' She paused, taking a sip of her wine. 'And their new striker.'

At training that week, the focus was on using Elías as the main striker, but Moreton was also keen to ensure that José Palermo felt very much part of Retama's new, and very inexperienced central striking options as well, and integrated him into the new patterns of play as much as possible. Whereas Santi had been a genuine leader of the line, able to compete effectively in the physical battles with defenders, Elías's style was very different, built on stealth and spotting opportunities to score that may have been created by others, rather than being the main man himself. The younger Palermo brother was much closer to being a like-for-like replacement for Santi, albeit a much younger and less developed one.

The other option was José's elder brother. In the corresponding home game against Costa Locos earlier in the season, a commanding performance by Retama had nearly failed to deliver victory, as they failed to turn a domination of possession into goals until Juan Palermo's heroic last-minute header. To do so again would be a setback for Retama, but sometimes lessons are only learned when a cost is demanded in exchange.

Moreton left the back line unchanged. He was tempted to give the returning Sebastián a starting berth, or at least consider using him as a substitute, but decided to allow another week of regular training before fully reintegrating him into the team. Samuel was brought back in to play alongside Revi with José Palermo on the right, Guido on the left and Swan behind Elías.

When the game reached the half-time break, Retama were in total command against a team struggling for confidence and belief in the lower reaches of the league. A brace from Swan, and a goal each for José Palermo and Elías had put Retama well clear, despite a home goal just minutes ahead of the break nibbling away at the arrears.

The Retama team returned to the dressing room in confident fashion with the goal conceded hardly registering in their consciousness. As with the game against Árboles Altos, Moreton felt twinges of concern that his players may just ease off too much in the second period and end up endangering the points. Three goals clear, however, it felt like over-exaggerated caution, and he convinced himself that he was worrying over nothing. When the second half commenced it took just ten minutes of playing time for him to realise the folly of his conclusion.

Almost from the kick-off, Costa Locos earned a corner as a Sanz tackle ran the ball out of play. As the ball was crossed in, both Kiko and Jiménez challenged for it, with neither getting a clean contact and the ball dropped invitingly for a home forward to tap the ball home from a couple of metres distance.

The nature of the goal hardly suggested that the home team were going to raise their game but, having now scored twice in a matter of four minutes of action, new hope was rising and they began to press forward with renewed vigour. Suddenly, Jiménez's goal was under sustained pressure.

On the sidelines, the alarm bells were now ringing in Moreton's ears as he shouted and cajoled his players to concentrate and pick up their performances again. The momentum of the game had changed though, and a third home goal was on the way. Jiménez tipped a long-range shot over the bar and, from the corner, Kiko headed the ball towards the edge of the area, where it fell to a Costa Locos player. Firing the ball into the still-crowded penalty area, his shot cannoned first off Kiko, then Sanz before being scrambled over the line. From being four goals up, Retama were now only ahead by the narrowest of margins.

Moreton needed to act and not only instil some urgency into his team who, by now were well aware of the danger, but also inject some defensive solidity. He called Matías from the bench, withdrawing Elías, and sent him on to play alongside Samuel and Revi to strengthen the team's defensive shield in front of what now looked like an increasingly vulnerable back line.

If the move added a little stability to the team, the situation began to look threatening again when Kiko suffered with a kick to his ankle and, after trying to continue, had to be substituted. Losing the muscular presence of the towering defender was a major problem, and Moreton sent on Juan Palermo, who had the height to fill the gap. With Felipe Blanco as the only real alternative, it looked like the best option and, after a further 25 minutes had passed, the danger seemed to have eased as frustration built up in the Costa Locos players' attacks.

Entering the final few minutes, despite having bitten nails, Moreton was beginning to think his team would escape with the three points and a valuable lesson without a tangible cost. The following 30 seconds would prove him wrong. A tired and clumsy challenge by Samuel conceded a free-kick 20 metres from goal and a curled free-kick left Jiménez as a mere observer as the ball ripped into the net for the equaliser. Moreton bowed his head and shuffled his feet as the home bench celebrated their recovery. 'How did that happen?' Sophia asked of no one in particular.

Moreton merely shook his head. 'My fault,' he said. 'I should have hammered into them at the break to keep concentration up. I should have used that late first-half goal as a warning.'

At full time, the demeanours of the two sets of players were as different as the scores were identical. The home team jumped on each other, high-fived and celebrated the draw like a cup final win. The Retama players headed back to the dressing room in sullen silence. Their run of three successive wins had come to an end in a game where they had been 4-0 ahead. Moreton and Sophia followed them in and the entire group sat in silence for a few seconds before Moreton spoke.

'We paid the price today. We learnt the hard way. We need to understand this lesson and remember it.' He stood up and walked out of the door with Sophia. As she closed the door, the voice of Alejandro Sanz was clear. Moreton paused a while to listen, but his Spanish was not good enough for him to understand the Retama captain's words. He turned to Sophia. 'He's saying that they all let you down, Jon,' she explained. 'That they should all be ashamed, and that you would have been right to yell and shout at them, but you showed the hurt in those few words.' Moreton nodded. 'He also says it must never happen again.' There were a few seconds of silence before Sanz spoke again. The man whose quiet authority meant he never needed to raise his voice to deliver a message broke the code on this occasion. '*¡Nunca más!*' he shouted. '*¡Nunca más!*'

Perhaps it was the sobering lesson of seeing a four-goal lead disappear, perhaps Moreton's brief comments, maybe the words of Sanz, or a combination of all three but the training sessions the following week were full of commitment, dedication and a determination to put matters right in the next game, especially as it would see the rapid return to the Estadio Antonio Núñez of Santi with his new team-mates from Sobrolepeña Industrial. The works team had already seen the benefit of their new player as Santi delivered a hat-trick in his debut game against bottom of the table club, Torre del Olmos.

All through the week Moreton considered which option was the best reaction to the collapse against Costa Locos. Should he name an unchanged team and give the players a chance to redeem themselves or make changes to demonstrate that the display was simply not good enough. By Friday, after talking it over with Sophia as the players went through their training drills, he had decided on the former. Anything else would have been saying that it was only the players to blame, when he felt that he was just as guilty about the outcome as they were. He had the chance to put things right, so it was only fair that they were afforded the same privilege.

It was therefore an unchanged Retama side that would line up against the yellow and green-hooped shirts of the visiting Sobrolepeña Industrial players at the Estadio Antonio Núñez the following Sunday. Before leaving the dressing room, Sanz had ensured that lack of concentration would certainly not be a factor in the game ahead. '*¿Somos Retama?*' he had asked, receiving the echoing call, in response. Then: '*¡Retama. Está en nuestras cabezas. Está en nuestros corazones!*'

Santi, wearing the colours of his new club, greeted each of them in turn with a warm embrace as they entered the field. There was little chance of that moment diluting the determination of the Retama players though. As the referee began the game. Sanz's rallying call of '*¡Somos Retama!*' once again echoed around the home team, both among those on the field and the substitutes. It was also quickly taken up by Moreton and Sophia as well. 'I think the guys are well up for this one,' Moreton said quietly to Sophia sitting next to him. There was no reply, however, her concentration was also very much on the game.

There was little doubt that Santi had improved the attacking threat carried by the team from Sobrolepeña. His hat-trick against bottom of the table Torre del Olmos may have been secured against weaker opposition, but it had also boosted his confidence and impressed his new team-mates. The previous evening Sophia had mused as to whether Santi would celebrate the goal if he scored against Retama. Moreton had replied that he didn't want to find out, and the avid attention that his defence was giving to their former team-mate suggested that his players were of a similar mind.

The opening 20 minutes were tight, and, even after that, as the play opened up a little, defences were on top. The visitors looked to free Santi with crosses and through balls, but Kiko and Victor were determined not to give their friend even a sight of an opening. Sanz berated his defenders for even the slightest slip and Adrián greeted Santi with one of his robust tackles, before pulling the forward to his feet and exchanging pats on the back with him. It was not so much one of the defender's 'Welcome to Retama' tackles, more of a 'Welcome back to Retama' one.

Despite the diligence of the defence, Santi still had a couple of brief glimpses of a goal. First, a cross from the right saw him flick a header just wide of the far post. Then, a turn and shot flew comfortably into the midriff of a waiting Jiménez.

At the other end of the pitch, the more subdued style of Elías meant that the home team rarely looked threatening and, while Swan prompted and probed looking to find the pass that would open the door for Retama's goal poacher, a more obvious threat came from the young José Palermo. His energetic work down the right flank, and willingness to cut inside to add his presence to that of Elías pulled the visiting defence around. At the break though, the game remained goalless.

If anything, the visitors had shaded the first-half and, with Santi looking the most dangerous forward on the field, had been the more likely to score. Moreton considered his options for change, but was still minded to utilise the determination of the players who had fallen short in the previous game to get them over the line here. Encouraging the young Palermo brother to keep making runs into the box and support Elías, he also asked Swan to look out for opportunities to exploit the movement coming from the right flank. The ploy would be rewarded ten minutes after the restart.

The visitors opened the second period with a sustained period of pressure. Neither goalkeeper had been overextended in the first-half, but that situation changed a couple of minutes after the referee restarted the game. First Sanz blocked a goal bound shot, throwing himself in front of the ball. Then Jiménez was called on to plunge to his right and divert a shot around the post. From the corner, Santi found space, as another Sobrolepeña player astutely blocked the run of Kiko as he marked the former Retama player. Fortunately, the effort was cleared from under the crossbar by Victor, with Jiménez beaten. As so often is the case, despite the early play being concentrated in and around the Retama penalty area, the opening goal came at the other end.

Sanz received the ball from his goalkeeper before exchanging passes with Kiko as he advanced along the Retama right flank. Closed down as he approached halfway line, he fed the ball inside to Revi who slipped past his marker and advanced into the visitors' half. Drawing his marker with him, Swan drifted out to the left to create more space for the head-banded Retama playmaker, before the Sobrolepeña defender identified Revi as the more immediate danger, recovering his more central position to close him down.

Seeing Swan in space, Revi played a square pass to the veteran, who had seconds to look up and consider his options. As instructed, José Palermo made his run into the box from the opposite flank, and Swan drove a powerfully hit pass towards him, just as a late challenge failed to block the pass. Reaching the ball at a run, some dozen metres from goal, the young forward powered his header on goal. Beaten by the sheer pace of the ball, the Sobrolepeña goalkeeper's dive was little more than a gesture, as the ball flew past him and into the net to give Retama the lead.

The Retama players celebrated as if a dam had been breached. For periods of the game, they had been second best and needed to prove that they could still prevail. The goal delivered on that. Jumping from the bench as the ball hit the back of the net, Moreton embraced Sophia. 'We needed that,' he said unnecessarily, but her attention was drawn to the pitch instead. As the celebrating group of players broke up, she noticed that Swan was limping. 'Look,' she said. 'Look at Billy.' The challenge intended to block Swan's pass had, instead, impacted on his ankle.

Experienced enough to understand that he needed to prevent the restart, Swan sat down in the centre circle, rubbing his ankle as the perpetrator of the tackle apologised to the fallen Retama player. The pain in Swan's ankle was hardly mitigated by its cause being accidental, and the referee called Sophia on to attend to him.

From 50 metres away, Moreton watched with concern as Sophia ministered to Swan, offering sprays and words of encouragement, before trotting back off the field as the player struggled back into position for the game to restart. 'He wants five minutes to see how it goes,' she reported to Moreton.

'OK,' he said.

'The challenge was late. I don't think the guy wanted to hurt him, but it's already starting to swell up. I really don't think he's going to be able to run it off.'

'OK,' Moreton repeated, telling Matías to get ready to go on.

Very much as Sophia had suspected, a few minutes later, with the game passing him by as he struggled to even break into a trot, Swan sat down on the ground again, his twirling fingers gesture confirming the need for a replacement. Matías was sent on to play alongside Samuel, with Revi pushed further forwards, as Sophia went to fetch ice for Swan's ankle.

'How is it, Billy?' Moreton asked as Swan slumped down on the bench.

'It's sore, Jon,' his friend replied as he removed his boot, rolled down his sock, and discarded the shinpad to reveal the angry-looking swelling already developing a deep blue and purple hue. 'You can't believe, at my age, I was too quick for one of these kids, can you?' he added with a wry smile, as Sophia returned with a bag of ice, strapping it around Swan's ankle. He flinched as the ice was taped securely.

'Why today, Jon?' Swan lamented.

'What do you mean?'

'Well, I'm supposed to go to a salsa dancing thing tomorrow night with Izzy.'

Moreton was taken aback. 'Salsa? Dancing?'

'Yeah, I know,' Swan explained. 'But she's been going on about it for days now. I told her that dancing ain't my thing, but she said that I'm a footballer and good on my feet, so it should be easy for me to learn. I told her that's fine, so long as there was a ball on the dancefloor, but she wouldn't take no for an answer.'

Despite the pressure of the game, and his friend's injured ankle, Moreton couldn't suppress a smile. 'So, you said you'd go?'

'Yeah, she can twist me round her little finger, she can.' Swan winced as he stretched out his ankle. 'I'm kyboshed now, but she'll think I'm swinging the lead.'

'Show her the ankle, Billy. I think it'll convince her.'

With his team holding a slender lead, sitting down next to Swan became as difficult for Moreton as standing would have been for the injured player. Retama's coach paced up and down nervously, shouting encouragement to his team as time ticked on, and the visitors continued to have the better of the game. Inside the final ten minutes the second goal came for Retama; and allowed a little of the tension on the home bench to drift away. A right-wing corner was headed on by Kiko and, stationed on the far post, Elías swept the ball into the net.

The home side's second strike effectively closed out the game and secured the points for Retama. Despite his team playing much better in a number of other games, the victory was particularly pleasing for Moreton, following on the back of the collapse against Costa Locos. Retama were back to winning ways again and, although the injury to Swan's ankle suggested at least one week out of action, Moreton felt things were moving in the right direction again – and they were – for the moment, at least.

All Shapes and Sizes

With Swan absent for the following week's game against the students from Universidad San Juan, Moreton had to decide who would replace him in the number ten role. One option was moving Revi forwards from his deeper role, but that would again imperil the efficiency of Retama's transition play as they moved from defence into attack. The other approach would be to play Antonio Vasquez in the middle. Moreton had tried this on a couple of occasions, but with only limited success. He was discussing the situation over dinner with Sophia on Monday evening when a phone call removed one of the options he was pondering.

As they were sitting on the balcony, the ringtone of Sophia's phone beckoned her attention. She left the table as Moreton sipped his wine. Returning with the phone to her ear, the troubled look on her face suggested to him that it wasn't good news. Moreton put his glass back down on the table and waited until Sophia closed out the call.

'Bad news?' he asked.

'I'm afraid so. That was Revi. You remember his grandmother, the one who lives in Sevilla, she was ill last year?'

Moreton nodded.

'She's been taken ill again, but it seems very serious this time.' She shook her head sadly. 'They were very close a while ago. Revi's family come from Andalusia, and they lived there for a long time, before he and his parents moved to Retama a few years ago. When he was very young, he used to spend a lot of time with his grandmother at the *finca* where she lived in the countryside outside of Sevilla. She grew strawberries there and sold them at the local market. Revi always said that they were the best thing he'd ever tasted. He would often go with her to the market in her little pony and cart, but he would eat as many strawberries as they sold. She never seemed to mind though.' She paused, looking down at the floor. 'From what Revi said, I think she's dying. He was very upset.' Sophia was struggling to hold back her tears.

'Oh no, the poor kid.'

'He's going there to see her tomorrow with his parents.' She paused. 'He could be there for a while.'

'Of course,' Moreton said getting to his feet and hugging her.

'Even now, he calls her Abuelita Fresa, Granny Strawberry,' she sobbed, recalling the phone conversation.

There was no knowing when Revi would return from Andalusia so, at training the following evening, after Sophia explained things to the rest of the players, Moreton set to work on getting Retama's erstwhile right-winger established in the centre of the field. Despite working on the new set up across Tuesday and Wednesday, the move looked to be anything but comfortable, with

Vasquez's natural tendency to drift out to his more usual wide position. On the second evening, Moreton and Sophia stood and watched the players in a short-sided game. The teams had been organised to help Vasquez adjust to the new role, but it was failing to do so. Standing next to him, the injured Billy Swan had his attention on other things. 'They look good together Jon,' he said.

'Who Billy?'

'Young Josie and Ellis. They're both kids, but one's all action and the other's a bit of a poacher. Give it a couple of years and they could be a decent partnership.'

The comment hardly registered with Moreton. His concerns were focused on solving how to make his team effective without either Revi or Swan, and yet part of the answer had just been suggested to him.

On the way back to their apartment, an hour later, with only Friday's training remaining to iron things out, Sophia made a suggestion. 'We could change the system, rather than the players, Jon.'

'How do you mean?'

'Well, I know playing with a number ten and a creative midfielder in a deeper position suited the players we had, in Billy and Revi, but we don't have either of them available now, not for this weekend at least. So, we could play a different way, and use a system that suits who we do have, not the players who aren't available.'

Moreton thought for a moment. 'Yeah, it's not a bad idea, but that system not only suited Revi and Billy but it also meant we could rotate Samuel and Matías keeping them both fresh, use Guido's pace on the flank and operate with a single striker.'

The more he thought about it though, the more the idea settled into his mind. They crossed the road by the roundabout in front of Carlito's Bar. 'Let's have a glass of wine, and talk about your idea,' Moreton suggested.

Along with the two glasses of wine that Elena brought to their table, there was also a bowl of olives and, for the next 20 minutes, each olive became a member of the Retama squad as Moreton and Sophia toyed with the idea of a number of different systems.

Playing with five at the back, as they had done against Torreaño at the end of last season was one option, but it was discarded as neither Sanz nor Adrián were really suited to a wing back role and even if one of them was deployed as the extra central defender it would mean them playing out of position and still not solve the problem of the flank positions outside of the central three, regardless of how Moreton moved the olives around reassigning them different identities as he did so.

They looked a 4-3-3 formation, but the olive in the centre of the midfield still looked more like a piece of fruit than a creative player. It was Sophia who came up with the next idea. 'What about this?' she suggested, shuffling the olives into two rough lines of four behind one of two.

Moreton was less than convinced. '4-4-2?' he scoffed. 'It's a bit 1970.'

Sophia was indignant at his reply. 'And trying to force players into patterns that they don't fit, is a bit short-sighted as well Jon! Or haven't you noticed?'

Moreton felt admonished. 'I'm sorry,' he said reaching for her hand. 'It's just that 4-4-2 is a bit rigid and doesn't offer much opportunity for flair players except on the flanks.'

Clearly still irritated by his dismissive remarks, Sophia raised her eyebrows at him. 'Well, think about it Jon. For this week at least, we haven't got any creative players, except on the flanks.' The final four words were delivered in exaggerated staccato fashion as she wobbled her head from side to side.

Moreton stroked his forehead with thumb and index finger, before running his hand through his hair. 'You're right,' he conceded. 'And I'm a pompous prat.'

'You're correct on both counts,' Sophia agreed, taking a sip of her wine. 'Certainly, the first at all times, and the second … well, sometimes … not too often.' She smiled. He replied in kind, relieved at being forgiven for his dismissive remark, and invited Sophia to flesh out the idea.

'We keep the back four as usual' she began. 'Play both Samuel and Matías in front of them. Guido on the left and Antonio on the right.' She paused a moment as Moreton nodded at each name in turn. 'Then, do you remember what Billy said earlier?'

Clearly Moreton didn't.

'We play José and Elías as a pair.'

Moreton was silent as he considered the proposal, but Sophia hadn't finished.

'And look at the flexibility it gives us, with options from the bench. Felipe can fit into the back line or midfield. Seb has had two weeks of training now and can fit in anywhere across the middle, or even as a wide player. Plus, we have Juan, who'll give everything wherever we play him.' Convinced that she had won the argument, she picked up one of the olives, flipped it up in the air, caught it and popped it into her mouth.

'That's all fine,' Moreton said rubbing his chin. 'Apart from one thing.'

'What?'

'You've just eaten Guido!'

As the players assembled for training on Friday, Moreton explained the change of plans, and how the team would now be set up for Sunday's game. The relief on Antonio Vasquez's face was there for all to see. He was clearly delighted to be returning to his natural position and his performance against the students would provide ample proof of that. There was also the boost that Juan Torres had now been cleared by the doctor to begin training again. Although Moreton had no reason to consider dropping Jiménez for the younger man, the luxury of a second goalkeeper available on the bench was a comfort he had been without for the previous six games.

Having already told the players the way the team would be laid out, there was little surprise when the selection was confirmed at the end of training. In the seventh game of the season, Retama had struggled to a goalless draw at home to the students in the game where Dani Barbieri had made himself unavailable to prove a point. In the return at the university, there would be plenty of goals.

The journey to the university town of San Juan was one of the longest in Retama's league programme, and unexpected roadworks on the *Autopista* hardly helped matters. A journey that should have taken around 75 minutes occupied the best part of two hours and the coach arrived barely in time to have the team officially registered with the match officials, changed and prepared to start the game, with the minimum of warm up exercises completed.

Getting the team onto the pitch felt like a scramble and their inevitable lack of preparation was illustrated when Retama fell a goal behind with just four minutes played. An innocuous looking cross into the box, from the right, was allowed to run through to the far post where it was crashed home with the Retama back line static. It had been a poor opening four minutes, and the final two at the end of the game would follow a similar pattern. Between those two periods, the reshaped Retama formation and Antonio Vasquez returning to the starting eleven for the first time in three games in his preferred role, would dominate the game.

Conceding the goal was a wake-up call for the eventual victors and, as they cast aside their slumbering start, Retama began to take control of the game. The extra solidity of having both Samuel and Matías patrolling in front of the defence allowed more freedom for both Sanz and Adrián to push further forward supporting the Retama wingers. Ten minutes after conceding, that freedom led to Retama's equaliser.

Sanz took the ball from Jiménez and advanced along the right flank, exchanging passes with Samuel before progressing into the other half of the field and feeding the ball into the feet of Antonio Vasquez. With José Palermo performing so well from the right flank in recent games, the slightly built, mop-haired Vasquez was not only refreshed, but also determined to prove his worth to the team. Controlling the ball and turning to face his marker, he feigned to move left, running his foot over the top of the ball before dragging it sharply back in the opposite direction, skipping past the off-balance defender and haring down the touchline.

The danger drew one of the home team's central defenders out of position to close him down, but a pause and then rapid acceleration left him floundering, and created gaps in the middle of the penalty area. Looking up, Vasquez spotted José Palermo advancing into the area and clipped a right-footed cross towards the penalty spot. The Retama forward met up with the cross, flicked the ball to his right and Elías volleyed home. If their late arrival had left the Retama players dozing for the students' goal, they were wide awake now.

For the next 20 minutes, Vasquez continued to give the home left-back a torrid time, turning him this way and that, with apparent ease, before delivering dangerous crosses into the box. It seemed the inevitable route for a second Retama goal and, five minutes before the break, that inevitability became reality.

This time, it was Victor advancing with the ball out of defence with the dual safety blankets of Samuel and Matías dropping deeper to cover the gap. Vasquez came short to receive the ball, closely followed by his marker. The pass was made and quickly returned as the winger pivoted and raced into space behind the defender. Victor's astute one-two found him again. As he cut inside, José

Palermo drifted wide to create space. Vasquez played the ball to the young forward, whose one-touch return rolled neatly into the winger's path and a low drive from the edge of the area found the corner of the net to put Retama ahead.

At the break there was little for Moreton to say. As he walked back to the dressing room, emphasising the need for concentration was at the forefront of his mind but, as he entered, it was clear that Sanz had already delivered the message effectively, as the second period demonstrated.

Five minutes after the restart, another dazzling run by Vasquez created more mayhem in the home defence and José Palermo side-footed his low cross home. A late home goal with just a couple of minutes on the clock served to concentrate Retama minds on seeing out the victory but, when the referee's whistle ended the game, the points were secured.

The journey back to Retama took just as long as the outward leg, but felt much less stressful. Sitting in their usual positions at the front of the coach, Sophia leaned drowsily on Moreton's shoulders, but sleep was far from the Retama coach's mind. He was already contemplating the club's next game.

'Let's see how Billy's ankle is next week, but I'm thinking about leaving the same team for the next game,' he said.

Sophia's reply was a barely audible mumble but, wrapped up in his own mental deliberations, Moreton took it as agreement.

'Torre del Olmos are bottom of the league and we should be able to beat them, even without Billy. Elías has notched five goals in five games now and José has scored in the last three. They deserve to play. We give the old boy a couple more games rest and then he'll be fit and firing for the run-in and, if all goes well, the play-offs.'

'Hmm. Uh.'

'Yeah, but I had a look at the league table this morning and the win today, plus another three points next week will have us back in contention towards the top again.'

'Huh, hmm.'

'Yeah, OK. I'm probably getting a bit ahead of myself talking about play-offs. Fair enough.'

By the following Friday's training session, Swan's ankle was recovered enough for him to take part. It wasn't up to taking on salsa lessons, as Swan insisted to Izzy, but at least he could run around and take part in a game of football. Moreton's one-sided conversation in the coach, however, had convinced him to retain the same set up for Sunday's game. After training he confirmed an unchanged starting line-up, but with Swan on the bench in case of need.

A typical poacher's strike from Elías, and a brace by Guido, had Retama comfortably ahead at the break and allowed Moreton to give both Matías and Samuel a rest for the second period. Sending on the enthusiastic Felipe Blanco and Sebastián was never going to endanger lack of concentration or effort, and the latter celebrated his return to the team by scoring the fourth goal with a long-range shot. The fifth was added by another substitute when Juan Palermo replaced his brother and nodded home a corner in the dying seconds.

The only players from the Retama bench not used in the romp were Swan and Juan Torres. Before the end of the season, however, both would have crucial roles to play in deciding Retama's fortunes. Moreton's team had now gone seven games since the reverse against San Esteban as the season resumed, winning six, and only that frustrating 4-4 draw away to Costa Locos blotting the otherwise perfect run of results. The next few games would see that form tested.

All Fall Down

Moreton and Sophia had been looking for an opportunity to spend more time with Swan and Izzy and suggested dinner in town on Monday evening. Swan quickly accepted, seeing it as a way of delaying his debut into the world of salsa dancing before trying, and failing, to convince Izzy that his introduction into the dips, tricks and spins of the Latin American dance had slipped his mind.

The two couples met at the Leveche restaurant just across the promenade walkway from the beach. Their table by the window offered a view of the setting sun causing dancing silver darts to rise and fall among the waves as they looked out onto the Mediterranean.

'This is a nice restaurant, Billy,' Moreton offered. 'How did you know about it? Been here before?'

'A couple of times. It's her favourite,' he said cocking his head towards the woman sitting next to him, who offered a playful tap on his arm in reply.

'Well,' Moreton said turning to Swan's companion. 'It's really nice here.'

'And the food is good too,' Izzy replied. 'I can seriously recommend the Paella de Pollo.'

'Erm, that's chicken paella guys, if your Spanish isn't up to translating.' Swan put in unhelpfully.

'Yeah,' Moreton said laughing. 'Cheers, Billy.'

They ordered the paella and, while waiting for it to be served, Sophia decided to pre-empt the inevitable course of the evening's conversation. 'There's bound to be lots of football talk tonight Izzy so, before we get into that, how's business?'

Izzy laughed softly. 'I like football Sophia,' she replied. 'Originally I come from Madrid, the Arganzuel area, not far from the river.'

'Ah,' Sophia said. 'So, you are an Atléti fan?'

Izzy reached down and opened her bag, pulling out her phone with an Atlético Madrid case wrapped around it, featuring a picture of Diego Simeone. 'I am,' she said. 'I love Cholo. He's crazy mad, but 100% Atléti.' She placed the phone back in her bag. 'But business. Yes, business is good at the moment. Mine is just a small office. I only have two people working for me but they are very good. They know the area and they know the market, so we do OK.'

'That's great,' Sophia said.

'Anyway, we've done business now,' Izzy said as the food arrived. 'We can eat and talk football.'

Moreton caught Swan's eye as his friend smiled at the woman he was becoming increasingly smitten with. A quick wink of the eye and nod confirmed to Swan that Moreton wholly approved.

As the evening progressed, CD Retama became the dominant topic for discussion. Initially, Moreton found the conversation difficult as they chatted about next Sunday's game against San Vicente and how important it was to keep the club's run of form going. Swan was fit again and, after a week's training, would be ready to return to the action. After two successive wins, however, and eight goals in the games playing a different formation – one that offered no place for a player of Swan's particular abilities – Moreton was loathe to change things to accommodate his friend's return. Fortunately, Swan removed the elephant from the restaurant.

'Unchanged team for the game then, Jon? Can't change a winning team without good reason, mate.'

'Yeah, Billy. I guess so. You were certainly right about José and Elías. They look good together and they've scored seven goals between them in their last four games. Actually, Elías has scored as many goals in the last seven games as Santi scored all season until he moved on. Plus, Antonio is on fire and Guido notched two against Torre del Olmos. The attack's going great guns.' He paused a little, realising that he had probably made Swan feel a little redundant. 'It'll be great to have you back in the team though, Billy,' without knowing how soon that would be and for how short a time.

'Don't sweat it, Jon,' Swan said calmly. 'I'll wait my turn. It ain't about me. It's about the club. If they keep winning and I keep sitting on the bench, I'll be well happy.'

Izzy reached out her hand and placed it on top of Swan's. 'And that'll mean no more injuries and we can go dancing.' She half-sang, rocking her shoulders, rhythmically. 'Salsa, here we come!'

'Argh,' Swan called out in mock horror. 'Get me on that pitch, Jon. I can take the knocks.' He affected a grimace, and then an idea struck him. 'Tell you what, Jon. In training tomorrow, stick me up against Adrián in a few one-v-ones. He can deliver a couple of his 'Welcome to Retama' tackles and I can escape the clutches of this salsa thing. No pain, no gain, yeah?'

They all laughed and, as Izzy squeezed his hand, smiling at him. Without thinking, Swan leant over and kissed softly her on the lips. It was their first kiss. They both knew it wouldn't be their last. After the meal and coffee, they walked down the steps out of the restaurant and into the pleasantly warm evening, cooled perfectly by the gentle breeze gently drifting in from the sea.

'We're going to get a taxi back home,' Moreton said. 'Fancy sharing one?'

'No, we're good thanks, mate?' Swan replied. 'We're going to walk along the front for a while and watch the sea. I'll catch you both at training tomorrow.' The two couples exchanged hugs and kisses before walking off in opposite directions.

'I don't believe it,' Moreton said quietly to Sophia, looking over his shoulder at the couple laughing together as they strolled away, arm-in-arm.

'Isn't it great?' Sophia answered.

'It is. It's terrific, but it's also… I don't know… unbelievable. I mean it's Billy Swan! I don't know if he's ever had a relationship before in his life. Not one of his one-night-stands after a drunken night. He's had plenty of them. I mean a real relationship.' He shook his head, as if trying to free himself from the clinging, impossible inevitability of his next words. 'I think he's in love. It's Billy Swan. And I think he's in love.'

They both laughed happily, and Moreton drew Sophia closer to him as they walked towards the Taxi rank. 'He won't break her heart, will he?' Sophia asked looking intently into Moreton's eyes.

'Have you seen the way he looks at her?' Moreton asked by way of reply.

'But what happens at the end of the season, when …' Sophia's words trailed off, but Moreton understood where they were leading.

'I don't know. I really don't know,' he said as they climbed into the taxi to head home.

Despite Swan's request at the restaurant, Moreton resisted the temptation of pairing the veteran with Adrián in the week's training session, noticing that there was still the hint of a limp in Swan's gait and that he did even less running than usual. Slightly concerned that the injury perhaps hadn't fully cleared up, he checked with his friend, but Swan assured him that everything was fine, that he was just building himself up slowly, and he'd be ready to come off the bench on Sunday if required. Announcing an unchanged team once more after Friday's training session, the Retama players and coaches were confidently looking forward to Sunday's trip to the small village of San Vicente.

Sophia woke on Sunday morning and turned over in bed expecting to see Moreton, but she was alone. Stretching, and climbing out of bed, she reached for Moreton's old training top and threw it on. She often wore it when they were alone, especially after showering or while relaxing before bed. It was hardly the sort of thing to wear in public, but she liked the effect it had on her lover when she wore it – and nothing else.

Looking out of the bedroom, she could see that the door leading from the living area to the balcony was open, but was cautious not to expose her semi-nakedness to the outside world.

'Jon?' she called leaning around the corner of the door so that the lower half of her body remained hidden.

'Yeah,' Moreton answered. The sound of the balcony chair moving suggested he was about to reappear.

'Hi,' she said, stepping from behind the door as he entered the living area, smiling coyly. 'What are you doing?'

The combination of the training top hanging loosely from her breasts and the exposed length of her legs, beneath it worked their charms once more. Moreton stood transfixed for a moment, a piece of paper in one hand and half-consumed cup of coffee in the other.

'I was just… Sorry, what?'

Sophia suppressed a giggle. 'I said what are you doing?'

Moreton's brain scrambled to recover his composure. 'I woke up early and was just looking at the fixtures from now until the end of the season,' he said, concentrating intently on the piece of paper to focus his concentration

'Really?' she replied. 'Is that what's on your mind right now?' She lifted her hand to ruffle her hair with a breathless sigh, the movement causing the hem of the training top to rise by a further few inches.

'Yeah listen,' Moreton replied, his eyes fixed on the piece of paper. 'After San Vicente today, we're home to UD Callosa and then away to Lacitana. We could win all of those and, if we do, we could go into the last seven games top, or near to it anyway, then we've got some tough games.'

Sophia sighed, but Moreton was in full flow. 'We've got Bugroño, Politanio B and Córuel at home and away games in Palancio and the local derby against Villanuevo, before finishing up with that game at Torreaño.'

Sophia coughed to gain his attention. 'Ahem.'

Moreton held his hand up to signal he had more to say. 'The only fairly uncomplicated game is against Palancio, but even that's away, too. The next few games are going to be really important. We're going to need to have a good points total going into that run in, aren't we?'

The noise of Sophia dropping the discarded training top onto the table, as she stood naked in front of him, eventually drew Moreton's attention from the fixture list he held in his hand. Retama's next three games would deliver far less points than their coach was hoping for. At that moment though, as Sophia slowly stroked the lower lip of her half-open mouth with her index finger, such things were of little importance and football was very much relegated to the back of Moreton's mind.

The game against San Vicente was hardly as Moreton had optimistically expected that same morning. The forward line that had looked so effective against bottom of the table Torre del Olmos now struggled to put together any kind of consistent threat. The team lacked cohesion and once the threat from the flanks had been largely curtailed, Retama had little else to offer. By the break, Moreton had become increasingly convinced that the five goals scored in the previous game had as much to do with the poor quality of the opposition, as it did with the effectiveness of the formation and performance of his team. He decided on changes.

Removing a player who had scored in each of his last four games, and seven times in the same number of appearances looked strange, but Moreton knew it was the correct thing to do. Elías was taken off and Swan went on instead for the second half.

Initially, things improved slightly, as Swan looked to be the conduit between the Retama defence and forward line that had clearly been missing in the first half, but the upswing was patchy at best. Although he saw a lot of the ball, and often linked the play well, creating space on the flanks for both Antonio Vasquez and Guido, at other times he seemed slow and ponderous in his movements. It wasn't difficult for Moreton to discern that something wasn't right and, as a heavy tackle on Guido by one of the home defenders saw Sophia trot onto the field to give the winger attention, he called Swan over to him.

'You OK, Billy?'

'Yeah, just trying to get into the pace of the game, Jon,' Swan replied, but Moreton was unconvinced.

'How's the ankle?'

Swan grimaced a little as he held up his leg and rotated the foot below the injured joint. 'It's still a bit stiff to be honest, mate.'

His concerns confirmed, Moreton pursed his lips in thought as Sophia headed back towards the sidelines with a restored Guido ready to re-enter the action. 'Do you think you should come off?' he asked, as Swan trotted back into the centre of the field.

Swan shook his head, calling over his shoulder, 'Give me ten minutes to see if it loosens up.'

Moreton was now even more convinced that Swan shouldn't be on the pitch, but was pushing himself through the pain barrier, convinced that it was the best way to keep paying back his debt to all at CD Retama. Sophia reached Moreton's side at the same time as Swan's words. 'What did he say?' she asked.

'He wants to give it ten minutes,' Moreton replied. 'But I'm not sure it's a good idea.'

Sophia shook her head. 'You're right. Guido says that Billy's playing like he can't stand on that bad ankle.'

'Stuff ten minutes' Moreton said. 'Let's get him off.' He called across to Juan Palermo to get ready to go on and, at the next break in play, he made the change, telling the older Palermo brother to ask his younger sibling to drop deeper, try and link the play, and drive forward in support whenever he could.

Seeing the change, and realising its inevitability, Swan walked dejectedly to the sidelines, head bowed as Kiko rushed forwards from defence and put his arm around his fellow Musketeer. Swan nodded slowly as the teenager whispered to him and patted him on the back, before returning to his position, with the game about to restart.

High-fiving Juan Palermo as he reached the touchline, Swan shook his head sadly at Moreton. 'I'm sorry, Jon. I thought I could just run it off, but the ankle's giving me proper jip.' He slumped down on the bench and put his head in his hands, pulling his blue shirt up to cover his face.

Sophia nudged Moreton to go and speak with Swan. He nodded, and sat down next to the player who, so many times in his career, would have been delighted to have spent so little time on the pitch; always assuming that it didn't diminish his financial returns. This version of Billy Swan was a different person and, even through the CD Retama shirt covering his face, Moreton could hear the emotional sobs.

'You OK, mate?'

There was no reply.

'Billy? You OK?'

'Yeah, Jon,' came the unconvincing reply.

'Want some water, mate?'

'Yeah, Jon. Cheers.'

Moreton reached down for one of the bottles of water from Sophia's bag. 'Here you go.'

Swan took the bottle, lowered his shirt and tipped some of the water over his head. Any tears were instantly mingled with the water and camouflaged, before he took a long drink from the bottle.

'I've let them down again, Jon,' Swan eventually said, bowing his head.

'What? You've let nobody down, Billy.'

'Yeah, I have. The guys needed me to perform and I can't. They needed me and I've fallen down again.'

'Nobody thinks that, Billy!' Moreton insisted, wrapping his arm around his crestfallen friend's shoulders. 'If it's anybody's fault, it's mine. You've had a bang on the ankle. I shouldn't have even had you on the bench. I saw you limping a bit in training, but I ignored it. There are plenty of games to come, big games. We need to get you fit, properly fit and then you can be the difference when it really matters.' Swan snorted as he took another drink, and looked a Moreton with a wry smile.

'What?' Moreton asked.

'That's exactly what Kiki Dee said.'

The game ended in a 1-1 draw. A late goal by Antonio Vasquez, equalising a San Vicente penalty, conceded when Victor was adjudged to have handled in the area, blocking a shot. Moreton's hopes of securing a good haul of points before going into the last half-dozen games of the season were already beginning to look fanciful.

The home game against UD Callosa had looked the easiest one of the three Moreton had considered as vital before entering the run in, but with Swan now relegated to the sidelines, probably for the next couple of games to ensure his fitness for the final six games of the season and Revi still missing, creativity was at a premium. The following Sunday brought only another 1-1 draw, with Juan Palermo starting and scoring in a changed line-up that also included Felipe Blanco and Sebastian as Moreton sought new impetus, but failed to find it. A draw was probably all that could have reasonably been expected from another uninspired performance. The faltering form of CD Retama was now casting realistic hopes of promotion into doubt, and a 1-0 defeat in the next game, away to Independiente Lacitana only confirmed those fears.

There was, however, still some measure of hope. With each having six games to play, four clubs, including CD Retama, were still in the chase for top spot. Despite, only taking two points from the last nine possible, the other clubs had been taking points from each other, denying anyone an opportunity to open up a gap. Torreaño topped the table with 54 points, so many of which were garnered on the back of Montero's goals. Del Hart's CD Bugroño were second, two points behind, with Retama a further four points back. FC Córuel were in fourth place, a single point behind Moreton's team. Any of the four, who could put a series of good results together, could end the season at the top, but with CD Retama having to face each of their rivals, theirs appeared to be the most difficult of run-ins.

Conversations and Inspirations

Moreton had spent much of the Sunday night following the defeat in Lacitana unable to sleep as the dream that held so many of his hopes and aspirations for the future looked to be slipping through his fingers. There were now just half-a-dozen games remaining in CD Retama's season and they were six points behind top of the table Torreaño. Plus, the five-goal defeat they suffered in the final game before the mid-season break meant that they would surely have an inferior head-to-head record against the club they just edged out of top spot last season. In reality, the difference between the clubs was, effectively, seven points with just 18 to play for.

He was painfully aware that the club was walking a tightrope. Any slip up now would surely be fatal to their hopes of promotion and salvation – and he felt helpless to prevent the fall. After all that the club had gone through – the players, the people who loved CD Retama, valued it, and had given their all for it – he was going to fail them, and this time there was no one else to blame. No one had been working behind the scenes to sabotage things It was down to him. When it came to the crunch, he, Jon Moreton, was going to fail – and then what?

A restless sleep had finally wrapped its weary arms around Moreton during the early hours of Monday morning, just as the rising sun was offering a promise of a brighter day ahead, but anything even approaching optimism felt a long way away. He drifted in and out of consciousness. Each time he awoke the worrying reality hit him.

The illuminated red figures on the clock by his bedside read 6.13 as Moreton's eyes blinked open. He rolled onto his back and let out a deep sigh. Next to him, Sophia slept and, despite an almost irresistible urge to move next to her, draw her close to him, he knew that he couldn't. She was out of reach, too far away, and his arm wouldn't stretch that far, except for the long black tresses of her hair that fell across the pillow. He touched her hair gently before rolling out of bed. Being careful to replace it exactly as he had found it in case she awoke and realised it had been moved.

For a few seconds, he sat on the side of the bed. The only sounds he could hear were the gentle hum of the air conditioner, Sophia's breathing and the rise and fall of the swifts' piercing whistles as they performed their aerobatic swoops and dives in pursuit of the early rising insects in flight. There was another sound as well. An owl? It sounded like an owl to Moreton, although he knew that he'd never really known what an owl sounds like. Perhaps it was an ostrich instead. They sound like owls he decided. It seemed to make sense.

Moreton rubbed his tired eyes and reached into the chest of drawers by his bed. After lifting out the trousers from his only suit, together with a tie from his time at junior school, he pulled out a pair of swimming shorts. Placing them on the ground, he stepped into the shorts with a little jump, raised them over his knees, up to his waist, and tied off the cord in an elaborate knot. Padding quietly out of the bedroom, he snatched one final look at Sophia, checking that her hair was still in the correct position, before blowing her a kiss, and closing the door behind him.

The swimming pool, situated in the middle of the complex, had become more and more popular as many of the apartments were occupied by holidaymakers from Valencia, Madrid, and from overseas, as the weather became warmer. It meant that enjoying a quiet period in the cool water, that guaranteed a welcome solace from the insistently penetrating rays of the hot Spanish sun as spring moved towards summer, was an increasingly rare pleasure.

Deciding to take the escalator with the red and yellow steps that had been installed overnight, Moreton moved silently towards the pool. He ignored the *'Normas de la Piscina'* sign that advised the *'Horarios de la Piscina'* were between 4am and 4pm, that he had never seen before and yet seemed perfectly natural, and stepped into the water.

On he went, deeper and deeper until the water level reached his chest. Then, standing by the side of the pool, he held his nose, curled up his feet and plunged his head below the surface. For a brief few seconds, he looked around, underwater. All was blue. The tiles at the bottom and on the sides of the pool, and even the sky above, as he looked up, was changing colour from semi-darkness into the bright blue of dawn. Everything was blue. Everything was quiet. Everything was still. In a strange, but eerily serene way he felt a comfort that had been denied him as he had tried to sleep in the long preceding hours. For an instant, he closed his eyes.

The next thing he felt was a splash about two metres away from him and a body bobbing about in the water. He pushed his head above the surface, shaking his hair and rubbing his eyes as he did so, to reacquaint his senses with the world above water. The newcomer was a youth of about sixteen. *'Hola,'* he said in an appealingly familiar accent, born of the midlands of England.

'Hi,' Moreton replied. 'Are you English?'

The youth nodded in reply.

'Me too,' Moreton confirmed. 'My name's Jon.'

'Really?' the teenager replied. 'Mine too!' The teenager reached down and rubbed his right knee where a scar betrayed a serious injury yet to be sustained.

Moreton looked around the pool area. 'Are you on your own, Jon? You really shouldn't be in here at this time you know.' He pointed to the *'Reglas de la Piscina'* Board detailing the hours of permitted pool use, even though they failed to support his assertion.

'Yeah, I know, but it's the only time you can be here on your own, isn't it? And, my dad will be here in a minute. He's just gone back to fetch the towels.'

'OK, mate. I can understand that.'

'Do you live here forever?' the youth asked Moreton.

'Yeah,' he replied. 'Well, I don't know that anything is really forever,' he added as the reality of his situation required a correction. 'What about you?'

'No, I don't think so. I'd really like to. We've been here a while now, about 18 months, I guess. I've got so many friends here, and there's this Spanish girl …' The voice trailed off into silence, but Moreton instantly understood perfectly.

Moreton smiled. 'I know what you mean about Spanish girls.' He could see that the younger man was unhappy about things. The smile was not returned.

'I'm going to lose her, aren't I? When things don't work out and I have to go home. I'm going to lose her.' Moreton felt an overwhelming sympathy for his new acquaintance and an irresistible need to reassure him.

'Perhaps you won't have to go. Perhaps things will work out,' he suggested, but received only a sad shake of the head in reply.

'My dad's job over here is going to be finished in a few weeks. He may get a promotion at the office, which would mean us staying, but there are other people after it as well. He thinks they're better than him, and he's almost given up on it. Things don't just work out. You have to make them work for you. Some of the people who he works with say he's really good at what he does, but he doesn't seem to believe in himself enough. I keep telling him to give it all he's got, not to give up. I can't understand why he thinks he'll fail. It's as if he's afraid in case he gives it everything and still fails. He wants to stay here as well. Last year, when we first came over, he met a Spanish woman, someone he works with. She's really nice and they've been together for a long time now. Why isn't he fighting for her as well?'

It seemed a strangely intense conversation to be having with someone that Moreton had never even seen before this early Monday morning encounter, let alone spoken to but, at the same time, it felt natural. 'Do you like your father's girlfriend?' he asked.

'Yeah, she's great,' the teenager replied. 'And she has the same name as my girl as well.'

'Wow, that's a coincidence,' Moreton said, but was hardly surprised by the revelation.

'Not really. His name's the same as mine and yours, isn't it?'

'Is it? I don't know. How would I know?'

'Come on now,' the teenager replied, dipping his head into the water for a moment.

Suddenly the next question felt inevitable.

'What's your dad's girlfriend's name. What's your girl's name?'

The teenager smiled knowingly. 'You know that already, Jon. Don't you?' He jumped in the air, his feet clear of the water, before plunging below the surface. The only word he said before disappearing into the water was 'Sophia!'

Moreton looked into the water, but could see no trace of the teenager. He plunged his own head under the surface, looking around frantically, his mind racing. "Where had he gone?" The pool was empty except for Moreton and the mermaid climbing the ladder at the other end of the pool. The long black tresses of her hair trailed behind as she lifted her perfect body out of the water. How could she climb the ladder without feet, he wondered, as she turned and waved to him saying something indiscernible that merely translated as bubbles. He knew it was 'Goodbye' though. And then she was gone. Now the pool was empty Moreton's new friend was gone. 'Jon,' he shouted underwater. 'Jon, where are you?'

There was no reply. He surfaced again and looked around the pool area. Had the teenager slipped out of the pool? Where was the mermaid? Moreton could see nothing. He tried to part the water with his hands to get a better look below the surface, but could still see nothing. 'Jon, Jon, Jon,' he repeated.

Then the voice shouting the name changed. It wasn't his. It was the teenager's father. 'Jon! Jon!' he called. Then it changed again. Now the voice was female. Was it the teenager's mother? Was it one of the Sophia's? It sounded so familiar.

Lying in bed, Moreton's eyes flicked open, to see Sophia's face inches away from his. 'Jon. Jon. Are you, OK?'

Still lost somewhere in the fog between the realms of REM and reality, Moreton struggled to find the right path, but Sophia's smile guided him home.

'You were dreaming, and talking in your sleep. In fact, you were almost shouting, and struggling around.'

'I'm sorry. What was I ...' he paused as the memory of the subconscious encounter with himself floated around in his mind, defying gravity, refusing to be pinned down and analysed. 'I was asleep?'

Sophia smiled at him and kissed him on the forehead. 'You were, my love,' she said. 'But where were you. Who were you talking to?'

Moreton rubbed his forehead and sighed. 'Myself, I think.'

'OK, but you're right there inside yourself, you don't need to shout to make yourself heard, Jon,' she said with an empathetic smile.

'Sometimes you do need to shout to make yourself understood, and to understand,' Moreton offered enigmatically, before adding, 'Can I just hold you for a while? Just lie in each other's arms for a few minutes. Hold on like we'll never let each other slip away?'

Sophia's beaming smile was enough of an answer as she fell into his arms. For an hour that was how they slept and when Moreton awoke again, he was filled with a new determination to save Club Deportivo Retama and stay in Spain with Sophia as the love-struck teenager, as the man he was now, and as the father he would become.

The dream was still echoing around semi-coherently in Moreton's head as he and Sophia sat on the apartment balcony eating breakfast when her phone rang. She went into the living room to answer it and, although he could not clearly make out the conversation she was having with the caller in Spanish, hearing the name 'Revi' mentioned suggested to Moreton who she was speaking to. A couple of minutes later, Sophia returned and sat down at the table, her face betrayed the story of the conversation.

'She died on Thursday,' she said sadly.

Moreton reached out his hand and gently squeezed hers. 'She must have been quite old,' he offered sympathetically. 'And she had clearly been ill for a while.'

Sophia nodded.

'How's Revi taking it?'

Sophia dabbed at her eyes with a tissue before answering. 'He's not bad,' she said. 'He was able to spend some time with her before she passed. I think that was very important to him.'

'That's good,' Moreton said softly.

'On the night before she died, Revi sat with her for a couple of hours before she slept. They just spoke about the old days when he was young and he used to eat all of the strawberries on the way to the market. It made her smile, and he loved that.'

Moreton just nodded.

'Just before she fell asleep, she told him: *"Siempre come la fruta cuando puedas. No espere hasta que sea demasiado tarde".*'

'I'm sorry,' Moreton confessed. 'I don't understand all of that.'

'Sorry Jon. It just sounds better in Spanish,' Sophia said. 'It means "Always eat the fruit when you can. Don't wait until it's too late."'

Moreton smiled. 'She was very wise, Abuelita Fresa.'

'It was the last thing she ever said to Revi. Apparently, she slipped away peacefully overnight, but he told me that when he saw that she was asleep, she still had that smile on her face.'

'I guess that's the best way to go, forever locked into happy memories.'

'Yes,' Sophia agreed, still a little tearful. 'I think it made things so much easier for Revi.'

'That's good ... Well, not good of course but if it eases the pain a little for him, it's got to help.'

'I think it did.'

'When's he thinking of heading back to Retama?'

'Tomorrow. The funeral is today. Then Revi and his mother will be heading back. His father, it was his mother, is staying there to sort a few legal things out about the property and her will. Revi wants to be at training tomorrow.'

'He shouldn't rush back for training.'

'No Jon,' Sophia argued. 'He wants to. I told him to take his time, but he said that you should always eat the fruit when you can. It's an important time for the club, for the town, for his friends. He didn't want to wait until it was too late.'

'Wow,' Moreton exclaimed. 'Retama. Está en la cabeza. Está en el corazón.' He paused as a thought struck him. 'I know where else it should be as well!'

An hour later Moreton and Sophia walked out of the Estadio Antonio Núñez, waving to Esteban as he locked the gate behind them. 'OK,' Moreton said. 'We're set. If you ring the guys and get them all to bring in their shirts tonight, Esteban will have everything ready.'

'I think it's a great idea, Jon.'

'I just hope the players do too.'

Amor Vincit Omnia

As he had promised, Revi returned for training on Tuesday evening. Everyone offered their sympathy to him, but he insisted that they should concentrate on training and preparing for the game at the weekend against Bugroño, saying that winning would be the best way to honour his grandmother. Moreton had been planning to give additional inspiration to the team after the training session, but Revi's words had already got them heading in that direction.

With the young playmaker back and available for selection, plus the return of a now fully fit Swan, the coach initially had a full squad to work with, although that was compromised when Jiménez damaged an ankle, landing awkwardly after catching a ball during a drill concentrating on crosses into the box. Frustratingly for Moreton, it came almost at the end of the training session and, although it wasn't a serious injury, it would mean at least a week out of action and a return to the team for Juan Torres. Fortunately, having the young goalkeeper ready to step up meant that the loss of the veteran should not be much of a problem.

After the players had warmed down, and showered, Moreton asked them to wait in the dressing room for a few minutes and have their Retama shirts with them. After Sanz signalled that all was ready, Moreton, Sophia and Esteban entered the dressing room. The old man carried two large bags, one empty and one full and closed at the top with a drawstring, its contents hidden. He placed both bags down in the middle of the room, as Moreton began to speak with Sophia translating.

'*Somos Retama,*' he began quietly. 'We all know that. And, as José told us', he said, nodding towards the younger Palermo sibling. '*Está en nuestras cabezas. Está en nuestros corazones...* It's in our heads. It's in our hearts.' He paused as everyone nodded in agreement, and Juan Palermo put his arm around his younger brother's shoulders. Moreton continued with his theme.

'But it should be somewhere else as well,' he said. 'It should be in a place where everyone can see how proud we are of being CD Retama, of being Retama, of being part of the town, of being part of this group of exceptional people, of being part of this family.' He raised his voice, clenching both of his fists. 'We should shout it out!'

Moreton paused again, before pulling open the closed bag and dipping his hand into it. He pulled out his zipped tracksuit top. On the front, was the club crest and the initials JM but, when he turned it around to show the players the back, all became clear.

On a patch of dark blue paint, the word "Retama" had been hand-painted in white by Esteban. Moreton held up the top, and then clutched it to his chest. 'Soy Retama,' he declared in a voice that resonated with quiet determination and drew cheers and applause from all in the room. 'And I want to tell all of the world who I am.' Then Sophia did the same to reveal her top, with the same wording on the back, and repeated the phrase. Again, the cheers.

Moreton then nodded to Esteban. This was going to be his show now. The old man reached into the bag and pulled out the number one shirt. On the chest was that same patch of blue paint and the bold claim "Retama" in white. Esteban held it out to Jiménez, who hobbled across to take it from him. He hugged the old man and then Moreton and Sophia in turn. Holding the shirt up he shouted. *'¡Soy Retama! Y quiero que todos sepan quién soy.'*

Next was Sanz, and then Adrián, then Samuel and so on. Each were gifted the last season's shirt with the name of "Broome Cerámica" painted over with Retama blue and the name of the club adorned in white. Affirmation of renewed ownership by the town. The only exception was Guido, whose shirt had been torn in the game against Desorio, but Esteban promised him that he would take his current shirt and apply the paint as required to make it part of the new set.

When all was finished, the initially empty bag was now filled with shirts that carried the sponsor's name of Bella Cucina on it, other than Guido's shirt, which Esteban held. Moreton spoke, as Sophia translated. 'Last season, in the play-off games, the other team laughed at these shirts.' He shook his head. 'They did not know what they were doing. We have six games to play before the end of the league season. We will wear these shirts in each of those games – and those beyond.' He paused again, gripping his top to his chest. 'We will wear them proudly and,' he added,' I promise you now, no one will be laughing at them now. Because we are Retama!'

The players all stood and cheered, clapping and stamping their feet. In the small dressing room, the noise echoed around and around. Esteban patted Moreton on the back and, despite the raucous clamour, Moreton clearly heard the old man's gruff voice declare, *'¡Eres Retama!'*

The other sessions of the week's training were taken up in preparation for the upcoming game against Bugroño. When Retama had played the away fixture, the three experienced players that Del Hart had brought across from England had been key to the way the home side played. Moreton was now looking for a way to turn that knowledge to his, and his team's, advantage. Santi had been subdued by the experienced George Clift at the heart of the home defence, and it was only Juan Palermo who had enjoyed much success. Moreton also remembered though that it was the speed of Guido and the guile of Elías that had conjured up Retama's equaliser late in the game.

He decided to start with the elder Palermo brother as the front man to work the ageing defender and then look to put Elías on late in the game when his fresh legs and sharp thinking could be most effective. He would also use the pace of Guido to ensure Clift was kept busy by encouraging the Retama speedster to look for options to switch with Palermo, offering Clift, and Karl Bryant in front of him, the threat of pace and direct running as a different problem to the physical challenge of Palermo. After a couple of sessions concentrating on how to constantly move the older Bugroño players around, Moreton announced his team on Friday evening.

With Juan Torres back in goal, it was reassuring to have the regular back four of Sanz, Kiko, Victor and Adrián in front of him. Matias partnered Revi in the centre of midfield with Antonio Vasquez and Guido on the flanks of the attack. Swan would return to his number ten role behind Juan Palermo. Swan's role was to look for Palermo making runs wide, drawing Clift with him, to create spaces in the middle where Vasquez and Guido could then drive at the defence. If Clift didn't follow the striker, Retama would have an overload on the flank. Swan would have to pick his option with care.

At the back, Moreton emphasised to Matías to be vigilant about picking up the astute runs of Feliciano from deep, and to cover for Kiko or Victor if they were drawn out of position. Retama's margin for error across the last six games of the season was narrow in the extreme, if they were to maintain any viable hopes of topping the league. With Torreaño having a comfortably winnable fixture away to San Vicente and FC Córuel at home to San Esteban, a win was essential. Otherwise, Retama's rivals would be disappearing away over the horizon.

On Saturday morning, as Moreton and Sophia lay in bed, locked in an embrace, the shrill whistle of the ringtone on Moreton's phone was hardly what they wanted to hear.

'Ignore it,' Sophia suggested.

'Defo!'

The phone rang out, but started again a few seconds later. 'Oh, come on,' Moreton said exasperated.

'I think you'd better answer it,' Sophia sighed, rolling back to her own side of the bed.

'It'll wait,' Moreton insisted, following her and gathering her back up in his arms. It did, but only for a few seconds before the ringtone insisted on a response.

Moreton flicked up his eyebrows and blew out his cheeks in resignation. He kissed Sophia tenderly. 'Wait there,' he said. 'Don't go anywhere.' Releasing her from his arms with a reluctant sigh, he reached for the phone sitting on top of the chest of drawers by his bedside, as Sophia drew her fingers playfully up and down his back.

'Billy!' Moreton exclaimed seeing the caller's name displayed on his phone. 'What the hell does he want at this time of the morning?'

Sophia sat up. Her attention now drawn from Moreton's body. 'Is something wrong?'

'There'd better be,' Moreton replied, as he answered the phone, and sat on the side of the bed.

The tinny sound of Swan's voice on the other end of the call was far from clear enough for Sophia to hear, but from Moreton's side of the conversation, it quickly became clear that their plans for the next half hour or so would have to be postponed for a while. She rolled out of bed and into the bathroom to shower. By the time she emerged again, wrapped in a towel, Moreton was dressed in a T-shirt, shorts and sandals.

'Is everything OK?' Sophia asked as Moreton was clearly going out.

'I'm not sure. Billy said he needed to talk about something important. He was on his way to the stadium to help Esteban with the painting, but asked me if I would meet him in Carlito's for a cup of coffee first.'

'Why?'

'I don't know. He said he'd explain when he saw me, but asked me not to tell anyone what it as all about. I told him that wouldn't be difficult because he hadn't yet told me what it was all about.'

'You'd better go and find out then, hadn't you?' Sophia said turning away to get dressed. 'And then you can avoid telling me all about it. And, don't forget, I'm meeting Elena for lunch in town so I'll probably be gone when you get back, yes?'

'Sure, OK.' And with that, Moreton left the apartment and headed for Carlito's bar for his mystery liaison with Billy Swan.

Five minutes later he was sitting at a table on the terrace of Carlito's bar opposite a clearly concerned Swan as the early morning sun was still rising, each with a cup of *café con leche* in front of them. 'So, what's so urgent, Billy? What's the big deal, then?' Moreton asked, the traces of frustration from his doomed earlier tryst with Sophia still fresh in his mind.

'Was it bad timing?'

Moreton's sense of irritation had hardly been disguised. 'Yeah, you could say that.'

'I'm sorry Jon. But I've got this problem. It's been going round and round in my head for days and I just need to get my brain around it.'

'OK, Billy,' Moreton suddenly felt guilty for his sullen demeanour. His friend clearly needed his help. 'Don't worry about me. What's on your mind, mate?' He asked, taking a sip of his coffee.

Swan took a deep breath. 'OK, here we go.' He paused and blew out his cheeks. 'How much does it cost to live in Spain?'

During the brief journey from the apartment to the bar, Moreton had considered the various things that may have been troubling his friend. The cost of living in Spain, hadn't been remotely near the top ten. 'What, Billy? Seriously?' Moreton had just raised the cup to his lips again, but immediately placed it down again. 'You've got me here to discuss the economic plight of the Spanish people?'

Swan shook his head. 'Jeez, Jon. For a bright bloke you're a bit on the slow side sometimes.' Moreton was confused, and Swan could tell. He would need to be more specific. 'Look Jon,' he began. 'You've seen me and Izzy together. It's a bit like you and Sophia. It works.' He nodded at Moreton, inviting agreement. 'You know what I mean, don't you?'

The clarification was sufficient. 'You're thinking about staying here?' Moreton asked.

Swan shook his head. 'No, of course not.' He paused. 'Except, yes. I guess I am.' He picked up his cup, took a drink and then looked up at the skies, seeking some kind of inspiration. 'Hearing you talk about just being six games left and then, perhaps a couple of play-off games, smacked me in the kisser. In a few weeks, I'll be going back to England. And then what? What about Izzy? I can't ask her to go back with me. She's got a business here and family, and what can I offer her in England? Sharing a small flat with me? So, I was thinking, if it ain't too expensive here, I could live here for a while, and fly back to work at the soccer schools for a few days and then fly back ...'

Moreton smiled, but also recognised his friend's dilemma. 'That won't work, Billy. You know that don't you.'

Swan sighed in resignation. 'I know Jon. But what can I do?'

'Look, mate. Living here is far cheaper than in England, but flying backwards and forwards every few days is going to cost an arm and a leg. Plus, you'll be exhausted all the time, and not giving sufficient time to the schools or to Izzy.'

Swan grimaced and nodded. He knew it was true. He'd known it for a while, but had clung on to an impossible dream, hoping that Moreton could somehow make it real. In the ten months since he had left Spain, full of shame and regret at what he had been compelled to do, Swan's life had been a whirlwind of change – all for the better. And now, for the first time in his life, he had found someone who he knew was more important to him than himself. He couldn't contemplate losing her. 'It's tearing me apart, Jon. I was even tempted to have a drink last night after Kiko came and took her home after dinner. I sat in the hotel bar and felt empty, but knew that if I went home and left her here, it would a million times worse. There was just me and the waiter in the bar. No one else. I could have a couple of drinks, to drive the worry away. Who would know? I ordered a large vodka and sat there looking at the glass for, oh, I dunno, ten minutes, I suppose, without touching it. Then I remembered that not drinking had led me to Izzy and if I went back down that road, I'd screw it all up anyway. So, l left it on the table and went to bed.'

For Moreton, all of the other things that he had thought Swan might have wanted to talk to him about paled into insignificance by comparison to the pain his friend was enduring. 'That must have been tough, Billy.'

Swan nodded.

'You should have called me.'

'I was going to, Jon, but what could you do about it, other than tell me that I was being a daft prat.'

Moreton felt an irresistible need to calm his friend and ease the turmoil in his head but, as Swan had said: "What could he do?" It was a question to which he had no answer at the time, but he had to convince Swan that there was a solution.

'Billy, do you love her?'

Swan sighed. 'Me? Love? Christ, Jon, what a question. The only thing I've ever loved in my life is me, and brass. I don't know what it feels like to love somebody.'

'Yes, you do.' Moreton replied. 'No one talks like you've just talked if they're not in love with someone.'

'Sodding hell, Jon. This is like being at an AA meeting or something.' Swan glanced around at the other customers in the bar. Some were drinking coffee. Others eating breakfasts of various kinds. No one was listening to their conversation but Swan felt a need for increased confidentiality. He leant forwards and whispered. 'Of course, I bloody love her, you muppet. Why do you think I'm telling you this!' What felt like a guilty secret had tumbled from his lips and with it came an acceptance that had been fighting for freedom, but entrapped in his subconsciousness for months.

'OK, Billy. In that case, there's no way we aren't solving this. I refused to lose Sophia and I'm not going to stand by and watch you lose Izzy. And, watch Izzy lose you too.' He pointed a finger directly at Swan's face. 'We'll find a way. Got it!'

Swan took hold of the hand with the finger pointing towards him, gripping it tightly. 'Got it!' he confirmed.

'Remember, Billy. Love finds a way. "Amor vincit omnia,"' Moreton added, throwing in the only phrase in Latin he had ever been able to commit to memory.

'Gotcha, Jon. Cheers, mate,' Swan declared confidently. 'But who's this Vincent geezer?'

Hours later, after Moreton had eaten lunch and swum for while in the complex swimming pool, he was sitting on the balcony, lost in contemplation, when he heard the door of the apartment open and Sophia return from her lunch date with Elena. Dropping her bag on the sofa, she walked out onto the balcony and sat down opposite Moreton. He smiled at her warmly. The last few hours had been filled with thoughts of Billy Swan, Isabella and how he could prevent what looked like being an inevitable and sad parting for them. It made him appreciate the strength of his relationship with Sophia more than ever.

'So?' Sophia asked. 'What's the issue with Billy? Or can't you tell me.'

Moreton drew a deep breath. 'I can only tell you if you promise to help solve the problem' he replied enigmatically.

'Well, I don't know if I can help you solve the problem unless you tell me what it is,' she said with a smile. 'And then I can tell you whether you can tell me or not.' It was a triumph of logic and despite concerns for his friend's dilemma, Moreton had to smile. He reached out and took her hand, squeezing it gently before releasing it and propping his chin on joined palms.

'Well, I guess it's nothing that you don't know anyway, but it's about Izzy. Well, about Billy and Izzy and what happens at the end of the season.'

'Is he wondering how to let her down lightly when he leaves?'

'Nope,' he said definitively. 'He doesn't want to leave. He loves her and wants to be with her. He knows he can't take her back to his small apartment in London. Her business is here. Her family is here.'

'You mean Billy wants to stay here in Spain? With Izzy? Be together with her?'

'Pretty much.'

'Wow! That's brilliant.' Sophia said, then paused. 'Isn't it?'

'It is, but how does Billy make it work, I mean financially and with his commitment to Bobby Broome after all that Bobby's done for him. What about the Soccer Schools?'

'Sorry,' Sophia admitted, deflated. 'Of course. I suppose the schools are not that much of an issue. Didn't Billy say that some other players were involved there and it was pretty much running itself with Señor Broome's management company?'

'Yeah, I guess so. But what about finance? Billy won't just live off Izzy. He wouldn't do that, even if she offered. If he stays in Spain, he'll have to find some way of earning his keep, and he can't keep playing much longer, not that CD Retama could pay him enough to live on in the longer term, anyway.'

'What about something to do with football, but not playing?'

'Yeah, but what? He's done a bit of radio work in the past, but it was all pretty much small-scale stuff in his local area, and because he was a bit of a name in England. That wouldn't work over here.'

'No, that's true. Perhaps something outside of football. What else can he do?'

'Billy? Well, he's played football and done his coaching at the Soccer Schools, but that's about it,' Moreton said with a resigned sigh.

'Don't worry, Jon,' Sophia said brightly trying to inject some positivity into a conversation that was heading remorselessly towards disappointment. 'We'll work something out. Look at us. Love finds a way. It always does.'

'Amor vincit omnia,' Moreton confirmed.

'That's right Jon. Love conquers all.'

'We just need to give it a nudge in the right direction then?'

'Yes. Let me take these shoes off, make a cup of coffee and I'll tell you about Elena and Nicolás.'

'OK, but I've told you about the problem now, so you have to help me solve it. That was the deal. OK?'

'That was the deal,' Sophia replied over her shoulder.

Moreton was still deep in thought when Sophia returned minutes later with two cups of coffee and sat down again. It jolted him back to the present.

'Thanks,' he said. 'So, all good with Elena and Nicolás?' For both of them, it was a relief to put the problems of Billy Swan to one side for a moment, and concentrate on something else. There was a link between the two subjects but Moreton and Sophia were yet to uncover it.

'Yes,' Sophia said with a smile. 'Elena seems very happy. Nicolás stayed with the business when Cerámica Internacional bought Broome Cerámica and he says that despite all the talk around the dodgy-dealing that Charlie Broome set up, they seem really good people to work for. Keen to invest in local people and develop them, both for the business and the locality in general. He's also been promoted twice.'

'That's great. Good for Nicolás. He always seemed like a decent guy. I'm glad things are going well for him and Elena.'

'Yes, he seems very happy according to Elena and things are great between them. In fact, she said that if the company ends up building their new factory somewhere different, Nicolás will be heading up a programme to train new staff there. It'll mean more money for him and they can then buy a house together, and will probably get married. All we have to do is win the league and ensure we get promotion. Then Nicolás will be earning money training people, which he really enjoys, and they will have their future together sorted. No pressure on us then, Jon.' She smiled at him, but received no response. Moreton's mind was elsewhere.

'I said, Jon, no pressure on us, then.' Then louder and with more than a hint of irritation at apparently bring ignored. 'Jon! Are you listening to me?'

For the final couple of seconds, it was clear that he hadn't been but, the smile slowly spreading across his face suggested that her words, ahead of that, had been fully appreciated. He clapped his hands together sharply as an idea solidified in his mind. 'You, my love, mi amor, are a genius!'

'What?'

'I asked you to help me solve a problem, and ten minutes later. There you are with the solution. Genius, pure genius. I'm just surprised it took you ten minutes.'

Sophia was baffled by Moreton's reaction to her news about Elena and Nicolás but, as Moreton jumped to his feet, kissing her on the head as he passed on his way back into the apartment, he clearly had no time to explain.

'Where are you going, Jon?' Sophia called after him.

'I need to speak to Joaquín,' he shouted back.

Nostalgia isn't always a thing of the past

By the time they arrived at the Estadio Antonio Núñez for the game against Bugroño, Moreton had explained his idea to Sophia and, after a couple of phone calls had set the wheels in motion. All he could do now was to wait and see if things panned out as he hoped. Sophia had suggested telling Swan that they were working on an idea, but Moreton was reluctant to build his friend's hopes up in case in case the plan then fell flat. Besides, with Del Hart sitting on the away team coaches' bench, this would be first time that Swan had played for Retama when the opposition coach knew all about him. There would be more than enough to occupy his mind, without complicating matters.

To even things up, Moreton had filled Swan in on the conversation with Hart during the away fixtures, that he knew his old coach had approached Swan and about the players that Hart had brought across to Spain, when Swan had rebuffed his offer. The names had meant little to Swan though. Whilst he was climbing the ladder to top tier football, Hart's recruits had been earning their money in the lower reaches of English football's pyramid. The one similarity though, was that each of Hart's players and Swan had qualified to be professional footballers by earning their diplomas at both the school of hard knocks and the university of life.

As the players assembled in the dressing room ahead of the game, Moreton took time to suggest that it would be highly likely that Hart, identifying Swan as the key creative asset in the Retama attack, would deploy Karl Bryant to man mark him and seek to limit his effectiveness. After speaking with the veteran earlier, Swan had suggested that if this did happen, he could drop deeper to either escape Bryant's attentions, or create space for Revi to move forward instead. Moreton emphasised to Revi that if Swan could draw Bryant out of position, it would be important for him to exploit the space and drive forward to take full advantage.

The importance of the game was emphasised by the crowd that had gathered to watch the game. Despite the poor run of late, fans of the club had broadly kept faith with the team, and a sizeable support was present. A loss, or probably even a draw, would see Retama's title hopes slide from the improbable to virtually impossible category. In the last three games, two draws and a defeat had seriously imperilled Retama's title ambitions. A win in this game, against one of their rivals was vital. The game in Bugroño had been difficult and Retama had been fortunate to escape with a draw after Elías scored his late goal. This game would be very different.

As the players trotted out of the dressing room towards the pitch, Moreton noticed the unmistakable figure of Del Hart waiting on the touchline to greet Swan. As the veteran player reached his old coach, the two men embraced and patted each other on the back. There was a clear affection between them and suddenly Moreton felt like an outsider, watching an event he had no part in. At first, he thought of walking over to join the two men as they chatted, but decided he would feel like an interloper and, instead, headed for the Retama bench, and sat down next to Sophia.

'They must have known each other a long time ago,' Sophia surmised as she watched Moreton's rapt attention on Hart and Swan.

'Yeah, even before the "new" Billy appeared, despite the way he was, he always remembered the people who stood by him and helped him.'

The two men were still talking when the referee called the captains forward for the coin toss. 'It's time,' Moreton decided aloud. Standing, he whistled to Swan and pointed to the pitch. Swan raised his hand and trotted away as his old friend walked back towards the benches. As he did so, Hart called out to Swan, and held his hand to his ear with only the thumb and the little finger extended, in the shape of a telephone receiver. Swan replied with a thumbs-up acknowledgement. Moreton and Sophia watched and then turned to each other. Before they had a chance to discuss what they had seen, however, Del Hart was approaching with his usual chirpy greeting. 'How you doing, kids?'

'Sorry about that,' he added. 'But I ain't had a chance to catch up with Billy for ages. It's great to see him again. He's looking pretty good for an old 'un. You must be looking after him.'

Moreton returned the greeting with a smile. 'Hi, Del. Good to see you again.' Then looked across to Swan. 'Yeah, this one here,' he nodded towards Sophia, 'keeps him pretty fit.'

'Well, I hope he's off form today, eh?' Hart nudged Sophia and chuckled with an impish wink. 'After that though, you can take as many points off those other geezers around us in the table as you want.'

Moreton smiled and took Hart's hand as it was offered. 'After the game, Jon,' Hart asked as he turned away towards his own bench. 'Can I have quick with on the QT?'

'Sure, Del. Of course.' As Hart walked away, Moreton turned to Sophia and shrugged his shoulders. Just then, the whistle sounded to start the game.

Very much as Moreton had expected, Karl Bryant made a bee-line for Swan and, for much of the game would be a constant shadow for the Retama player. For the first 15 minutes or so, Hart's attempts to subdue his former charge's influence on the game looked to be effective but, as Swan wandered deeper, drawing Bryant away from his comfort zone in front of the Bugroño defence, gaps began to appear in the visitors' back line. With 20 minutes played, the first goal arrived

Remembering his coach's instructions, as Swan drifted deep and to the left, Revi received the ball from Samuel and, after exchanging crisp passes with Antonio Vasquez darted forward into the Bugroño half of the field. Realising the ploy, Bryant tried to chase back, but the passing years had stolen much of the zest from his legs, and he couldn't prevent Revi closing in on the penalty area. Using his muscular physique, Juan Palermo cleverly blocked George Clift's attempt to challenge and, from 25 metres, Revi hit a rising shot that ripped into the top corner of the net to put Retama ahead. Celebrating, he ran towards the corner flag, before turning to face his teammates and raising his shirt to reveal a white vest with a crudely drawn strawberry on it. He kissed both of his index fingers before raising them to the sky. Abuelita Fresa looked down and smiled at her *nieto favorito*.

Too late, Del Hart realised how Swan had taken Bryant for a walk down the garden path and, at the next break in play, he called the rugged midfielder across to him, instructing him to stay in position and just pick Swan up as he advanced. The damage had been done, though, and Retama were in the ascendancy. They doubled their lead five minutes later. With Bryant now more permanently stationed in the heart of the Bugroño midfield, Moreton's ideas of Guido and Antonio Vasquez utilising any spaces in the middle created by Swan were limited. On the flanks, however, they were enjoying more success.

The right was particularly productive where Vasquez was causing repeated problems for his defender with trickery and acceleration. On three separate occasions, he escaped his marker and provided crosses into the area. Only the experience and canny defence-craft of Clift had prevented Juan Palermo profiting from the winger's deliveries. On the fourth occasion, though, the defender's luck was out. Palermo found a couple of metres space and the precisely delivered ball was bound for his head before a nudge by Clift sent the striker tumbling. The fall to the floor was undoubtedly exaggerated but, much as the defender had escaped a couple of similar examples of gamesmanship, this time he was the fall guy as the referee pointed to the spot. Swan stepped up and delivered with his usual aplomb. At the break, there seemed little way back into the game for the visitors and Moreton's insistence to his players on a solid first 15 minutes of the second period was overly cautious, if understandably so.

The Retama players responded precisely as their coach had demanded. Despite their forward threat being diminished somewhat by a dogged concentration and determination not to concede, as the hour mark passed, Feliciano had hardly been a factor in the game. Had his adoring young support choir been in attendance, their attention might well have drifted away.

With 15 minutes to play, and a job done, Moreton removed an exhausted Juan Palermo who had worked the ageing Clift almost to a standstill. It was time to deliver the coup de grâce. Elías was sent on. Across the last twelve months or so, Moreton had come to regard the elder Palermo brother as an indispensable and hugely valuable member of the Retama squad. Always reliable, always fully committed. Whatever task Moreton had given him, he had delivered. Despite the incident when he collided with the goalpost in the play-off game against Atlético Santa Kristina at the end of the previous season, he had emerged with all parts still in place and, regardless of all the efforts of this term, when others would have described his commitment as working them off, that remained the case. Juan Palermo had *cojones*.

At 2-0, the game was done and dusted, but the full vindication of Moreton's game plan was delivered with six minutes to play when Elías scored the third goal. Receiving the ball from Guido, Swan elegantly turned the attendant Bryant and slipped the ball through the Bugroño back line. Running onto the pass, Elías dragged the ball around the goalkeeper and rolled it into the net.

At the final whistle, Moreton punched the air before hugging Sophia and congratulating his players as they left the field. Ten metres away, Del Hart was commiserating with his players instead. When all had left the field, Hart walked across to Moreton, arms outstretched, palms upwards.

'Ah, what can you do, eh? Billy's still got it, ain't he?'

'Yeah, Del. He's exceptional. But we were lucky today. Things went our way.'

'Nah, give over, mate. We were second best today, a bit like your lot were at our place, but you escaped with a draw and we got "Swaned" today.' Hart lifted his cap and wiped his balding pate before replacing the headpiece that Moreton had never previously seen him without. 'It ain't over yet though, Sunny Jim,' he said. 'Looking at the fixtures coming up, and your games, we've still got a chance and we'll be fighting to the end.'

Moreton smiled and nodded politely, as Sophia waved at Hart before walking away. 'What did you want to talk about, Del?'

'OK, Jon. Here's how it is.' He sat down on the Retama bench, inviting Moreton to join him. 'I'm a straight up sort of bloke and can't be doing with any of this back of the hand sort of talk, so I wanted to give you the grift on things. The guys at my club still want Billy to join us, so I've told him that, wherever you guys are at the end of the season, there's a home for him at Bugroño. We can offer him a deal for a couple of years, pay him decent money and there's a couple of other things that might be attractive to him as well. To be honest, the thought of pairing him up with Alfie has me licking my lips, Jon.'

Suddenly, the significance of the "telephone" gesture Hart had made to Swan ahead of the game was clear. For a moment, Moreton was silent, as Hart's words sank in.

'I just wanted to be honest with you, Jon. I know Billy will be a free agent then, and can do what he wants, but I don't work like that. I'm sure he'll tell you about it anyway, but I wanted you to hear it from me first. It's the way I always work.'

Moreton's question was inevitable, if inappropriate. 'What did Billy say?'

'He said he'd think about it and ring me.'

'OK,' was the full extent of what Moreton could offer. 'Thanks,' felt a strange thing to add, but he also appreciated Hart's honesty.

'Good luck for the rest of the season, Jon.'

'Cheers. You too, Del.'

As the two men parted, Moreton headed for the Retama dressing room. His celebratory mood of a few brief minutes ago was now overshadowed by the cloud of doubt and concern hanging over him. He opened the door to be met by a chorus of cheers and raucous celebration. It was difficult not to get swept up in the emotion and, for a few minutes, the conversation with Del Hart was pushed to the back of his mind. Thirty minutes later, though, as he waited outside the dressing room, shaking the hand of each of the players as they left, it was front and centre again, especially as the shuffling figure of Billy Swan appeared in the doorway, inevitably accompanied by Kiko and Victor. Moreton beckoned Swan to one side and, after asking Kiko to wait for him, Swan ambled over to join the

The gap to Torreaño was still six points and now there were just five games left to play. The following Sunday, Retama would travel to Villanuevo for the 'Derby' game. Anything other than a win was unthinkable.

Since Moreton's first experience of this fixture, the tension between the sets of players of each club had eased a little, and although the rivalry was just as fierce, the reduced feeling of animosity had been maintained. Despite that, there was still an enhanced tension in training the following week, as the importance of the game added fuel to the fire inevitably still alive between the two neighbouring clubs. And, just to raise the temperature even higher, Moreton's concerns about Swan's intentions continued to trouble him. They would have their day.

Ahead of training on Friday, sitting on the coaches' bench as the players arrived, Moreton confided to Sophia that, given the likelihood that Sunday's game would have a physical edge to it, he was thinking of making changes to both the formation and the players selected, to avoid being muscled out of the game. Sophia was far from convinced by his logic. She argued that if you go looking for trouble, you're bound to find it. And that was what he was doing. When he told her the team he planned to announce after training, however, she suspected that a different rationale was being played out.

'Is this about Billy?'

'No,' Moreton protested, but Sophia was unconvinced.

'Have you said anything to him yet?'

'No, and he's not said anything to me either. So, that's where we are.' The almost petulant reply virtually confirmed her suspicions.

'Jon, you're wrong, and I think you know that you are.' It was a witheringly accurate assessment, but given Moreton's state of mind, it only encouraged him to dig deeper into the entrenched opinions that were shaping his thinking.

'Well, let's see. Shall we?'

The evening's training was completed with the minimum of communication between Retama's two coaches and as they gathered together in the dressing room with the players afterwards, Sophia sat on the bench alongside Kiko, Swan and Victor, rather than, as normal, standing next to Moreton. The difference wasn't lost on anyone in the room as he announced the starting eleven for Sunday's game.

Moreton would have been reassured to welcome the vastly experienced Jiménez back into the team as a steadying influence behind the back line for the 'Derby' but, with Sophia having advised him that to do so would be risky, it was decided to allow the veteran goalkeeper an extra week to recover. He would be on the bench with Juan Torres retaining the gloves. It was an obvious selection. When the rest of the team was announced, however, it was anything but obvious.

The back four would be Sanz, Kiko, Victor and Felipe Blanco. Adrián was pushed forward into a midfield three, alongside Samuel and Matiás. Ahead of them would be Antonio Vasquez, Juan Palermo and Guido. Revi and Swan would be on the bench. Both had scored in the convincing win over Bugroño, but that wasn't deemed sufficiently persuasive for them to retain their places. It was a team built for belligerence and one that fitted with the coach's mentality at the time. As the players dispersed and began leaving, Swan caught Moreton's eye and beckoned him to one side.

'My ankle's fine, you know, Jon,' he said by way of seeking an explanation for being excluded.

'It's not your ankle I'm worried about.'

'What's that supposed to mean?' It was a reasonable question, one provoked by Moreton's aggressive and dismissive comment. It caused the Retama coach to run for cover rather than admitting that his own frustration and lack of faith in his friend had fuelled the decision.

'It's going to be a hard game, proper physical. I've left Revi out as well. You guys are too valuable to be kicked up in the air and then injured at this stage of the season.' It was an explanation almost devoid of logic and Moreton knew it. He was trying to convince himself as much as Swan, and failing on both counts.'

Swan shook his head slowly. 'OK, mate. You're the coach. It's your decision. I'll be on the bench if you need me.' He slapped Moreton on the shoulder and turned away. 'See you Sunday.'

The remaining hours of Friday evening and all of Saturday were difficult for Moreton and Sophia. Tension over team selection, and the real reason, for it was coming between them, but neither felt inclined to make he first move on the road to reconciliation. For much of Saturday, Moreton was alone. Over breakfast, Sophia had brusquely informed him that she was spending the day with Elena, and might not be back until late, and that he shouldn't wait up for her. He didn't and, when he woke the next morning, the space in the bed next to him remained empty.

He sat up and scratched his head vigorously, before rubbing his eyes and letting out a deep, troubled sigh. For a week now, Moreton had been angry at Swan, the world and himself. The resentment had festered in his mind because no one seemed to understand how he felt, particularly Sophia. He was the good guy in all of this. He was the victim, so why was he now beginning to feel like everything was his fault. There was a simple answer to that question. For the moment, however, it remained beyond the reach of his reasoning.

He climbed out of bed and padded out towards the bathroom, noticing that the door to the spare bedroom was closed. He opened it quietly, and saw Sophia sleeping.

For the remainder of the day, ahead of the game at Villanuevo, the atmosphere between them was as cold as the empty space in Moreton's bed had felt when he woke up. Even on the short coach journey to the game, they hardly spoke, and his final team talk ahead of kick-off was translated in flat, unemotional tones. For the players, that there were issues between the two CD Retama coaches was as clear as the nose that Moreton had cut off to spite his own face. As the players left to warm up, Jiménez took hold of Swan's arm and spoke to him urgently. Each of them was being assigned a task.

Trying to isolate Moreton from Sophia so that Swan could speak with his friend and Jiménez could fulfil his role as her knight in armour, was hardly difficult. Sophia walked ahead and sat down on the visitors' bench as Jiménez settled beside her, motioning the other substitutes to keep their distance for a while. At the same time, Swan trotted after Moreton and, taking his arm, guided him to a quiet spot at the side of the dressing room.

'All right, Jon. Enough of this crap now. What's going on?'

By this time, Moreton's self-righteous indignation was paling, it's supply of self-doubt and angst almost exhausted. He looked Swan in the eye. 'I know,' he said flatly.

'You know what?'

'I know about Del Hart. He told me. I know about the offer. I know, Billy.'

Swan bowed his head and shook it slowly, before rubbing his hands through his hair. 'Is that what this is all about?' he asked with undisguised indignation. 'Are you telling me all this bollocks with me being dropped, messing the team around, falling out with Sophia and sulking like some bloody kid, is all because Del Hart made me an offer?'

Instantly Moreton felt a wave of shame and embarrassment wash over him, but he reached for dry land. 'No, it's about you not telling me, Billy. About what might be going on behind my back. Shit, how do you think I feel after what happened last year? And now at the crucial time of the season, I find out about you keeping things from me.'

In any other circumstance, Swan would have felt justifiably angry at the mistrust but, given the pain he had inflicted on his friend at the end of last season, there was more than a hint of empathy in his reaction. 'OK, Jon. Perhaps I should have told you but, do you know why I didn't? Because of this sort of thing. I didn't want you worrying about something that wasn't there.' He rubbed his face in frustration. 'I should have realised Del would say something to you. He's a straight bloke, but I never thought it through.' He paused. 'Right, here's the facts. Del made me an offer before the game. We didn't talk figures, but he said it would be good money. Plus, because the blokes who own the club were big in the estate agent game, he said they could be of advantage to Izzy's business. I was never going to do go, Jon. Stuff the money, but I had to speak to Izzy first to tell her about it and why I wasn't interested. That's where I was going after the game when we spoke. Remember? I rang Del up that same night, from Izzy's, and told him thanks, but no thanks. He understood. He said he never thought I'd be interested but had been asked to make the offer. And that was it, Jon. Finished. Kaput. Over. He wished me good luck and I did the same to him.'

Moreton's head was bowed by the weight of guilt now bearing down on him. He remained looking at the ground as Swan spoke again. 'Jon, that's the truth, straight up. You can ask Izzy if you don't believe me. I said nothing to you, 'cos there was nothing to say.' Moreton slowly raised his head, and blew out his cheeks. He wasn't sure whether he felt more relived or ashamed.

'Hey, Jon.' Swan added. 'This bloke here,' he said pointing to himself. 'Soy Retama, amigo!' He smiled, inviting Moreton to reciprocate.

'I'm sorry, Billy. It's just that the thought of going through that hell again. It haunts me,' Moreton confessed. 'It haunts me. I couldn't stand it.'

'Well, don't sodding worry about it then. Cos it ain't gonna happen, is it.'

Now Moreton was smiling too. 'But what about you and Izzy, Billy? With Del's offer you could have everything sorted and be with her over here.'

Swan exaggerated his apparent surprise a little at Moreton's comment. 'That's all going to be sorted any road, ain't it,' he said cheerfully. 'You've got that Vincent bloke on the job, yeah?'

Moreton smile broadened a little. 'Sure, Billy. Sure.'

'Well, there you are then.' Swan reached out a hand, placing it on Moreton's shoulder. 'Look, Jon, I trust you, OK? And you can trust me. I've come here to pay debts and the biggest one I owe is to you.'

'Cheers, Billy.'

'Look, Paco's over there talking to Sophia. You two better get things together now. Paco and me we're like the Reunited Nations, you know, when they get people to stop fighting and be nice to each other. So that's what you're going to do.'

Moreton nodded.

'Right, so sod off over there. Give her a kiss and stop pissing everybody off. There's a game to win here.'

Just then the sound of shouts and laughter from the pitch demanded their attention. Players were facing up to each other, pushing and shoving aggressively as the referee repeatedly sounded his whistle in vain. 'Come on, Billy.' Moreton said as they both ran over to where Sophia was standing alongside Jiménez as some semblance of order was restored on the pitch.

'What happened?' Moreton asked as he arrived.

'One of their players was pointing to Juan's shirt and started laughing. He shouted to the others that they were just playing a load of Pintores.' She looked at him. 'It means painters, like decorators, Jon. Then they started shouting at each other and it got out of hand.'

Moreton looked into her eyes. 'I'm sorry,' he said. 'Billy's straightened me out. I was just worried, scared really, about what happened last year. I couldn't bear that again.'

'Paco's spoken to me too.'

'Are we OK?'

'We're always OK,' Sophia confirmed. 'Sometimes, we just need a kick to realise it though.'

On the field. The referee called Juan Palermo and one of the Villanuevo players. He reached into his pocket and flourished a red card at both of them. Players from both teams surrounded the official, forlornly pleading their case and, for a few minutes, disorder returned.

'Quick,' Moreton said to Sophia. 'Get José ready to start.'

'Jon, Juan's been sent off. We can't just send a substitute on to start instead.' And then she doubted herself. 'Can we?'

'Yes,' he confirmed. 'We can. I just hope the ref is up on the laws of the game.'

Fortunately, he was and, to offer a balanced approach as well help defuse the explosive situation, as Moreton prepared to send on the younger Palermo brother, the official approached the Villanuevo bench and informed their coach that he too could replace his dismissed player.

Ten minutes later, 15 minutes after the scheduled start, the game began amid simmering anger and smouldering resentment. Moreton had chosen to use the hand-painted shirts as way of building a siege mentality among his players. On this occasion, though, the passion engendered had spilled over and, with a team designed to be aggressive, the danger was that more of the same would follow.

Tension was clearly the order of the day in the early part of the game as robust tackles flew in from both sides. With the uncompromising Adrián sequestered into the Retama midfield alongside Matías and Samuel, Retama weren't short of physicality, but the erstwhile full-back would soon be returning to more familiar territory. A dozen minutes in, Sanz slid into a tackle to put the ball out of play as his opponent fell across his legs. It looked entirely accidental but, with the temperature of passions reaching boiling point, the incident was unlikely to be perceived in that way. As Sanz lay on the floor, holding his knee, a crowd of players gathered around the stricken Retama captain, pushing and shoving as the referee called Sophia onto the field.

Kiko arrive on the scene and used his physical presence to ease his team-mates away from confrontation. It was too late to save everyone from the referee's sanction, however, as Samuel followed one of the Villanuevo players into the official's notebook. The caution meant that the midfielder would be suspended for the next game. Potentially worse for the team, however, was the sight of Sanz limping heavily as he climbed to his feet and made his way to the touchline after Sophia had spent time working on his injured knee.

In typical fashion, he insisted on staying on the field but, as Sophia returned to Moreton's side, she confirmed his fears. 'He'll have to come off,' she said. Moreton called Revi across to him. The game restarted and Sanz hobbled back onto the pitch. He was clearly struggling though and the home team was quick to capitalise before Moreton could put any kind of temporary cover in place. He was already signalling for Adrián to go back to the left flank of the defence and Felipe Blanco to switch and cover Sanz when Retama conceded.

Seeing Sanz was clearly immobile, the home attack concentrated on Retama's right flank, as their wide player easily eluded Sanz's laboured challenge before cutting into the area and driving the ball into the net via the far post. Sanz bowed his head as Moreton called him off and sent Revi on to play in midfield.

'He should have come off,' Sophia said. 'It's cost us a goal.'

Moreton agreed. 'I know, but sometimes emotions, hope, fear, get the better of us,' he said, patting the dejected Retama captain on the back as he passed them before slumping down on the bench. 'It's exactly what I've been doing for the past couple of days and that's what led us to this. It's my fault, not his.' He offered a wry smile of confession and Sophia responded in kind before going to find ice for Sanz's knee.

For the remainder of the first half the game was largely played in midfield. Villanuevo seemed satisfied with their one goal lead, as Retama's attack was hardly offering any threat with the three forward players largely isolated and any possession that found its way to Vasquez, Guido or José Palermo was quickly squandered.

By half-time, Moreton had accepted that a change was necessary if Retama were to gain anything from the game and keep their faltering title hopes alive. With Samuel now suspended for the next game, Moreton gambled on his discipline not drawing another caution, and therefore a sending-off, leaving him to play out the game alongside Revi. Instead, he removed Matías, reasoning that he would be needed fresh and fit for the next game, and sent on Swan. Retama had returned to their usual formation, but with just 45 minutes of the game left, they needed to score twice, or their tenuous hold on hopes of promotion would drift away.

Over the years of his career, Swan had played in a number of games that had been critical for his employers in the hurly-burly of English football, but each time the urgency of the situation had failed to percolate into his attitude. They were all just games that translated into money. Anything else was largely irrelevant. On this occasion though, things were different. This time his desire to get his team a win matched those of his club. For the next 45 minutes, he would deliver a performance where his undoubted ability was matched by a determination and dedication to the cause of CD Retama.

From the restart, the whole pattern of the game changed. With Swan now pulling the strings and providing the link between the front line and the remainder of the team, Retama assumed control and Villanuevo were forced onto the back foot, compelled to defend a lead that suddenly looked worryingly slender. The link between Revi and Swan became a conveyor belt of possession with chances accruing for the Retama forwards.

A shot from Guido struck the top of the crossbar and a header from the younger Palermo brother was blocked on the line following a corner. Swan prompted and probed, drilling holes in the Villanuevo back line with precision passes, but, with the entire home team now forced into defensive mode, gaps were at a premium and each passing chance that went unconverted merely increased the pressure. Freed from any defensive duties, Revi pushed further forward, allowing Swan to drift both wide and into more dangerous positions up against the home defence. A chest control and shot on the turn from the veteran brought a plunging save from the home goalkeeper and then a dancing, shimmying dribble almost had him through on goal before a hefty challenge brought him down on the edge of the box. From the resulting free-kick Revi's effort struck the post, and the rebound was hoisted clear before José Palermo could pounce.

Time and again, Swan had possession and threaded balls into dangerous areas, but last-ditch tackles and bodies thrown in front of shots denied Retama a breakthrough and now, increasingly, the clock's unforgiving hands became a nagging concern. There was hardly any threat from the home team, and with 15 minutes to play, Moreton waved Kiko into the attack and sent on Elías for Victor, leaving just Samuel, Adrián and Felipe Blanco to provide security at the back. Time ticked on, and still there was no breakthrough as the final ten minutes were breached.

Moreton instructed Guido and Vasquez to keep as wide as possible, stretching the home defence, and hopefully creating more spaces in the middle. Now with Kiko's height added to the forward line, crosses had a new dimension of danger but, although headers on, flicks and nods down were won, there was no tangible reward. With the temptation to consistently throw the ball into the area, though, Swan was the model of composure, cautioning against what was usually a pointless exercise and insisting his team kept possession and probed for openings. With six minutes to play, his patience was eventually rewarded.

Yet another pass from Revi found Swan a few yards outside the penalty arc, with a defender closing him down. Neatly allowing the ball to run through his legs, before swiftly pivoting, he played the ball first time to Kiko, who returned the pass into the small amount of space that Swan's move had created. Feigning to shoot, he drew a defender into a rash dive to block, before flicking the ball past him. Closing on the goalkeeper, he coolly lifted the ball over him and into the net. It was a goal of consummate skill, with a level of calm composure that had drained away from many of his team-mates, but there was even better to come.

Now being roared on from the sidelines by Moreton, Sophia and the removed players, the call was to play the ball to Swan. 'Billy! Billy!' they yelled in urgent demand. Moving forward on the left, Adrián complied as Swan dropped deeper to collect possession around the halfway line. Dropping his shoulder, he drove inside of the first challenge and played the ball wide to Guido who was hugging the touchline, adhering as tightly to his coach's instructions, as he was to the whitewash demarking the edges of the pitch. Swan then looped outside of the Retama flyer and collected the ball again running towards the corner flag, before jagging back inside towards the edge of the penalty area.

The box was crowded with players of both teams, but what may have been perceived as an impediment by many, Swan used to his advantage. Realising that the Villanuevo goalkeeper would have little sight of the ball through the crowd scene in front of him, Swan rolled the ball outside of his right foot, then dragged it back to his left as the defender closed him down. There was the merest hint of a gap down towards the goal line, but precious little space to work with. As the ball lay outside of his left foot, Swan took half a step forward then clipped an elegant "Rabona" shot with his right foot. The ball arced towards goal and, as the goalkeeper advanced expecting a cross, too late, he realised that the ball was heading into the far corner of the net. He reached back to try and divert the shot over the bar, but was beaten by the flight of the ball. As it nestled gently into the back of the net, the Retama bench erupted and Swan fell on his knees before being engulfed up by a delirious wave of blue.

Having defended for so long, Villanuevo launched a flurry of desperate attacks to try and rescue what they believed for so long had been secured. Without any player with the guile of Swan however, they resorted into high crosses that Kiko majestically headed clear or Juan Torres claimed. At the final whistle, Retama had kept their dreams alive, and everyone swarmed around Billy Swan, with Kiko lifting his fellow musketeer off his feet in joyous celebration.

Reaching the sidelines eventually, Moreton held his arms out towards Swan. 'Billy, that was stunning!'

'What, that Rabona? Nah, that was nothing. It's a salsa move that Izzy taught me,' he said with a wink.

Upturns and upsets

The journey back from Villanuevo was short and, by the time the coach arrived outside of the Estadio Antonio Núñez there was no news available from the other games that had taken place that day. The victory was vital for Retama but, their hopes of winning the league, and then progressing to promotion through the play-off games were still dependent on other clubs dropping points.

Moreton and Sophia walked home from the stadium with mixed emotions. The elation of the victory, and Swan's virtuoso performance was still fresh in their minds, but they knew it could all count for nothing if other results today, and in the next few games, didn't turn out in their favour.

With Torreaño at home to Córuel, at least one of the clubs involved in the race with Retama would drop points today. A draw would be the ideal result, meaning both would only gain a single point and with Retama collecting three from their trip to Villanuevo, they would gain ground on both. By the time they reached the gates of the complex, Sophia had checked her phone half-a-dozen times without finding the required information.

'Still nothing,' she advised Moreton as he unlocked the gate and held it open for her.

'Look, don't worry about it, there's nothing we can do anyway,' he replied. 'Let's get showered and walk down to Bella Cucina for dinner. OK?'

'That's a good idea, Jon.'

Entering the apartment, Moreton threw his bag onto the sofa. 'Shall I go first?' he asked.

Sophia nodded absently as she checked her phone once more. He shook his head with a smile as he closed the bathroom door behind him. Throwing his clothes into the laundry basket he stepped into the shower and let the warm water wash over him for a few seconds basking in its soothing effect. Then a banging on the door drew him back. He turned the shower off. 'What's the matter?' He called through the door 'Are you OK?'

'They drew!' Came the excited voice from the other side of the door. 'They drew 3-3. They drew!'

'That's great,' he shouted back, as he stepped into the shower once more.

Ninety minutes later as they sat in the restaurant, Sophia related the implications of that day's games. The draw was good news for Retama. Less encouraging however was that Bugroño had beaten Politanio B. The club coached by Del Hart was fast becoming serious contenders. Torreaño still led the table on 58 points, but Hart's team had closed the gap to just three points, with Retama a further point behind and Córuel apparently slipping away on 51 with each club now having just four games to play. The club now supported by the *El Celo* organisation would still have plenty to say in the final outcome of the season. After playing at home to Desorio the following week, and then again at home to Torre del Olmos, their final two fixtures were both away, first to Retama and, on the final day, when Moreton's team travelled to Torreaño, they would play their last fixture away to Bugroño.

Moreton scratched his head as he tried to work out the permutations from the information Sophia had given him as she gazed at her phone while the pasta went cold in front of them.

'You know what we need to do?' he asked.

'What games we need to win and how many points will get us to the top?'

'Not really. We should eat this pasta before it gets too cold.' They both laughed. 'And,' Moreton added, 'we should just try and win all of our games, because we can't do much more.' With that, he reached out and took Sophia's phone, placing it down on the table face down and placed a fork in her hand instead. 'Tonight, I'm out with the most perfect woman in Spain. We have a lovely meal in front of us and later, we can go back put on some music and lie on the sofa together in each other's arms. Yes?'

'That sounds perfect, Jon.' And it was.

The injury to Sanz and the suspensions of both Samuel and Juan Palermo meant that changes would be required for the home game against Politanio B. At training on Tuesday evening, as they were discussing how best to plug the holes left by the absentees, Sophia suggested that the game may not be too difficult with Politanio pursuing a policy playing their less accomplished players in away games. Moreton wasn't so sure though.

'The problem is,' he said as they watched their players go through a press, support and cover drill, designed to focus on regaining possession high up the field, 'that these players designated as the less gifted, and shunted into the "away" squad will be desperate to prove themselves. They'll only have four games left to convince the club, that they're worth retaining and push for a place among the more favoured players for next season. They'll have a massive incentive to show Francisco that they're good enough. This could be one of our toughest games of the season.'

They decided that Felipe Blanco should come in as cover for Sanz, with Matías taking the midfield slot alongside Revi. Juan Palermo had been selected for a specific purpose in the Derby game, albeit perhaps by a misguided logic of Moreton, and may not have been in the starting eleven for this game whether he had been suspended or not, but Moreton sought to tweak his forward line anyway. José Palermo was drafted into the left flank of the attack with Guido given a break. Swan was in the number ten role with Antonio Vasquez on the right and Elías leading the line. The training sessions across Wednesday and Friday concentrated on settling the players into the line-up, with special attention on Vasquez dropping deeper to support Felipe Blanco. When the team was announced following training on Friday, both Moreton and Sophia were convinced that they'd prepared well and selected the best starting eleven for the game. It was just as well. As Moreton had suggested would be the case, Retama would face a strong challenge from an enthusiastic and determined Politanio B second string team determined to prove themselves worthy of ascent or, at least, retention.

As the teams left the dressing rooms to warm up for the game, Moreton and Sophia spotted Francisco walking towards them. The man in the red tracksuit with white piping and prematurely greying hair, now also receding, smiled warmly at them.

'*Hola, Jon,*' he offered shaking Moreton's hand, and then Sophia's. 'Your team is doing well.'

'Thanks,' Moreton replied. 'How has your season been?'

'Results are not that important for us. This league is about preparing players for first team football.' He paused and looked at the players in red shirts and white shorts warming up on the pitch. 'If these coaches can get me three or four players for my first team, that is all I ask.' He paused again as he rubbed his chin pensively. 'But they will always come from the stronger squad who play the home games. You understand what I mean?'

Moreton nodded in acknowledgement, but a question was brewing in his mind. 'So, why have you travelled with these players then?'

'Ah,' Francisco replied with a nod and smile. 'My coaches tell me that there are two, no wait, three, players here who could make it and time is running out.' He held his arms open. 'So, I come here to meet you two again, and to see if my coaches are correct.'

'Which players?' Moreton asked hopefully.

Francisco laughed and patted Moreton on the shoulder. 'Now, Jon. I can't give away all my secrets to you, can I?'

Moreton joined in the laughter. 'It was worth a try.'

'Well,' Francisco concluded as he turned to go back to join his coaches. 'I hope you'll find out during the game anyway.'

Fifteen minutes later, the game was under way and within five minutes, Retama were ahead. A long clearance downfield caused confusion in the Politanio ranks and, as goalkeeper and defender left the bouncing ball to each other, Elías nipped between them to head the ball over the former and into the net. It was an early fillip for the home team, but a brief period before the visitors assumed dominance of the game with both Moreton's concerns and Francisco's suggestions being borne out.

The red-shirted Politanio players, clearly conscious of the club's head coach being present, and bruised by conceding a careless early goal, were clearly out to impress. They busied themselves when out of possession and, when they had the ball, runs demanding a pass and astute interplay were the order of the day. For the first quarter of the game, the away team dominated and the Retama defence was hard pressed to keep them at bay.

As Moreton had worked on during training the previous week, Vasquez funnelled back to help out Felipe Blanco, who, for all his youthful exuberance and passion, lacked the solid game nous and experience of the Retama captain he was replacing. In the centre Kiko and Victor worked hard to defend crosses and Matías stood sentry duty in front of the back line. Further forward, Swan and Elías were, for the most part largely isolated, with the younger Palermo sibling also forced into auxiliary defensive duties. Juan Torres was both diligent and fully employed in goal.

The pressure was becoming relentless and, when a shot from distance required Torres to touch the ball onto the crossbar, the goalkeeper was unable to regain his feet before an eager Politanio forward tapped the rebound home for the equaliser. It was a goal that had been coming and, for the reminder of the first half, a second goal for the visitors looked likely.

At the break it was clear that, unless something changed, the one-way traffic of the first half would surely condemn Retama to defeat with Elías' early goal, by now, a distant memory. Moreton needed to change something. After his opportunistic poaching, Elías' skills had been rendered redundant by the lack of possession Retama could establish further up the field, and Moreton replaced him with Guido. Whilst most of the players assumed that this meant a left flank role for the substitute, with José Palermo switched to the centre, Moreton confounded their expectations. Guido would play in the centre, but also deeper, looking to make runs into space as the Politanio players pushed forward.

When the second period got under way, with Guido operating almost alongside Revi and Matías, and Swan the most forward Retama player, if anything, the play was even more concentrated in the Retama half of the pitch. Sensing little threat from the pedestrian pace of the veteran Swan, the visiting defence eagerly pushed forwards, determined to impress their watching coach. It was precisely what Moreton had hoped would be the case and, as the next ten minutes rolled by without any goals, the established pattern of the game only intensified. Despite his team being pressed back, Moreton retained hopes that his plan would deliver and, with 25 minutes to play, it did.

A cross from the left was plucked out of the air by Juan Torres who rolled the ball out to Guido. Laying the ball off to Victor, and then on to Revi, the Retama speedster trotted innocuously forward, ostensibly to offer support for Swan. Revi eluded the overly enthusiastic challenge of a Politanio player and ran forward injecting a sudden burst of pace into the move. It was mirrored by Guido who was now approaching a sprint as he drew level with Swan. Revi's ball was perfectly weighted and Swan deftly flicked the ball on with the outside of his foot as Guido burst into the clear grass of the Politanio half of the field with defenders trailing in his wake. On he went towards the edge of the area as the visiting goalkeeper approached to narrow the angle, a deft clip eliminated Politanio's last line of defence and the ball bounced towards goal before striking a post and bouncing out. Fortunately, Guido had been following the ball and smashed it into the net from two metres out. Against the run of play, Retama had stolen the lead. Sophia embraced Moreton as Guido cavorted around the field celebrating and, for a few seconds, eluding the chasing pack of team-mates before being caught and dragged to the ground by them.

Two thirds of the game had passed as the referee blew the whistle to restart. Moreton hoped that his defence could hold the Politanio attack at bay until full-time, but his back line would fail to sustain the lead for more than sixty seconds. After playing the ball to Revi, Victor had been felled by a desperate late tackle. The incident was caused by over eagerness rather than any malice, but the effect was hardly reduced by that fact. At the heart of the Retama defence, Victor was now little more than a limping passenger and, while Moreton was considering options to reshuffle his team, Politanio equalised. A ball played into the heart of the Retama half eluded Matías and, as Kiko tried forlornly to cut out the move, a visiting forward controlled the pass, eased past the incapacitated Victor and slid the ball past Torres. The scores were level again and, if results mattered little to Francisco, the requirements of the Retama coach were very different.

Sebastián was the only replacement left for Moreton, but leaving Victor on, limping around was not an option. Before the game restarted, he called the blond-haired defender off and sent his last available player on. Matías was dropped into the back line alongside Kiko with Sebastián taking over alongside Revi. Retama had it all to do again, if they were to keep their title hopes alive, and this time, they had to do it with a depleted team.

For the next 15 minutes, any goal looked likely to come at the other end of the pitch as the Politanio players attacked almost incessantly. Having finally breached the Retama defence, the momentum was strongly in their favour and they pursued the victory with renewed vigour. Moreton's defence stuck to their tasks and, despite the inexperience in the blue-shirted wall in front of Torres, each player was committed to keeping the visiting forwards at bay. Inside the final six minutes the attacks began to wane in intensity, as fatigue, frustration and a growing acceptance of a draw set in for the Politanio players. It offered Retama a brief chance to go forward and, from a break, a shot by José Palermo was deflected behind by a defender's leg for Retama's first corner of the game.

Revi crossed the ball in as Kiko challenged the goalkeeper, and the ball spilt to the floor. Attempting to hack the ball clear as José Palermo reached for it, a Politanio foot cut the young forward's leg from underneath him. It was the most obvious of spot kicks. As Palermo struggled to his feet, Revi grabbed the ball and placed it into Swan's hand. With time ebbing away, it was surely Retama's last chance. Score and their hopes would remain alive. Miss, however, and the dream would surely have died.

The latter was never a possibility as, in typical fashion, Swan rolled the spot kick home with the Politanio goalkeeper falling in the other direction. With injury time almost up, Kiko headed Retama's second corner of the game home to close out what, for so long, had looked likely an unlikely victory. Retama had the win their coach required and, with results of less importance than further information on his players, the Politanio coach could also deem the game successful.

At full-time they embraced warmly and Francisco parted with the words. 'Now go and win the league, Jon!' He waved his arm around indicating the crowd that had come to watch the game. 'You can't let all these people down.' With Retama still fighting for that title and promotion spot, they were attracting increasing numbers of fans back to watch them. Moreton just smiled. He felt the pressure.

As was the case after the Villanuevo game, there was then a tension-filled wait until the results from the other games became available online. Moreton and

Sophia hung around with a number of the players and Esteban wearing his number eight Retama shirt, long after the stadium had emptied of fans and the Politanio party had left. Along with the coaches and Esteban, the Three Musketeers, Jiménez, the injured Sanz and the Palermo brothers were gathered in a small knot standing around the coaches' bench by the side of the pitch, many of them repeatedly pressing the 'refresh' button on the phones, anxious for news of the other games.

The first of the key results was a comfortable 3-0 win for Bugroño over Costa Locos. Feliciano had apparently scored a hat-trick. 'I can hear old Del leading the "Alf-eee" chorus from here,' Swan quipped. Then another result was added. This time, it was no news at all, but still provoked a response from Swan. 'Hey, we won,' he shouted. 'Beat Politanio 4-2. I wondered who scored, eh?' he asked, winking at Kiko. 'We know who didn't though don't we?' he said ruffling Victor's hair with a smile. 'Save it for the big game like last year, Meldrew, eh?'

Just then Sophia's phone rang. Torreaño had been visiting Árboles Altos and, while her parents were away from the village, they had asked a friend to let them know the final score as soon as they could. Sophia quickly glanced at the caller's name. 'Papá!' she exclaimed opening the call.

'*Si. Si*,' she repeated, as the others watched her, looking for any hint of what the result had been. Two seconds later, detective work was hardly required to discern that the news was good. Sophia jumped up and down with a huge smile on her face as she spoke breathlessly to her father. Then with a quick '*Gracias, hasta luego*,' she closed the call and, drawing a deep breath passed on the news. 'They drew 3-3!' They didn't win. They were winning 3-2 but a late penalty made it a draw.'

Suddenly everyone's attention was back on their phones, working out how the league table would look now, but Moreton was musing on the fact that despite scoring six times in a couple of games, the team at the top of the table had conceded just as many. In the crucial game last season, Moreton had concentrated his tactics on blunting Torreaño's attack, and particularly Montero. Perhaps focusing more on their defensive weaknesses than attacking strengths might pay dividends this time around.

Sanz got the official news first, along with the information that FC Córuel had surprisingly lost 2-3 at home to lowly Desorio. Now with just three games to play, their hopes were surely finished. Realistically, the race was down to three. Sanz turned the screen of his phone to face the others. They crowded around it as the updated league table was revealed. Torreaño were still top on 59 points, but their lead had almost vanished. Bugroño had closed to within a point of the leaders and Retama were third on 57. FC Córuel home defeat had left them on 51. Although they would still have a major say in who would win the league, having to visit both Retama and then Bugroño in their last two games, their role from here on would be as potential spoilers, rather than rivals.

After a few minutes mutual backslapping and speculating about how many points they would need to make a strong challenge for the title, the party broke up and headed for the gates with Esteban locking up behind them. Outside, Swan and Victor waved as they entered Kiko's car and drove off, but Jiménez and Sanz waited until Esteban had left and they were alone with Moreton and Sophia.

'Do you have time to talk?' Jiménez asked. His demeanour suggested that a light-hearted chat about the weather was not what he meant.

Glancing from the goalkeeper to the Retama captain's face merely confirmed Moreton's concern. 'Sure,' he said looking at Sophia who nodded in turn.

Ten minutes later the four of them sat around a table in Carlito's bar. '*Hola Elena, Que t'al?*' Sophia asked as Elena came across to take their order. The two women chatted briefly as the men watched and then Sophia placed the order. 'Tres vinos blancos por favor y un agua sin gas.' As the drinks arrived, they toasted each other's health and Moreton asked the inevitable question.

'What's wrong, Paco?'

'It's about Juan?' Jiménez revealed. 'Juan Torres,' he clarified.

'OK,' Moreton answered hesitantly.

'He has spoken with me, and now he has also spoken with Alejo.'

'What about?' Sophia asked.

'OK,' Jiménez began. 'At training on Friday, before the Villanuevo game, he told me that he felt not well, and it was not good to play if I was fit instead. I told him that it was normal to be nervous in front of a bigger game and that I trusted him, and we all trusted him. He seemed OK. After the game, he said the same thing and in front of the Politanio game said that I should play instead.' The veteran goalkeeper sighed. 'I should have told you then,' he said, directing his words to Moreton. 'But it would have seemed like I was trying to put myself back into the team on his expenses. I did not want that.'

'I understand Paco, but you must always know that I trust you too, and whatever you tell me, I will believe you.'

'Thank you, Mister.' Jiménez replied before continuing. 'Now, after this game, he thinks that talking to me is not working. He talks now to Alejo and said the same. We shouldn't ignore this.'

'Do you think it is just nerves?' Moreton asked. 'Let's face it, we're all stressed at the moment with the way things are. Is he still worried about the wrist he injured?'

'I think so,' Jiménez replied. 'Alejo?'

'Si. Creo que está muy nervioso,' Sanz agreed.

Moreton grasped enough of the phrase to understand the meaning. 'I think you're right, guys. I …' he began, but was stopped by Sophia.

'I'm not so sure. Perhaps he is unwell. I've been feeling like that for a couple of days now as well. Nothing terrible, but just having an upset stomach. Perhaps there's some kind of illness going around. With us all working so closely together it could soon pass get passed around.'

'OK,' Moreton said. 'We all trust Juan and, if he thinks he's not well enough, we shouldn't put him under pressure to play. Paco, how's your ankle?'

'It is good. I can play if you need me.'

'Right, we'll leave it for now and see how things go in training next week. Perhaps Alejo, you can ask Juan how he is feeling by Friday and, if he still feels unwell, we'll bring Paco in and give him a rest, yes?' Jiménez quickly translated for Sanz who hadn't understood all of what had been said, but nodded in agreement afterwards. He and Jiménez drained their wine, stood up and left.

Moreton looked at Sophia with concern. 'I didn't know you weren't feeling well. I'm sorry. I guess I've just been too engrossed in the team.'

'Jon, I'm fine,' she insisted. 'It's probably just some kind of bug that I caught from Juan, or the other way around.'

'OK, but I'm keeping special attention on you now, young lady. I don't want you bunking off with a sick note at the big games,' he said waving his finger in the air at her playfully. She slapped his hand and they both laughed.

Fortunately, the knock sustained by Victor was only slight and by Tuesday he was able to take a full part in training. Throughout the week, Moreton watched Juan Torres with increased vigilance and, while he seemed to have no obvious problems physical problem during training, he did look uncomfortable at times. With Sophia also still feeling nauseous, it added weight to the conclusion that perhaps there was some kind of illness going around. When, on Friday, Sanz confirmed that Torres had again said he was feeling unwell, it all fitted with the theory and Moreton decided to bring Jiménez back into the team.

Sanz's injured knee was still troubling him, so Felipe Blanco would deputise on the right flank of the Retama defence again. Aside from that though, the remainder of the eleven to face UD Palancio was much more akin to what Moreton would consider to be his best team. Victor, Kiko and Adrián completed the back four, with Samuel and Revi in front of them. Guido and Antonio Vasquez were on the flanks and Swan would play behind Elías.

That Saturday evening, Moreton and Sophia had arranged to meet Swan and Izzy for dinner in town, but Sophia had asked Moreton to postpone it as she had felt unwell in the morning and, despite the nausea passing later in the day, said she felt tired and wanted to rest instead. Moreton quickly agreed and rang Swan. So far, the stomach bug had only seemed to affect Juan Torres and Sophia. The Retama squad of players was quite small and if the illness spread to others, it could cause problems for the club in the next few vital weeks. He decided that it was best to keep to keep the rest of the players away from the young goalkeeper and Sophia as much as possible.

He asked Sophia to ring Torres and tell him to take a break on Sunday and stay at home, and sit out the next week's training as well to give him time to recover, but turn up for the team selection after Friday's training. When she closed out the call, the look on Moreton's face told her something she didn't want to hear.

'I think you should do the same. At least for the game tomorrow. A couple of coach journeys are no fun when you feel a bit off.'

'Jon, I'm fine,' she insisted, but Moreton wasn't prepared to take any risks.

'Look, here's the deal. You stay here tomorrow. Put your feet up and rest. Then, if you're feeling better next week, come to training as usual and we'll take it from there.'

'What if someone gets hurt,' she protested. 'What if you need someone to translate if something happens.'

'I don't care. We'll cope.' He paused. 'Please Sophia. For me.'

She sighed deeply. 'OK, I still think you're making a drama out of it. I'm not even sure it's an illness. It's probably just a bit of stress and worrying about things. It's mainly just in the mornings, after that I'm better. I'm not sleeping well and that doesn't help. That's all it is.'

Moreton was unmoved though and, as the coach left the Estadio Antonio Núñez the following morning for the journey to Palancio, the seat next to him was vacant.

The club in the town of Palancio had suffered since Francisco had left them to return to Politanio. After just falling short of promotion with him in charge the squad had been diminished as players left to join Estrella Azul. While their new club achieved promotion through the play-offs, Palancio had drifted down the table and finished last season just one place above the relegation zone. The new season hadn't been much better, and the club was still hovering dangerously close to the bottom three places. It meant that, regardless of any potential lack of talent in the team, the Palancio players would be fighting to preserve their status in the league. Points were just as important to them as they were to Retama. There was another link between the clubs as well. After this fixture, each would face games against table-topping Torreaño. Palancio would entertain them the following week, before Retama's visit to the town of San Julio del Rio to play the same club for the final game of the season.

Retama's home game against Palancio earlier in the season had served to underscore that no game should be taken for granted, despite any apparent travails of the opponent. After starting well, two controversial refereeing decisions had seen Retama reduced to nine men by the final whistle and a 1-1 draw meant two precious points, that would be so valuable now, had slipped away. Retama couldn't afford that happening again.

Keeping his team talk as simple as possible, and leaning on Jiménez to take up Sophia's role, Moreton drilled into his players the importance of treating their opponents with all respect and to expect a fight in the game as they battled for survival. Regardless of any problems in translation, the message had been delivered effectively. At full-time, a brace from Elías, a goal in each half, had more than outweighed a home goal in the last minute of injury time. It had been a thoroughly professional performance.

As had now become almost a ritual for the coach and players of CD Retama, as soon as they left the dressing rooms after the game, phones were the centre of attention to check the results of other games. Moreton had a different use for his phone first though.

'How did it go?' Sophia asked as she answered the call on the first ring.

'All good. We won. No problems. The boys did well.'

'That's great Jon. But don't ever ask me to sit at home when we have a game again. I've been worried sick, literally. The nerves are terrible when you don't know what's going on. I've been sitting here thinking I should call you, but didn't want to break your concentration on the game. What was the score? Who scored, and ...' Sophia's words flooded from her mouth as if a sluice gate on a dam had been opened.

'Slow down, *mi amor*,' Moreton said laughing a little. 'It was 2-1. Elías got both goals. Typical poaching. One after Billy's shot had been palmed out to him. The second was a header from Guido's cross. Right place, right time. They scored a late goal. It pissed Paco off, but didn't really matter. How are you feeling?'

'Well, I'm better now I know we won. Oh, yes. Something else. Papá called an hour or so ago. They are coming to Retama next week. He says that he has good news about your plan for Billy, and something very important extra as well.'

'That's great news. Well done, Vincent!'

'Vincent?'

'Don't worry, I'll explain later.'

'Are you going to tell Billy now?'

'No, not yet. Let's wait until we get the full story from Joaquín first, so we know where we are.'

'OK, that makes sense.'

'I wonder what the other thing, the 'very important extra' news is,' Moreton pondered aloud.

'I don't know, he wouldn't say. He wanted to tell us both at the same time.'

'I guess we'll just have to wait then.'

Just then raucous shouting erupted around the coach. 'What's going on?' Sophia asked.

'I don't know. Hang on a bit.' He stood up and looked back down the coach to see knots of players peering into phones. 'Paco?' he shouted, with arms outspread, inviting information.

'Bugroño,' Jiménez shouted, holding up an index finger on each hand, indicating that the club in second place had only drawn 1-1 against Lacitana. Retama's win had sent them up to second place.

'Torreaño?' Moreton asked.

Jiménez shrugged his shoulders. Moreton picked up the phone again.

'Bugroño only drew at home to Lacitana,' he said to Sophia.

'I know Jon. While you were away, I opened my laptop. They were losing until the last couple of minutes then George Clift scored. Must have been up for a late corner perhaps.'

'Anything else?'

'Hmm, yes. Not such good news. Torreaño beat Castello Viejo 4-0. Montero scored all four goals but then ...' She paused mid-sentence.

'But then what?' Moreton asked.

'Sorry, I was reading. He was substituted. I think he must have been injured, but it doesn't say any more. There's only a couple of sentences. One more thing. FC Córuel beat Torre del Olmos 3-0. Here's the league table ...'

This time it was Moreton's turn to halt the sentence in mid flow. 'Don't worry,' he said, looking at Jiménez's phone held in front of his face. 'I've got it here from Paco. We're two points behind Torreaño and Del's boys are a point behind us. Córuel are out of it now. Even if they in their last two games, they can only get to 60 points, and Torreaño have 62 already.'

'Yes, that's it,' Sophia confirmed.

'I'll see you when I get home.'

'I'll be waiting for you. Yo te quiero.'

'*Yo te quiero.*' He repeated closing out the call.

Wonderful News. Terrible News

After convincing Moreton that she was feeling better and perhaps it was all just a matter of nervous stress, Sophia attended training on Tuesday, and returned to the apartment to find Joaquín and Dolores Garrigues waiting for them. Hugs and kisses of greeting were exchanged before the four of them entered the complex and climbed the stairs to the apartment. Even before they sat down, Sophia made a suggestion.

'Jon, you go and shower first, then you and papá head down to Carlito's. Then I'll take my shower and mamá and I will join you. Yes?'

It sounded like a *fait accompli* to Moreton, but he had little reason to argue. Thirty minutes later he was sitting in the bar with Garrigues retelling the tales of recent matches and discussing how things were looking ahead of the last two games of the league programme.

'Three points between the top three teams with two games to play, Jon.' Garrigues said. 'It's all very tight.'

'It is, Joaquín. And there's some really difficult games as well. We have Córuel at home next. They've slipped out of contention, but are still a good team. Winning that one, won't be easy. Then we have to go to Torreaño on the last day.' He puffed out his cheeks. 'Both hard games, but the other clubs haven't got it easy either. Before they play us, Torreaño are away to Palancio. They're struggling at the bottom and, after we beat them last week, they dropped into the bottom three, so they'll be fighting for their lives there. Plus, I understand that Montero may miss that game through injury, although he'll be back when we go there. Bugroño are away to Politanio B. So that's their better team.'

Garrigues looked confused by the term, and Moreton explained the way Francisco's club had split their squad into home and away teams. 'The kids in that team will all be up for a place with the big boys next term, so they'll be giving it all they've got. That'll be a battle to win points. Then, in the final game they're playing FC Córuel at home.'

'It all sounds very intricate Jon,' Garrigues commented taking a sip of his wine. 'How many points do you think you need to top the league and get directly into the promotion play-off.'

'I've no idea, Joaquín. Each of those games, and ours could go either way. All we can do is try to win our games and see where it takes us.'

On that, Sophia and Dolores Garrigues walked into the bar. The two men stood as each woman sat down next to their partner. Elena brought across another glass of wine and one of water. 'Jon, papá and mamá are staying here for a few days. Papá has some business meetings tomorrow, so mamá and I are going to spend the day shopping in town, OK?'

'Sure' Moreton agreed.

'First though, mamá insists that we have to hear papá's news. Moreton and Sophia looked intently at Garrigues.

'Ah,' he said, in feigned surprise. 'I suppose you want to hear the news, yes?'

'Papá!' Sophia scolded gently.

'OK, here we go. If all goes well and the club gets promotion, my group have succeeded in brokering a deal between the ayuntamiento and Cerámica Internacional. The ayuntamiento will sell them the land at the site they wanted on the edge of town near to the Valencia *autopista* and allow them to build their factory there. In exchange, CI have agreed to make an annual donation to the ayuntamiento to be used for the promotion and improvement of Retama's young people and their health and well-being for a period of no less than ten years, renewable by negotiation after that. In short, they will fund a youth development programme at CD Retama, covering all costs, including the salary of a new coach – namely one William Swan.'

Moreton reached up and punched the air with both fists as Sophia jumped to her feet, and leant across the table to kiss her father on his forehead. 'Joaquín that's brilliant. You're an extraordinary man!' Moreton exclaimed.

Garrigues chuckled to himself, briefly enjoying the acclaim, before a thought struck him, and he recalled the phrase that Moreton had used at the airport many months previously. 'As a very wise young man once said, Jon. "Not really. I just know some people who are." And, I have to say that, as I understand it, CI were quite willing to comply. They have a policy of building good relations with the communities where their businesses are located and, although this one is a little more expensive than their usual plans, they saw the positive business benefits and good PR opportunities.'

Moreton and Sophia raised their glasses. 'Whatever, Joaquín. To extraordinary people then. Whoever they are. Wherever they are.' They all took sips from their drinks.

'You both must remember though.' Garrigues added injecting a note of caution. 'All of this only happens if Retama win promotion.'

'Of course,' Moreton said. 'But now with this to sell to Billy as well, he'll be unstoppable. And we couldn't have the fate of the club in the hands of a better group of players.' He turned to look at Sophia. 'Could we?'

She smiled in agreement.

'Or a better pair of coaches,' Dolores Garrigues added. 'Now, tell them the other news as well,' she prompted to her husband, clearly excited by what was about to be revealed.

'Yes, well you two. If you were impressed by what I've just told you, this will, well, I don't know …'

'*¡Date prisa, Joaquín!*' Dolores Garrigues insisted.

'Vale,' Garrigues said softly to his wife, before turning to Moreton and Sophia. He was about to change their lives for ever. 'You may not be aware of this, but Billy has been speaking with Bobby Broome, yes?

'I think they speak a couple of times a week,' Moreton suggested. 'To see how things are going back at the Soccer School.'

'Well, yes,' Garrigues agreed. 'But also, about more than that. Billy has told him all about Isabella and how he wants to stay in Spain, to be with her for a long time.'

'I didn't know that,' Moreton confirmed.

'Well, yes he has. And I know that because the solicitor in my group, the one who dealt with all of the financial agreements to guarantee the money when Barbieri withdrew his support, has had a number of telephone conversations with Señor Broome and his legal team over the last week or so. Señor Broome has agreed that the school Billy set up in London is now running perfectly well without him, so he is no longer required to be there. The school will maintain his name, and he can visit there a couple of times a year for publicity purposes, but that's all he is required to do now. Señor Broome has therefore suggested setting up a similar organisation here and have it linked to the club. The funding will come from the €150,000 that will be redeemed from the guarantee if promotion is gained. Señor Broome has agreed to donate this amount to the club. The people in my group have agreed to look after all of the management and administration details. It means that, together with the CI money promised, the youth set up at the club will probably be one of the best financed in the region, if not the very best. We can also upgrade the facilities at the stadium. CD Retama could be reborn.'

'Bobby Broome is such a good man,' Moreton said unnecessarily.

'He certainly seems to be,' Garrigues concurred. 'But he told Ricardo, the solicitor in my group who has spoken with him, that he considers it a matter of paying a debt that his family owes to the town of Retama.' He paused for a moment. 'I don't want to put any added pressure on to you but, again, all of this only goes ahead with promotion.'

'Wow,' Moreton exclaimed as the weight of responsibility settled onto his shoulders.

'There's one other thing,' Garrigues added teasingly. 'And this is not dependent on anything.' He paused slightly. 'Well not on promotion anyway.' Next to him, Dolores Garrigues sighed in irritated frustration at her husband's equivocation, but Garrigues continued in his usual measured tones. 'Señor Broome has also been told, by Billy, that you two were living in that little apartment of mine and that, apparently, it was too small for you both.' He paused again. 'Jon, I understand that some time ago, Señor Broome offered to buy you a house over here, if you wanted that, yes?'

'Well,' Moreton began. 'Well, he did, but I'm not sure that …'

'I think it's a little too late to turn down the offer now, Jon. As I understand things, after what Billy had told him, Señor Broome made a decision. He has arranged with Ricardo to transfer a very significant sum of money over here for you, for that purpose. There will be taxes to pay of course. Ricardo and I will resolve all of that for you, but I would estimate that there would be something around €228,000 for you to spend on that property.'

Moreton was stunned into silence. All he could do was shake his head in disbelief. His mouth opened and closed but, for a few seconds, no words came out. 'I can't believe it,' he said at last. 'This can't be true. It can't.'

Garrigues merely smiled and nodded. 'It is, Jon. It is.'

Moreton turned to Sophia, who was also shocked into disbelief. Then they fell into each other's arms.

'I should say,' Garrigues added after at least some measure of composure had been restored on the opposite side of the table. 'That it will take a few weeks for all the legal administration to be worked through, so it will give you both some thinking time, yes?'

'Er, yes, of course, yes,' Moreton stuttered. His world would never be the same again. If he and Sophia could now deliver promotion as well, everything he could have wished for would be there for the taking. Or so he thought. 'I must call Bobby and thank him. This is so generous. What a man!'

'I'm afraid you can't do that Jon,' Garrigues counselled. 'The last message Ricardo received was that Señor Broome would not be reachable for a number of days. Ricardo thinks he was going on holiday and that's why he wanted to get these things sorted out and all tied up before he went away.

'A holiday?' Moreton said in surprise. 'That's not like the Bobby Broome I know. But, if anyone deserves a holiday, it's him. He picked up his glass and raised it across the table. 'Bobby Broome,' he said. They all echoed the toast.

That night, after Joaquín and Dolores Garrigues had left for the Hotel El Barco, Moreton and Sophia sat on the sofa at the apartment. Both were still in a state of shock about the news her father had delivered. There was so much to take in. The things now in place that would follow if the club achieved promotion would have been sufficient for to occupy anyone's thoughts but, for the young couple, sitting in the small apartment, the prospect of owning their own house, pushed everything else to the margins of their consciousness. They were giddy with the excitement. Eventually, Moreton jumped to his feet.

'I've got to call Bobby,' he said resolutely.

'He won't be able to receive the call Jon. He's on holiday, perhaps somewhere without phone access.'

'Yeah, I know,' Moreton agreed, pressing the numbers on his phone regardless. 'But I'll leave a message and he can pick it up later, when he gets back or reconnects his phone.' He paused as the ringtone began. 'I've got to do it,' he confirmed, pausing again as the messaging service opened.

'Hi Bobby. It's Jon. I had to call and say thank you so much for what you have done for everyone. The money for the house is an amazingly generous thing to do. Sophia and I are so grateful. We can't possibly thank you enough. And the way you've sorted things out for Billy and the club it's … Well, it's just amazing. I know I keep saying things are amazing, but it's the only word I can think of. Sophia and I, and Billy, and all of the players at the club will work so hard to get promotion, and make everything happen. OK, I'll speak to you when you get this message. Please call me. Cheers and thanks again. Oh wait. One more thing. Will you promise to come over to Spain some time and stay with us? We'd love to show you the town and, if we get the promotion, the club and what you have done for its future. OK, thanks again, Bobby. I'm sure we'll speak soon.' He closed out the call, and placed the phone down on the table. 'OK, I hope he rings back soon. I can't wait to speak to him and thank him properly.'

'We have to tell Billy, and the other guys as well. Let's meet up with Billy tomorrow and give him the news,' Moreton suggested, his mind still befuddled with excitement.

'I can't tomorrow, Jon. I'm out with mamá, yes?'

'Oh, sorry, I forgot. OK, we can tell him with the others tomorrow at training.'

'No, you can't keep him waiting. Why don't you see if he's free for lunch tomorrow and you can tell him then and then we can get all the players together before training.'

'I wanted us to be together when we told him,' Moreton reflected. 'Especially the news about the money for the house. After all, from what Joaquín said, some of it is down to him.'

'That's fine, Jon. You tell him everything. It's best he knows as soon as possible.'

Moreton called Swan and asked if they could meet for lunch as he had something he wanted to talk to him about. With Izzy being engaged with a prospective client for the day, Swan was happy to accept the invitation, little knowing what the nature of Moreton's "something" was.

Sitting in the bar of the Hotel El Barco, the following lunchtime, Moreton watched Swan happily as the news and what it meant for the former bad boy of football was delivered.

'Are you havin' me on, Jon?' It was a question, but not one that required an answer.

Regardless, Moreton shook his head slowly, beaming.

'Bloody hell. What? Really? That's amazing,' Swan echoed Moreton's choice of adjective from the previous evening.

'You've got to remember though, Billy. None of this is happening unless we win promotion. We've got two games left and will probably need to win them both to top the league, and then win the play-offs. It's not going to be easy, mate.'

'Look, Jon. After all that Sophia's old man and his mates have managed to arrange, and what Bobby's done, if we don't get the club promoted, we need our arses kicking. They've set things up for me and Izzy. For you and Sophia. I ain't gonna be letting 'em down. Are you?'

'No way, Billy. That's what I thought you'd say.'

'When are you telling the boys, tonight?'

'Yeah, I want to do it with Sophia, so that we're all together. It'll give them such a lift.'

Swan nodded.

'You can tell, Izzy, though, if you like, but ask her to keep it under hat until later.'

'No worrries, Jon. She's on an all-dayer with this couple from Germany apparently looking for a proper swanky gaff, big commission for Izzy if she pulls it off, so I won't see her until later. She's picking me up after training, So I can tell her then.'

'OK, Billy.'

'One question though, Jon.'

'Sure, Billy, what?'

'Well, Sophia's dad and his mates have sorted things out with the council and the deal, yeah?'

Moreton nodded.

'And Bobby's volunteered to leave that extra wedge of dosh with the club?'

He nodded again.

'So, what did this other geezer do?

'Other geezer?'

'You know, Vincent, that bloke you said would sort it out. What did he do?'

That evening, raucous cheering broke out in the home dressing room of the Estadio Antonio Núñez as Moreton and Sophia relayed the news of the deal, and Bobby Broome's gift, to the players and Esteban. High-fives and embraces followed as everyone revelled in the prospect of the club not only surviving, but also prospering with the potential investment. As Moreton was quick to counsel however, none of it would happen unless the club achieved promotion. It was an ideal way to start the training session as exuberance and excitement transformed into commitment, with the players going through their paces, under Moreton's guidance.

After the announcement, he had noticed that Sophia looked distracted, despite joining in the celebrations. When he enquired, however, she merely told him that she was feeling tired after a long day shopping with her mother. Accepting that her recent nausea, be it due to excitement and stress or a stomach bug, had probably left her feeling drained before a hot day walking around town, he advised her to just sit down and watch the session and relax. A couple of hours later, as he ran through the warm down drill to end the session and send the players off to shower, he was pleased to see that Sophia looked much better as she walked across to him. She kissed him tenderly.

'OK, thanks,' he said. 'What was that for?'

'Do I need a reason to kiss you now?'

'Nope,' he said, putting his arm around her waist. 'Listen, while the players are changing, I want to talk to you about the team for Sunday.'

They sat down on the bench, and Moreton pulled his notebook from the bag. After I met with Billy, I was thinking about how we should approach the game. Do you remember when we played Córuel earlier in the season, away?'

'Yes, we had Kiko and Adrián suspended and had to change the defence. Didn't we play with a back five?'

'That's right, and we got a draw there. This time, we have our first-choice players available, but I'm wondering whether we should go to a five again for this game. What do you think?'

'I'm not sure, Jon. It means sacrificing a player from somewhere else in the team.'

'Yeah, I know. I was thinking of adding Matías in the back line, have Revi and Samuel in their usual role, then have Billy play behind Elías and José Palermo with Alejo and Adrián pushing forwards to provide the width in midfield and attack. It'll give us some flexibility because we can drop into a five when under pressure and spring into a 3-4-3 when we have the ball, or even have Matías carry it out of the defence.'

'It's a gamble, isn't it?'

'Yeah, you're right. I just wanted to run it past you, to see what you thought. Nah, let's leave it. Perhaps give José a game though. He's always hungry to play and, after Santi left, he probably expected to move up to first choice until Elías started scoring regularly. What do you think about starting him on the right and giving Antonio a break?' Her expression indicate approval without words. 'Sorted,' he said.

After training on the Friday, Moreton announced the team to face Córuel two days later. Juan Torres was back with the group and looking much more like his old self, but Jiménez was retained in goal. The regular back four was in place, with Sanz, Victor, Kiko and Adrián lined up in front of the veteran goalkeeper. No one knew at the time, but it would be the last time that the five would play together this season. Samuel partnered Revi in midfield, with the younger Palermo brother replacing Antonio Vasquez on the right. Swan was in the centre, Guido on the left and Elías as the striker completed the line-up.

Twenty minutes later, Moreton stood outside the gates of the stadium chatting with Swan. He was waiting for Sophia to return after checking with Esteban that he could lock up and Swan was waiting for Isabella to collect him. Both women arrived at the same time and, after brief greetings, Isabella and Swan drove off, leaving Moreton and Sophia to walk home.

The ringtone of Sophia's phone halted their progress after a few steps as she fumbled in her bag to find the phone. 'Papá' she said to Moreton, opening the call. The conversation was brief and, from Sophia's expression as she closed out the call, was clearly concerning. 'He's waiting for us at the apartment,' she revealed. 'He has some bad news.'

With ill tidings awaiting, the logical tendency is not to be in any hurry to receive it. With myriad thoughts and concerns running through their minds, however, Moreton and Sophia covered the fifteen minutes' journey in far less than the usual time, to find Joaquín Garrigues standing outside the gate of the complex. They exchanged brief embraces as Garrigues asked if they could go inside to talk.

'You should sit down,' he said to them both as they entered the apartment. 'It is very sad news.'

They complied and subconsciously, Sophia took Moreton's hand in hers.

'I have to tell you that Señor Broome sadly died earlier today,' he revealed solemnly.

Moreton shook his head sharply as if trying to free it from the reality now planted in his consciousness. 'What? How?' He put his hands to his head, and bowed it down till his elbows rested on his knees. 'How?'

'I'm very sorry, Jon,' Garrigues sympathised. 'I know this must be very difficult to hear.' He reached down and patted Moreton on the shoulder as Sophia drew her lover's head down onto her shoulder.

'What happened, papá?'

'He had been ill for some time. He had heart problems. I think you know this from when you spoke with him at his house, Jon. Yes?'

Moreton raised his head from Sophia's shoulder and nodded slowly. 'Yes,' Moreton confirmed, 'but he didn't say it was serious.'

'No,' Garrigues said. 'I'm afraid that it was though. I told you that Ricardo had spoken to one of his legal people last week about the club donation and the money for the house, yes? Well, Ricardo took another call this evening and the full picture was given to him. Señor Broome's condition was getting very much worse. Last week, his doctors told him that he needed to have an operation. It was a last chance, and it only had a 50/50 chance of success. Now we can see that what he did last week was to ensure that all of his plans were completed. Ricardo had been instructed to set up a trust fund as organised in Señor Broome's will to ensure that the Retama soccer school had enough financial support for years to come. He also wanted to ensure that he had done all he could to put things right after his son had caused so many problems here in Retama – and for you, Jon. This is why he had the money for the house transferred without telling you about it. He didn't want to risk you turning it down. When he went into hospital, this was why he told people that he couldn't be reached by phone.'

'The operation wasn't successful?'

'No, I'm afraid not. Ricardo was told that Señor Broome never woke up after the operation.' He paused a moment for reflection. 'At least he passed quietly, in his sleep, with no pain,' he offered, but knowing it was of small solace.

'OK,' Moreton said, dragging himself to his feet. 'Thank you for coming here to tell me, Joaquín. That can't have been an easy weight to carry around.'

'I must go,' Garrigues said. 'I have left Dolores back at the hotel. Your player Sebastián is with her. He said he would sit with her until I got back.'

'Of course,' Moreton said opening the door of the apartment.

'Oh, one final thing,' Garrigues added as he began to walk down the steps towards the gate. 'The funeral is on Thursday, Jon. I thought you'd want to know.'

'Yes, thanks,' Moreton said. '*Hasta luego, Joaquín.*'

Moreton closed the door and leant against it, sighing deeply, as Sophia fell into his arms.

'I'm so sorry, Jon. What a terrible thing to happen. Life is so precious.'

Moreton kissed the top of her head. 'I have to go to the funeral, Sophia. I have to pay my respects.'

'Of course, you do, Jon,' she said, but, as with the telephone message that was never received by Bobby Broome, Moreton would be denied that opportunity as well.

Losses

The following morning, Moreton awoke after a largely sleepless and restless night to the sound of retching from Sophia in the bathroom. He jumped out of bed and padded to the bathroom door. 'You OK?' he asked.

'Ye … yes,' came the stuttered reply between sharply taken breaths. 'Just give me a minute.'

He stepped back from the door and sat on the side of the bed, waiting. A couple of minutes later, he heard the toilet flush and then a drained Sophia appeared in the doorway. 'Sorry,' she said. 'It's just all been too much.' She started to cry. Moreton jumped up and took her in his arms.

'Hey, it's OK,' he reassured her. 'Everything will be fine.'

'Will it?' she asked earnestly. 'Will it, Jon? Everything? Even the things you don't know yet? Do you promise me?'

'Of course, it will.'

'Promise me, Jon. Tell me that you promise.'

He lifted her head up and looked into her eyes. 'I promise. Everything will be OK.

She smiled through the tears. 'I love you, Jon Moreton.'

'And I love you Dolores Sophia Isabella Medina Garrigues. And that's why I know, why you should know, that everything will be OK. Everything. From the tiniest little thing to the biggest thing. Everything.'

Sophia raised her hand and wiped a tear away. 'Sometimes, Jon, the tiniest little thing is the biggest thing, isn't it?'

Sleep had been elusive across the last six hours or so. Moreton's mind was hardly at its sharpest, and an ability to penetrate elusive word play was seriously lacking. He went with the easy answer instead. 'I guess so.'

Sophia eased herself away from him. 'I'm sorry, Jon. I'm OK now. Everything is just happening so quickly. So many things, all at once. The club, the things that can happen if we get promotion, the things that will happen if we don't, Billy and Izzy, and there's just two games left and hopefully then play-offs. Then there's the issue over the money for the house, and then Señor Broome dies. A really good man Jon. It's so much to take in. Too much.'

'He was ill, Sophia, but he's not suffering any more. In fact, I bet he's having a bacon sandwich for breakfast up there somewhere, right now' he said, flicking his head upwards towards an unseen celestial breakfast room where bacon would always be on the menu.

This time it was Sophia's turn to be puzzled. 'OK, Jon. You make the bed, I'm going to shower, then we'll have breakfast too.'

An hour later, although a bacon sandwich was offered, Moreton sat down with Sofia to their usual yoghurt and fruit breakfast, with *café con leche*. 'We'll have to let everyone know,' Moreton said, sipping his coffee.

'Sebastián knows already. Papá said last night. He may have told some people. And then there's Billy.'

'The mention of Billy Swan and having to tell him about Bobby Broome brought Moreton to a stop. 'Oh wow, Billy. That's not going to be easy.'

'Might he know already? Perhaps Seb told him.'

'No, I don't think so. I think he stayed at Izzy's last night. So, unless he's back to the hotel early, and Seb tells him, he won't know.'

'OK,' Sophia declared. 'Here's the plan. I'll speak to Seb and see if he's told anyone yet. Knowing Seb, he'll understand the need for discretion and won't have. After that, I'll call everyone and put them in the picture. You ring Billy.'

'OK.'

'But don't tell him over the phone, Jon. It's different for the players, they only knew Bobby Broome as a name. He meant much more than that to Billy. You have to tell him face-to-face.'

Sophia had hardly eaten anything as they rose from the table and Moreton went to find his phone to make a call that he really didn't want to make. 'Billy,' Moreton said as his call was answered.

'Wotcha, Jon. You OK?'

Moreton ignored the question. 'Where are you, mate. I need to talk to you.'

'Well, young Jon,' Swan replied in cheery tones. 'Isabella managed to pull off that big deal I was telling you about, so, we're off to have a nice breakfast by the beach to celebrate. There's even talk of champagne, I'll have you know.' Swan was clearly in high spirits and Moreton knew that what he had to say would bring his friend's happiness tumbling down, but he had little option. He could at least let him enjoy his celebration breakfast first.

'Sounds good,' he said trying to sound positive. 'Tell you what. I'll meet you both back at the hotel at 11.00, is that OK?'

'Both?' Swan asked.

'Yeah, if Izzy is OK for the time. It might be good if she's there as well.'

'This doesn't sound good, Jon.'

'Don't worry about it for now, Billy. You and Izzy enjoy your breakfast and I'll see you later.' He put the phone down on the table and rested his head in his hands as Sophia walked in from the kitchen where she had been washing up.

'How did it go with Billy?' She asked.

'He's so happy at the moment, and what I'm going to tell him will destroy it all for him.'

Sophia walked over to him and kissed him on the head. 'I know, Jon. But it has to be done. I've spoken with Seb. He hasn't told anyone. So, while you're out, I'll ring all the guys up.'

At 11 o'clock, Moreton was sitting in the bar at the hotel, when Swan and Izzy walked in. 'Hi guys,' Moreton said standing up to greet the newcomers.

'I can't stay long,' Izzy said. 'I have to go and meet my clients in 30 minutes to get all the papers signed.'

Moreton nodded.

'What's up, Jon?'

'I think you'd better sit down, Billy,' Moreton said softly and began …

Ten minutes later, all three sat in silence. Moreton had passed on the heavy weight of sad reality to Swan and Izzy, but his burden felt no lighter.

'I'm sorry, Billy. But I had to tell you, mate.'

'Yeah, course you did, Jon. Yeah, thanks mate.' Swan paused before smashing his right fist down onto the table, twice. 'Shit!' he shouted. 'How can that be right?' He reached up to his forehead and rubbed it vigorously with both hands. 'You know, you do things right and this crap is what happens. What's the sodding point?'

Isabella put her arm around Swan's shoulders drawing him towards her. 'Ssshh,' she whispered as Swan's body shook with the emotional turmoil. She looked at Moreton. 'I have to go,' she said slowly to Moreton. 'Will you stay with him for a while? Please?'

'Of course,' Moreton replied, as she rose from her chair. She whispered into Swan's ear and he nodded slowly. She kissed him on the head and squeezed his hand as she turned to leave. 'I'm so sorry, baby.'

'What kind of shitty world is this, Jon?' Swan asked earnestly, raising his head after Izzy had left. 'Tell me!' he shouted.

'I don't know, mate?' It was all he could muster.

'Then what's the point? What's the point of anything?'

'I know it's crap, Billy, but at least he's not suffering any more.'

'Don't give me that bollocks, Jon. When you're dead, you're dead. That's it. There's no better place to go to. That's just religious cobblers.'

Moreton sighed deeply. His friend was tumbling into despair. 'Look, you've still got Izzy, mate. Hang on to that.'

'Have I? Or is that just something else being dangled in front of me before it's snatched away. You know what's going to happen? We'll miss out on promotion and I'll have to go back. She'll be here and I'll be fucked up again. Everything gone. Back to normal. This sodding world must really hate me. "Oh, here's Billy Swan, let's give him another kick in the balls." That's how it's always been for me. That's me. That's my life.'

For the next two hours, Moreton sat with Swan as his mood drifted down, launching into repeated bitter rages against his perceived fate. Eventually the anger evolved into a brooding melancholy and sad acceptance of his fate.

'Look Jon,' he said. 'Thanks for coming over and talking to me. Thanks for letting me rant at you as well. I'm sorry, mate. You must be feeling like shit as well. It's just that in my life, you can probably count on one hand the people who have given a sod about me, and he was one of them. I know it sounds stupid, but he was like the Old Man that I never really had. When I was down, he did so much to lift me up. I didn't deserve any help. I'd been a total shit, but he didn't care about that. I owe him so much. I don't know where I'd be today if he hadn't kept bothering me with phone call after bloody phone call.' In spite of himself, he smiled at the memory. 'I wanted to pay him back, pay my debt, now it's too late.' Swan leant back in his chair. 'Ah, sod it,' he said. 'Jon, you should get back to Sophia. You don't want to sit here listening to me moan about things. You've got enough to worry about. I'm going to go for a walk and then to see Esteban for a bit of painting. It'll be like therapy. I can moan at him for an hour and he won't even know what I'm talking about.'

'You sure, Billy?'

'Yeah, sod off home, mate.'

'Are you meeting up with Izzy later?'

'No, she's having dinner with her clients. Look, I know what you're doing. I'm OK. When I get back from the ground, I'll sit here and read. It'll take my mind off things.'

'OK, I'll see you tomorrow for the game.'

'Yeah, see you then.'

Moreton rose and the two men embraced. Swan went up to his room to change and Moreton headed for home to Sophia and the comfort of her arms.

The following day, at the Estadio Antonio Núñez the Retama players were assembling as the visiting FC Córuel coach parked outside. Walking in alongside the visiting party, Victor and Kiko chatted as they approached where Moreton and Sophia stood by the bench. 'Where's Billy?' Moreton asked them. Despite rapidly improving their ability to communicate with Swan in Estuary English, they found it easier to answer in Spanish and Sophia related the information to Moreton.

'They normally meet Billy by the bench outside the hotel, but sometimes, if he's been with Izzy, she drops him off. He wasn't there today, so they assumed that was what had happened.'

Moreton frowned in concern.

'They could have just been delayed a little,' Sophia suggested, more in hope than conviction. 'Give it ten minutes?'

'Yeah, OK? Wait, tell you what? Can you call Izzy and see if they're on the way?'

Sophia walked away and made the call, returning with a shake of her head. 'She's at home. They were going to meet up this evening.'

Moreton raced over to his bag and, pulling out his phone, tapped in Swan's number. The ringtone sounded for a few seconds, before handing over to the messaging service. 'Billy, where the hell are you?' Moreton barked into the phone and hung up. 'Is Seb here yet?' he asked Sophia. She nodded and rushed away to find the son of the people who owned the Hotel El Barco. 'Billy, Billy, Billy,' Moreton said quietly to himself as he waited looking towards the gap in the concrete wall leading towards the gates of the stadium, hoping to see the missing veteran appear, but also convinced that it wouldn't happen. A few minutes later Sophia returned. Her expression told the story that Moreton had been both expecting and dreading.

'Seb's parents checked his room. He's there, but he's asleep. They say he's very drunk, Jon. There are two empty vodka bottles on the floor. They've tried to wake him, but he just goes back to sleep.'

Moreton sighed deeply. 'OK, they might as well leave him there. He's no good to us in that condition anyway. Let's go and talk to the boys. We'll put

Matías in alongside Samuel and push Revi forward into Billy's role.'

Sophia took Moreton's arm, stopping him as he headed to the dressing room. 'Do we tell them the truth, all of it.'

Moreton thought for a moment. 'I think we have to. Billy's in a bad place at the moment. He's trying to wash the bad things away. They'll understand. They'll want to help him. We're a family and, when one of us is down, we all help. Anyway, we can't ask Seb to lie and cover things up.' Sophia squeezed his arm and they hurried off to make the late changes to the team and explain why they were happening.

The loss of Swan from the starting line-up, and the reasons why, had an inevitable destabilising effect on the team and with the Córuel players working desperately to secure a place in the play-off system from a top three finish, the half-time break saw the visitors two goals up. Retama were in serious danger of a defeat that would surely fatally wound their title hopes. In the dressing room, Moreton tried to lift his team, reminding them of how far they had come this season and how important it was not to let things slip away now. After he had finished, Jiménez stood up and in slow measured tones, spoke in Spanish as Sophia translated for Moreton.

'We need to do this now, for Billy. He is Retama. We are Retama.'

¡Es para Billy! Sanz said. The call then echoed around the room.

Ten minutes after the restart, a goal from José Palermo cut the arrears as he chased through, and converted, a pass from Revi after a clever "dummy" from Elías had deceived the Córuel defence. '¡Es para Billy!' the enthused forward yelled, rallying his team-mates to press forward at the restart.

The swing in momentum was clearly evident as the blue-shirted Retama players took control of the game, pressing for an equaliser. Guido, Elías and Revi all had shots saved by the Córuel goalkeeper, and a towering Kiko header from a corner looked destined for the net, before it was headed from the line by a recovering defender.

With just ten minutes to play, though, the eagerness of the Retama players proved their downfall, in more ways than one. With more players committed to attack, the opportunity for the visitors to break and score the third, killer, goal was always present and, when two visiting forwards broke clear with just Sanz as the lone sentinel at the back, the result was inevitable.

There was further trouble for Moreton though when, in an attempt to gain possession, Sanz felt his studs stick in the artificial turn and his recently injured knee buckled under him. Sophia was already on the field tending to Retama's fallen captain as Jiménez fished the ball from the back of the net, and her twirling fingers gesture confirmed that Sanz's race was run for this game, and probably for the remainder of the season. Moreton sent Sebastián on to replace the defender and seconds before the final whistle, it was the substitute firing in a shot that was deflected wide of the goalkeeper for Retama's most insignificant of consolation goals.

Seconds later, as the Córuel players celebrated the victory, the Retama team headed for the dressing room, contemplating what would now surely be a long-drawn out play-off programme of half-a-dozen games, each one carrying the threat of defeat and the death of the club. And even that would, in all probability, only occur if they could go to Torreaño in their last game and win. Watching his players' downcast demeanours, after shaking hands with the Córuel coaching team, Moreton made a point of greeting each of his players as they left the pitch, encouraging and thanking them for their efforts. Even to him, it felt like commiseration rather than the intended inspiration.

As they waited for the players to change, Moreton and Sophia stood by the coaches' bench.

'We can't let them give up now. We can't give up now,' he told her. 'If we have to finish below top in the league and go through the long play-off programme route, that's what we'll have to do. We're a long way from dead yet.'

'Yes, Jon, that's right. We need to keep the players positive. Shall I see if I can find Esteban. We can get him involved as well.'

'Sure,' he said. 'Why not.'

Moreton slumped down on the bench. Despite his encouraging words to Sophia, he had hardly convinced himself that Retama still had a chance, let alone her. If Torreaño had won at Palancio, they would be five points clear of Retama, and assured of the title. Even if they hadn't, a win for Bugroño would put them ahead of Retama anyway, and if either won their last game, the title would be theirs. Fifteen minutes had passed as he sat in deep contemplation before Sophia returned. 'I can't find him,' she admitted.

'Don't worry about it,' he said, just as a raucous noise came from the Retama dressing room. The door opened and Victor appeared, beckoning them. Moreton and Sophia looked at each other briefly before hurrying across and into the dressing room, where they found Esteban and the players all celebrating. The old man had received a telephone call from his daughter who worked at a radio station in Valencia. She had seen Retama's result cone into the studio there, and also those of the games involving Torreaño and Bugroño. In the centre of the room, the old man was jumping around waving his phone in the air. Moreton and Sophia were baffled, but Sebastián explained. With Montero injured, Torreaño had lost 1-0 to the Palancio team fighting against relegation, and Bugroño had lost by the same score to Politanio's "home team". All of the top three clubs had been beaten.

Moreton grabbed a piece of paper and began scribbling down the table and working out the possible permutations from the last games. It all meant that with one game to play, Torreaño were top on 62 points, Retama were still second on 60, with Bugroño on 59. The scenario from last season had almost been perfectly replicated. Even victory for Del Hart's team from their final fixture would be insufficient for a title win. The race was now between Retama and Torreaño. It would be decided when Moreton's team headed for San Julio del Rio to face the league leaders. A win or draw for Torreaño would make them champions, and just two games away from promotion. A win for Retama would do the same for Moreton's club. His calculations completed, Moreton stood up to try and pass on the message. By this time, though, everyone had already come to a similar conclusion. Club Deportivo Retama were indeed a long way from dead.

An hour later, Moreton and Sophia were sitting in the apartment, trying to catch up with the whirlpool of events careering around in their heads when her phone rang. Kiko and Victor had volunteered to go back to Hotel El Barco with Sebastián and check on Swan. It was Kiko, explaining that Billy was OK, but upset that he had let everyone down. They had explained that everything was fine. Everyone understood, nobody blamed him and it was all forgiven and forgotten. Kiko said that Swan had told them he'd fallen off the wagon. They said it was all OK, if he just climbed back on it again.

The ringtone on Moreton's phone an hour later however heralded a text message from a far less welcome source. Moreton picked up the phone to see the name on the text message read "Chaz." He hadn't changed the name in his phone Contacts directory, and there had been no conversations with the man who had so nearly destroyed CD Retama since that fateful day almost twelve months ago. At first Moreton was tempted to delete the message unread, but thought better of it. He clicked to open it. It was brief and matter of fact. Even the sign off carried no warmth.

"Jon. The old man's funeral is strictly family only, so please do not try to attend. I think it's for the best. Hope you are OK."

Moreton shook his head at the words of Charlie Broome. He passed the phone to Sophia for her to read the message, blowing out his cheeks as he did so. 'I don't know whether I should still go,' he mused. 'Who's he to keep people away?'

'Probably best not to,' Sophia counselled. 'I never met Bobby but, from what I've heard, the last thing he would want, would be some kind of a problem at his own funeral.'

'You're probably right. It's just that Charlie's taking away my chance to pay my respects and thank the man who has given me, us, Retama so much.'

'I understand, Jon. But perhaps there's other ways that we can show him respect.'

Gains

Billy Swan had not been looking forward to training on Tuesday, unable to shake the nagging feeling of guilt that he had let the club down, and that their defeat had at least in partly been due to his absence. He arrived in a subdued mood with Kiko and Victor, but with everyone welcoming him back like some returning prodigal son, things soon returned to normal and, other than a quick wink from Moreton, the matter was quickly closed. The coach had far more pressing matters on his mind.

After talking with Sanz, Sophia advised that the injury to his knee would benefit best from rest and he should sit out training for the week and be considered as highly unlikely to be available for the game at Torreaño at the weekend. Replacing the many qualities of the Retama captain was not an easy task. Felipe Blanco could, as he had done a number of times across the season, slot in at full back and do a more than competent job in the role, but he lacked the experience and charisma of Sanz. Replacing those lost elements was less easy. The armband would pass to Adrián and, although his commitment was clear to see for all, his naturally introvert demeanour carried much less air of authority.

The injury also meant that any plans Moreton may have been considering for again deploying Sanz as a man-marker on Montero were to be abandoned. The Torreaño marksman was likely to be back in the starting team after his absence in the loss to Palancio, but how should Moreton deal with the goal threat that the returning striker brought with him? The question occupied Moreton's mind and many of his conversations with Sophia across the week.

The recent games against Árboles Altos and Córuel where Torreaño had conceded three goals in two successive games had given Moreton cause to think that perhaps an aggressive, front-foot approach to the game would be more beneficial than last season's doggedly defensive tactics. Last term, a draw was sufficient. This time, the stakes were just as high, but only victory would suffice. By Wednesday his ideas had taken the form of a suggested starting line-up to share with Sophia. After breakfast that morning, he laid out his idea.

'It may look like a back five, and we may need it to be like that at some stages in the game, but it's really 3-4-3,' he said, arranging condiments and cutlery to illustrate his plan on the breakfast table. 'Sanz is out so let's use that situation if we can. We can drop Guido back into Sanz's role. Do you remember that he used to play as a defender when I first arrived and you told me all about the squad?'

'He wasn't brilliant there though.'

'No, I know, but whoever we put there isn't going to be Alejo, and what a weapon to have coming from deep with his pace.'

'OK.'

'We drop Matías between Kiko and Victor to play as the spare man looking to pick up Montero's runs and cover if he drags one of the others out of position. Then to add some solidarity we partner Felipe and Samuel in front of them. We'll have plenty of cover then if Guido gets caught up field or if Matías sees a chance to come out with the ball. Upfront, we can pair Revi with Billy and start with José up as the striker, but have Elías or Juan as options to change if we need to.'

Sophia looked at the table, up at Moreton and then at the table again. 'OK, I like the idea of having Guido to attack from deep and encouraging Adrián to look for chances to get forward as well, but is Samuel and Felipe a little too defensive and one-paced in the middle?'

'Perhaps, what do you think is better.'

'I think play Seb with Samuel instead. He's got more pace than Felipe, and it means we can keep Felipe fresh on the bench to fill in elsewhere if we need him to.'

'I like it. That's what we'll do. Let's work on it tonight and Friday with the guys.' Moreton stood up and started to clear the table. 'I have to go into town for a couple of errands after this.'

'I'll come with you if you like,' Sophia suggested. 'I haven't got a lot to do here.'

'No,' Moreton said, a little too quickly. 'I can get things done quicker on my own, and you can put your feet up, perhaps go for a swim.'

Sophia was a little mystified by Moreton's response, but agreed. The thought of a swim was attractive as the Spanish spring was turning into another hot summer, and the time would give her the opportunity to carry out a plan she had been hatching in her mind since the text message from Charlie Broome had upset Moreton. Five minutes after Moreton had left, she followed him out of the door and headed towards the Estadio Antonio Núñez.

The remaining training sessions had gone well and, when Moreton announced the team and formation for the visit to Torreaño it had been received positively. All was settled and Moreton was ready to break things up when Sophia asked him to wait a moment. She opened the dressing room to door and called Esteban in. The old man was carrying a small black bag, and passed it to her as he entered. Sophia reached inside and pulled out a blue Retama shirt. She held it up to reveal the now familiar patch of blue paint that had been applied to cover the 'Bella Cucina' logo with the word 'Retama' in white on top of it. She smiled at Esteban in thanks for his work, before turning it around to show Moreton and the players its reverse. When the numbers had been allocated to the players only one was left unclaimed, number 20. That was no longer the case. Above the numbers, in the same white paint, Esteban had added the name "Bobby Broome".

'I wanted to make sure we honoured a man who has done so much to help us to save the club. Now,' she said, nodding towards the name as she held up the shirt with both hands. 'Bobby Broome will be with us at all times. He'll be in the dressing rooms with us. He'll be on the pitch with us and, when we score, we'll make his shirt dance in the wind as well.'

She had spoken in English so that Moreton and Swan would understand, but as the words were translated to others in the group applause began, and spread around the room. Swan stood up, walked across to Sophia and kissed her on both cheeks, taking the shirt from her and holding it up proudly. Moreton pulled her close to him, whispering his thanks and appreciation in her ear.

After a couple of minutes, the applause died down and Sanz stood up. *'Señor Broome. ¡Él es Retama!'* CD Retama's captain said in his quiet authoritative way, before adding, *'Está en nuestras cabezas. Él está en nuestros corazones. Para siempre.'*

Swan lowered the shirt and embraced Sanz. The unmistakable evidence of tears was in his eyes as he broke away and tried to pass the shirt back to Sophia. Easing herself away from Moreton slightly, she shook her head. 'No, Billy. You look after the shirt. You look after Señor Broome's shirt.' Swan nodded with a shy smile. Neither Moreton or Sophia knew at the time, but that gesture would guarantee a virtuoso performance from the emotional Swan on Sunday – and a setback that would accompany it.

In sharp contrast to the weather across the recent weeks, Sunday morning dawned cloudy and dull, with a strong wind blowing. As the coach carrying the Retama party edged up the narrow roads towards San Julio del Rio, and then on, climbing further, before parking outside the stadium of Torreaño CF, it was buffeted by the increasing ferocity of the wind. Stepping down to enter the stadium, Moreton cast his eyes around and towards the pitch. 'This wind is going to be a big factor in the game,' he confided. She nodded. As assessments go, it was hardly a revelation.

In the dressing room, with Sophia translating, as the players were about to depart for the pitch, Moreton advised stand-in captain Adrián to play with the strong wind behind them in the first-half if he called the toss of the coin correctly. Twenty minutes later, it was clear that Adrián had been denied that option and Retama would face the wind in the first period. 'This is going to be a tough 45 minutes,' he said to Sophia. 'If we go into the break two or three down, as they use the wind, we'll need a miracle in the second-half.

Five minutes after the referee began the game, Moreton's concerns took flight. A long punt downfield from the home goalkeeper found Montero deep in the Retama half of the field. Samuel closed him down, preventing a turn and shot. Seeing his options limited, the Torreaño striker instead played the ball off to a team-mate who thundered in a shot from fully 35 metres. On any normal day, from such a distance, the effort would have had little chance of evading the experienced Jiménez. Powered by the strong wind however, the ball seemed to accelerate in flight and, as it found a home in the top corner of the net, was still rising. Torreaño had taken the lead in a game that Retama needed to win.

For the next 20 minutes, the home team pressed to increase their advantage and Retama's changed formation, designed to provide a flexible attacking platform now served as a strengthened rear guard, as the back three became an almost permanent back five. With his team dominating possession, the red and white shirted players looked certain to carve out opportunities for Montero as they pressed incessantly. Ahead of the back line, Sebastián and Samuel looked to limit the supply line but, with the ever-present danger of wind-assisted long-range shots flying towards goals, they were being both overworked and often overrun.

Twice in that period, Montero broke clear of the defence chasing a through pass and homing in on goal. The first time the wind that had assisted his team worked against him as it sped the ball on and into the welcoming arms of an advancing Jiménez. On the second occasion however, he collected, turned inside Victor and then outside the stretching leg of Matías to curl the ball around the stranded Retama goalkeeper, only to see it thud against the post and bounce wide. It was highly questionable as to whether Retama's luck would hold until the break with just a single goal conceded. On the half hour mark, the answer came.

A cross into the box was headed away by Kiko but, with the wind howling against the direction he powered the ball in, it held up and dropped towards the edge of the box and a waiting Torreaño forward. Matías raced forward to close down the threat, but was beaten by a drag inside and his leg left dangling was an irresistible target, advancing into the box, the home player cleverly contacted the leg and sprawled forwards to the turf. The referee pointed to the spot and Montero sent Jiménez in the wrong direction to double the lead. Moreton put his head in his hands, as he felt the game slipping inexorably away from his team. To win from two goals down against the team topping the table would be a big ask. 'No more goals before half-time please,' he asked of the unseen forces above as he looked to the heavens.' The plea wouldn't be answered.

With 15 minutes still to play while they held the metrological advantage, Torreaño continued to press knowing that a third goal would surely settle the contest. Throughout the game, Revi, Swan and José Palermo had been mere observers in the attacking third of the pitch, and desperate now to avoid any further damage, Moreton had called the young striker back to help out the defence. Conversely, the defensive move would be key the Retama's renaissance.

The half was drawing to a close as another Torreaño attack broke down on the edge of the Retama area. Samuel slid into a tackle diverting the ball towards Sebastián. The home team had committed a number of defenders forward and the young Retama player saw a chance to break up field and, at least, give his defence a respite. Running with the ball close to his feet to avoid it being blown away from him, he drove forwards towards the halfway line, before threading a pass towards Revi. Instinctively, the head-banded midfielder stepped over the pass, allowing it to run on towards José Palermo. Suddenly, there was a huge gap as the Torreaño defence, denuded by their ambition to score that third goal, chased back in a vain attempt to recover their positions.

The younger Palermo sibling advanced towards the home goal, before firing in a shot from the edge of the penalty area. Throwing out a right hand, the goalkeeper diverted the ball into the air. At first it looked likely to drift into the net anyway but, as it rose into the air, its direction was buffeted and instead it fell short and drifted wide. Running from deep, Swan had been unable to keep pace with his younger colleagues, but read the flight of the ball as the wind pushed it from goal. Collecting by the goal line, towards the edge of the penalty area, he turned to be confronted by the goalkeeper, having eagerly recovered to place himself between goal and ball. Swan trotted towards him, dragged the ball right, then left, before slotting it through the goalkeeper's legs and into the net via the far post. In the last minute of the half, Retama were back in the game.

The blue-shirted players celebrated wildly realising the difference that the goal could have made, but Swan ignored the dancing throng of joy, instead heading towards the coaches' bench, beckoning to Sophia as he did so. Understanding what was required of her, she reached into her bag, from where Swan had placed it an hour or so earlier, and pulled out the number 20 Retama shirt. Taking it from her, Swan held it up in the air. As she had predicted would be the case, a couple of evenings earlier, Bobby Broome's CD Retama shirt danced in the wind.

There was barely time for the referee to restart the game before halting it again for half time. Back in the Retama dressing room there was a feeling of relief, that those last few seconds of the first half had at least given them a chance of redeeming the deficit in the second period, and pushing on for the win with the wind now in their favour. With the changed circumstances, Moreton looked to take full advantage.

It was likely that there would be little need for a reinforced back line now, with the play probably concentrated in Retama's attacking half of the field. Withdrawing Matías, he replaced him with Felipe Blanco, deploying him on the right flank of the defence and pushing Guido into a more regular attacking left flank position. Revi and Sebastián swapped positions with the former dropping back into his deeper role and the latter switching to the right flank of attack. Sophia suggested sending Antonio Vasquez on and using him on the right instead of the inexperienced Sebastián, but Moreton decided to hold fire on that move, reasoning that the tricky winger would be much more effective against a tiring defence that had been under pressure for a while. Just three minutes after the restart, keeping Sebastián on the field looked like a masterstroke.

The momentum of the game had clearly changed, not only by the goal, but more conclusively by the fact that the wind that had forced Retama to defend in the first half, was now at their backs. From the start, they pressed forward and a long range shot from Swan nearly brought the scores level, but it clipped the top of the bar with the home goalkeeper an impotent spectator.

Three minutes in, though, that equaliser arrived. Possession was established deep inside the Torreaño half of the field as the ball was transferred out to the right and Sebastián. Initially looking to feed a pass back to an advancing Revi, instead the youngster fed the ball low into the box towards the feet of José Palermo, before advancing to follow it. Offering a sharp return, Palermo's quick thinking had opened up a gap and, as Sebastián drilled the ball low across the face of goal, Swan was on hand to tap home on the far post. Again, as the others celebrated on the pitch, Swan raced across to collect the number 20 shirt from Sophia and flourish it. Moreton patted his friend on the back as he stood by the bench. The Retama coach was convinced things were now inexorably moving in his team's favour.

The following minutes certainly fed into that assumption. With Torreaño now compelled to defend deep, Montero became an almost irrelevant figure further forward as the Retama players pressed for the all-important lead goal. It came just seven minutes later and, if Swan's first two goals had been largely assisted by his team-mates, this one was purely down to the veteran himself.

The move began with Revi carrying the ball forward and exchanging passes with Guido on the left flank. With the home defence compressed, there had been little opportunity for the wide man to use his pace, and the ball was fed back to Revi. Sensing that the massed ranks of red and white striped shirts had the look of an impenetrable wall, Swan dropped back out of the area to find some space and received a short pass from Revi after calling for the ball. The view presented to Swan was little different to the one that had faced Revi, but the veteran had faced many similar situations before.

Rolling the ball under his foot, he hopped backwards five paces, drawing a defender forward. Then, with a swift change of direction, he pushed the ball forward and, dropping his left shoulder, drifted right of his opponent and past him. He reached the edge of the area as two other defenders closed him down, but they were too late. Striking the ball with the outside of his right foot, Swan arced his shot wide of goal, before it curled back inside the post and into the back of the net. It was a strike of rare quality, and this time, before he could race off to the bench, Swan was hauled to the ground by his team-mates. A few seconds later as he rose to his feet, he looked across to see Sophia waving the shirt in his absence. A raised thumb acknowledged her actions, and his gratitude. For both sets of players, there was a feeling of things now being settled. There was however still 35 minutes to play, and more drama to follow.

Despite the wind still dictating the momentum of play and Retama dominating, the lead was still fragile. One goal, either way would make a dramatic difference. A fourth for Moreton's team would surely put the game beyond Torreaño's reach, whilst an equaliser – no matter how unlikely that seemed at the time – would surely end all Retama hopes and dreams.

For the next 25 minutes or so, both teams played as if the growing realisation of how narrow Retama's lead was, edged out any thoughts of things being settled.

Inside the final ten minutes, with the setting sun apparently easing the force of the wind, the home team sensed a last chance and began to push further forward in hope of creating a late chance for Montero and saving the day. The growing sense of hope in the Torreaño players fed into a concern festering in the minds of the Retama players, and encouraged the home fans who roared their team forward. The finishing line was in sight, but with each passing second, the chance of any response, should Torreaño find an equaliser, was becoming slimmer.

Moreton's watch suggested barely six minutes to play when he glanced at it for the fourth time in two minutes. The Retama players, now almost bereft of the assistance from the wind, were sinking deeper and deeper, protecting their fragile advantage as the Torreaño bench urged their players forwards. A shot from distance clipped the heel of Victor on its way towards goal, wrong-footing Jiménez, but the ball drifted just wide of the post. Moreton blew out his cheeks in relief, but the reprieve would be short-lived.

From the ensuing corner, a subtle block from a Torreaño forward compromised Jiménez's leap to punch the ball clear, and it drifted over his head towards the far post. Up from the back to support the attack, a Torreaño defender headed it towards goal. For a brief second, there was silence as 22 players watched the ball drift towards the top corner of the Retama net, before hitting the crossbar and bouncing down a couple of metres from goal. Throughout his career, Montero had made his living by exploiting such moments. His instincts blaring, he jabbed out a foot and prodded the ball towards the line as Felipe Blanco just failed to intercept. As the ball rolled over the line, the Torreaño bench exploded in celebration jumping around and hugging each other. In contrast, the Retama bench sat in silence, momentarily stunned into sullen acceptance of a fear that had now become harsh reality. It was a scene repeated on the pitch as the goal-scoring hero of CF Torreaño was mobbed by his team-mates. Big goals in big games are what define top marksman and Montero had, once more, proved himself to be one.

Quickly shaking off his disappointment, Moreton called to Antonio Vasquez to go on to the pitch and, by the time the celebrations had been quelled by the referee, he had replaced Sebastián on the right of Retama's front line. There was little surprise that, for the next minutes as time drained away, Retama gambled everything on a late goal. Each time the Torreaño goalkeeper caught a cross and fell to the ground, face down, clutching the ball safely, or when a clearance sent the ball spiralling downfield, the relief was met with a cheer from the home fans and Torreaño bench, as if another goal had been scored.

Kiko was sent forward to help out the attack as more and more desperate crosses were thrown into the Torreaño box, but to no avail. Moreton checked his watch again, and again. Five minutes left, now four, now just two. The sad realisation that Retama would fall short again began to settle like bile in the pit of his stomach.

Another cross, another header clear. Last minute of the game thought Moreton as Revi looked to drive another ball forward. Instead, he looked right to Vasquez. As Moreton had hoped, playing against a tiring defence was a big advantage for the dribbling skills of Vasquez, but there was precious little time to exploit that dominance. One man was beaten, but a second jabbed out a foot, sending the ball out for throw-in, to more raucous home acclaim.

Blanco threw the ball in towards Vasquez. Once more he beat his first man, flicking the ball past him. Closed down quickly by a covering defender, he decided to hit in an early cross. The ball flew over the massed ranks of players in the box, towards Swan lurking at the far post, but marked by two defenders. The cross was over-hit, denying the veteran the chance for a header on goal. With the ball destined to drift out of play, he turned and threw himself into a bicycle kick connecting powerfully with the ball. It smacked against the underside of the bar – at the very spot where Victor's shot had stuck the woodwork 12 months earlier – and dropped into the net.

This time it was Moreton, Sophia and the Retama bench celebrating as the blue-shirted players headed towards the figure of Swan, who was painfully dragging himself to his feet. As they reached him, he held out his hand to stop them jumping on top of him, his other hand reaching down to the back of his right thigh. Realising the problem, the players called over to Sophia for some attention.

Even as she trotted onto the field, Swan was already shaking his head sorrowfully, twirling his fingers indicating a substitution was required. Confirming the diagnosis took just a few seconds and Juan Palermo, fresh from completing his suspension was sent on as the replacement. His return would last only a couple of minutes. There was time for Torreaño to launch a couple of hopeful balls into the Retama box, one headed clear by Kiko, the second claimed and clutched to his chest by Jiménez and the game was over. Retama had topped the table and were heading into the two-legged play-off to decide promotion.

Back in the Retama dressing room, the celebrations were tinged with a concern for Swan. He insisted that it was only a slight twinge and that he would be back for the second leg even if it was inevitable that he'd miss the first, but both Moreton and Sophia were less confident.

Eventually, as things calmed a little, Moreton held out his arms asking for silence.

Everyone was expecting the coach to address the players, but Moreton had other plans. When all was quiet, he took Sophia by the shoulders and stood her by the dressing room door, standing in front of her with the players sitting in a horseshoe shape around him. He drew a deep breath and fumbled in his pocket, eventually pulling out a small box.

'Estás en mi cabeza y estás en mi corazón,' he said softly and slowly. After another breath, he sank to one knee, opened the box and raised it towards Sophia. The diamond ring that he had collected as Sophia organised the number 20 Retama shirt for Bobby Broome, glistened as the last rays of the setting sun filtered through the frosted glass of the dressing room window. '*Dolores Sophia Isabella Medina Garrigues. ¿Quieres casarte conmigo?*'

The dressing room erupted in cheers and her answer was lost in the noise. The smile, however, was not, and any verbal confirmation was hardly necessary.

Going Home

The coach journey back to Retama was both boisterous and quiet. Apart from the front two seats to the right of the driver, where Sophia sat silently propped up against Moreton, his arm around her as she looked at the ring on her finger every couple of minutes or so, celebrations and recollections of the game were the order of the day. Even Swan, despite his injury joined in, and a few choruses of "I've got the music in me" provoked banter and laughter.

Despite many handshakes and hugs for Moreton and kisses for Sophia before they left the Torreaño dressing room, the congratulations were repeated as the party exited the coach at the Estadio Antonio Núñez, and dispersed in their different cars. Eventually, as the coach drove away, Moreton and Sophia were alone.

'Wow, Jon. It's been a dramatic day,' Sophia said smiling.

'Yes, but in a good way?'

'In a very good way.' Sophia kissed him. 'And it's not over yet.'

'Really?'

Sophia took him by the hand and led him to a bench under a tree by the side of the road. She sat down indicating him to sit beside her.

'I'm really sorry,' he said.

'Sorry? Why?'

'I should have done this a long while ago, but the timing never seemed right. Too many things going on to complicate matters. I wanted to do it at a happy time.' He smiled a little sheepishly. 'Plus, I thought if I proposed in front of the guys, you couldn't really turn me down, could you?'

'Did you think there was a chance that I might?'

'Honestly? No. I think that fate had brought us together. It was meant to be and, seriously, I couldn't live without you now. Really, I couldn't.'

'Well, you don't have to. Do you?' The evening was now moving on and the last rays of sunlight were dipping down behind the mountains.

'Shall we go?' Moreton asked.

'In a moment. I want to introduce you to someone first.'

Moreton was confused. He looked around but there was no one in sight. 'Who?'

'This person here, with us. Now, just say "Hello".'

'OK,' Morton was even more puzzled now, but complied hesitantly. 'Er, hello?'

Sophia reached out and took his right hand, placing it on her stomach. 'Now,' she said, looking down at her stomach and his hand. 'Say hello to Daddy.'

Instinctively, Moreton moved his hand, before placing it back again. 'What? Really? Are you … ? Are we … ?'

Sophia laughed and smiled and cried all at the same time. 'Yes, Jon. I'm pregnant.'

Moreton jumped to his feet, then settled onto his haunches so that his face was level with Sophia's, then jumped up, running and punching the air. 'Yes!' he shouted, and then again to the echo, before returning to sit next to a still smiling Sophia. 'OK,' he said. 'I'm calm now,' he lied. 'But when? How?'

'How!' Sophia repeated. 'How do you think, Jon?'

Moreton laughed at his own inelegant question. 'You know what I mean, precautions and all that.'

'Well, sometimes these things happen, don't they? It's a bit like you said. Perhaps it was meant to be.' She paused for a moment and her tone became suddenly intense. 'Are you happy about it, Jon? Truly happy?'

'Are you kidding? Did you see me just then? I'd be doing cartwheels if it wasn't for my dodgy knee,' he fired out quickly, before catching his breath. He took both her hands in his. 'I've never been happier in my life and,' he added. 'That's got nothing to do with football. It's all because of us two.' He released one of Sophia's hands and held his index finger in the air indicating something important was to follow. Then he placed his hand back on Sophia's stomach. 'Us three,' he corrected himself.

Walking back to the apartment five minutes later, Moreton could hardly keep the smile from his face as Sophia explained further. She had mentioned to her mother a while ago that she thought she may be pregnant, and when they were supposed to go shopping together, instead they had been to the doctors to have a test. It confirmed things. She also explained that it was the reason why she had been feeling so nauseous, and suggesting that it was nerves or a stomach bug was just to delay telling him until she was really sure and found the right moment. And, when he had proposed that afternoon, she decided it was the perfect time.

Climbing the steps up to the apartment Sophia said, 'I must phone my parents to tell them that you know, Jon.'

'Of course,' he replied. 'And we need to start thinking about houses now as well.'

'Perhaps not yet, Jon,' Sophia suggested as she opened the door. 'We need to know about the club first. If we don't get promotion, we'll both need to think about jobs, and we may need to move somewhere else.'

Walking in behind her, Moreton took her by the arm and turned her round to face him. 'Promotion is happening now. It has to. There's too much riding on it for us to fail. The club, and all the investment that could come into it, the players, Esteban, Billy and Izzy, the whole town. And us, the three of us. I want to be here in Retama with you and this little one,' he smiled at her stomach and then back at her face. 'It's too perfect to fail. It has to happen. It has to.' And in that moment, the full enormity of the consequences if it didn't, hit him. 'It has to,' he repeated more quietly. There was so much to lose if it didn't.

It was a thought that settled in his mind and battled with hope against fear as he sat on the balcony with a glass of wine, while Sophia spoke to her parents in the living room. When she returned and joined him, he was glad to be rid of the thinking time that isolation had offered free rein to. 'How are they?' he asked.

'They're very happy, and asked me to pass on their love.'

'That's great. Look, I've been thinking. I'll need to tell my parents too.

They'll be over the moon and will make such a fuss of you when they meet you. We must go and see them after the season ends, OK?'

'Sure, of course. It will be great to meet them.'

'Wow, a grandkid. They'll never believe it. They'll be so happy.' Sophia smiled.

'Look, I've been thinking,' he continued. 'Should we tell anyone else yet?'

Sophia shook her head a little. 'No, Jon. Let's not. Not yet. Just in case … you understand.'

'Of course, that's what I was thinking.'

'Good, it's very early yet and nobody will be able to tell anyway for a few weeks yet, so there'll be no awkward questions to face about me putting on weight and overeating, eh?' They both laughed. 'I'll just take things a little easy at training and not get involved with participating.'

'Yes, all good with that.'

'Oh, one other thing, I forgot to mention.'

'What! There's something else! Is it triplets?'

Sophia kicked him playfully under the table. 'Idiot,' she scolded with smile. 'No, papá said that we will be playing Puente Norte in the play-offs. The email from the league arrived as I was speaking with mamá.'

'Puente Norte? Is it far away? Do we know much about the club?'

'Not really. I've heard of the town. It's in Ciudad Real, about 250 kilometres away.' It will be a long journey. About five hours I'd say. It's very dry and flat there, and very hot. The town is famous for its wine and, of course, La Mancha is the home of Don Quixote, yes?'

Moreton nodded knowingly, but with less than total honesty. He'd heard of the book, but knew little of it. 'OK,' he said. 'I think we've had enough excitement for one day.' Let's get some sleep and tomorrow we can do a bit of research on Puente Norte.

The following morning, Moreton woke early. Stretching, he sat up and rubbed his hands through his hair, before turning to look at the still sleeping Sophia. Then he remembered. She was going to marry him. She was carrying his child. He shook his head and smiled. It was all too good to be true, and yet it was true. He kissed the tips of his fingers and then touched them lightly on her forehead, being careful not to disturb. 'Sleeping for two now,' he said to himself.

He threw on a pair of shorts and a vest, made a cup of coffee and sat at the table on the balcony, basking in the still cool early morning. Opening his iPad, he tapped the words "Puente Norte, Spain" into the search engine. By the time Sophia joined him, an hour later, his knowledge of the town of Puente Norte – and Don Quixote – had grown.

'Coffee?' he asked as she sat down.

'No, just water please,' Sophia replied.

'OK, wait there and I'll tell you what I've found out.' He returned seconds later, passed a glass of cold water to Sophia and, picking up his pad of notes, he began. 'You were right, it is a fair bit away. And it is likely to be very hot there. The name comes from an old stone bridge in the north of the town. It used to be over a river, but it's just dry for most of the year now. It's an old town, with about 100,000 people living there, dating back to around the 10ᵗʰ century and they produce a famous wine. Apparently, there's even a grape named after the town that they use for making a Tempranillo wine. The football club is officially called Club Deportivo Puente Norte, and they're nicknamed Los Campesinos and the stadium is called El Hogar.'

Sophia was finding it hard to stifle a laugh.

'What?' Moreton protested with affected indignation.

'Did you swallow an entire Wikipedia entry, Jon?'

'Perhaps,' he confessed reluctantly. 'But here's something. There's a hotel in the town called 'Hotel Dulcinea. Do you know who Dulcinea was?'

'No.' Sophia lied.

'Ah, then let me tell you. She was the woman who Don Quixote swore allegiance to. Although I'm not actually sure whether she was even meant to be real. Anyway,' he declared. 'That's me done. Over to you.' He had expected that Sophia would have had nothing to add, but when she briefly left the balcony and returned seconds later with three sheets of printed paper, he realised that his Mastermind specialist subject on of the town of Puente Norte was about to be trumped.

Sitting down again, Sophia confirmed his suspicions. 'Papá sent these over last night,' she revealed waving the papers in the air. 'They have been in their league for eight years and never finished near the top before. This year however, they came top due to their head-to-head record against the runners-up. They played 34 games in the season and scored 47 goals, but only conceded 14. They only lost one game at home all season and only one team scored more than a single goal against them. They also had eight players sent off and, across the season, their opponents had six dismissed playing against them, including three in one game. El Hogar,' she continued, sneaking an impish smile at Moreton, 'Is situated by the stone bridge, with one goal backing onto the dry river.'

'Well, OK. You win,' Moreton said with a smile. 'I guess your info is more relevant than mine. I'll just tap Joaquín up myself next time.'

'You can try, Jon. But remember I'm still his little girl. So good luck with that one.'

'Yeah, OK. Understood. Anyway, it seems that these guys are going to be difficult to break down if they don't concede many goals; just 14 in 34 games is pretty impressive. Those red cards worry me though. Do you think it's likely that they're over physical?'

'I'm not sure. They've had a lot of players sent off against them as well. Perhaps the referees in that league are a bit over the top.'

'Hmm, perhaps. I don't suppose Joaquín had any info on that sort of thing, did he?'

Sophia shook her head as she flipped the sheets of paper back and forth. 'Doesn't look like it. I just asked him for anything he could find out about Puente Norte.'

'Fair enough. Let's work with what we have then. I guess, realistically, we're not going to have Billy fit again for either game?'

'Well, the second leg is a remote possibility, but you have to take into account his age, Jon. I think it's extremely doubtful.'

'I agree. But that means without our main creative source going forward, against such a miserly defence, scoring is likely to be a major problem, especially in the away leg. Winning would be great of course, but coming back with a goalless draw, or at worst a single goal defeat is probably the best we can get. If we set up to be strong at the back for the first game and then, with or without Billy, try to win the home leg, that seems the best approach. It'll be good to have Alejo back for such a game. What do you think?'

'Without Billy, that's probably the best tactic. But, to be honest, I'm worried about all those red cards. Whether it's because the games against Puente Norte are just very physical, or the referees are very harsh, either way, we have a small squad and if we lose any of our key players for the home leg, it could make things very difficult.'

For much of the rest of the day, Moreton and Sophia exchanged ideas for team selection and a formation that would offer the best chance of returning from La Mancha still in with a chance of winning the play-off tie and clinching promotion. Playing with a back five, including the returning Sanz and Matías, as they had started against Torreaño, with a defensive midfield pair in front of them, looked a solid defensive unit. Further forward, they could then deploy their two wide players, Vasquez and Guido to offer support at the back when needed, but also to offer a threat up front, with Elías in the middle hopefully on hand for any chance that may come his way. Unfortunately, at training on Tuesday evening, those plans required a rapid re-evaluation.

Swan arrived with Kiko and Victor as usual, but his heavy limp across the pitch confirmed his absence from the upcoming game. 'It's not good, Jon,' he confirmed unnecessarily. 'Give me another week though, and I'll be raring to go.' The bravado convinced no one. In truth, not even Swan himself. Being without the veteran was disappointing, but hardly unexpected. That Sanz would also be missing was not.

Despite throwing himself into a third-man running drill with typical application and determination as the session got under way, it was clear to Moreton and Sophia that the knee was clearly still bothering him. Moreton asked Sophia to have a chat with the captain and see how things were, while he continued with the drill. Minutes later, she returned as Sanz sat down by the side of the coaches' bench and the assembled water bottles next to Swan.

'Alejo says he's fine to play. But he's not. I told him that if he trains now and plays on Sunday, he'll last ten minutes and then have to come off because he can't run and then he'll miss the home game as well. If he rests though, he'll probably be OK to pick up training next week, probably Wednesday, and then play in the home game.'

'Did you convince him?'

'Eventually.'

The absence of Sanz required a solution, and a quick conversation between the two Retama coaches settled the issue. Guido would drop back into the right flank of defence to cover for Sanz. Samuel and Sebastián would play in front of the back line and José Palermo would replace Guido on the left of the attack. Although losing the team's captain for a second successive game was hardly ideal, identifying the problem so early in the week at least left plenty of time for Moreton and Sophia to work on the adjusted team and the formation he wanted them to play in. By Friday, everything was set and Moreton confirmed the team for the long journey to Puente Norte in La Mancha on Sunday. Despite being unavailable to play, and against the advice of Sophia who suggested that rest would be far more beneficial than two five-hour coach journeys, both Sanz and Swan insisted on travelling with the team. Retama would not be short of cheerleaders from the bench in the game.

The long journey required an early start on Sunday morning and, when Moreton's phone alarm shocked him into abrupt consciousness at 7a.m, he rose reluctantly to find Sophia was already out of the bed. The sound of vomiting from the bathroom confirmed the reason why, and hardly suggested that a long and uncomfortable coach journey would be ideal. When she appeared, ashen-faced at the door moments later, it was a brief visit. Moreton was making coffee.

'Oh, that smell,' she said before disappearing back into the bathroom, closing the door. Moreton cursed himself for the lack of consideration and threw the coffee away, rinsing the sink out and spraying air freshener. Instead, he filled two glasses with cold water and sat on the sofa, waiting and feeling guilty. When Sophia opened the door again, he jumped to his feet.

'I'm sorry. I wasn't thinking.'

'It's not your fault, Jon. It's just one of those things, but I can't even think about coffee now, let alone be able to smell it.' He handed her the glass of water and she took a small sip.

'Thanks, that's better.'

'I don't think you should come to the game today,' he said. 'It'll be a terrible journey. You'll be stuck in the sun all day and feeling ill. It's not worth it.'

'I'm fine,' she said.

'No, you're not. You look terrible.'

'Thanks, Jon. That helps a lot,' she said barely trying to hide the sarcasm.

'Moreton rolled his head from side to side. 'You know what I mean,' he insisted, pulling her close to him. 'Remember what you said to Alejo?'

'Yes,' she replied, her voice muffled with her face buried in his T shirt. 'But he's going anyway, isn't he?'

Moreton sighed deeply. 'Look, I really don't think you should go, but it's your call.'

She pulled herself clear of him for a moment. 'It is a long journey, isn't it?'

He nodded.

'OK, you win. I'll stay here, but you must promise to phone me at half-time and full-time, yes?'

'Sure.' Then he sighed.

'What?'

Moreton shook his head and exhaled deeply. 'I ask you not to go and you say you're going. I said OK, it's up to you and then, you decide not to go.' He sighed in resignation once more. 'Women.'

Sophia smiled and kissed him on the lips. 'I know,' she said patting his cheek playfully. 'Delightful, aren't we?'

The journey was indeed long and uncomfortable and with the added feature of numerous bumps and potholes along secondary roads, the decision to leave Sophia back in Retama looked increasingly sensible. After the excitement of the first hour of the journey had passed, a silence descended over the party. Some slept, others gazed out of the windows, transfixed by the parched uniformity of the landscape. Moreton had little experience of the interior of Spain, away from the coast and mountains. This environment was very different to Retama. It was dry, flat and consistently unchanging for the final three hours of the journey, until they arrived into the town of Puente Norte.

Driving through the sleepy Sunday streets, the coach was followed by a billowing cloud of dust in hot - very hot - pursuit. By the time it turned right, into the grounds of the stadium just ahead of the stone bridge, the vehicle's air-conditioning was conceding defeat to the temperature outside and everyone was glad to step out into fresh air, although opening the coach door was like someone turning a hair-dryer on.

Moreton was first out of the coach, and greeted by a portly man with an elaborate moustache and long greying hair, tied back in a pony tail, wearing a black and white tracksuit. He introduced himself as Luis. When the rest of the party had alighted and gathered their bags and equipment from the coach's luggage compartment, Luis guided them all towards the visitors' dressing room, passing by the pitch where a number of players wearing black and white striped shirts and black shorts were either warming up or standing around in small groups. Even at first glance, Moreton noticed that, almost without exception, the players of Puente Norte were all tall and muscular. His thoughts went back to the conversation he'd had with Sophia about the number of red cards recorded in games where this club were involved. A sense of trepidation drifted over him.

The dressing room was compact, but perfectly acceptable and as the players sat down on the benches and began to unpack their bags, Swan walked over to Moreton. 'These lot are a bunch of big geezers, ain't they, Jon?' Swan offered. 'It could be a right battle if we ain't careful, mate.' Moreton could only a wry smile in agreement. The caution would form a large part of Moreton's pre-game comments.

Once changed, Moreton sent the players out to warm up, although given the temperature under the blazing sun and cloudless sky, that was hardly necessary, but it did allow the players to become a little accustomed to the ground and its surroundings. Unsurprisingly, the pitch was bone dry and most of the grass had been scorched to a bleached yellow, making the playing surface more of an ochre colour than green. There were no stands or terracing, but a steel rail, a metre high, surrounded the playing area, supported by concrete posts, five metres apart. Despite the sparse surrounding, there was feeling that the playing area was locked in.

Moreton stood and watched his players go through their regular warm-up procedure, led by Sanz in Sophia's absence, as the match officials walked past him and onto the pitch. Moreton smiled and nodded as they passed but, from the opposite bench, Luis ran forward and greeted the yellow-shirted referee and his assistants like long lost cousins. At the same time, a number of the Puente Norte players began to walk into the Retama half of the field and offer handshakes to the blue-shirted players. On the surface it looked like a sporting gesture ahead of the game, but Moreton couldn't shake the feeling that it was more coordinated than spontaneous.

After the players had returned to the dressing room, Moreton offered his final words of encouragement, emphasising the importance of a solid start and to avoid getting drawn into confrontations of any kind. It was almost like walking a tightrope for the Retama coach. Inspiring his players to maximum effort but also preaching the importance of a calm approach. When they left the dressing room, Moreton hoped that he hadn't fallen off, either side.

Sitting on the bench as the game got under way, he subconsciously turned to the place where Sophia normally sat next to him. He suddenly felt alone and eased across towards where Swan and Sanz were sitting, next to the substitutes. It lessened his sense of solitude a little.

The early period of the game revealed that, despite the physical stature of the Puente Norte team, their players were less technically proficient than the Retama players and Moreton was pleasantly surprised as his team's neat passing gave them an early ascendancy. Annoyingly however, the inconsistent bumps and dips of the bone hard surface hardly assisted fluent football and the home team's more direct play opened up a couple of early chances, despite their limited possession. First Jiménez fell to his left to gather in a low shot and then he was happy to wave another effort on its way over the crossbar.

The bobbling journey of the ball across the uneven surface of the pitch not only made accurate passing difficult, but also compromised control of the ball when it was received. Often, a late unexpected bobble would mean it bouncing away from a Retama player inviting a robust challenge and, despite there being a helping hand from the opponent to help the fallen player to his feet, the increasing amount of jarring late and high challenges began to take their toll and, on occasions drew resentful reactions from the Retama players. Swan tapped Moreton on the shoulder.

'Have you clocked this, Jon?'

'What, Billy?'

'See what they're doing? When they pull a player up, they'll be treading on their foot, or crushing their hand or the pat on the back is more of slap or a strong pinch. It looks all innocent, like. But it's a proper wind up. You watch.'

Sure enough, the next challenge, as Vasquez collected the ball and skipped past his marker saw him tumbled to the floor. The challenge looked innocent enough, albeit a little late but, as the defender reached down to offer a hand, he stood on the winger's foot. Having been the victim of the ruse for a few times already, Vasquez was reluctant to accept the proffered hand and waved it away, climbing to his feet with a painful and pained expression, and turning his back on his assailant. The defender looked towards the referee with his arms outstretched in a gesture of wounded innocence. It was clearly a well-practised denouement of the underhand tactic. Prompted into action, the referee called Vasquez to him, insisting that he calmed down.

Moreton now better understood the plethora of dismissals in games involving Puente Norte. Their direct approach would simply overpower opponents and allow them to dominate and win games or this devious provoking of reaction would lead to an astute referee spotting the move and delivering the appropriate sanction, or the opponent would react and receive their marching orders after biting on the baited hook, with Puente Norte then looking to score against depleted opponents. Vasquez had been the first to reach that point, and Moreton was concerned that more of his players would follow.

At the break, there had been precious little action in either goalmouth, but a number of the Retama players were feeling the effects of the Puente Norte tactics. Moreton had primed both Swan and Sanz to go round the players and explain the importance of not being provoked into retaliation and, after allowing a couple of minutes for the team to take on valuable lost liquid, they darted from player to player delivering the message. "Do not react," were the watchwords. But words are easier to deliver than deeds.

The second-half started in much the same way as the first period had ended. Retama were as composed in their play as the playing surface would allow them to be. The home team were as deviously aggressive as they could get away with but, as Moreton's team remained restrained in their reaction, the aggression became more open.

With 20 minutes to play, an attack down the home left flank saw a forward push the ball too far ahead in his dribble and the quick Guido stepped in to intercept. As he did so, the forward lunged into a studs-up challenge that missed the ball but contacted the Retama player just above the knee, cartwheeling him into the air. Stung by the ferocity of the action and feeling a darting empathic pain in his own knee, Moreton jumped to his feet, hurling his water bottle down in anger. Grabbing the medical bag to attend to the fallen player, he turned towards the home bench. *¡Mierda total!* He yelled, but the Puente Norte bench was implacable. They simply sat looking straight ahead, offering no reaction. It hardly calmed Moreton's ire.

The Retama coach had feared the worst, but fortunately, Guido's feet had been off the ground at the time of impact. It meant that the aggression of the challenge was transformed into that aerial cartwheel rather than more serious damage across the knee. The sight of the Retama player hurtling through the air was enough to convince the referee however and by the time, Moreton reached the stricken Guido, a red card had been flourished and the home team were down to ten men.

The damage could have been far worse, but it was still bad enough for Guido to be taken off. From the pitch, Moreton signalled to Felipe Blanco to be ready to replace him and was careful to take as much time tending the injury as possible to allow the substitute to be ready. As he helped Guido to his feet, he called Sebastián to him, ostensibly to help him support the player off the field. As he did so, he also cautioned the multi-lingual youngster to warn every one that the referee would be looking to even things up, and to be careful not to make that easy for him. As he continued to help Guido towards the sidelines, waving Blanco on as he passed him, Sebastián hurried around his team-mates ensuring all were aware of the warning. Returning to the bench after applying some ice to Guido's knee, Moreton sat down next to Swan.

'How's Giddy?' Swan asked.

'I think it's just bruising. It'll stiffen up a bit, but the boot caught him above the knee, not on it, or it could have been much worse.'

'They're like sodding psychos, Jon. Someone could get really hurt. A few of our lot can look after themselves. Nobody's going to try and stick one on Ady, and Kiko's big enough to deal with anything, and look after Victor as well. What about Seb though and Joe, they ain't been around the block yet.'

Moreton nodded.' I know.'

He looked across at the substitutes. Revi had the skill to turn the game. Score now and they could be on their way, but it would be a gamble. The roughhouse tactics of the home team were hardly the ideal environment for a player like that. Juan Palermo was the obvious candidate but, when the next substitution came, Moreton's hand would be forced, and none of those he'd considered would be involved.

With time drifting away and the chances of a goal at either end looking less and less likely, the prospect of a goalless draw and the home leg to come looked increasingly inviting. The Puente Norte bench were now becoming increasingly agitated as a similar conclusion was dawning on them. The game was in the final five minutes when a hopeful cross into the box was collected by Jiménez under challenge from a home forward. As he landed though, he fell to the ground holding his side. With the ball now less than secure, the same player kicked it from his hand and was about to drill it over the line when Kiko shoved him away and hacked the ball clear as multiple urgent sounds from the referee's whistle halted the game.

Unseen by the official, the Puente Norte forward had delivered a sharp elbow into the goalkeeper's side, causing the fall to the ground. It was clear that some kind of contact had taken place, but what? With Jiménez climbing slowly to his feet, tenderly touching the area of his ribs and ruefully wincing as he did so, the referee walked across to speak to the linesman covering the left side of Retama's defence. The Retama players shouted to him about the elbow, as the guilty player pleaded innocence. A minute passed, and then another as Moreton went on to tend to the Retama goalkeeper. The ice spray hardly helped and it was clear that Jiménez couldn't continue. Moreton called to Juan Torres and the young goalkeeper, whose nerves at the big occasion had been a source of concern recently, readied himself to come onto the pitch. As he did so, the conversation between the officials ended.

The referee produced the red card from his pocket, and Moreton applauded vociferously at justice being delivered – but then stopped. The referee walked past the black and white shirted forward, towards Kiko and flourished the card at him instead. With his view obscured by the players in the penalty area, and unable to gain any contrary information from the linesman, the referee concluded that any contact in the challenge on Jiménez was incidental and the first offence was Kiko's push which denied a clear goal-scoring chance. The red card was the consequence, as was the award of a penalty to Puente Norte.

Moreton was incandescent with rage at the injustice and it took both Adrián and Victor to usher him from the field along with the wounded Jiménez, and the dismissed Kiko. It made little difference though as he ignored the advice he had given to his players, and was rewarded with a yellow card from the referee as he reached the Retama bench. Back on the pitch, Juan Torres who had only played three full games since his injury was facing the penalty.

The ball was placed on the spot, ironically, by the same forward whose elbow had initiated the series of events leading to the spot kick. Standing on his line, Torres waved his arms in the air, swaying from side to side, attempting to distract the forward's concentration. The referee blew the whistle and Torres threw himself to the right as the ball flew in the opposite direction. Looking back over his shoulder, the moment was frozen in time as Torres watched the ball clip the bar and fly over. The Retama players and bench jumped in the air celebrating. Even Jiménez raised his arms, but winced as he did so. The referee's whistle brought the joy to a halt though. Deciding that Torres had advanced from his line before the ball was struck, he ordered that the penalty should be retaken.

'That's nonsense!' Moreton shouted, before Swan calmed him down. Regaining a little composure, he explained. 'Unless the goalkeeper's action causes the player to miss, there shouldn't be a retake. That idiot doesn't know the rule.' He shook his head in frustration as the penalty was lined up again. This time, Torres waited as the forward was about to shoot, he leaned left, but didn't move his feet. The penalty was struck down the middle again, but at a lower height and Torres caught the ball in his midriff, falling forward as he held onto it. This time there was no whistle and the game restarted as Torres pumped the ball downfield. The young goalkeeper was instantly mobbed by his team-mates and the joy on the Retama bench was uninterrupted.

Five minutes later, the game ended and, for the first time in his time as a coach, Moreton turned his back on the opposition coach as a handshake was offered. He feigned not to have noticed, intent on getting his injured players back to the dressing room as quickly as possible.

The rebuff felt appropriate at the time, but he would regret it soon afterwards.

No more than 30 minutes later, the Retama party changed, but unshowered, left the dressing room and boarded the coach. They had wanted to get away as soon as possible. Moreton was the last to leave the dressing room, closing the door behind him. As he followed the players, he noticed Luis leaning against the home dressing room, talking to another coach. He dropped his bag to the floor, walked across to his opposite number and offered his hand. Looking surprised, Luis took it. *Próxima semana,*' Moreton said, before turning away, collecting his bag and joining the rest of the party on the coach. As it pulled away from El Hogar, Moreton looked out of the window and shook his head. He picked up his phone and dialled Sophia. The call at half-time had been necessarily brief. Now he could tell her the full story.

When the players assembled for training on Tuesday it was as much an opportunity for Moreton and Sophia to assess who would be available for the return game on Sunday, as it was to maintain players' fitness. Jiménez had spent an uncomfortable couple of nights trying to sleep but the vivid colour of the blossoming bruise on his side painted a picture for others that only he could feel in pain. There was precious little chance of him being fit for the game, but insisted to Moreton that he should be put on the bench just in case. For the training that week, he would work with Torres and try to build on the boost that the young goalkeeper's confidence had received from the penalty save.

The prognosis on Guido was much more encouraging. As Moreton had thought was the case, with the impact of the challenge being just above the knee and the swirling motion of his body in the air absorbing much of ferocity of the challenge, the soft tissue bruising was very much less than could have been the case. By Tuesday, the leg was still a little stiff, but Guido could still run and train with it and there was no reason to doubt his availability for the game.

Sanz's situation was very much the same. His knee was much improved by the rest prescribed by Sophia. He took a full part in the training and, he too, would be available for the game. Swan was an entirely different case. Still walking with a noticeable limp, five days seemed like too short a time to return to fitness. He assured Sophia that, by Friday, he'd be ready to train properly and would be able to play. It sounded hopeful, rather than convincing. The main problem, the two coaches faced however was the absence of Kiko. The red card meant he would miss the game and the gaping hole in defence left by his absence would be a major problem, especially against such physically intimidating opponents as Puente Norte.

Sophia had suggested moving Sanz inside to replace the centre back, and playing Felipe Blanco at right back. It seemed sensible but, as Moreton explained, the Puente Norte team would be full of players six foot tall, and more. Sanz would never be second best in determination and dedication, but his lack of height, especially playing alongside the small Victor would invite trouble. Other options were considered, including slotting Samuel into the back line and, for a day, that was the solution they settled on. On Wednesday, however, a clash of knees during a practice game rendered the idea redundant as a heavily bruised leg suggested that a place on the bench for the quiet unassuming midfielder was all that could safely be considered. With just one training session to go, Juan Palermo was drafted in to play alongside Victor for what was Club Deportivo Retama's most important game in their recent history.

On Friday evening, alongside Kiko and Victor, Swan turned up with his full kit on ready to train, but there was still the hint of a limp as he walked across the pitch. Sophia watched him approach, before turning to Moreton.

'No chance,' she whispered.

'Here we go, Jon boy,' Swan chirped enthusiastically as he joined them. 'Fit and ready to rock and roll. Told ya so.'

For all that Moreton wanted it to be true, he knew that it wasn't. 'Tell you what, Billy,' he said. 'You come over here with me for a minute. I want to run something past you.' As the other two Musketeers joined the rest of players to begin warming up, Moreton guided Swan towards the bench and sat down, patting the space next to him, inviting his friend to join him.

'You can't play, Billy. You're not fit.'

'I am, Jon,' Swan insisted. 'Look, try me out and you'll see.'

Moreton shook his head. 'Here's the deal Billy. If you train today, you're done. There's no way the leg will stand up to it. Got it?' He paused. 'Sit this one out though, and I'll stick you on the bench for Sunday. It'll give you another couple of days recovery time and, if we need you for ten minutes or so, I'll consider putting you on. That's the only deal there is, Billy. Your choice.'

Swan looked down at the floor and kicked at the dusty surface. 'Shit, Jon. I've got to do this for the lads. For the club for everyone.' He paused. 'For Izzy. For me and Izzy as well.'

'You'll be helping nobody if you knacker yourself up completely, mate. Rest up and you'll give yourself an outside chance for Sunday.'

Swan looked up to the heavens. 'Yeah, OK. You're right.' He paused. 'Bollocks!'

Moreton stood up and walked across to tell Sophia just as she was completing the warm up. Before the session started, Kiko and Victor walked across to Swan and sat either side of him. Moreton watched as they consoled their friend. Three players, three people, so different, and yet so alike. He gave them as much time as possible to talk, but the most important part of the evening was to help the older Palermo brother to become as accustomed as possible to his emergency centre-back role. He whistled towards the bench, called Kiko and Victor back and the training got underway.

With the emphasis on creating some semblance of defensive understanding and coordination, much of the time was spent with an Attack v Defence set up from various angles of threat. Free play from the flanks, crosses coming in, set pieces and positioning. It was hard, concentrated work but, in typical fashion, Juan Palermo gave it everything.

As the session was winding down, Moreton walked across and sat next to where Swan was still sitting, watching the players being put through their paces.

'He's doing OK,' Moreton said.

'Juan? Yeah, he's good as gold. He'd run through a brick wall for the club, for his mates. Meldrew'll look after him anyway. He'll be fine. If those geezers cut up a bit rough, they won't get much change from Juan. Especially with Sanz back and Ady on the other side as well.

'That's true,' Moreton agreed, looking around the ground as he did so. 'Ah,' he remarked. 'I see all the painting is done. The wall's finished.'

'Yeah, pretty much. We locked it out last Saturday. 'There's one last job to do, but we'll have it all sorted by Sunday for the game.'

'Last job? It all looks finished to me.'

'Don't you worry about that, Jon boy. Me and Esteban have got everything in hand. You'll see.' The smile on Swan's face suggested that he had told Moreton all that he was going to.

On Sunday afternoon, Moreton and Sophia closed the door of the apartment, walked down the steps and through the gate of the complex on the way to the stadium. Since returning from training on Friday evening, the time had dragged so slowly. A visit to the town on Saturday had helped eat into the long hours but a day still felt like a week with so much depending on Sunday's game, and having to field a depleted team. Sleep had been an infrequent visitor on Saturday night and Moreton got up out of bed a couple of times, ostensibly for a drink of water, but more realistically, just for something to do. As was often the case in such sleep-deprived situations, when at last he did relax sufficiently to drift off, he slept longer than usual, but at least that also brought the game closer. Now it was here.

As they walked Sophia had a confession to make. 'Jon, there's something I haven't told you.'

'What's that?'

'Well, you know how we allocated the number 20 shirt to Señor Broome?'

'Yes.'

'Well, there was something else that we wanted to do. Me and papá.'

'What's that?'

'You'll see. We couldn't get it all agreed until last week, but it's all done now. I'll explain later.'

Moreton thought little of the conversation as they walked along with a number of fans also heading the same way. It was only when they arrived outside of the stadium that he understood. Instead of the rusting sign, proclaiming the Estadio Antonio Núñez in faded lettering, a new sign was in place. On a blue background, the white lettering announced the inauguration of the Estadio Bobby Broome.

Moreton stepped back to gain a better perspective of the sign. 'Wow,' he said, shaking his head. 'That's amazing.'

'Isn't it great?' Sophia beamed. 'It was papá's idea. I told him about what I was doing with the 20 shirt and, ten minutes later he rang me back with the idea. I thought it was a great way to pay tribute to Señor Broome for all he had done, whatever happens from now. I think Billy and Esteban did the work yesterday.'

Moreton nodded slowly. 'So that's what he meant,' he said to himself.

Kick-off was still more than an hour away but, as they walked past the coach that had delivered the Puente Norte party to Retama, and through the gates, the crowd was already starting to grow, and blue was certainly the colour.

Walking towards the dressing room they saw Joaquín and Dolores Garrigues already seated behind the coaches' benches. Embraces and congratulations were happily, if secretively, exchanged and Garrigues asked Moreton about the name change. 'Do you approve?' He asked.

'Oh yes. It's brilliant. But won't Señor Núñez mind?'

The entire Garrigues family laughed softly. 'Not really, Jon,' Garrigues explained. 'Antonio Núñez was a local council official many, many years ago.' He waved his arms in the air. 'Even before I was born. I don't even know why the stadium was named for him. But, when Sophia told me about her idea with the shirt, it seemed the perfect way to honour you and Billy's generous friend. The council agreed and Billy wanted to make sure it was all completed before today's game.'

'I can promise you Joaquín, Señor Broome would be delighted, and honoured.'

'Well, that's all good then. Debts paid all round,' Garrigues said with a smile. 'Now what about the game?'

Moreton blew out his cheeks. 'Well, they're a very physical side,' Moreton said.

'Yes, I know. Sophia has told me.'

'If we had all our players fit and available, I'd be more confident, but with injuries and missing Kiko, it's going to be a battle.'

'I appreciate that, Jon. But, you understand, if it's a battle we have one strong thing in our favour, don't we?'

'I'm sure we do, but what?'

'*¡Somos Retama!*' he exclaimed, punching his right fist into his left hand.

Moreton smiled and the two men embraced before Garrigues sent Moreton and Sophia on their way. 'Get our team sorted please.'

As they were walking away though, a female voice called after them. It was Izzy. They waited until she caught them up. 'Don't let him play!' She insisted. 'He wants to, but he knows he's not ready.'

'Don't worry,' Moreton counselled. 'We know. We put him on the bench to keep him involved, but he's not going to play.'

'Do you promise?'

'Of course.'

'OK. Good luck,' Izzy said as she turned to return to her seat, and Moreton and Sophia headed towards the Retama dressing room.

They waited by the door as each of the players arrived. Even those not available to play, turned up. It wasn't a time not to feel part of the team. Once everyone had arrived and changed into their kits, there were 30 minutes before the game, and Moreton sent them out for a steady warm up, before calling them back 15 minutes later.

Opening the dressing room door and walking in, Moreton and Sophia immediately noticed how quiet it was. Usually, there would be lots of chatter between and across small groups of players, with plenty of banter about the game ahead. Now, there was barely any audible conversation at all. The tension from the importance of the game was clear to all. Moreton knew that he needed to act – and quickly.

Clapping his hands, he gathered their attention. 'One more game. One more. *Uno mas.* You men, wearing blue shirts have Retama written across your chest, but it's not only there. *Está en nuestras cabezas. Está en nuestros corazones.* This game will be difficult and it is so very important. But, I, we, the town, Retama could not wish for our future to be placed into more trusted hands. There are around two thousand people out there. They believe in you, and everyone in this room believes in you too. We are Retama. *¡Somos Retama!*' came the echoing call from everyone in the room. Moreton opened the door and sent his players out for the game that would decide the future of the club, and that of so many people there too.

Taking Sophia by the hand, they followed the line of blue along the short walkway out onto the bench and headed towards the coaches' bench.

'Here we go,' he whispered to her.'

She smiled and answered with a single word. 'Believe.'

The visiting contingent were already sitting there, and Luis offered a barely noticeable nod as Moreton and Sophia approached their seats. The Retama coach was not prepared to leave things like that though and walked along the touchline to the black and white track-suited coaches, offering his hand to each in turn with a cheery smile and *Bienvenidos a Retama*'. He wanted to demonstrate to his players how they should meet any provocations with a studied calm.

The game started much as the one in Puente Norte had done. The visitors were aggressive and robust, while Retama's more technical play allowed them to take an early ascendancy. Although the playing surface at the newly designated Estadio Bobby Broome was some way from perfect, it's flatness and consistency were much more suited to the home team's play than the pitch at El Hogar. Revi found room in his deeper role to dictate play and prompt those further forward and, despite José Palermo lacking much of Swan's guile and game nous, his energetic style still allowed him to keep both Vasquez and Guido in the game, and support Elías.

In defence, what Juan Palermo lacked in experience, he made up for with application and a back line consisting of him, Sanz and Adrián were never going to be intimidated by the pulling, pushing and punching approach of the Puente Norte forwards. And yet, when the first chance came, it fell to the visitors. Twenty minutes had passed, with Retama largely controlling the game and pressing forwards without any tangible reward when a pass from Revi was intercepted in the Retama half.

Sensing a chance for a rare opportunity to attack, the ball was transferred out to the right and then swung into the Retama box. Understandably lacking any established understanding, both Torres and Palermo hesitated hoping each other would deal with the danger. Too late, Victor raced in to try and block the advancing run of a Puente Norte forward, but couldn't prevent him firing a fierce header that flew inches over the crossbar.

On the bench, Moreton looked to the heavens and blew out his cheeks in relief, as the Puente Norte coaches jumped to their feet, applauding the effort and urging more of the same. The opening exposed the deficiency in the Retama back line and, from that point, any attacks that the visitors were able to muster looked to exploit that weakness with balls into the box.

After a couple of hesitant moments however, the relationship between goalkeeper and stand-in centre back settled down and, by the break, the perceived weakness had largely disappeared. In attack, although their domination of possession had gifted Retama plenty of the ball in advanced situations, there was a lack of penetration to offer serious threat as Elías struggled against the physically imposing Puente Norte defenders and many of the crosses provided from the Retama flanks were comfortably dealt with. Tactically, they were controlling the game, but hardly looking like scoring. Approaching half-time Moreton shared his thoughts on options with Sophia.

'We could send Seb or Felipe on to play alongside Matías, push Revi further forward and use José to replace Elías. I'm not sure his style makes him particularly suitable for this match against those defenders.'

'Perhaps. José would add more energy as the striker. Elías needs something to happen for him, but José could make it happen for himself.'

They'd decided to make the change at the break but, with seconds to play ahead of half-time, José Palermo received a pass from Revi and played it first time into the box. Executing a nimble control and turn that deceived his marker, Elías created a half chance, but his curling shot from around the penalty spot struck the far post and rebounded into the goalkeeper's arms. Taking the striker off after that would have seemed harsh and, instead of making the change, Moreton used the half-time break to encourage his players to believe the goal would come. So far, the Puente Norte team had been physical but largely with an absence of the late challenges and premeditated 'accidental' collisions of the first game. As time went on Moreton had cautioned his players that may well change, especially if Retama could find that all-important goal.

Ten minutes after the restart, it became clear that, rather than heralding a number of similar opportunities, Elías' late effort on goal had instead been an isolated oasis in a desert of chances for the forward. Moreton made the changes, and José Palermo moved into the striker's role with Sebastián joining Matías in front of the Retama back line and Revi moving into the number ten role. The change had a galvanising effect on Retama's goal-scoring prospects. Whereas the poaching style of Elías had barely ruffled the composure of the visitors' defence, José Palermo's energetic, all-action approach, drifting left, then right, dropping deeper and then looking to spring goalward on the turn suddenly created a whole raft of new problems for the Puente Norte defence. Their response was hardly a surprise to Moreton.

A couple of heavy challenges were clearly designed to slow the boisterous young forward down and the kicks, punches and elbows delivered off the ball aimed at discouraging his enthusiasm. Neither really worked and, first a shot on the turn drew a plunging save from the goalkeeper and then a header from Vasquez's cross drifted narrowly wide. It looked likely that Moreton had found the key to unlock the Puente Norte defence but, reaching the same conclusion, the visitors resolved to take that key away.

There were 20 minutes remaining when Revi fed a pass to Guido, looking to pull a defender out of position, José Palermo, ran out left towards the wide man offering support. A quick pass saw him hold the ball up, allowing Guido to scamper down the touchline, screaming for a return. Instead, Palermo faked the pass, turned and was approaching the area when felled from behind. The defender then contrived to fall on top of Retama forward in an awkward looking slip managing to tread on the back of his right calf with both feet and before falling to the ground with an elbow to the back of Palermo's head. As the young forward lay flat out on the floor, the defender hauled himself to his feet, arms outstretched in a gesture of innocence. The referee had a decision to make. Was it a clumsy challenge followed by an inadvertent tangle of legs, or a premeditated move, stamp and elbow? He opted for the latter brandishing a yellow card.

Running forward from his defensive position bent on vengeance, Juan Palermo was furious at the assault on his younger brother, and made a beeline for the assailant. Seeing the infuriated charge, Moreton screamed out to stop him, knowing that any retaliation would surely bring a red card and hand the visitors a maximum return of ill-gotten gains. Fortunately, by the time the elder sibling had run the 60 metres or so, composure had got the better of ire and instead of confronting the defender, he ran straight past him to where Sophia was tending to his fallen brother.

It took a couple of minutes to evaluate the extent of the injury but there was little surprise when Sophia indicated to Moreton that a change was required. Expecting it to be the case, he had already called Samuel across and prepared him to go on. He would slot into the back line and Juan Palermo would replace his brother as the striker.

Samuel jogged onto the pitch as Moreton helped Sophia ease José Palermo out of the action. As word of the changes were spread around the Retama team, the information eventually reached the elder Palermo. He nodded calmly, walked forward into the mist of the Puente Norte defenders preparing to face the free kick and spoke quietly to each of them in turn.

For the next 15 minutes, the play was concentrated into the Puente Norte half of the field. Juan Palermo was buffeted, pushed, pulled and elbowed by the defenders, but the Retama player felt perfectly at home in that sort of play. He'd happily take two blows in exchange for being able to deliver one and, after Elías and then José Palermo, the Puente Norte back line was now facing an ordeal by combat. It was their rules but Juan Palermo knew them so well.

Crosses delivered now homed in on Palermo's head. Flicks-on opened up spaces and chances for team-mates, while others were directed at goal. The visitors were now under intense pressure as the rugged Palermo led the attack with a fierce determination hungrily feasting on a need for revenge. With time running out, extra-time seemed inevitable, and Moreton began to contemplate the unthinkable. Should he gamble everything and send Swan on? It would mean breaking his word to Izzy, but for five minutes, perhaps a free-kick, one moment of magic could make all the difference. Then fate took the matter out of his hands.

A long clearance into the Retama half found a lone Puente Norte forward with just Victor and Samuel to beat, Sanz and Adrián had pushed up field. His control let him down though and Victor coolly guided the ball back to Torres. A side foot pass from the goalkeeper found Samuel, who moved the ball on to Sebastián and then to Revi. Juan Palermo came short to receive and play a one-two with the head-banded playmaker, receiving a rap on the back of his legs as he did so. The ball was moved to Guido. He spun away from his marker and hared down the touchline, falling away as he crossed the ball from the corner flag. Hobbling from the earlier challenge, Juan Palermo hadn't been able to make up sufficient ground to be in the box for the cross and the ball was headed out towards Revi, who moved the point of attack to Vasquez on the right. The wide man jinked past one defender and then another. Suddenly there was space, compelling a centre-back to come out and to close him down. The limping Juan Palermo was now hobbling by the penalty arc as Vasquez slid a low pass towards the penalty spot. Without even attempting any disguise, a covering defender saw the danger and slid into Palermo just before he entered the box, knocking him off his feet. Taking one for the team, he'd accepted the sanction from the referee to stop Palermo from reaching the ball. As he watched though, Palermo reached out a hand and half maintained his balance for two steps, before throwing out a foot as he finally hit the ground. Hooking the ball as it passed him, the shot headed for the far corner of the net. A gloved goalkeeper's hand finessed its flight, diverting it onto the post, but it rolled along the line and into the opposite corner. With two minutes to play, Retama had salvation with all of its rewards in sight.

The Retama bench exploded with joy, as the blue-shirted players hauled the heroic Palermo to his feet like some wounded hero of battle. Half-limping, half being carried, he found his way back into his own half of the field as the referee prepared to restart the game.

'Quick,' Moreton said to Sophia. 'Get Felipe ready to go on. Juan's done.'

Sophia shook her head. 'Leave him, Jon. Leave him.'

'He can hardly walk.'

'It doesn't matter,' Sophia assured him. 'There's no way they will score now. After what Juan just did, the players won't allow it. Juan won't allow it. Ellos son Retama. El es Retama.'

Moreton looked back at the pitch as the game started again. With nothing to lose now, Puente Norte threw all of their players forward and hoisted long balls into the box. Three, four, five times the ball was lofted in. Twice Torres came to punch clear. Then the wounded Palermo threw himself into the air to head the ball up field to huge cheers from the crowd. On the fourth occasion the ball flew long, giving Torres an opportunity to eat away at the seconds remaining before finally clearing long. There was time for one last cross. The ball was arrowed into the box, to be flicked on by a Puente Norte forward. Was it destined for the corner of the net? No one would know. The blue-shirted figure of Juan Palermo hurled himself horizontally to head clear. Not all heroes in flight wear capes.

As he hit the ground, the sound of the final whistle confirmed that the dreams of CD Retama had become real. Promotion, salvation. A future that had teetered on the very brink of the precipice now was full of hope and anticipation. Moreton, Sophia, the substitutes and removed players, plus Swan and Kiko ran onto the pitch, the latter two brandishing their rapiers as they head towards Victor to complete the triumvirate. Jiménez headed for Torres. Sanz and Adrián, the two rocks on the flanks of the Retama defence, melted into each other's arm and tears. The big circle though was around the Palermo brothers as José hugged his brother and Juan winced in pain as he jumped into the air.

An hour later, after the crowds had dispersed, the Puente Norte party left for the long journey home, the dazed and delighted Club Deportivo Retama players emerged from their dressing room celebrations. Embraces, cheers and tears had been the currency of joy, and now, blinking in the bright light of the setting sun, they headed across the pitch and towards the stadium exit.

Sitting on the wall, surrounding the pitch, Izzy sat waiting alongside Esteban, as Swan, Moreton and Sophia were the last to emerge. Seeing him walking towards her, she stood up and held her arms out for him. He fell into them and then lifted her off the ground in celebration. She whooped in both delight and surprise causing all of them to laugh. Esteban beamed at Moreton and offered his hand.

'*¡Este año ganamos!*' he said, repeating the words he'd given to Moreton before the season has started. '*¡Ganamos, te lo dije!*'

Moreton took the old man's hand but then hugged him as well. '*Si amigo, ganamos.*' The two couples then left the beaming Esteban and walked across the pitch, over the wall and through the gates of the Estadio Bobby Broome. 'What you doing now, Jon?' Swan asked. 'Going home to see your folks?'

Moreton pulled Sophia towards him, and kissed her on the head. 'I'll probably go and see them, yes. I need to introduce this lady to them.' Then he paused. 'I'm not going home though. I am home.'

Acknowledgements

The experienced guidance of a publisher is invaluable to any writer, regardless of format. This is just my second novel and I still very much feel like I'm feeling my way into the genre. Such being the case, I'd like to acknowledge my sincere thanks to Steven Kay of 1889 Books for his continuing tireless work, infinite patience and professionalism in assisting in the production this project. Without his help and diligent attention, Jon, Sophia, Billy, *et al*, would still be just wandering around in my mind, like lost souls looking for a place to tell their story.